RICHARD REINKING

POX

ISBN: 1463547218
ISBN-13: 9781463547219

Library of Congress Control Number: 2011909284

This is for Karen, the love of my life.

PROLOGUE

The air smelled of death. Yet it was unlike anything Ahmed Musa Mohammed had ever experienced before, and he had seen and smelled death many times. The odor was sickening but also faintly sweet, causing a burning in his nostrils; Mohammed had noticed it long before climbing out of the front seat of the Range Rover and stepping down on the hot, desert sand. As he approached the mud-covered hut, the smell grew to be almost unbearable, and he instinctively covered his mouth and nose with the heavy sleeve of his white linen robe. He waved toward the three Arab men traveling with him, indicating for them to wait near the vehicle. Two covered their faces and turned away while the third man, the youngest of the group, was already doubled over vomiting. "If he's sick now," Mohammed thought, "how will he do once inside?"

The four men had traveled from Mogadishu north and east toward the Ethiopian border, crossing two hundred miles of flat, monotonous desert. Few Somalis inhabited this region, most having fled to the cities to avoid falling victim to the constant civil war or dying from starvation or disease. The hut was the only structure Mohammed had seen for miles, and even with the help of the handheld GPS, he felt he was fortunate to find the mother and child here. *Al-hamdu lillah*. Praise be to Allah.

They had arrived when the sun was setting, and as it disappeared over the horizon, an intense blackness rapidly enveloped the desert. In the soup of darkness, an oil lamp from inside the hut flickered through the woven sticks of the wall, casting a faint light on the ground around Mohammed's feet. The temperature had dropped, yet still exceeded ninety degrees, and despite being in the desert, the humidity was stifling. A hot wind

1

blew hard from the north, rattling sand against the dry mud of the hut, as tiny fragments stung Mohammed's coarse face and hands.

Mohammed paused momentarily to say a brief prayer. He uncovered his face and drew in a deep breath. Now, finally, after many months of training and much patience, his jihad against the Americans was beginning. He was ready.

A round hole cut in the base of the wall made an entrance. Draped over the opening was a brown, tattered cloth that was flapping briskly in the wind, and Mohammed pushed it to one side before ducking inside.

The light of the lamp illuminated the interior. His eyes rested on a young Somali woman who looked barely twenty years old. She sat on the dirt floor, cradling the head of a small boy in her lap, his body lying on a bed of dry sticks and bits of cloth. The mother's shabby, dirty white dress fell off one shoulder, partially exposing the left side of her chest. Her frame was emaciated. She obviously was starving. She didn't cover herself or look up when Mohammed entered. Instead, she busied herself with the child, dipping a rag into a wooden bowl of brown water beside her and squeezing drops into the young boy's mouth.

The boy was dying.

He lay naked in his mother's arms. His entire body was covered with hard, firm pustules, many weeping a foul-smelling fluid and most coalescing into a solid layer of decaying and dying flesh. The boy never moved but constantly followed Mohammed with his eyes. The whites of his eyes had turned solid black. Mohammed met his gaze, and it was obvious to Mohammed that the child was alert and not in the coma he had expected. The boy's lips oozed blood and pus, and a red discharge trickled from his right nostril. His breathing was rapid and shallow. He smelled of vomit and excrement, but the worst odor came from the boy's infected, necrotic skin, which was caused by the disease that had brought Mohammed to the hut.

From outside, the wind blew through the cutout opening, covering the mother and child with a fine layer of yellow dust. Dozens of flies crawled on the child's body and swarmed around him. Maggots were eating at the flesh of his legs. Occasionally a gust of wind would scatter the swarm of flies but only for a brief moment. His mother appeared too weak to brush them away. Even if she could, the effort was pointless.

Mohammed felt the content of his stomach rise into his throat, and he swallowed it down hard, hoping it would stay.

It was evident that the child's illness would kill him before dawn, and with his death, Mohammed thought, the child would die a martyr. By the will of Allah, and through his servant Ahmed Musa Mohammed, both the boy and his mother would soon be in heaven.

CHAPTER ONE

DECEMBER 2, 11:00 A.M. MST
VAIL, COLORADO

The powdery Colorado snow fell briskly, partly obscuring the view of Vail Mountain through the plate-glass window of the conference center. Dr. Harry Bennett glanced at his watch. The last lecture would conclude in an hour at noon, and with the additional powder, the skiing would be nearly perfect. As he leaned back in his chair, he could visualize himself racing down the mountain with the wind in his face and the snow spraying off his skis, as he sliced sharp turns back and forth on Vail's slopes. Rather than this long, boring medical lecture, he would have preferred to strap on his skis for the first time in more than five years. But the meeting would be over in an hour, and then the vacation would begin. He supposed he could wait. Except for the few required lectures and other such distracting responsibilities, coming to Vail for the winter conference of the Illinois Academy of Family Physicians was a great idea.

Harry's wife and twin daughters, identical twelve-year-olds, were already on the mountain. His wife, Maureen, was teaching the twins to ski, and today's advanced lesson was on the moguls. Maureen was an accomplished skier, state champion in high school, cross-country on the Michigan ski team in college. During the past few years, she and the twins had been skiing several times, but this conference was his first opportunity to break away from his busy medical practice long enough to join them. He would be a bit rusty, and he wouldn't be surprised if the twins were skiing the difficult black diamond runs by the time he joined them for lunch. They probably would ski circles around him.

Harry had been an athlete in high school and college but had enjoyed mostly indoor sports like basketball and volleyball, and might have excelled if he'd grown a few more inches instead of staying an average height. Now it was a struggle to keep up with Maureen and the girls. He felt fortunate to be healthy, particularly at fifty-three years old, but his joints ached more, his hair was thinner, and the lines around his eyes seemed to deepen with every passing year. His wife said he looked distinguished, especially with his wire-rimmed glasses and the touch of gray along his temples and peppered through his dark hair. He always dressed conservatively, even to the point of a jacket, tie, and dress slacks at a casual meeting such as this one. He was serious minded yet was known for his generous smile. His medical practice was successful, oftentimes overwhelming, and the Vail conference was a refreshing break from his normal, hectic routine.

The speaker for this session, Dr. Hugh Jackson, was lecturing on bioterrorism. Since 9/11, every family physician in the United States had been exposed to a huge amount of information about a variety of biological agents and weapons of mass destruction they had never seen and most likely would never see in their lives—plague, sarin gas, smallpox, anthrax, Ebola, monkey pox, and endless others. In fact, this was the third lecture on the subject Harry had attended in the past six years. With the passage of time since 9/11 the sense of urgency seemed less intense, but in his heart he knew the reality was greater. The world wasn't less dangerous. Though Harry felt he needed to know this stuff—maybe it was even a patriotic duty—he couldn't help but think the diagnosis and treatment of these unlikely infections and nerve gases was a complete waste of his time.

The program guide billed Jackson as the world's foremost expert on bioterrorism. His qualifications as a world authority had grabbed Harry's attention. Jackson was over seventy years old, wore a crumpled and slightly frayed gray suit, was overweight, and walked with a limp—not the typical hotshot doctor on the speaker's tour. He was in charge of bioterrorism at the Centers for Disease Control and had flown in for this meeting from Atlanta. In the 1970s, he had worked for the World Health Organization and supervised the eradication of smallpox in eastern Africa. Though his lecture was smooth and informative, Jackson had obviously given the same talk many times, and his singsong delivery was beginning to neutralize the benefit of the caffeine in Harry's third cup of coffee. He felt like taking a nap, but he still had fifty-five minutes to go.

The Pines was one of Vail's premier resorts, and the only one with a view in the lecture hall. The view was fabulous: snow-covered mountains, endless blue sky, majestic lodgepole pines rising from the white, snowy slopes. As Jackson droned on, Harry wanted to sneak out, but he was stuck. The meeting's coordinator had asked him to moderate the last session and help with the Q & A at the end. He wished now that he had declined so he could have met his family early on the mountain. Hindsight.

The conference room was set up for two hundred attendees, which in this case were all family physicians. Most of the seats were filled. The physicians attending were a diverse group—different nationalities, as many females as males, and a variety of ages, though most were younger than Harry. Some were likely fresh out of training, but Harry thought they looked fresh out of high school. As the moderator for the session, Harry sat in the front row. Jackson stood behind a lectern in the center of a raised platform, and his computer-generated slides were projected on a screen to his right. The incredible postcard view of the mountains completely filled the window directly behind him.

The view had an unfair advantage.

Jackson continued on about the serious possibilities of bioterrorism. "The purpose is to cause terror," Jackson said, "not necessarily to kill people. An example is the anthrax attack in two thousand one. Though there were only twenty-three infected and five deaths, it caused incredible panic. Despite the low numbers in that case, we shouldn't underestimate anthrax—a hundred pounds of anthrax spores sprayed upwind of a city of a million could kill fifty thousand people."

Jackson flipped through a series of slides. The list of his examples was lengthy: botulism, Marburg virus, tularemia, Q fever, plague, Ebola, and even SARS. Harry yawned. All the names were running together and the symptoms were sounding the same.

He needed more coffee.

Jackson stopped, pausing briefly, and Harry looked back up at the screen. The picture was grotesque, showing an African child of about two, obviously miserable, her tiny face disfigured with a hundred round, raised pustules.

"This is a smallpox victim from east Africa," Jackson said. "This child has *Variola major*, also known as ordinary smallpox." He pointed to one of the pustules with a laser pointer. "Note the discrete, individual lesions. This poor soul died a few hours after this photograph was taken."

Jackson showed a dozen more slides, commenting on each one. The scenes were heartbreaking—African children and adults, all emaciated and pox covered, and very likely near death, being tended to by Western doctors, who were kneeling on the dirt floors of their grass huts in their white shirts and ties, khaki slacks, and white lab coats. The close-ups of the faces of the dying children were especially haunting.

The lecture room was silent except for the sound of Jackson's voice. He now had the audience's full attention.

"Smallpox killed over three hundred million people in the twentieth century," Jackson said. "I know that number sounds incredible because it equals the current U.S. population. The virus has been around for over four thousand years, and its epidemics have shaped world history. The plague of Antonine accounted for six million deaths in the Roman Empire in one eighty AD and was a contributing factor in the decline of Rome. Smallpox decimated the Aztecs and Incas, killing, by some accounts, fifteen to twenty million when introduced by the conquering Spaniards in the fifteen hundreds. Pharaoh Ramses V, Marcus Aurelius, Queen Mary II of England, Tsar Peter II of Russia, and King Louis XV of France all were its victims. Would an epidemic today likely change our future? God forbid that we should ever find out."

The next slide showed a picture of a young, thin black man standing bare chested in an open desert, superimposed over a map of Africa in the background.

"This is Ali Maow Maalin, a cook in Somalia, who had the last known naturally occurring case of smallpox, diagnosed on October twenty-six, nineteen seventy-seven. He survived *Variola minor*, the least serious form. The very last case of smallpox was an unfortunate lab error that caused the death of Janet Parker in nineteen seventy-eight. A minor mistake then that emphasizes the danger now. The only two known locations of live virus in the world are the CDC, where I work in Atlanta, and Vector, the State Research Institute of Virology and Biotechnology, outside Novosibirsk, Siberia. We believe the Soviets at the height of the cold war were manufacturing tons of weapons-grade biological agents, including smallpox virus, but we can't confirm it. Imagine making vats full of these terrible poisons. Unfortunately, when the cold war ended, the security of Vector was questionable. It is rumored that Soviet scientists and technicians may have defected and set up labs in other countries. Candidates are Iran, North Korea, and maybe China. Some believe several other nations may be seeking biologic capability—India, Pakistan, Israel, Cuba, Serbia, and some former Soviet republics. Who knows for sure, but the threat is real. How real, we're not certain."

Jackson showed more slides. He projected a picture of a young adult male who looked far worse than any of the others. He lay on a bed, propped up on pillows, and bare from midchest; every inch of visible skin was covered with thick, black pox lesions. Harry felt a twinge in his stomach. How could a human being possibly look so terrible?

"This is hemorrhagic smallpox," Jackson said, pointing to the screen. "Smallpox takes many forms that can vary greatly, and though I saw thousands of cases, even I couldn't identify some of them just by their initial appearance, especially early in the course of the infection. That's why it might be difficult for physicians like you who've never seen a case to recognize it. Two of the worst forms are *flat* smallpox, where the pox lesions are flat, coalesce, and the skin slips off in sheets, and *hemorrhagic*, which you see here, where the person's membranes disintegrate and blood oozes from all the victim's orifices. Notice how his eyes are black from blood. Hemorrhagic smallpox is a terrible sight. Both of these forms are nearly one hundred percent fatal. Ordinary smallpox, which is the more common type, is between twenty and forty percent fatal.

"As you are aware, there is no cure for *Variola*. That's why vaccination is so important. Even though Edward Jenner invented the vaccination in seventeen ninety-six using *Vaccina* or cowpox virus—hence the name *vaccination*—smallpox was not eradicated until the nineteen seventies by using what we call "ring" vaccination campaigns. In these campaigns, each case of smallpox and all contacts of that case were quarantined and vaccinated, thus providing a ring of protection. In Africa, we isolated entire villages for weeks and vaccinated everyone. Obviously, ring vaccination was a success. Of course, quarantining people today may not be as simple."

Jackson concluded with a brief discussion of the CDC's rapid response plans and its communication systems. "Family physicians and other primary care physicians are the backbone of America's response," he said. "You are our public health system. If a bioterrorist attack should occur, you'll be seeing these cases, maybe even the very first ones. You need to be ready."

Harry jotted down the emergency phone numbers he would never use in his notebook. He looked around the room. Hardly a doctor had left. His watch showed exactly noon. At least Jackson finished on time.

Harry stood and faced the audience as Jackson flipped off the projector. "We thank Dr. Jackson," Harry said, "for his excellent discussion. I know you all are anxious to get out on the slopes, but we do have time for just a couple of questions. Does anyone have a question for Dr. Jackson?"

An arm shot up in the back, and Harry pointed to it. A thin, elderly man stood. Harry knew him. The old doctor, now in his eighties, had practiced for more than fifty years in a small town in southern Illinois and came to almost every conference, even to Vail, though Harry thought he looked too frail to ski.

"This ring vaccination you were talking about," the old doctor said, "in fact, this whole smallpox vaccine thing is a scam, isn't it, Dr. Jackson?"

Jackson stepped back to the microphone. "I'm not sure I understand the question, Doctor."

"Then let me ask it in another way," he said. "My understanding is that a mass vaccination program would require the use of the stockpiles of old vaccine. So you take a vaccine made of cow parts that was only eighty percent effective when it was new, then store it for forty years under questionable conditions, then dilute it to one-tenth its previous potency, and then spring it on the population based on the safety and efficacy data from decades ago. That's your plan?"

"I understand your concerns," Jackson answered smoothly. "And I assure you every effort has been made to make the vaccine as safe as possible." He may have heard such a question before. "Though the original vaccine appears to be highly effective, a cell-culture grown vaccine was approved in two thousand seven, and it is now being used by the military and some select first responders."

"Aren't we seeing problems already? I've read about serious inflammatory heart conditions and other side effects. I'm one of the few doctors here old enough to have actually given smallpox vaccine in my office, but that was before HIV, organ transplants, and immune-suppressive medications, which will make using the vaccine dangerous for patients. *And* it was before the glut of liability attorneys who will make using the vaccine dangerous for us doctors—or at least our pocketbooks."

Harry moved to the microphone to save the speaker. "Thank you for your comment. Since everybody's ready to ski, we appreciate the questions—"

"I have a follow-up question," the elderly doctor interrupted, with an insistent tone that Harry couldn't tactfully ignore. "I'd like to ask another question if I could."

"Of course," Harry replied reluctantly. "That's fine. What's your follow-up question?"

"Dr. Jackson, you expect us to believe that this so-called ring vaccination that you say creates a protective zone around the smallpox will work today in the United States?"

"It's been effective in other countries."

"That was years ago, and this isn't Africa. So you plan to quarantine large populations in this day and age without quarantine laws, immunize them without an effective public health system using an old vaccine that's dangerous or the new vaccine that's unproven and potentially unsafe, and then keep them from traveling for several weeks to see whether or not they're infected? That's the plan?"

"As I said, there will be some challenges. Congress is looking at some contingency legislation."

"I hope to hell we don't have to find out how well your plan works."

"That's all the time we have for questions," Harry cut in. As moderator, Harry was the timekeeper, and their time on the mountain was dwindling. Besides, he shouldn't let the participants beat up on the lecturer. "Please, doctors," Harry said, "have fun on the slopes. And be careful out there."

The doctors quickly filed out of the conference room. At the end of most lectures, someone would usually come up to the front to ask a few additional questions but not today. Obviously, they were ready to ski.

Harry stood with Jackson as the speaker gathered his papers and shut down his laptop. Harry waited because the moderator was tasked with closing the lecture hall. Jackson was almost done.

"Thanks for the lecture," Harry said. "It was very interesting. Sorry about those questions at the end."

"No, they were good. There *are* some tough issues."

"He's getting crotchety in his old age."

"So am I."

They both laughed.

"Actually," Jackson said, "the old doctor is right. Nothing about this topic is easy."

Jackson picked up his computer case, and they walked down the aisle toward the back of the conference room. Harry turned off the lights and pulled the doors shut.

"Then, Dr. Jackson, may I ask a question of my own?"

"Call me Hugh."

Harry nodded. "Then call me Harry."

"Harry it is," Jackson said, flashing Harry a smile. "Your question?"

"What are the chances that we're really going to see a serious bioterrorist attack in this country?"

Jackson paused a moment, growing more somber. "Unfortunately, Harry," he said, "the chances are high. Sooner or later it will happen."

"And you don't think we're ready?"

"After anthrax we've made some strides, but no, we're not ready. A lot of good people have been and are working hard, but the public has a short memory."

"You mean without a recent event."

Jackson nodded. "It's the reality of what we do."

They walked down the empty hallway and rode the elevator up to Jackson's floor. The doors opened, and Jackson stepped out.

"One thing's for certain," Harry said, holding the doors open. "Our doctor's right about the last part."

"What's that?"

"I hope to hell we never find out how good your plan works."

"Yeah," Jackson said. He looked away briefly, as if he were watching the consequences play out in his head. "Neither do I."

CHAPTER TWO

DECEMBER 2, 7:15 P.M. UTC+3
BAIDOA, SOMALIA

The dust swirled around the interior of the mud hut like a miniature cyclone, fueled by the constant, brisk wind blowing through the cutout doorway. The flies had multiplied a hundredfold since Mohammed had arrived, possibly drawn by the light inside. The terrible odor seemed to penetrate right through his skin, reaching to his very core. He hadn't expected the smell.

Mohammed stood solemnly over the mother and child. He was pleased he had found them still alive and exactly where they were supposed to be. Intelligence on this mission was crucial, and he felt fortunate theirs had so far been accurate.

He leaned over her. "Allah is great," he whispered in Somali to the young mother.

The woman held her eyes down and didn't respond, but he saw a subtle nod. She squeezed another drop of water into the dying boy's mouth and shifted some grass underneath his body. Mohammed whistled softly to signal the other men standing outside by the Range Rover, and one by one they stepped through the opening into the single room.

The space inside the circular hut measured about ten feet in diameter. The sidewalls curved upward to a round point six feet from the ground. Mohammed stood opposite the woman, his head bent over slightly to fit underneath the top, while the others crowded in around the child. Mohammed waited until all of the men were settled and then began speaking to them in Arabic.

"We now begin our jihad against America," he said in a low voice. Mohammed was a native Egyptian, with olive skin, black hair, and dark eyes, and he favored the thin, precisely trimmed mustache above a full beard that was common among Islamic males. At forty-five, he was the oldest of the four men. He had personally chosen each one of them to come with him. "Our fight is against the enemies of Allah," he continued, "and we have been called to war against America. The Americans are tyrants and oppressors who have brutally slaughtered our mothers, our daughters, and our sons. And they call us terrorists! The Americans are the terrorists! With the grace of Allah, we will bring the battle to their doorsteps. Yes, even to their very homes. Homes where they sleep peacefully, confident of their security. Allah, guide us in our jihad."

Mohammed paused a moment as he held his hand over the boy.

"This is the child I told you about," he said. "This is smallpox." He knelt down beside the boy. "There have been a number of cases of smallpox in eastern Africa that have gone undetected by the authorities, harbored by the impoverished nomads of this region. Some suspect it is because so many die of starvation and AIDS that there has not been an epidemic. Our contacts have known about it for some time. We think the West does not."

Mohammed looked up at the mother, nodded, and then leaned over the boy, coming to within an inch or two of his mouth. He took in a deep breath and held it. He batted away a few flies, and then breathed deeply several more times before he looked back up at the men.

"Neither the United Nations," he said, "nor the World Health Organization come to Somalia. The Somalis hate the Americans as much as we do." He turned his head back to face the child. "The Americans thought smallpox was eradicated in nineteen seventy-seven, but it's clear they were wrong. Allah is greater than the medicine of the West. Few in America have immunity to smallpox, and if our plan is successful, we will kill millions of Americans. *Allah-u akbar*. Allah is great."

Mohammed breathed for several minutes near the child's mouth and nose before standing up. He pointed to one of the men. The man was Abdul Bin Khalid, a Kuwaiti, though no one, not even Mohammed, knew his real name. He was a principal in the bombing of the U.S. embassy in Kenya and the USS *Cole*. Khalid was short, medium build, with a full, dark beard. He knelt down beside the boy and began to breathe deeply next to his face.

"They hope," Mohammed continued, "that their vaccines will save them, but they are old or unproven, and the American public is hesitant about the mass inoculation of the population. With the first cases of smallpox, they will panic. If we are able to infect only a hundred in each of the four cities we have targeted, we will paralyze the United States. It will be a great victory."

Khalid stood and the third man, Muhsin Al-Musaleh, knelt. Al-Musaleh was Egyptian like Mohammed, and they had known each other since they were boys, fighting side by side many times for the greater glory of Allah. Al-Musaleh had lost a brother in Afghanistan to an American laser-guided bomb that struck the Tora Bora complex before he could escape with Osama over the mountains and into Pakistan. Allowing Al-Musaleh to live after the fall of the Taliban was a mistake, and he would make the Americans pay.

"Smallpox is a slow death for them," Mohammed said, "but as effective for causing terror as any bullet, bomb, or plane. Allah be praised. Once you are contagious, you will go to big markets that they call department stores or shopping malls. You will be surprised at the excess and greed. In fact, you will be amazed at the infidels in a frenzy, buying worthless items for their religious holiday. The stores in all the cities will be packed with Americans. You should avoid government buildings and airports where the security is high. In the stores, the security personnel, even the police, are only looking for people who are stealing. Because of this, you will be safe there. The Americans have everything, yet they steal, and their security forces only protect the merchants from thieves. Incredible!

"It would be best if you seek American, not international, crowds if you can. For me, how ironic it would be if I could stand with a group of Americans viewing what they call Ground Zero, the site of our greatest triumph, the destroyed World Trade Center. They witness our strength while I am infecting them with the smallpox virus! They think they are safe! *Al-hamdu lillah!* Praise be to Allah!"

The others chanted in unison. "*Al-hamdu lillah!*"

The fourth man, Nazih Al-Sabai, a Libyan, knelt. At thirty-two, he was the youngest of the men. Both of his parents and a younger sister had been killed during the 1986 U.S. bombing raids in Libya. Mohammed watched him lean over the child and breathe near his mouth. Al-Sabai had been the one who had vomited outside, but he appeared fine to Mohammed now.

"We must get to within six feet of the Americans to infect them," Mohammed said, as he continued his briefing. "Americans don't like to get close to each other, but they will crowd into subways, trains, and lines for restaurants or museums. Each of you will have a map of your city with the best places marked. Having a map won't be suspicious—everyone has a map. Go to popular places. Get close to them and politely cough. Talk close to their mouths. Be friendly. If you are rude, they will remember you.

"As the rash gets worse, you must hide it. After the blisters, it turns into hard pustules like you see here. Cover your face with makeup. If the rash is too noticeable to hide, you must leave. By then you will be experiencing severe backaches and headaches, and probably vomiting. This means you are sick, and you must not wait too long. They must not find you, or they will know. I can't emphasize this enough. You have completed your jihad. You are prepared for heaven, and it awaits you. May Allah grant your families solace. You are a martyr. *Allah-u akbar*."

Nearly two hours had passed since their arrival, and it was pitch black outside when Mohammed watched the three men leave the hut to return to the Range Rover. Mohammed was confident that each man had been infected. The jihad against the Americans would be a success, and the Americans would not be prepared.

As Ahmed Musa Mohammed had planned from the beginning, he stood behind the mother, reached down, and in a quick motion easily snapped her neck. The boy's eyes turned to Mohammed, and he watched as Mohammed knelt beside him. Mohammed gently placed his large hands around the child's small neck. The boy did not move. He was too weak to struggle. His eyes never left Mohammed's, and Mohammed did not turn away as he applied a firm and steady pressure, holding his hands tight until the young boy's rapid, shallow breathing had completely stopped, forever ended.

The boy was dead. His soul was in heaven. Clear, running water. Sweet, abundant fruit. Paradise.

Before leaving, Mohammed buried both bodies beneath a thin layer of sand inside the hut and set the hut on fire. He stood near the Range Rover and watched the red and yellow flames climb upward into the black sky.

For Mohammed, his jihad had just begun, but for the mother and the child, their jihad was now complete. *Al-hamdu lillah*. *Praise be to Allah*.

CHAPTER THREE

DECEMBER 2, 1:00 P.M. MST
VAIL, COLORADO

Harry stepped out of the lobby of the Pines at Vail into the bright sunlight. The snow, heavy earlier, had let up, and only a few flakes drifted down. The wind was still. The temperature was in the low twenties, and several inches of fresh snow covered the slopes. Perfect skiing conditions.

Harry turned down Bridge Street and walked through Vail Village. He wore a red and black jacket over black ski pants and carried his skis on his shoulder; he looked like any one of the many skiers heading to the lifts. The village was quaint with boutiques, small shops, restaurants, and the famous Vail clock tower. The shops reflected Christmas at full tilt; there was a wide assortment of ornaments, trees, Santas, snowmen, elves, and reindeer—every imaginable Christmas decoration at every possible price. The village was crowded with people. Obviously those who weren't skiing were shopping. As he crossed Gore Creek, he stopped at the railing and admired the view. The sparkling clear mountain stream roared and tumbled through the rocks and snowy banks, carving its way through the very heart of Vail. "Its wildness is contained," Harry thought, "but not tamed."

After purchasing a lift ticket and waiting a short time in line, Harry stepped onto the lift platform, and the chair smoothly swung in from behind him, plucking him up for the trip up the mountain. The Riva Bahn Lift rose sharply toward the top of Two Elk Lodge, and with the swift movement upward, the air grew much cooler. Harry inhaled deeply and watched the pointed tops of the narrow pines sweep past him, the limbs of the tall trees touched white with a fresh snow. The valley's panorama opened up behind him. This was a spectacular display—the snow, the mountains, the trees, the sun, and the pleasant smell of the Rockies—and he had missed it all. Why had he taken so long to come back?

At the top, the lift dropped him off, and he skied down a little embankment to a gentle slope toward the restaurant. His wife and two daughters were sitting at a table on the outdoor deck. All three were dressed in identical ski outfits with black jackets and bibs, and had their blond hair pulled back in ponytails held by matching red scrunchies.

His daughters saw him and began waving. He waved back. His wife was initially facing the opposite direction, but as he approached, she turned around and smiled. Harry was glad to see the smile. Maureen seemed more relaxed, even happier, than he had seen her in a while. Lately there had been too much tension between them. He blamed himself; he was often too busy and distracted, as he struggled with the balance of home and work. Their first few years had been even rockier, and they had almost split, but ultimately they decided to stick it out. After nineteen years, it seemed to Harry to be the right decision. He hoped his good fortune would continue.

Harry's twin daughters, Amy and Audrey, favored their mother. The twins were *exactly* identical, and at times even he had trouble telling them apart, which was the joke of the family. Amy was fifteen minutes older and the better athlete, which was evident by her participation with the swim team, soccer, and softball. Audrey was the intellectual—a poet, artist, and musician. Both were fun and enjoyable company most of the time, but they could sulk and be temperamental in a flash. Maureen blamed preteen hormones. Friends with teenagers reminded them it would only get worse.

Harry jammed his skis and poles in the deep snow and walked up the stairs. He kissed Maureen and both his daughters, and then slid in next to his wife.

"We ordered you a hamburger and fries," Maureen said. "We're eating salads."

She knew him all too well.

"How's the skiing?" he asked.

"It was awesome," Amy said.

"The Northeast Bowl was all powder," Audrey chimed in.

"You went to the Northeast Bowl?" Harry said. "I thought you'd wait for me. Weren't you doing moguls?"

Both girls rolled their eyes. "Dad!" they said in unison in that tone Harry hated.

"We never know when you're coming," Amy added, as she gave him a little smirk.

I was here, and I was on time, he wanted to say. But often he wasn't, if he made it at all, and his family knew his pattern better than anyone.

"We've skied there most of the morning," Maureen said. "The snow earlier made the moguls hard to see, but it's almost stopped. Look at this view. It's just beautiful."

Harry knew Maureen was attempting to change the subject, her eyes flashing the *we're-on-vacation* plea.

"You're right," he said, agreeing with her. "The view is wonderful."

The snow-capped peaks, framed by an endlessly blue, cloudless sky, stretched out fifty miles in all directions. Harry had forgotten how breathtakingly beautiful the view was from the top of a Colorado mountain. He was pleased they were spending the afternoon together—something he didn't do often enough, especially with the girls. He had missed more than his fair share of their life events—sports, plays, programs—either on call or in the delivery room. It was an occupational hazard. But then he'd apologize, ask for their forgiveness, and they would, but it often didn't seem enough. As hard as he tried, the pattern would only be repeated, as he fell into the usual grind at home. Sometimes it was difficult for him to recognize that unless he was away.

Harry glanced up noticing a man with a slight limp and saw Hugh Jackson walking out of the restaurant carrying a tray of food. Harry was surprised—Jackson seemed a bit too old to be a skier. Jackson stopped and turned a slow circle searching for a place to sit. Harry scanned the deck and saw that all of the tables were filled.

"Hey, Hugh," Harry yelled across the deck as he stood and waved his arm at Jackson.

Jackson saw Harry and waved back.

"Would you care to join us?" Harry asked.

"I'd hate to interfere with your family time."

"Please, you'd be welcome."

As Harry pulled up a chair, he introduced Jackson to his wife and two daughters. Jackson set his tray down and shook hands with Maureen.

"Pleasure to meet you," he said. He turned to Harry's daughters. "And these beautiful young women must be twins."

The girls smiled shyly.

"Identical," Harry said.

"Can you tell them apart?"

"Most of the time," Harry said, "unless they switch places."

They all laughed because they knew it was true. Jackson sat in the chair next to Harry.

"Hugh was one of our lecturers, Maureen," Harry said. "He's from Atlanta."

"Atlanta is beautiful," Maureen said. "My sister lives there."

"It's a lovely city."

"So what is it that you do," she said, "besides lecturing at meetings in wonderful resorts?"

"That's the best part, but my real job is the head of the bioterrorism department at the Centers for Disease Control and Prevention."

"My goodness," she said. "That's a mouthful. Bioterrorism—is that like anthrax and smallpox?"

"That's correct."

"Harry has told me that he's had several lectures on that topic over the years. It's a shame anyone would ever use one of those terrible diseases as a weapon."

"Terrible, indeed," Jackson said.

"Your job is to make sure we're ready just in case anything like that happens?"

"That's right."

"So, are we?"

Jackson shook his head and glanced up at Harry before he answered her. "Do you want the truth?"

"Of course," she said.

"Actually, we are ill prepared."

"Why is that?"

"We're approaching this from an intellectual and scientific viewpoint. Our enemies are strategic. They're biding their time, waiting for the right opportunity, while we're studying systems and vaccine side effects."

Harry thought Jackson sounded much more pessimistic than he had in the lectures. And Jackson, Harry thought, was a person who should know when to worry.

"Sounds grim," Maureen said.

"Maybe not so grim. I could be wrong."

"I hope you're wrong," Maureen said. "And I hope your plans are a complete waste of time. You know…because it never will happen."

"I'd be happy if that were true," he said.

Harry glanced at his daughters' faces. They seemed oblivious to the conversation and were busy watching the skiers around them. Soon, though, knowing them, they would grow bored and become impatient.

"But it's a good topic for a lecture," Harry said, hoping to change the subject, "especially when the skiing is good."

"That's for sure," Jackson said, taking the hint. "And the skiing certainly looks great today."

They finished their meals. The twins were already chattering about the black diamond runs, but Harry wanted to practice in the basin first. Everyone said their goodbyes to Jackson, slipped on their skis, and headed for the lift.

Harry and his wife followed their daughters as they scampered up to the lift line to start their afternoon. As Harry watched the twins laughing and smiling, he couldn't shake the images of the children dying with smallpox, especially their desperate, hopeless eyes. He thought he saw a reflection of the sadness in Jackson, the toll of the tragedy, as if a part of his soul had been left there in eastern Africa.

In his lifetime, Harry had never seen such a tragedy. He hoped he never would.

* * *

DECEMBER 2, 4:00 P.M. EST
NEW YORK CITY

The Saint Joseph Hospital emergency room was always busy, but the last twenty-hours had been insane. Dr. Vicky Anderson looked at the rack with fifteen charts and moaned. She was working as hard and as fast as she knew how, yet the number of patients who were waiting grew faster than she could see them. The flu season had started two weeks earlier, and it was in full swing and not likely to let up anytime soon. She was working a double twelve-hour shift for the second time this week. At 6:00 P.M. she'd be off duty after twenty-four hours straight, and she couldn't wait to go home and crash.

Influenza was hitting the staff, too. Half were home sick, and several staff members still working in the ER probably should have been. A couple of the doctors were out, too. Hadn't anyone heard of flu shots?

Vicky picked up three charts at a time from the rack. She thumbed through the first chart quickly. The emergency room was designed as a pod with a central workstation for telephones, computers, and medical-record charting. Sixteen rooms were in a square surrounding the workstation, four on each side, with a blue curtain separating each of the rooms from the hallway. This afternoon, every room was taken, and the curtains were all closed. Six or seven patients also occupied stretchers crowded into the hallway. A couple of patients sat on chairs. The waiting room was packed, and there was a line checking in at the reception desk. It would be one of those days.

From the very beginning of medical school, Vicky's goal had been to be an ER doctor, but the constant grind was taking its toll. She felt like she had been working 24/7 all her life. She had been told she was attractive. Her auburn hair was cut short and flipped up stylishly. Her facial features were pretty and certainly not ordinary, and her complexion was flawless. She had a slender figure and a good sense of humor. Yet she didn't date and had no social life. She couldn't remember the last time she had gone to a movie or enjoyed a fancy candlelight dinner. The reason was mostly her career but raising two young children didn't help much. And neither home nor work was likely to get much better, especially during the flu season.

Vicky closed the patient's chart. As she started toward the first exam room, one of the nurses approached her.

"Dr. Anderson," the nurse said, holding out a chart. "I think you should see this one next."

"Sure," Vicky said, taking the chart from her. "What's she got?"

"Probably the flu. When she arrived, I thought she was going to stop breathing. Her pulse oximeter was down to fifty percent oxygen. Her respirations were increased at forty. So I started bipap on her, which I think helped."

The nurse pulled open the curtain for Vicky and then followed her into the room. Vicky stood beside the bed. The patient was old, frail, and looked quite ill. A bipap mask fit tightly over her mouth and nose, and Vicky heard the constant hiss as the bipap device forced air into her lungs.

"She looks better now that she's on the oxygen," the nurse said. "I ordered the routine lab, cultures, and X-rays. IV is next door and will be here in a minute. You want me to start any meds?"

"Let's use the pneumonia protocol. We need it quick."

"Okay," the nurse said, moving toward the doorway. "I'll get on it."

The mask made it difficult for the patient to talk, but when she didn't even try to answer a couple of questions, Vicky decided she was either hard of hearing or demented.

An elderly woman sitting in a chair next to the bed spoke up. "Mother has Alzheimer's. I'm not sure she can understand."

The daughter must be eighty years old, Vicky thought, which would make the patient…well…ancient. "Your mother's very ill," Vicky said. "It could be influenza. We're seeing a number of cases."

"I wouldn't be surprised," the daughter said. "It's going around at the nursing home. Mother has always refused the flu shot. She's old-fashioned. Doesn't like modern medicine."

"How old is your mother?"

"A hundred and four."

"My goodness," Vicky said. "Your mother did pretty well without modern medicine."

"She said she doesn't want to be kept alive. I'm not sure she'd want this breathing machine."

"It's called a bipap. It simply pushes the air in to get the oxygen deeper into her lungs. It doesn't actually breathe for her. We can stop it if you think it would be against her wishes."

Tears formed in the daughter's eyes. "No, why don't we continue it for a little while and see how she does. I just want her to be comfortable."

Vicky nodded. "We will certainly do that," she said gently. "I promise you."

Vicky stepped outside into the hallway. The nurse saw her and started toward her.

"Pharmacy's getting the antibiotics STAT," the nurse said. "Should be just a few minutes."

"Thanks. She doesn't look very good. I'm still afraid she's going to stop breathing."

"We couldn't put her on a ventilator even if we wanted to. There's not a ventilator left in the hospital. In fact, this is our last bipap."

"We may want to try to wean her off of that as fast as we can. We'll need it for someone else. Let's call her attending physician and see if we can get her admitted upstairs."

Vicky sat at the workstation and wrote her progress note. She still had three charts in her hand.

"Good morning, Vicky."

She turned to the voice behind her. It was Dr. Jack Newton, the medical director of the emergency room. Lately, his presence invariably indicated a problem. Besides, it wasn't morning. It was actually already afternoon. Knowing Newton, this was probably the first time he had stuck his head out of his administrative office.

"Hello, Jack," Vicky said. "What do you need?"

"I'm really in a pinch. I need you to work another shift."

"That's impossible. I haven't stopped for twenty-four hours. I'm exhausted. I just can't work another shift."

"How about six hours? We don't have any other options. Simmons called. He has a fever of a hundred and five, and can't move a muscle. He says he's so sick he can't raise his head off the bed."

"If I work six more hours, I won't just be sick, I'll be dead."

"I know, but what choice do we have?"

"You could try working a shift or two."

Newton smiled. "I've been away from it so long. I'd kill people."

"We wouldn't want you to kill anyone, would we?"

"So it's a yes?"

"I guess. I'll have to call my mom. She's watching the kids."

"Sure, give her a call," Newton said, walking away. "It'll just be another six hours."

Vicky watched him walk down the hallway. Six more, then six off, and then another twelve. "Thanks a lot," she said under her breath.

Vicky picked up the phone and dialed her house. She hated calling her mother again. It was the third time this week. Though her mother was the children's grandmother and would never complain, Vicky didn't like taking advantage of her. For the past three years, the two children, girl ten and boy eight, had been her responsibility after her sister, Kelly, had died of ovarian cancer at the age of thirty-four—Vicky's age. Their deadbeat dad had moved to Hawaii one month after Kelly's diagnosis, and he had missed the six months of grueling chemotherapy, tortuous surgical treatments, and excruciating pain she had suffered to the very end. Vicky hadn't heard a word from him since and never expected to see a dime of support. Good riddance. The children were her responsibility, but without her mother, she couldn't manage.

The phone rang a couple of times before her mother answered.

"Hi, Mom."

"Hi, Vicky. Shift about over?"

"No, Mom. That's why I'm calling. They want me to work another six hours."

"How can you do that? You've already been working twenty-four straight."

"I know, but there's no one else. Simmons is out with the flu."

"Did Newton ask?"

"Yes, Mom. He's my boss."

"You shouldn't let him run you around like that. You have a life, too."

"Simmons is too sick to come in. I don't have a choice."

"You'll be sick, too."

"I know. I told him. How are Becky and John?"

"They're fine."

Vicky could sense her mother wasn't finished with her comments about Newton, the emergency room, and the number of hours that Vicky had to work, but thankfully her mother let it drop.

"Becky has a lot of homework," her mother continued. "I'm trying to help her, but my old brain is just too slow."

"I don't think mine's much faster. I'll help when I get home."

"You'll go straight to bed when you get home. I'll have some supper waiting."

"Thanks, Mom. I appreciate you."

"I know. Aren't you lucky?"

Her mother hung up and the line went dead. Vicky sat for a moment and listened to the sounds of the busy ER around her. She closed her eyes and tried to relax the tension she felt in her shoulders; she allowed herself a few seconds of slowly breathing in deeply. But this was no time to stop. If she did, she might not be able to start again. In fact, she thought she'd probably benefit from another cup of coffee, especially with six extra hours—six long, busy hours.

Despite this day and her fatigue, her mother was right. She *was* lucky. She enjoyed a busy, fulfilling career. Her mother was great. And she had two wonderful kids. Now, if she could just go home and get some sleep.

CHAPTER FOUR

DECEMBER 3, 7:00 A.M. UTC+3
DAY TWO OF EXPOSURE
CENTRAL SOMALIA DESERT

The sun rose over the horizon as Mohammed and the three men faced Mecca, knelt on their prayer rugs, and recited their morning prayers. The sky turned a brilliant red, streaked with purple clouds that faded overhead to total darkness behind them. Mohammed prayed especially earnestly this morning for the day might well be hazardous. He felt particularly vulnerable in Somalia, but Allah would protect them.

"There is no god but Allah," he prayed, "and Muhammad is his prophet."

After finishing their prayers, the men rolled up their rugs and placed them in the rear of the Range Rover. Muhsin Al-Musaleh had brought an old soccer ball, and he and Nazih Al-Sabai began kicking it around, enjoying a few minutes of exercise to break up the monotony of their long trip.

Before they left, Mohammed buried both the GPS unit that they'd used to find the child and the night-vision goggles he had used during the night, as planned; it was better not to have any technology with them when they arrived at their destination. He had mixed feelings about the equipment. Both had been useful, but only an unexpected deviation from the schedule would necessitate their use again.

Mohammed drove and, just as through the night, the Range Rover struggled over the potholes and crevices that pockmarked the dirt highway. The going was easier now that Mohammed could see the highway in the daylight. During the night, they had traveled using the night-vision goggles but not the headlights. A bright light in darkness was an easy target. What passed for a road was more a remnant, built by the 43rd Engineer Combat Battalion of the U.S. Army during the ill-fated American occupation in 1993. It had been neglected, washed-out in spots, and lacked a single smooth or level surface. Yet it was better than driving through the rough and rocky countryside, especially with the hundreds of unmarked landmines left over from the years of war between Somalia and Ethiopia, and the dozens of clan conflicts that continued to ravage the countryside. They were heading north and east, not far from the disputed and unde-marcated Ethiopian border, but would soon turn due west and into Somaliland, where the Issaq clan had declared an independent state from the rest of Somalia.

The men had spoken very little through the night. None had asked any specifics of their mission, and Mohammed didn't expect that they would. After their prayers, they had eaten their morning meal of bread, dried fruit, and nuts in the car. All the men were awake and alert. It was cool in the car, yet Mohammed knew the temperature wouldn't stop climbing until it hit a hundred degrees. They had plenty of drinking water, and except for an occasional stop to relieve themselves, there would be no breaks until they arrived at their destination.

"How much farther, Ahmed?" Al-Musaleh asked.

"About five hours," Mohammed said. "We should be there by noon. We will be staying with a man named Fazul Qaarey. Because the virus must incubate within our bodies, we will need a few days here in Somalia. Qaarey is a local warlord, and a pay-ment has been made to him. He and his men are Islamic, but we cannot trust them. Each of you has the passport that I gave you in Mogadishu. You will receive new pass-ports and identities in Cairo, but for now, you must memorize the identities in your current papers. I am certain they will scour your documents, so you must be perfectly correct. We need these clansmen for safe passage, but we will tell them only what we want them to know about us."

"You do not need to give us details," Abdul Bin Khalid said. "It would be better if you did not."

"I understand," Mohammed said. "But each of you already knows the most impor-tant detail—you are going to America with the smallpox virus inside you. However, we do not wish to let these Somalis find this out. You must not say anything." Mohammed's momentary pause emphasized his point. "Each of us has a different route to the United States, but we will all leave from Cairo." Mohammed pointed to Muhsin Al-Musaleh. "Muhsin, you will have a direct flight to America. The rest of us will make connections through Athens, Rome, or Singapore. Our destinations are Chicago, New York City, Los Angeles, and Washington, DC. After our stay in Somalia, we will leave. We will be in

America seven to ten days—two weeks at the most—before the illness begins. During this time, you will be in hiding. You will suffer from headaches, muscle pain, and fever. You will be contagious when the rash first appears. It will appear in your mouth, then on your face, and then on your entire body. Blisters form first. As soon as they do, you must begin to infect the Americans with the virus. You will only have a matter of days. Then you must go to the airport's long-term parking and find the car waiting there for you. You will get in the trunk. Allah is great. A large, plastic bag is in the trunk, and you will slide your body into it. Allah be praised. Tie the bag closed. Say your final prayers. And when you are finished with your prayers, take your cyanide capsule. Your jihad will be finished. *Allah-u akbar!* You will be in heaven."

Mohammed paused and the men remained silent. Mohammed said a prayer to himself before he began again.

"We will be staying outside Hargeysa for several days, and then we will travel on to Djibouti and board a vessel bound for the Port of Suez via the Red Sea. We will board in groups of two. Each pair will make its way to Cairo by bus, then on to the airport by taxi. If we traveled in a larger group, we would raise suspicions. Our new documents will be in a locker at the airport, and I will distribute them to you one at a time.

"I want to tell you about your destinations. In Cairo, I will give you a packet of information about your cities. You will have hotel information, maps, and a list of popular tourist sites. All this will be from an American tourist company so it will look very innocent. You will each have a small carry-on bag with a few clothes and toiletries. The authorities can search you—expect them to do this—but you will have nothing suspicious, except the cyanide capsule. It will be wrapped in a package marked aspirin."

"So, Ahmed, my brother," Al-Musaleh said, "we shouldn't take it for a headache, right?"

The men laughed. Mohammed allowed the light moment before continuing.

"You must carry the capsule with you at all times," he said. "You will have two credit cards and adequate American dollars. Your hotel will be first class. Ask for room service for your meals. Do not let the maid clean your room. You hang a plastic sign provided by the hotel on the doorknob outside your room. If at all possible no one should enter your room, and you must not have any women." Mohammed paused a moment. It would be immoral for them to have a woman, but they were men, and he had learned to be specific. "Muhsin, you will go to Chicago directly from Cairo and land at the O'Hare

Airport. I have seen this airport, and it is one of the largest in the United States. You will take a taxi to your hotel, a Holiday Inn near Michigan Avenue. There are many shops along Michigan Avenue, and there will be many Americans shopping.

"Nazih, you will go to Athens and then to Washington, DC; you will arrive at the Dulles Airport. You will take a taxi to your hotel, which is a Marriott near the Washington Mall. The Mall is where many museums and monuments are located. Go only to the tourist sites but not the government offices or the Capitol. The White House is there also, but it will be impossible to go there. Your hotel has many stores nearby with many people shopping. For your own safety, you must stay close to this area. There is much crime in Washington, DC."

"One could hope," Nazih Al-Sabai said, "that a secretary to the American president or a servant employed in the White House could be infected."

"We have not planned specific targets," Mohammed said. "It is too risky."

"Then may Allah strike as a great serpent," Al-Sabai said, "with this virus as its poisonous venom."

"Yes, Nazih," Mohammed said. "It is as we hope."

"Thanks be to Allah," Al-Sabai said.

Mohammed nodded, and then he continued. "Abdul, you will be going in the direction opposite to the one taken by the rest of us; you will go to Singapore. Your target city is Los Angeles. You will be traveling a few miles south to a hotel in Anaheim. Abdul, consider yourself lucky. You will be going to Disneyland. Many thousands of Americans will crowd together to see Mickey Mouse, and you will easily walk among them."

Abdul Bin Khalid nodded.

"I will be going to New York through Rome," Mohammed said, "and staying near Times Square. I may be genuinely the most fortunate because I should have the opportunity to see the site of the World Trade Center, the blessed fruit of jihad. Praise be to Allah. For all of you, you must remember that America is not safe. It is not only the danger of your mission that concerns me, but it is also the rampant crime in America. You must stay in public areas and not wander down side streets. Many of their criminals carry guns. For a few dollars, they will leave you a victim on the side of the road and our objectives could be jeopardized. These infidels are a godless people. But Allah is faithful and will be with us."

Mohammed finished, and for the next couple of hours there was no conversation in the vehicle. The windows were down, and the air blowing in from the outside was warm, but the car was growing hotter as the sun bore down on its black metal surface. The men were beginning to sweat. Thick dust billowed out behind the car, and Mohammed knew they were visible for miles. They had passed no other vehicles, which seemed odd. Mohammed occasionally glanced in the mirror to see if someone was following them. He saw no one.

It was not a coincidence that they had not seen anyone and had not been stopped. The clansmen would choose their own time and place.

As they turned west, they encountered increasing signs of human habitation. Along the road were a number of single-story cement-block buildings. All were meager, simple structures. Some were dilapidated, and some were in ruins. Regardless of their condition, most appeared to serve as dwellings or homes. Only occasionally did they see an adult outside, and then only women. Young children in tattered rags, some without any clothing at all, played in the dirt. Every mile or so he saw a child on a rooftop talking into a cellular phone. Mohammed was aware the cellular service in the urban areas of Somalia was excellent, and obviously service was available in this area. Their progress was being tracked and reported.

As they approached the outskirts of the village of Laascaanood, the number of buildings increased, and he saw more people. He thought he caught a quick flash of metal over the edge of a roof. Was it a gun or was he paranoid?

Mohammed glanced up at his rearview mirror. This time two *technicals*—paramilitary open-bed trucks—were driving side by side and approaching fast from behind him, barely visible in the cloud of dust stirred up by the Range Rover. A large-caliber machine gun was mounted on each truck, facing forward and pointed in their direction. Six or seven clansmen, their faces covered with scarves and each holding an automatic rifle or a grenade launcher, were standing on the open bed. Mohammed stayed on his course and was very careful not to change speeds or appear to drive erratically.

They would soon meet Fazul Qaarey.

Mohammed slowed down as they approached an intersection. One-story, seemingly empty buildings lined both sides of the road. As they drew nearer to the intersection, a large two-ton truck pulled out just past the last building ahead to block the road. Mohammed brought the Range Rover to a complete stop. The two trucks that were following them stayed back about fifty feet. On each side of the cross street a truck, also mounted with a machine gun and carrying a dozen armed clansmen, waited. Other armed men stood on the ground around the trucks and in the doorways of the buildings. The local warlord had chosen this time and this place.

Mohammed slowly opened the car door and stepped out to the street, lifting both arms high into the air. "There is no god but Allah," he said loudly in Somali, "and Muhammad is his prophet."

A man exited the building on the corner to the left of the Range Rover and casually approached Mohammed. He was a short and stocky black man with gray hair and a gray beard; he was wearing a white linen shirt and black slacks that were crisply starched, which was unusual in the hot, humid desert. He was unarmed and appeared as if he had no cares. A small stub of a cigar hung from his mouth, and he reached up for it, flicking the ashes to the ground. When he was within five feet of Mohammed, he stopped.

"Praise be to Allah," the man said in Somali. His voice was coarse and guttural.

"And the blessing of Allah be upon you," Mohammed said. "I am Ahmed Musa Mohammed."

"My name is Fazul Qaarey."

Mohammed counted to himself the number of armed men on the rooftops of the buildings around the intersection, in the doorways, and on the trucks. Two large-caliber machine guns were behind them and one was on each side. This man liked protection.

Mohammed signaled his men, and they climbed out of the Range Rover. They gathered in a group behind him, far enough away from Qaarey so as not to appear potentially threatening. As they had been trained, their arms and hands hung loosely at their sides, out in the open, without hostility or provocation.

"We welcome you to Somaliland," Qaarey said. He dropped his cigar and rubbed it in the ground with his foot. He reached into his shirt pocket and pulled out a fresh eight-inch Cuban Partagas. After lighting the cigar and drawing in the smoke, he gestured to Mohammed, offering him one.

Mohammed shook his head. "We are grateful for your hospitality," he said.

"Please follow us."

The two-ton truck in front of them backed out of the street, and a black, late-model Mercedes sedan slowly advanced toward them. The car was in near-perfect condition, freshly washed and polished, with few dents or scratches. The shiny, dark surface reflected the bright overhead sun like a mirror. Its windows were rolled up and heavily tinted, obscuring the interior. Somali flags—blue with white stars scattered in the center—were attached to each side of the front hood, imitating an embassy vehicle or a presidential limousine. Mohammed suppressed a response to the pompous display. When the Mercedes stopped, the driver jumped out of the car and opened the passenger door for Qaarey. The driver, who couldn't have been more than sixteen, wore a ball cap backward and had a Russian AK-47 with a short metal stock slung over his shoulder. He raised his arm to signal the other drivers to start before climbing back into the Mercedes. Mohammed and his men returned to the Range Rover, and Mohammed started the engine. The Mercedes turned around and waited until one of the armed trucks from the side street was positioned in front and the other from the opposite side moved in behind. As Mohammed pulled in behind the second truck, the two remaining trucks formed a single column to his rear.

The convoy began to move slowly, then quickly picked up speed. The road was much smoother here than during any other part of their trip. As they reached forty miles per hour, the dust kicked up, and Mohammed rolled up the windows and turned on the air conditioning. They were approaching their destination.

Mohammed followed along in his place in the convoy, but he was uncomfortable surrounded by Qaarey's armed men. He was a warrior. He and his men were unarmed. They were safer without weapons, but the situation made Mohammed feel exposed and defenseless. Allah would protect him. This was their jihad, and it was against the Americans not these Somalis. But he would kill them, too, if he had to.

CHAPTER FIVE

DECEMBER 3, 2:00 P.M. EST
DAY TWO OF EXPOSURE
ATLANTA, GEORGIA

The glass and masonry office building housing the office of Dr. Hugh Jackson rose above suburban Atlanta with a perfect view of the sprawl of urbanization—the evidence of the South's new prosperity. The Centers for Disease Control and Prevention, known around the world as the CDC, had more than ten Atlanta locations and thirty buildings, including central facilities stretching along Clifton Road. Jackson's office occupied a small corner of the fifth floor. Assigned the job and the office fourteen years earlier, his list of credentials was as long and impressive—Stanford undergrad, Harvard Medical School, the New York Public Health Department, the World Health Organization for eastern Africa, the Department of Health and Human Services in Washington, DC, and finally, instead of the long-anticipated retirement he had planned and deserved, head of the Bioterrorism Department at the CDC.

The CDC was huge, employing 8,500 people in forty-seven states and forty-five countries; there were 5,000 employees in Atlanta and 1,600 at the headquarters complex. The headquarters was such a maze of hallways and corridors, extensions and additions, that Jackson frequently got lost trying to find his office, partly because he had a terrible sense of direction and partly because he was seldom there. He had traveled so much in his fourteen years, especially since September 11th and the wars in Iraq and Afghanistan, that he occasionally joked that his designated parking spot had been given away at least ten times because he so rarely used it. The administrators must have concluded, he would quip, that he had died, retired, or left the country.

Though responsible for a wide variety of services, the CDC was especially known for infectious disease monitoring and recommendations for treatment. The Atlanta site stored and studied the most dangerous infectious materials in the world, including HIV, anthrax, Ebola, and 400 different strains of smallpox. It was the only location anywhere in the Americas that stored the smallpox virus, which was given the highest precaution—biosafety level four, which meant scientists working with it wore protective suits, gloves, and helmets. Security was absolutely rigid both biologically and militarily, and the site was inaccessible to all but a select few. Although Jackson was considered the country's top expert on smallpox, even he did not have clearance for biosafety level four.

The smallpox virus should have been destroyed in the 1990s, Jackson had argued, as did many of the world's leading scientists. The World Health Organization had met in Geneva in 1996, and the representatives of a hundred and ninety countries had agreed. The date to incinerate the smallpox stocks had been set for June 30, 1999, but the designated date passed without action by the United States or Russia, the only known sites of the virus. Testimony before the U.S. Congress by a former Russian scientist relating the extent of the former Soviet Union's bioterrorism plans using smallpox had scuttled support for destruction. More worrisome, Jackson thought, were the reports of the attempts to alter the genetic structure of the virus. If this could be done, aggressive new strains of smallpox or entirely new viruses could be created. Even more disturbing, as if straight out of a science fiction nightmare, the new strains of viruses might be unaffected by the current vaccines and could therefore potentially cause the greatest, most deadly epidemic in human history. Jackson still believed the stored smallpox virus should be destroyed, yet his contrary position didn't seem to bother the current CDC and Washington administrations. He still had his job.

Jackson decorated his office in what he called controlled clutter. Stacks of medical journals were piled around the floor. The walnut desk, only partially visible under all of his papers, was over a hundred years old. It had belonged to his grandfather, a country doctor in rural Maine. Next to it was the dark brown leather chair Jackson favored, its edges worn from extended hours of use. Two maroon upholstered chairs in front of his desk would have invited visitors to sit, except that both were loaded with unopened mail. Books were stuffed in total disarray in a bookshelf along one wall. Three file cabinets were crammed with papers, without hope of ever closing again. A large flatscreen monitor overwhelmed a credenza behind his chair, and a wireless keyboard leaned against the wall. His laptop was open and perched precariously on a solid inch of loose papers on his desk, waiting for the slightest vibration to send it plummeting. His secretary, Nellie, sitting outside in the adjoining office, was in charge of filing, except he had strictly forbidden her to touch anything beyond the threshold of his office. He'd find his stuff if he needed it, he told her. If she touched one thing, as far as he was concerned, it'd be lost forever.

Jackson was hunched over his desk, vigorously typing on his laptop. He had much to do. He would finish the article for the *New Yorker* magazine first. Next, he'd tackle the unanswered e-mails filling the flatscreen on the credenza. Since 9/11 the e-mails came nonstop. Indeed, since the Twin Towers and the anthrax attacks, the realization of American vulnerability, his workload had increased enormously. Jackson had authored several books about bioterrorism, updated the CDC newsletters weekly, served as an adjunct professor at Emory University in Atlanta for three classroom hours a week when he was in town, and testified as an expert at Congressional committees and endless, and frequently pointless, meetings at the Health and Human Services Department. He traveled extensively, lecturing about bioterrorism to medical groups, universities, and health departments—just about anyone who would listen.

He essentially had no personal or family life. His wife of forty years had died of breast cancer two years earlier. The pain of his loss was on his mind daily. He had two boys, both grown and both workaholics like their old man; one was in Philadelphia and one was in Denver. Neither had children. He hadn't seen the boys much after his wife died, but with no grandchildren to motivate him, it didn't seem to matter. He'd call, or they'd call occasionally, and that was enough. He had no ties to property after he sold the house and moved into an apartment. No hobbies. No golf. No dogs or cats. His life consisted of nothing but work—exactly the way he wanted it.

Mike Lafitte walked into Jackson's office and plopped into one of the chairs across the desk. He didn't bother moving the mail.

"How was Vail?" Lafitte asked.

"It was great," Jackson said, looking up, "but I'm paying the price now."

"Snowed under with paperwork?"

"Very funny."

Lafitte was the supervising epidemiologist in the bioterrorism department. Tall, slender, an avid runner with a quiet manner and good looks, he was the consummate Southern gentleman, born and raised within a stone's throw of Augusta National, home of the Masters golf tournament. He was single and a gourmet cook, and Jackson had frequented his dining table in the months following his wife's death. At first, Jackson ate very little, and Lafitte talked a lot. After a time, Jackson talked his heart out, and Lafitte quietly listened—a kindness Jackson would never forget.

Jackson pushed away from the desk. "It's amazing how much accumulates while I'm gone. I was hoping you'd do some of it for me."

"Oh, I meant to do that," Lafitte said, smiling. "How long have you been back?"

"About an hour."

"Good skiing?"

"Very nice. Great weather. Good powder."

Lafitte sat up and pulled a memo from his briefcase. "While you were vacationing at the taxpayers' expense, we've been slaving away."

"I'm sure of that," Jackson said. "What have you got?"

"Actually, about the same." Lafitte slid the memo across to Jackson. "Nothing major. We've seen a big drop in the unconfirmed anthrax reporting. Of course, the West Nile virus has fallen off since the fall. Influenza is hitting hard, especially in the Northeast and Midwest. A smattering of the usual stuff. I won't bore you."

"Good. I hate being bored."

"One of the grad students did a study that showed a direct proportional increase in CDC reports with the number of government terrorism alerts."

"Like that would be a surprise."

"So without any recent alerts, it's actually been a little quieter around here. We did have a couple of interesting cases. A patron at a restaurant outside of Minneapolis reported that a person of Middle Eastern descent had sprayed the salad bar with a biological agent. We did investigate that one."

"What did you find?"

"It turns out that a man of Iranian descent, but who was born in the United States, had used his asthma inhaler while he was in the line."

"You know, though, that's the exact scenario that worries me. If a biologic agent had been used and made the media, it could literally shut down our produce and restaurant industries. Panic with the public is an odd thing."

"The other was a woman in Phoenix who thought a perfume tester in a department store had a toxin in it and made her sick."

"Did it?"

"Did it have a toxin in it?"

"No, did it make her sick? Some of those women's perfumes make me sick."

Lafitte rolled his eyes. "We sent out teams on both. The budget people are putting the pressure on us because we keep coming back empty-handed."

"We *always* want them to come back empty-handed. Do we have to have a biologic attack before our existence is justified?"

"Probably," Lafitte said, "if we're going to satisfy the accountants. Public interest is waning. Budgets are tight. The politicians listen to the polls."

"We have to hope for sensible leadership."

"Maybe, but sometimes I think it'd be better if we found a few actual terrorists. Find them before they strike, of course. Then we'd have a budget."

"Start looking. They're out there."

"I bet you're right," Lafitte said, "but still I hope you're wrong. Lots of bad people in the world are capable of bad things."

"Actually, I've heard there's been some grumbling in the intelligence community."

"How so?"

"Friend of a friend in Washington. You know how that goes. Something 'troubling.' Biologic. Unlikely to be picked up by our surveillance, whatever that means. That's all he could say."

"Credible?"

"Hard to know, isn't it? It always seems *something* is out there, and probably it always is, but this one was enough to perk my ears up. Timing would be good."

"Any special precautions?"

"Let's keep it low key for now, but we should keep our guard up. Look for coincidences and unusual patterns. One day it will be real. The trick is to know which day."

"Okay, boss."

"I should have retired when I had the chance," Jackson said, shaking his head. "Smallpox, anthrax, and terrorists. All I ever wanted was to be a good doctor. But if this becomes a reality, I'm not sure I'm ready to see it."

"Let's hope we don't."

"I pray to God we don't."

CHAPTER SIX

DECEMBER 3, 11:00 P.M. UTC+3
DAY TWO OF EXPOSURE
HARGEYSA, SOMALIA

Fazul Qaarey's residence was on the outskirts of Hargeysa, built in the center of a compound of buildings. It had the security of a military installation, with razor-wire fence surrounding the entire property and electronic sensors and video cameras aimed in every direction. Patrols of armed men walked the perimeter under floodlights powered by several large generators that kept the compound totally illuminated.

At the entryway of the house, Mohammed and his men removed their shoes and set them with the other footwear lined neatly at the doorstep. Two of Qaarey's men who looked to be no older than teenagers, carrying AK-47s, showed the visitors to their quarters. The room was plain and windowless but acceptable. It was equipped with cots and mosquito netting, and all four would sleep there. Mohammed would have preferred to have eaten a light meal and retire to the sleeping quarters where he could meditate, pray, and recover from the fatigue from the previous twenty-four hours. But Qaarey insisted they all dine together, and Mohammed did not wish to appear inhospitable.

The visitors were escorted from their quarters through the house to the dining room. As they passed through the hallways and living areas, Mohammed noticed oriental rugs, ornately carved furniture, and the latest electronic equipment—several flat-screen televisions and an advanced computer system. On the walls was a variety of artwork, including a painting of a nude woman reclining. Mohammed was repulsed but held his tongue.

In the dining room, three wooden tables were aligned end to end across the room and covered with white tablecloths and place settings of fine china, lead crystal, and silver flatware. Thirty or so men sat on metal folding chairs around the tables.

Plain, white walls enclosed a room that lacked any other furniture or decoration, in stark contrast to the excess of the living areas. Qaarey was sitting at the head of the table, and as they entered, he pointed to some empty chairs near him. Mohammed and his men took their seats. Qaarey introduced the mayor of Hargeysa to his left, the chief of police to his right, and at the other seats a few of his friends and relatives. All the men in the room wore *futas*, long rectangles of cotton cloth wrapped on their heads as turbans, and an impressive display of gold, silver, and carved ivory jewelry. Qaarey spoke in English, though Mohammed was told he knew several languages besides his native Somali, including Italian, French, and Arabic. He failed to introduce five of the men sitting closest to him, and Mohammed assumed they were his bodyguards. All the men around the tables, except for Mohammed and his men, were armed. Each carried personal sidearms, and some had two. A stack of rifles and automatic weapons, mostly Russian-made AK-47s, leaned against the wall in a corner of the room. Among them were a couple of handheld antitank missiles and a grenade launcher. "Practically an arsenal," Mohammed thought. "Offense was the best defense."

After all were seated, the food was served, with Mohammed and his men receiving the first portions. The meal was lavish: tender roast kid on a bed of rice steamed in a variety of spices, lamb on kabobs with onions, several types of fish, a couple of pasta dishes, *muufo*, a Somali flatbread, corn, black beans, and piles of bananas, mangoes, plantains, figs, raisins, and grapes. Three heavyset women dressed in brightly colored flowing gowns from their necks to their toes, their heads entirely covered with white burkas, carried in the food on silver trays. Mohammed suspected that the traditional veils were probably for their benefit, but of course he wasn't certain. These were the only women Mohammed had seen at the compound. He had observed no children.

"The rice is imported from Kenya," Qaarey said. "The pasta from Italy. The fruit, fish, and lamb are local. Do you like?"

"Delicious," Mohammed said. He had eaten very little.

"You would like more? Your men have not eaten much either."

"We're not very hungry after our long journey."

Qaarey was a heavy man and ate like he was starving. He tore off a piece of lamb and talked as he chewed. "My uncle has asked me why you are here," Qaarey said. "I could not tell him."

"We are on a journey for religious reasons," Mohammed said. "Praise be to Allah. We will be meeting with the holy clerics in Cairo."

"You travel through Somalia to reach this destination?"

"It is our belief that Allah has directed our path."

"Allah guided you to stop in the night in the desert of Somalia, and for this you needed my protection?"

"Our vehicle overheated," Mohammed said calmly, without hesitation. He had anticipated such a question. "This required that we stop."

"And you traveled at night with no lights?"

"We had a mechanical failure."

"Oh, I see. I am to believe this?"

Mohammed did not answer, and no one else spoke. Of course, both Qaarey and Mohammed knew it was a lie.

The questions were rude and in poor taste. Qaarey should have no need to know the nature of their travel nor was it his business. Mohammed hoped Qaarey's interest merely reflected idle curiosity.

As the men finished eating, the women began clearing the dishes. Several of the men pulled out small pouches and began chewing *khat*, a mild narcotic-like reed common to Somalia, stuffing small amounts in their cheeks. For twenty minutes, no one in the room said a word.

"I do not believe," Qaarey said finally, breaking the silence, "that you are speaking the truth."

"The call to wage war against the infidels and enemies of Islam has been made to all Muslims," Mohammed said, his voice soft but his eyes fixed directly on Qaarey. "One should be cautious when interfering with the will of Allah."

Qaarey laughed. Several of his men began laughing with him. Mohammed said nothing. Qaarey stood. He walked to the corner and picked up an AK-47, pushed the stock up against his shoulder, and pointed the weapon at the ceiling.

"I also ask for Allah's protection," Qaarey said, looking down the sights. "There is an Arabic proverb that says She accused me of having her malady, then snuck away." He dropped the weapon, replaced it in the stack, and looked back at Mohammed. "We have no morals in this country, but it is no different in the world. We have our clans—I am Issaq—but it is understood that I preserve myself ahead of my clan. You are Allah's servant, you say, but you do no less."

"That is where you are wrong," Mohammed said politely. "The crimes committed against the Muslim nation are a stain on every true believer. Muslims have been slaughtered and robbed of their honor and property, and the oppressors who subject the Arab nations to aggression should be punished."

"America?"

"America leads the list for desecrating the soil of our holy mosques, supporting the Zionist expansion into Palestine, and attacking and murdering our Arab brothers. Muhammad's call is to all mankind, and his message is to all nations. We ask America to embrace Islam. Our fight is against unbelief."

Qaarey returned to his seat. "I have prayed diligently about your mission," Qaarey said. "All should fight against America and the Zionists."

"Pardon me, my brother, but we are not on a mission. We are on a religious trek to Cairo."

Qaarey shook his head. "You insult me."

Mohammed opened up his arms. "It is not my intent to insult you," Mohammed said. "If I did so, my brother and most generous host, I regret it greatly."

Qaarey clapped his hands and one of the women came back into the room. She was carrying a silver tray of small glasses, each filled with a light-brown liquid.

"It is scotch," Qaarey said as the woman began passing out the glasses. "Please join us. It is imported from Scotland. Thirty years old."

Mohammed stood. "It is forbidden for us," Mohammed said. "We are grateful for your hospitality, but we must retire. We will be staying several days, so maybe we can continue our enjoyable conversation at a later time."

Qaarey took a glass from the tray and drank the liquor. He took a second glass and lifted it toward Mohammed. "To the destruction of America," Qaarey said and quickly drained the second glass.

Mohammed nodded slightly. His men stood, and Mohammed moved to the doorway.

"May Allah grant each of you a peaceful sleep," Mohammed said.

Qaarey snapped his fingers and two guards, both armed, came forward to escort the four guests back to their quarters.

When the guards left them alone, Mohammed checked for electronic listening devices and found none. He believed they were present nonetheless, but no one would discuss anything of consequence anyway. He had worked out a sentry schedule before they had arrived. Each would take two hours. His was first. Mohammed rolled out his rug and said his prayers for the fifth time this day before taking his position as sentry. He would be up again for prayers at dawn.

* * *

Mohammed was instantly awakened by the sound of the metallic click, but before he could move, the steel of the AK-47 was shoved against his forehead. A bright flashlight blinded him, the light flipped on a few inches in front of his face. As his eyes adjusted, he saw ten of Qaarey's heavily armed men aiming guns at him and his men. Qaarey stood in the doorway. He was holding an automatic pistol in his left hand. His head was bare, and he wore the same white linen shirt and black slacks he had worn earlier.

Mohammed glanced at Al-Sabai. He was sitting on the floor near the door. A uniformed black male held a large, serrated knife against his throat from behind. Two other soldiers aimed pistols at each side of his head. Al-Sabai had been the sentry while the others slept. At Mohammed's gaze, Al-Sabai cast his eyes downward.

Mohammed slowly rose to a sitting position, pushing the gun barrel forward as he moved. "What time is it, my brother?" Mohammed asked without emotion. "And why this rude awakening?"

"Shut up," Qaarey growled.

Qaarey was chewing *khat*. He reached into a pouch slung over his shoulder and stuffed another pinch of the narcotic into his mouth. He seemed to be enjoying the moment.

"While I was dreaming," Qaarey said, leaning against the doorway, "an angel of enlightenment came to me. The angel said to me, 'These men are a disgrace to Islam. They cheat, and they lie in the name of Allah.' The angel said to me, 'They have come here to harm you, and you must protect yourself. These men have weapons that are great and powerful, and yet they are deceptive. They are the enemy of Allah.'"

"I assure you, my brother, that this is not true." Mohammed extended his arms in a gesture of peace. "We are brothers in Islam, and our war is with the unbelievers. You harm all Muslims by harming us."

"Where is your proof? If you are warriors, where are your weapons?"

"We have no weapons. We are armed only with the truth."

Mohammed dropped his arms, but his eyes did not leave Qaarey's. He sat quietly, his face showing no emotion, yet on the inside he was fuming. This ignorant African peasant was threatening him. The man would regret his disrespect.

Qaarey nodded to his soldiers. Some held their automatic weapons on Mohammed's men while others began taping the men's arms behind their backs with duct tape. They wrapped the men's legs together and stretched several strips across their mouths. Mohammed was left unbound.

"I assure *you*," Qaarey said, "that we *can* and *will* kill your brothers if need be." Qaarey pointed his pistol at Mohammed. "You. Come with me."

As Mohammed stood, two gunmen stepped beside him; he stepped over his bound and gagged men, and followed Qaarey out of the room. The soldiers escorted Mohammed down a hallway and through the kitchen, then out a back door to the compound grounds and into the night air. The compound was well lit with floodlights. The sky was dark, and Mohammed estimated it was around three in the morning. Al-Sabai's shift as sentry was to have ended in an hour. Qaarey crossed an open space behind the residence and around a series of one-story buildings to the back of the compound. The razor-wire fence along the perimeter was twenty feet tall. Floodlights projected fifty yards beyond the compound on to flat, barren ground until the light faded into darkness. The night was cool but without wind, and the sky was starless. Mohammed felt his pulse quicken and his mouth become dry. Why was he feeling nervous? He was prepared to die. *Allah, grant me strength*.

As they reached the back of the buildings, Qaarey stopped. Scattered about was the Range Rover, completely disassembled into a thousand pieces spread out over the entire area between the buildings and the fence. Eight or ten of Qaarey's men were shuffling through the parts, holding them up, examining each one.

Qaarey picked up a door handle and held it to within a few inches of Mohammed's face.

"What do you make of this?"

"It looks like our Range Rover."

"Do I care about your door handle?" Qaarey said, tossing the part back among the other pieces. "You know what we're *really* looking for."

"I'm not sure that I do."

"You think we're idiots?" Qaarey yelled, moving close to Mohammed's face.

Mohammed did not answer.

Qaarey's thick veins protruded from his forehead. His neck muscles were tense. He was so close that Mohammed could smell his foul breath.

"This is all we have," Qaarey shouted. "No guns! No money! No explosives! No weapons!"

Mohammed felt the sting of Qaarey's pistol as Qaarey raked his gun across Mohammed's face. The unexpected blow caused Mohammed to fall backward, and he landed in the dirt. For a moment he lost his breath. Instantly, Qaarey's two men moved their weapons to Mohammed's head, pushing hard against his skull. Mohammed saw their fingers at the triggers.

Qaarey aimed his pistol at Mohammed's forehead. "Tell me now," he barked, "or you die. *Where are your weapons?*"

"We are on a religious journey," Mohammed said softly. "And, as you have now confirmed, we are unarmed. Allah will protect us."

"No!" Qaarey shouted. "Only *I* will protect you. *If* it is my pleasure."

Mohammed said nothing. He did not reach up to his face, though he wanted to rub his cheek. He felt a trickle of blood flowing down his chin. He had moved his jaw when he had spoken and did not think it was broken. His lower back hurt, but he didn't think his back was seriously injured either. Mohammed was thinking about killing Qaarey first, then the two guards closest to him. He could probably kill all three before the others killed him. Qaarey was pacing back and forth. Occasionally he would walk away and kick a piece of the Range Rover. Mohammed noticed the soccer ball sliced into pieces. Several times Qaarey reached into his pouch for more *khat*.

"I should ask for more money," Qaarey said finally. "Your protection is expensive."

Mohammed did not respond. Qaarey stopped in front of Mohammed and leaned over him, glaring down at him for a moment. Suddenly with a vicious yell, he kicked Mohammed hard in the abdomen. Mohammed let out a groan and doubled over in pain. He lifted his knees to his chest, holding them to his abdomen with both hands.

"Are you worthy of my protection?" Qaarey shouted at Mohammed.

Mohammed's insides contracted, and he thought he would vomit. "We are men," he managed to say, "who have no value." He tried to breathe slowly to ease the pain. "We are unworthy...of even Allah's protection."

Qaarey reached down and held his pistol against Mohammed's forehead. Mohammed closed his eyes.

"What are you doing here?"

"We are on a religious—"

"Shut up!" Qaarey yelled in disgust. "I don't want to hear that."

Qaarey dropped his gun from Mohammed's head and began pacing again. The two gunmen did not move theirs.

Mohammed sensed Qaarey's dilemma. The warlord had hoped his visitors had arms or cash or something of value he could steal or trade. Without anything of value, all he had was them. He could demand more money, but from whom? He could kill them all and bury them in the desert, but he had been paid to protect them, and even in this dishonorable country, he would answer for such a dishonorable action. He could hold them hostage and wait, and this possibility worried Mohammed the most. If their smallpox infection started here, it would likely become an epidemic and alert the world, and the Americans would then be prepared.

Qaarey returned to Mohammed and signaled his men to pick him up from the ground. Mohammed attempted to stand straight, but the pain from the blow to his abdomen caused him to bend over slightly. He lifted his eyes to look Qaarey in the face.

"You can no longer stay here," Qaarey said. "Your car is inoperative." He pointed his pistol over his shoulder at what remained of the Range Rover. "We will transport you to Djibouti and assure your safe passage through Somaliland. Then we will be done with you."

"May Allah's blessing be upon you," Mohammed said.

Qaarey raised his arm as if to strike him again. Instead, he waved toward the residence, and the two men each took one of Mohammed's arms to lead him away.

"And my brother," Qaarey said.

The soldiers stopped and forced Mohammed around to face Qaarey.

"You should know," Qaarey said, his eyes fixed on Mohammed.

Mohammed met Qaarey's gaze without flinching.

"The Range Rover's lights were working. There was no mechanical failure."

"Of course there wasn't, you fool!" Mohammed thought.

Mohammed shoved his arms outward, pushing the two men away from him. He turned his back on Qaarey and headed for the residence.

CHAPTER SEVEN

DECEMBER 4, 7:00 a.m. CST
DAY THREE OF EXPOSURE
DEKALB, ILLINOIS, NEAR CHICAGO

Dr. Harry Bennett placed his hand gently on the baby's head and looked at the loop of umbilical cord wrapped around its tiny neck. The baby's face was a terrible dark blue. At the sight, Harry felt an intense wave of anxiety rush up from the pit of his stomach, and his heart instantly began pounding like a sledgehammer in his chest. He had only a few seconds.

"Don't push, Mary," he said firmly. "I need for you to breathe through this contraction. It's very important."

Mary Beckstrom nodded and immediately started breathing in short, rhythmic breaths. She squeezed her eyes tightly closed, the pain evident on her face. Harry carefully slid a finger underneath the cord and tugged it gently. The loop of cord was tight, but loose enough that he could slip it around and off the baby's head.

"Okay," Harry said, relieved. "I think the cord accounted for those brief decelerations. It's fine now, Mary, so let's give it a push."

Mary's legs had been positioned in metal stirrups, and a nurse stood on each side holding her thighs. Mary grasped both of her knees and pulled them toward her chest. Fred, Mary's husband, stood at the head of the bed next to her, gently touching her face.

"You're doing great," her husband said. "The baby's almost here."

Light blue surgical drapes covered the lower part of Mary's body, and a ceiling-mounted lamp cast a bright light on the area where the baby's head protruded. Harry sat on a stool at the end of the bed, dressed in surgical scrubs and wearing a mask, a paper gown, and sterile gloves. His hands supported the baby's head, which had regained some of its color. The baby had a thick mane of black hair, and its small eyes were firmly shut as it grimaced in the bright lights. Mary took a deep breath and let out a slow, constant groan as she bore down and began to push.

"You're doing fine, Mary," Harry said. "Keep pushing. Just a little more."

Harry applied gentle traction with both hands as Mary pushed. Within a few seconds, the baby's shoulders began to appear. The top shoulder slipped out first, quickly followed by the rest of the body.

"It's a boy!" Harry said.

Mary and Fred let out a simultaneous shout of joy. Harry briskly rubbed the bottom of the baby's feet to stimulate him to breathe, and the newborn started crying vigorously, immediately turning a bright pink. As Harry lifted the baby onto the mother's abdomen, she reached out to hold the infant, sweet tears rolling down her cheeks.

"Hey, proud Dad," Harry said to the father, "want to cut the cord?"

"Sure," Fred said, "if you'll show me how."

Harry held out the cord, and Fred snipped through it at a spot between Harry's hands.

"See," Harry said, "we have an expert."

The nurse from the newborn nursery took the baby to a warmer. She suctioned the baby's nose and mouth, and wiped the infant clean. Harry delivered the afterbirth and massaged the uterus a moment to make certain it was contracting. The baby weighed in at eight pounds two ounces, and he measured twenty inches. With each announcement, the parents hugged and kissed. Harry examined the infant at the baby warmer, and the exam was normal. When Harry saw a healthy baby with ten fingers, ten toes, and normal color, he always felt better. It wasn't always this easy.

"He's perfect," Harry said, handing the father the baby. "Why don't you carry him to the nursery?"

Mary was smiling. "Dr. Bennett," she said, "we're really glad you made it back from Vail."

"I wouldn't have missed it."

The parents were celebrating, and Harry loved to see it. Delivering a newborn was one of the most enjoyable parts of his practice. Though he had delivered over a thousand babies, it never grew old and was especially fun when the new parents were so excited. Harry was smiling almost as much as the parents themselves.

After completing the required paperwork, Harry changed clothes for the wards. His watch showed eight o'clock. Nearly all his deliveries seemed to come at night, and

Mary's was no exception. Her labor had started at midnight and proceeded rapidly, and he had made the quick dash to the hospital when the nurses had called him at five, arriving just as Mary began pushing. Two hours later, he was holding the crying infant. His day had started with a little excitement, but his brain was in the Colorado mountains, smelling the pine, breathing the crisp, clean air. Home from Vail at nine o'clock, awakened at one, up at five, and a baby at seven—he was back at work. His brain would have to adapt.

Five patients were on his hospital list for morning rounds. Two of the patients were post-ops and doing fine; one had chest pain that he thought was unlikely to be cardiac; another had congestive heart failure but was improving; and the last was his next-door neighbor who was hospitalized with pneumonia. His partners had covered them for him in his absence, but he would resume their care this morning. Five patients to see before his office began at nine o'clock. He'd have to hurry.

DeKalb County Hospital was located sixty miles due west of Chicago. His office was in Sycamore, ten minutes to the north. He would likely be late this morning, but in a town as small as Sycamore, his patients would understand. Mary was the mayor's daughter, and Harry would hear more questions about the birth than complaints about the time. On his first day back from Vail, with or without the questions about Mary, he would fall further behind as the day progressed. All his sick patients would have waited for him to return and would want to be seen immediately. He was in for a long day.

After finishing with his first four patients on rounds, Harry sat at the computer at the doctors' workstation and clicked on the last name on his list, opening Chester Jurney's record. Jurney had lived next door to Harry for several years, yet they seldom saw each other except when doing yard work. Though seventy, Jurney had always seemed vigorous and healthy. According to his partner's notes in the chart, for a couple of weeks Jurney had been coughing, and over the last two days he had developed fever, chills, and shortness of breath. Harry scanned the chart and reviewed the diagnostic tests and treatments. His partner had ordered two antibiotics, intravenous fluids, and breathing treatments. All looked fine. After clicking off the computer, Harry walked down the hallway to Jurney's room.

"Good morning, neighbor," Harry said as he entered the room. "How are you feeling?"

Jurney was in a private room. His breathing seemed comfortable, without distress or particular effort. Oxygen ran from an outlet in the wall behind the bed to a plastic nasal cannula in Jurney's nose, and IV fluids flowed through a tube inserted into the back of his right hand.

"Better now, Doc, since they started the oxygen. How was Vail?"

"Relaxing. I could have stayed longer. I reviewed your chart. Looks like pneumonia."

"That's what they said. When I came in, I was sick. For a week I had a cough, really high fever, headaches, and chills so hard I shook the bed. I vomited twice."

"Then I'm glad you're better. My partner started you on two strong antibiotics. Good choices. Should do the job."

"They're helping."

They talked several minutes, and Harry examined him, listening to his lungs.

"I'm glad you're back, Harry," Jurney said when Harry had finished.

"Glad to be back. I think we'll have you on your feet in a couple of days."

"That's good to hear. I hate hospitals."

"Don't blame you."

Jurney was Harry's last patient. After finishing on the floor, Harry grabbed his jacket from the coatrack in the doctors' lounge and slipped on his gloves and hat. As he opened the door to the parking lot, the stiff December wind hit him full in the face. An Arctic front had charged through the area the night before and dumped more than six inches of snow in its path. The temperature plunged to a frigid zero degrees. He knocked an inch or so of snow off his windshield and slid into the front seat of his four-wheel-drive SUV. Colorado was cold, Harry thought, but nothing like northern Illinois. The fierce winds blasting off the lakes caused an awful wind chill that consistently guaranteed a miserable winter. He had grown up here and lived his entire life in this area. For him, cold winters were routine.

DeKalb County Hospital had been brand new when Harry first joined the staff, and almost every day for the past twenty-five years he had driven out of the doctors' lot at the rear of the hospital and left for Sycamore, just as he was doing today. He calculated he had made roughly six thousand visits to this hospital. The hospital was a two-hundred-bed facility, and he was one of a hundred and fifty physicians on staff. He had delivered babies, assisted in surgery, and had treated patients in the intensive care unit, on the floors, and in the emergency room. He was chairman of the family medicine department this year and would be president of the medical staff next year. It was the type of practice he had always dreamed about in medical school. Yet sometimes after a vacation, he would wonder if he should find a practice with less work and fewer hours, maybe one of those nine-to-five insurance jobs where he denied authorizations for hospital stays or MRIs. Maybe he could give up twenty-five years of his practice and twenty-five years of relationships with his patients. His life would definitely be easier. Maybe one of these days.

Harry drove the ten minutes up highway twenty-three to Sycamore. Most of the traffic was going in the opposite direction, heading south for the East-West Tollway and on to Chicago, looking for better jobs or big city excitement or simply an early start on the Christmas crowds. The highway was already plowed and sanded, which made the driving easier and quite a bit faster than he had expected. A few minutes later he entered Sycamore and the traffic slowed. The speed of the traffic and the pace of life were slower in Sycamore, and like many small towns in the Midwest, there was none of that big-city craziness. That was fine with Harry. His four years of medical school and three years of residency were all in Chicago, and that had been enough for him.

Harry followed Main Street downtown past the brown and red brick buildings dating back to the late 1800s. Sycamore's historical district, quiet tree-lined streets with Queen Anne, gothic revival, and Victorian homes, had ninety-nine acres within its boundaries that were on the National Register, and the citizens of Sycamore were proud of that fact. He and Maureen had tried to tackle a Victorian fixer-upper. They spent every spare minute working to save it from falling apart, but Harry didn't have enough spare minutes, and the house finally won. They built a new house on the outskirts of town, with their enthusiasm for historic homes having somewhat deteriorated.

Sycamore had received a few more inches of snow than DeKalb, and the drifts on the streets were contributing to the slower pace. The town was still waking up, and only a few people were out and about. Harry turned off Main Street and into his office lot and parked. His office was a one-story, brown brick, flat-roofed structure surrounded by four towering, stately sycamore trees. The sycamores were some of the oldest and largest in town. The office, though nearly twenty-five years old, was one of the newer buildings. He had started as a solo practitioner but in the ensuing years had added three partners.

Harry noticed that the sidewalks had been shoveled and salted. On more than one occasion, he had shoveled the sidewalks himself before beginning his morning schedule of patients. On those days he had wished he practiced in sunny Florida.

After hanging his jacket and hat on the coatrack, he walked across the employee lunchroom to the coffeemaker. Thanks to his nurse, his Chicago Bears mug was waiting for him on the counter, and he poured himself a cup of black coffee. Harry picked up the mug and stepped into the hallway.

"We're packed today, Dr. Bennett," his nurse said. She was approaching him with the day's schedule. "You should quit taking vacations."

Jill O'Dell had been his nurse for thirteen years. She was his right hand, and his patients loved her. Her two children were both grown and living out of state, and her husband was usually traveling as an international agricultural consultant. Jill lived on several thousand acres of farmland outside of town that had been handed down through four generations, but she leased out the land and didn't farm. Instead, she worked for Harry. She was a local girl who loved his patients. For Jill, Harry's practice was her life.

"Mary Beckstrom delivered," Harry said. "It was a boy."

"Eight pounds, two ounces, and twenty inches," Jill said with a smirk.

"You know everything," he said, a little surprised.

"Of course," she said, "and don't you forget it."

Harry found an empty spot on his desk for his coffee mug. His office was simple and plainly decorated. An oversized teacher's desk from the old Sycamore High School sat in the center of the room. Two antique wooden bookshelves along the wall held his collection of medical textbooks. His office chair across from the desk was purchased new—brown bomber leather, walnut arms, and brass studs. It was pricey but classy, and one of his few luxuries. The floor was cluttered with the latest medical journals that he intended to read soon. Older journals were piled high in one corner. A week's worth of unopened mail was piled on his desk and nearly covered his computer keyboard. He'd tackle the mail at lunchtime.

Jill stuck her head in the doorway. "Everybody and his uncle has the flu. I've resorted to getting influenza swabs on just about everybody."

"Fine with me."

Jill held out her wrist and tapped her watch. "Are you going to see patients this morning or what?"

"Nothing like the harassment of an ill-tempered nurse to make a person want to be back on vacation."

"Lauren Randall is the first patient," she said, pretending to ignore his comment. "She's got a rash."

"Which room?"

"Room one. Both Mom and Dad are in there with her."

Harry opened the door. Lauren, a cute, petite six-year-old girl, was sitting on the exam table cradling a doll in her arms. When she looked up at Harry, she immediately jumped off the table with a big smile and ran to him, her blond ponytail bouncing. She wrapped her two small arms around Harry's waist and gave him a big hug.

"That's the greatest greeting a doctor ever had," Harry said, smiling. He bent over and picked her up, gave her a hug in return, then plopped her down on the exam table.

"What's the doll's name?" he asked.

"Kirsten," she said in her little voice.

"Good name," Harry said. "The doll is pretty, but not nearly as pretty as you are."

Harry enjoyed watching her giggle at the compliment. He talked to the parents for a few minutes and caught up on their family. Frank, the father, worked at a local electric tool company and had just received a promotion to foreman. Kathy, the mother, taught second grade in nearby Yorkville; this was her third year. Harry asked about them because this was a special family. Lauren had nearly drowned four years earlier in a neighbor's pool. Her parents had rushed her to his office where he had resuscitated her, and then he had ridden in the ambulance with her to DeKalb. After a month in intensive care and another month on the pediatrics floor, Lauren spent six months in rehabilitation. Her recovery was near miraculous.

Lauren's mother explained her daughter's current illness, which was the reason for their visit. Lauren was feeling well, maybe just a little irritable, but had broken out in a rash the day before. Mom noticed the red spots first on her face and chest. This morning the rash had become worse and now she had blisters. The mom had bundled up the child and brought her over as soon as the office opened.

"I knew you had gone skiing," she said, "so I hated to bother you."

"No bother. I promise."

"Do you have any idea what this is?"

"Let me look."

Harry examined the lesions on Lauren's face, arms, and trunk. There must have been twenty or thirty. The lesions were blisters on a round base of red skin about a quarter of an inch in diameter. Lauren wasn't acting at all sick.

"It's chickenpox," Harry said. "We don't see much of this anymore."

"She had the immunization."

"I thought she did." Harry sat at the desk, pulled out the computer keyboard, and clicked on her immunization record. "Yes, here it is. She had it at twelve months of age and at five years old—right on time. The Varicella vaccine doesn't completely eliminate the chance of chickenpox, but it usually lessens the severity of the illness and, more importantly, the serious complications."

"I don't know anyone else's child who's broken out," Kathy said.

"I haven't heard of any other cases, but, of course, I've been gone a few days. It's classic for chickenpox. See the lesions coming out in what we call crops?" Harry pointed to her face. "A few of these are just red bumps, some are blisters, and later they will be developing a yellowish honey-colored crust. The spots are in different stages."

"Is she contagious?"

"She is for now. When all of these crust over, she won't be."

"So you think she'll be fine?"

"I doubt she'll be sick much longer." Harry wrote down his recommendations for an antihistamine and oatmeal baths for the itching. He told them she should be isolated until she was no longer contagious. "We used to see chickenpox all the time. With the immunization, it's pretty rare now."

Harry finished their visit, saying his good-byes and getting his last hugs from Lauren; then he stepped into the hallway. His nurse was immediately at his side.

"Chickenpox?" Jill asked.

"It's a mild case."

"Thought so. We haven't seen a case in a year." She looked at her watch. "But it's time for you to stop socializing and get to work." She was pointing to his next room.

"You're such a slave driver," he laughed.

"That's why you pay me those big bucks."

Harry shook his head in mock disgust. He picked up the chart for the next patient, a first-time pregnant mom. She was due in a week, which meant she could go into labor at any time. He hoped it wouldn't be tonight.

Twenty patients were on the schedule before lunch, and that didn't include Lauren who was a walk-in. He glanced at his watch. He was already thirty minutes behind.

Only twenty-four hours earlier he had been strapping on a pair of skis and waiting in a lift line.

Colorado felt far away.

CHAPTER EIGHT

DECEMBER 4, 3:00 P.M. UTC+3
DAY THREE OF EXPOSURE
PORT OF DJIBOUTI

Mohammed leaned over the metal railing to watch the blue-green waters of the Golfe de Tadjoura lap up against the rusted hull of the old steamer. The brilliant afternoon sun hovered in a cloudless blue sky and reflected in the shimmering water across the Gulf of Aden to the distant horizon to the east. The vessel, *El Shaza*, was registered as Egyptian. It held mostly freight but also carried seventy-five passengers. Mohammed thought the ship must be at least sixty or seventy years old, possibly built in the 1950s, around the time Egypt became a republic. Rust covered much of its surface. It smelled of rank, burnt oil. Below deck, the accommodations were basic. Yet, the ship appeared to be seaworthy. Mohammed was pleased to be onboard and even more pleased to be away from Somalia.

Fazul Qaarey had dumped them at the border without their cash, credit cards, or vehicle. The unassembled Range Rover stayed at the compound in pieces, and Qaarey would likely reassemble it for his own use. Qaarey only gave them their personal documents, but this was simply so they could cross into Djibouti. Otherwise, they would have had to stay in Somaliland, and Qaarey certainly didn't want that. But Mohammed had anticipated such a contingency, as he had been cautious to plan for many possibilities, and a contact had been previously arranged in Djibouti City long before their arrival.

The four men had jogged the few miles from the border into the city and had arrived before dawn. A man they could trust, a Saudi shopkeeper, lived in a small room behind one of the businesses near the port. When they had arrived unexpectedly before daylight, the man was naturally startled and frightened, but he allowed them in. The package that had been sent to him had not been opened, exactly according to instructions. Inside it were new credit cards, currency, and passports, should they need them.

Khalid had slipped behind the unsuspecting shopkeeper and had easily snapped his neck. The faithful Muslim had completed his jihad and was in paradise.

Arranging for the steamer was easy with their new cash. The boat would travel out of the Port of Djibouti north through the Red Sea to Suez. The trip would take two and a half days. In Suez, they would board a local bus for Cairo and arrive at the Egyptian capital that evening. The next day they would fly out of Cairo, make their connections in four different cities, and each arrive at their destinations in America late that night. They would be in America on the sixth day after exposure to the child, a few days earlier than planned. The symptoms could begin anytime between the seventh and seventeenth day.

Mohammed and Khalid stood at the bow of the boat with several other passengers as it pushed away from the pier. Below them, the pier was bustling with people. Vendors were doing a brisk business in teak African crafts, brightly colored gowns, and other worthless items stacked along the dock. The worst of the merchandise, Mohammed thought, were the dirty, vicious monkeys on leashes that were for sale, a Djibouti tradition. Djibouti, a former French colony and currently a base for the French Foreign Legion, was poor and filthy, and though a Muslim country, Mohammed was disgusted with it. As he watched the crude and unpleasant port fade into the distance, Mohammed thanked Allah for their good fortune. Hopefully, the difficult part of the journey was behind them.

A fair number of passengers were milling around on deck. The majority of them were Arab males, and none of them wore Western clothing. A few of the passengers were women, and they wore full burka. Mohammed was pleased to see this. There were several Europeans, all males, and they appeared to be French. Al-Musaleh and Al-Sabai must have gone below deck, Mohammed thought, because he had not seen them, yet they no doubt were on board.

As the ship moved out to sea, the water was less calm and the boat rocked with a gentle sway. The water was the color of emeralds, and the sky a deep blue. After a few hours of steaming north, they approached Bab el Mandeb, the Gate of Tears, an ancient gateway named for the tears shed for those lost passing through its treacherous waters. Here the Gulf of Aden narrowed to a mere twenty miles before entering the Red Sea, one of the world's most strategic "choke points" and likely a hot spot for future conflicts. On their right, a soft haze obscured the coastline of Yemen a few miles away.

"The Yemeni port of Aden must be near," Mohammed said.

"It is there," Khalid said, pointing off to the east.

"Aden was the site of the bombing of the USS *Cole*," Mohammed said. "It was a great victory for Islam." Mohammed knew Khalid had an essential part in the attack, though he knew Khalid would not speak of it. "The courage of the martyrs should make us fearless as we are resolved to our purpose. The Americans are not invincible."

"Allah be praised," Khalid said.

"Because of the bombing of the *Cole*," Mohammed said, "No American ship is safe in these waters."

"Yes, this is true," Khalid said. "Because of what we carry now, no American will be safe in his own country."

"Allah be praised," Mohammed said.

The sun dipped to the west and the air was cooler, and because of this, very few passengers remained on deck. As the sea lane narrowed at Bab el Mandeb, the wind gathered strength, and began to blow at nearly gale force, causing Mohammed and Khalid to hold tightly to the railing. Merchant traffic through the narrow strait was heavy, and several ships, mostly freighters and oil tankers, passed through with them. The region, of course, was known for oil. To their right were the nations of Saudi Arabia and Yemen, which had become wealthy from the sale of oil. On the opposite side was the Sudan and eventually Egypt, both of which had relatively little oil and were poor. Mohammed thought that oil had brought great wealth to the oil-rich countries, yet the oil polluted the land just as the wealth polluted the minds of the faithful. The faithful had become impure, and their Islamic countries had become unfaithful when they created relationships with the Americans, the greatest of the infidels and the protector of the Zionists. The West was dependent on petroleum. The Saudis, Kuwaitis, and other oil-rich Arab nations were dependent on the money, and their faith was eroding like a malignant cancer.

Mohammed believed Egypt was no better. The cursed Egyptians had made peace with the Zionists and the Americans because they wanted American dollars so that rich, fat tourists could ride camels around the pyramids. Peace with the Americans was impossible. All pure and true Muslims were required to rise up and overthrow any corrupt government with ties to the infidels. It was their moral duty.

"We must drive the Americans forever from Islamic soil," Mohammed said to Khalid. "You will need all of your skills in America, just like in Yemeni."

"Yes," Khalid said, "but this time I'll be going to paradise."

Khalid looked up at Mohammed for a moment and then turned away, facing out to sea. It was the first time on the trip that Khalid had made eye contact with Mohammed, but his expression was distant. Khalid's reputation was solid, but much of his past was unknown, and Mohammed was not completely comfortable with that fact. However, it was too late for second thoughts now.

"Allah willing," Mohammed said, "Muhsin, Nazih, and I, too, will join you. Soon all of us will be in paradise…and many, many Americans will be dead."

* * *

DECEMBER 4, 3:00 P.M. EST
DAY THREE OF EXPOSURE
NEW YORK CITY

Dr. Vicky Anderson's pizza had been reheated three times and was cold again. Two motor vehicle accidents, an overdose that was a medical train wreck, and a steady stream of assorted infections—typical for her emergency room—had once again kept her from eating lunch. No wonder she stayed so trim.

She had lost her appetite anyway. The overdose, a twenty-five-year-old suicide attempt on diazepam, alcohol, and antidepressants, was belligerent and violent, especially when receiving charcoal through a nasogastric tube Vicky inserted. The staff held her down and applied four-point restraints, as she screamed and cursed at the top of her lungs; then she promptly blew chunks from her stomach contents all over the room in appreciation for everyone's efforts. Vicky cleaned herself up and changed into a new set of scrubs, but the alcohol-charcoal-vomit smell lingered for a couple of hours.

The ER was packed as usual. Vicky had hoped it would slow down a little since the temperature was dropping and a light freezing rain had coated the streets with a thin layer of ice. Instead, the bad weather had increased the number of accidents and also the frequency of ambulance runs. Patients would call EMS, the emergency medical service, claiming an emergency rather than drive themselves, but when they weren't sick enough to be admitted to the hospital, they found themselves without a ride home.

And the ambulance certainly wouldn't take them back. As a result, the waiting room was overflowing. Many were planning to spend the night.

Vicky was standing at the workstation, scribbling a quick note on her last patient. She stretched on her tiptoes to work out a cramp in her legs from the nine hours on her feet.

"Studying ballet?"

Vicky turned to see Justin Carmella. At the sight of him, she blushed, despite herself. She had met him two days earlier during a code blue gunshot wound to the chest. Justin, a paramedic with EMS, had brought the critical, nearly dead patient into the ER already intubated, with two IVs, MAST trousers for support of the blood pressure, and a chest tube. Because of his efforts, the patient had survived. She was impressed and told him so. Later, she found out it was Justin's first day on the job. Since then, she had seen him in the emergency room four or five times a day, most of the visits medical, but some of the reasons for his presence seemed contrived. One of the nurses said he was an ex-navy SEAL, and she believed it. He had the prerequisite body with broad shoulders, thick muscular arms, and a sculpted chest, and he stood upright with confidence and a certain brashness. He was handsome, with almond eyes, a light tan, and his brown hair was cut in a military style. What she liked the most about him was his smile: big, friendly, and genuine. A person could tell a lot about someone by his smile, she always thought.

"Just stretching my legs," she said, smiling back at him. "It's been a long day."

She noticed that he stole a glance at her legs as she mentioned them. It had been a really long time since a guy she liked had checked her out. She was wearing green hospital scrubs, which weren't particularly flattering. They were baggy in the legs and the shirt was too big, yet it cinched tight at her small waist and accentuated her ample bosom. He appeared to notice that, too.

"And you'd make a pretty ballerina."

Vicky felt the warmth in her cheeks. It was a corny statement, but he was complimenting her, and she was enjoying it. She didn't receive compliments that often.

"Would you be interested," Justin said, his voice soft, "in getting a bite of dinner when you're off duty? If that would be okay?" He now seemed almost shy as he asked, despite his formidable presence.

The invitation was tempting. He seemed nice enough, though she didn't really know him. Yet, a date was as good a way as any to become acquainted. On the other hand, for the past week she had hardly been home at all, and her mother needed some relief from the kids. But she knew if she asked for her mother's advice, her mother would probably insist she go to dinner. He acted interested in her, but Vicky wasn't sure she wanted to start a new relationship. Relationships were time consuming, and the one thing she didn't have right now was extra time. And dating was risky; it meant exposing the heart to injury and a chance of pain or a wound even a doctor couldn't heal. What the heck was she was thinking? Relationship? Dating? He had only asked her out to dinner.

"I'd really like to," she said, "but unfortunately I've got plans." She couldn't believe that she was turning him down.

"I'm sorry to hear that."

"Thanks for asking."

"I'll ask again sometime," he said, "if that's okay."

"Please do."

"If you change your mind tonight, here's my cell phone number."

She took the number and watched him walk down the hall and out the double doors of the hospital. He was pleasant to look at, no doubt, but that wasn't what interested her the most. She missed having a decent conversation and a chance for friendship. She could never tell if this moment might be her one and only chance with a guy. In the past, she had been asked and not called back. It had happened more than once. Maybe the doctor title intimidated them. Maybe it was just her. If this *were* her only chance with Justin, was he really worth it anyway?

"We really don't have time to socialize, do we?"

Dr. Newton's voice came from behind her, and Vicky cringed. She turned around sharply to face him.

"It's really none of your business," she said, a bit harsher than she had intended.

"The two-hour waits for patients *are* my business," he snapped back, his face turning red.

"A couple of more doctors," she said, not backing off, "and a few more nurses would help."

"It's the volume, not the staffing."

That made no sense to her. "Then we should go on divert. Our ICU is full. Patients are stacking up. The ice storm is bringing them out in droves. We can't keep up this pace."

"We're not going on divert," Newton said. "Every hospital in the city is in the same situation. We're not turning away paying customers. That's out of the question."

"Then I'm wasting my time with you." She started to turn away.

"Dr. Anderson," he said, "what I really wanted was to see if you'd work another shift."

She shook her head. He had to be kidding. "I'd really love to," she said with obvious sarcasm, "but I have dinner plans." Dinner with Justin after her shift just suddenly seemed a much better idea.

"Just thought I'd ask," Newton said.

"I'll let you know if I change my mind."

CHAPTER NINE

DECEMBER 7, 12:30 P.M. CET
DAY SIX OF EXPOSURE
ROME, ITALY

The flight from Cairo to Rome was uneventful, and though this part of the trip was the most critical, Mohammed felt increasingly more confident that he would arrive in New York without incident.

The four men had traveled the two and a half days on the steamer north on the Red Sea to Suez and taken the bus to Cairo. Mohammed had found the locker at the Cairo airport, and inside there was a complete set of new passports, credit cards, and American currency, as well as casual Western clothing and tourist information. He gave each man his new items and briefed them on the last leg of their trip. They all had different destinations from Cairo and would be traveling on their own. Their jihad was approaching its final victory.

Security was strict in Cairo, but he was not searched and his documents and identification were not challenged. The documents, of course, were perfect. Each man was given several thousand U.S. dollars, not so much cash as to be questioned but enough to be useful, though most of their purchases would be made with the false credit cards. Mohammed was seated in the coach section next to the window, a location purposely chosen to create less suspicion. On his arrival in Rome, the customs agent, an intense young female he suspected was military, spent an eternity examining his passport. She asked him about each of the stamps from the various countries. He had not actually visited any of them but was prepared, and he calmly answered her questions. He had experienced a similar subtle interrogation several times; the theory, he thought, was to elicit anxiety by the continued questions and weed out those who had reason to be nervous. Mohammed remained unemotional but friendly, and she passed him through without comment.

The Aeroporti di Roma, named Aeroporto Leonardo da Vinci-Fiumicino, was new, immaculate, and expansive. He arrived at Terminal C from Cairo and into the reality of the Western culture. Most of the men were dressed in business suits, dress shirts, and ties, but some wore jeans, T-shirts, casual shirts, or shorts. The women were unveiled and were wearing dresses and short skirts with their legs exposed, tight blouses or sweaters not covering their arms, even halter tops where their breasts and nipples showed through shamelessly. They were provocative and seductive. The women of the West were infidel whores.

Mohammed dressed in Western garb. He was wearing blue jeans, sneakers, a braided leather belt, and a Florida State T-shirt. He had taken a class there during his stay in the States and knew the campus. His hair was short but not too short, and he was clean-shaven. He stopped at a food counter for two bagels and a black coffee. The coffee was weak and stale, typical for Italy and most of Europe. The bagels were fresh, so he bought two more. He sat at an empty table near a young couple with two small children. He would stay in crowds and not appear isolated. This is what he had also instructed the other men to do. The couple was Italian; Mohammed understood a smattering of several languages but was fairly fluent in Italian. The husband was complaining about traveling with a toddler and an infant, but mostly about the planned visit to his mother-in-law.

Mohammed finished his light breakfast and took the automatic shuttle across the Sky Bridge to the new terminal for international flights. As he exited the shuttle, a long line stretched down the hallway, waiting to pass through security. Mohammed had been to the United States several times in preparation for this mission. If he were unable to enter the United States this time, his part of the mission would fail. Twice before, he had traveled from the Rome airport to New York City without problems, even after September 11th and the creation of America's Homeland Security department. He had worried more about the portion of the trip preceding his arrival in Rome, but this was the most critical part of the entire journey. The security in Rome was very high, and he must be careful. Once he entered New York City, he would blend in and never be found. New York City had 160,000 residents of Middle Eastern and northern African descent. He would walk around infected there without a concern. But he had to reach New York City safely first.

The line moved slowly, initially four or five wide, eventually narrowing into a single file directed by a series of black nylon ropes on metal posts. After proceeding through the metal detectors, which Mohammed passed through without difficulty, the line continued on the opposite side. Farther down the hallway it stopped directly in front of a stern-faced Italian woman, nearly sixty years old and barely over four feet tall. She was examining every passenger's documents and dividing them between two new lines. The new line to the left led directly to the gate. The new line to the right was for those being searched. When Mohammed reached her, he handed her his papers. He had nothing suspicious that might alert the authorities except for his documents. His Egyptian passport was forged, but it looked perfectly authentic, so he wasn't especially concerned. The Bureau of Documents in Egypt was so inept that his passport was essentially unverifiable. The woman spent a couple of minutes thumbing through his papers and closely examining his tickets. Without looking up, she handed them back to him and directed Mohammed to the right.

A security guard, a giant of a man of nearly seven feet who towered over Mohammed, stood next to a metal folding table in an area partially cordoned off by curtains. The guard was dressed in a blue uniform and was wearing a holstered 9mm Beretta on one side and a large radio on the other. His huge hands were covered by flesh-colored latex gloves and were folded across his chest. As Mohammed approached, the man pointed to the table.

"Sir, please place your carry-on on the table," he said in Italian, "and remove your shoes." Though polite, his statement was not a request.

Mohammed followed his instructions. The guard waved a metal detector over Mohammed's body and then asked him to sit in a nearby chair.

"Sir," the guard said, "do we have permission to search your belongings?"

Mohammed nodded. He had little choice.

The guard rubbed a pad over the outside of the carry-on and handed the pad to a female guard who slid it into a device that presumably detected explosive residue. The male guard shuffled through the carry-on, removing a couple of articles of clothing and placing them on the table. He pulled out a small bag from the carry-on that held Mohammed's personal items—toothbrush, toothpaste, shaving cream, and such, as well as four or five small packets marked aspirin. The guard picked up a small nail file and held it up.

"Sir, this is not allowed."

"It's just a fingernail file," Mohammed said in his best Italian.

"No pocket knifes, nail clippers, or fingernail files are allowed, sir. It's the rules."

Mohammed remained polite. "What harm would that do?" he asked.

"Sir, no exceptions." The guard stood firm. "I didn't make up the rules. I can discard your file or you can return to the ticket counter and check it in. What is your preference?"

"Throw it away, then," Mohammed said, a little disgusted. "No wonder people aren't flying these days."

The guard dropped the nail file in a nearby trashcan. Mohammed was certain that his protest wouldn't sound unusual. The guard had probably had the same conversation with the same result many times that day.

After roughly stuffing the items back into the carry-on, the guard examined Mohammed's shoes. When finished, he handed both the bag and the shoes back to Mohammed, and then waved Mohammed through. Next in line behind him was a gray-haired elderly woman in her seventies who was stooped over, frail, and as slender as a reed. Maybe it was her cane that worried them.

Mohammed stepped up to the gate and handed his ticket to the agent. He walked down the ramp and into the plane. He sat in his seat next to the window and suppressed a smile. They had confiscated his nail file! They were concerned about a harmless piece of metal while he was carrying the smallpox virus, the most deadly and dangerous virus in the world.

Ignorant infidels! They are weak and vulnerable, unable to detect the danger in front of them. Yet they fear old women with canes! How powerful is the god of Muhammad.

The flight was scheduled to leave at one in the afternoon and would arrive at John F. Kennedy International Airport that evening at four twenty-five Eastern Standard Time.

Only customs in New York remained before the last phase of his jihad against the Americans would finally begin.

* * *

DECEMBER 7, 3:00 P.M. CST
CHICAGO, ILLINOIS

The direct flight from Cairo to Chicago was twelve hours, and Muhsin Al-Musaleh never left his seat near the window. Walking in the aisle attracted attention and might look suspicious. They had practiced many times even this mundane detail by withholding fluids.

The jetliner dropped out of the clouds, followed the approach to the runway, and landed smoothly. The passengers exited the plane in an orderly manner, and most followed the signs to the baggage claim area. Al-Musaleh bypassed the luggage and went directly to customs. Hundreds were waiting in the ten or twelve separate lines. The process was slow, but he was patient.

When it was his turn, the agent asked several basic questions. One question was about his lack of luggage, especially considering the chilly weather in Chicago. "No understand," Al-Musaleh managed in broken English. His bag was thoroughly searched, and he was passed through.

Al-Musaleh ate a sandwich and a few chips and drank a cola at a fast food counter. He found a gift shop in the terminal and bought a solid black Chicago Bulls team jacket and a blue and red Cubs ball cap. Mohammed had instructed each of them to buy clothing with the emblem of a local sports team as soon as they arrived in their city. The quicker they could fit in, the better.

Outside the terminal, the taxis stretched nearly a block, but the line of people was short. The slate-gray sky spit out a few flakes of snow. The air was cold, and a stiff wind caused Al-Musaleh to feel a brief chill, despite his new coat. A bored Oriental female in a red uniform directed the passengers to available taxis by the wave of her hand, all the while talking constantly on her cell phone. She pointed Al-Musaleh to a yellow cab, and he climbed into the backseat.

"Good morning, sir," the driver said. "What is your destination?"

"Holiday Inn, Michigan Avenue," he replied in perfect English.

"Yes, sir," the driver said and pulled out into the airport traffic.

Al-Musaleh shifted in his seat. His lower spine ached and the change of position helped. The soreness he noticed might have been caused by the long flight, but he also felt a slight throbbing in his head and a mild nausea. He reached up and touched the side of his cheek. His skin seemed warm, especially considering the cool air.

Were these the symptoms of smallpox? He wasn't sure, but he'd know soon enough.

"Where are you from?" the taxi driver asked in Arabic.

The driver's accent sounded Saudi. He was clean-shaven, had short hair, and wore American clothes. Al-Musaleh had heard about Muslim traitors who came to the United States and lived the decadent American lifestyle, became greedy, and quit practicing their faith. He wondered if this man supported the jihad with his finances and prayers, whether he was part of a network, or whether he had been corrupted. An impure Muslim was worse than an infidel.

"I'm sorry," Al-Musaleh said, "I didn't understand you."

The driver switched back to English and tried to small talk about the weather, but Al-Musaleh said nothing, and the driver finally took the hint. They proceeded down Interstate ninety from the airport to downtown in heavy traffic, at times slowing to a stop. Several feet of snow were piled on both sides of the roadway. Growing up in Egypt, he had never seen snow, and he first experienced it in Afghanistan. It wasn't a pleasant experience with the snow in Afghanistan: memories of bitter cold, frozen hands and feet, and the white snow turned red with the blood of the martyrs. Before now, he hadn't thought much about snow in Chicago.

The cars in Chicago were newer and much more expensive than any Al-Musaleh had ever seen, but the drivers were actually more subdued. Al-Musaleh noticed he was continuously in the midst of the city as they traveled mile after mile. Even Cairo seemed small in comparison. As they eventually made their way toward downtown, the mass of skyscrapers grew taller and soon towered overhead. The interstate exited on to Ohio Street and across the north branch of the Chicago River. They continued several blocks until they reached Michigan Avenue, and as they passed through the intersection, the brilliant lights of the storefronts and Christmas decorations illuminated the street in both directions as far as Al-Musaleh could see. He had never seen so many lights.

"This is known as the Magnificent Mile," the driver said. "High-dollar stores. Very expensive."

Al-Musaleh felt exhausted. His head was beginning to pound, and he felt worse than he had expected. He had broken out into a sweat and was sick to his stomach. It shouldn't be the smallpox, he thought. This was much too early. His exposure had been less than a week. The first symptoms weren't supposed to occur for ten or twelve days. Maybe it was the flu or a cold or even the long trip.

Two blocks past Michigan Avenue, the taxi turned into the circle drive of the Holiday Inn. Al-Musaleh paid the driver in cash and went inside. The lobby was light and airy with floor-to-ceiling beige columns, white plaster walls, and a dusty rose carpet. A solid wall of windows separated the lobby from the street. A group of people sat in chairs around a glass-topped coffee table, drinking wine and loudly conversing about some movie they had just seen. Al-Musaleh thought they were drunk and obnoxious— typical wealthy Americans. One side of the lobby opened on a restaurant, and he could smell the rich food and hear strains of a piano playing softly. The front desk consisted of a dark, wood-paneled base topped with an elegant beige-and-white marble. A young African American woman greeted him and smiled. He was the only person checking in. She found his reservation, verified his credit card, and slid a check-in form in front of him. He signed it and pushed it back to her.

"Sir, are you feeling all right?" she asked.

She was looking intently at him. Her interest seemed genuine, but her concern worried him. Did he look sick?

"It was a long flight from Los Angeles," he said, "and I didn't get much sleep."

"Do you live in Los Angeles? My grandmother lives in Pasadena. I've been there."

"I live in Long Beach." Of course it was a lie, but he was prepared. "It's not too far away."

"Home of the *Spruce Goose?*"

"The what?"

"You know. The wooden plane Howard Hughes built. I saw it."

"Oh, yes. I remember. When you live someplace, sometimes you don't see the tourist attractions."

"I know what you mean. I've never been to the Shedd Aquarium. Same thing."

She handed him a plastic room key, and the key to the courtesy bar. She pointed out the elevators.

"I hope you sleep well tonight," she said.

"Thank you. I know I will."

Al-Musaleh rode the elevator to his floor and found his room. He slipped the Do Not Disturb sign on the doorknob, locked the dead bolt, and secured the chain. The windows were open to a view of an office building across the street, and he pulled the curtains closed. "Why was the woman so worried," he wondered. He undressed completely and carefully examined his body. In the bathroom mirror he looked at his face, neck, and scalp. He inspected the inside of his mouth and along the cheeks and gums.

He found nothing.

Al-Musaleh rolled out his carpet toward Mecca and knelt down with his head bowed against the floor. *There is no god but Allah*. His head and back ached, and his nausea was worse. All of a sudden, he felt a hard chill rake through his body. *And Muhammad is his prophet*.

* * *

DECEMBER 7, 6:00 P.M. EST
NEW YORK CITY

Mohammed's flight and entry into the United States went as smoothly as his previous visits had. On arrival, his documents were carefully examined, but security did not search him or his carry-on bag. During the flight the pilot had announced they were being diverted to Baltimore because of an ice storm earlier in the day, but apparently the weather had improved sufficiently to allow their plane to land at Kennedy Airport on schedule. The terminal was full of people because of the cancelled and delayed departing flights, but he had no difficulty finding a cab, and within a few minutes he was on his way.

The ride to Manhattan was an hour and forty-five minutes through Queens in rush hour traffic. His driver was Pakistani and was dressed in Western clothing. A Christian cross hung from the mirror.

Mohammed leaned forward. "Are you practicing your faith, my brother?"

"I am a Christian now. My wife converted me."

"There is no god but Allah and Muhammad is his prophet."

"Abraham is the father of all religions, including Islam," the driver said. "We are presumptuous to think our god is the only god." The driver looked over his shoulder at

Mohammed. "Besides," he said laughing, "my wife threatened to cut me off, if you know what I mean, if I didn't go to church with her."

Mohammed leaned back in his seat, suppressing his anger, and did not reply. He would be required to control his emotions often in America.

As they approached the East River, he looked at the skyline of Manhattan. He smiled when he noticed the gap where the Twin Towers of the World Trade Center had stood. The driver took the Queens Midtown Tunnel north to Forty-Ninth Street, drove by Rockefeller Center, and then turned west to Seventh Avenue. Although he had been to New York many times, Mohammed always found the hundreds of skyscrapers amazing. A mass of taxis like a swarm of bees moved up the street with horns honking, maneuvering in and out of tight spaces with astounding speed. The sidewalks were jammed with pedestrians. The bright lights of Times Square lit up the night sky with marquees for sodas, alcohol, electronics, and movies. New York City exemplified, even celebrated, the total decadence of the Americans. The excess and greed of the infidels here far exceeded that found anywhere else in the world.

Mohammed would cherish the part of the mission he would play here.

The cab pulled up to the main entrance of the Renaissance Hotel, which was a black glass complex wedged between Seventh Avenue and Broadway.

"That will be forty-four dollars," the driver said.

The price was outrageous, Mohammed thought. "May I have a receipt?" he asked.

Mohammed wasn't feeling bad at the moment. He felt no nausea, no headache, and no back pain. He was certain he had no rash. It was too early, yet he leaned forward as he handed the driver the cash and coughed in the face of the Pakistani.

"Pardon me," Mohammed said. "It's my allergies."

The driver pulled back. "Certainly," he said.

The driver wrote out a receipt and turned to hand it to Mohammed. When he did, Mohammed coughed again. Mohammed hoped he was contagious. He hoped the smallpox virus was in his cough and in the very air he exhaled. This man, this traitor of Islam with his Christian whore wife, should be the first to die!

Mohammed checked in and went to his room. He pulled out his prayer rug and faced Mecca. He felt confident his prayers for success would be answered.

* * *

DECEMBER 7, 11:00 P.M. EST
WASHINGTON, DC

Nazih Al-Sabai sat on the hotel bed and turned on the television he found inside a cabinet that was placed against the wall. The day had gone much easier than he had expected. His flight from Cairo to Washington, DC, had connected through Athens, an airport well known for its confusion and disorganization. Yet, his boarding went smoothly and his flight was uneventful. He had slept most of the trip. On arrival, customs at Dulles International Airport and his taxi ride to the Marriott were completely unexciting, just as he had hoped.

He told himself that his room was quite adequate, but in fact it was the most elegant room that he had ever seen. The bed had eight pillows, and the sheets looked as if they had never been used. The shower was marble, and the hot water flowed from jets that massaged him. His first shower in America had lasted for over an hour. Afterward, he ordered a meal from room service, and when he had eaten it all, he ordered the same meal again.

Al-Sabai fluffed the pillows behind his back and changed channels with the remote. The television blared some game show or a music video or a news talk show, and Al-Sabai couldn't decide what he would watch. He had seen American television once before, yet he was surprised at the wide variety of programs, which was in sharp contrast to the meager selection offered in his own country of Libya.

Mohammed had instructed him to only leave his hotel room to send an e-mail message to confirm his arrival. Then he was instructed to stay in the room until his smallpox was contagious, which Mohammed said would be from seven to twelve days.

"Almost two weeks," he thought, "alone in the room. I'll be watching a lot of television!"

Al-Sabai pushed the pillows aside and swung his legs around to sit up. He dialed the phone and ordered desert—American apple pie topped with vanilla ice cream.

At least he wouldn't go hungry while he waited.

CHAPTER TEN

DECEMBER 9, 6:00 p.m. CST
DAY EIGHT OF EXPOSURE
CHICAGO, ILLINOIS

The holiday display at Marshall Field's on State Street—Harry wasn't sure he could ever call it Macy's—was bright, colorful, and extravagant, particularly the series of windows outside detailing the Twelve Days of Christmas. All the characters—a partridge in a pear tree, lords a' leaping, and French hens—were displayed in life-sized pageantry. Harry and Maureen ambled along with a crowd of people on the sidewalk, peering in at the windows, oohing and ahing, following the well-known song of Christmas.

"This is lovely," Maureen said. "I wish the twins could see it."

"Me, too," Harry said. "But it's nice that it's just you and me."

The annual outing had been a tradition for them for the past fourteen years. Harry would schedule an afternoon off, and they'd drive to Rosemont and ride the Blue Line into town to State Street in the Chicago Loop. Afterward, they'd agree on a restaurant and do a little shopping, just the two of them— without friends, relatives, or kids.

Walking inside the popular department store, their eyes followed a forty-five-foot pine as it stretched upward toward the Tiffany dome, its branches richly decorated in multicolored bulbs, wrapped with waves of gold ribbon, and topped by a two-foot-glass star. Several thousand sparkling white lights illuminated every inch of the star's surface. Each year Harry would ask a complete stranger to take their picture in front of the tree, and this year he exchanged favors with a man with five children. Keeping another tradition, Harry bought two boxes of chocolate mints, one for Maureen and one for the girls, hoping they would share some with him. They always did.

After choosing several presents for the twins, they caught a cab to Michigan Avenue and were dropped off in front of the John Hancock Center. They walked down the stairs to an open courtyard, watching a water fountain spray and splash amid a sparkle of lights and ice.

Though they had reservations, they waited at the restaurant twenty minutes before being seated. The waiter took their order and brought their drinks. Maureen held up her glass, offering a toast, and Harry clinked his glass with hers. They drank wine and talked about the girls until dinner came. The food was piled high, and smelled of oregano, basil, and garlic.

"I'm glad you were able to get away tonight," Maureen said. "You've been awfully busy lately."

"It's the cold and flu season," Harry said. "Hard to control my schedule."

"I know, but…" She hesitated for a moment. "I'm not mentioning this so much for me, but for Amy and Audrey. You haven't had much time for them lately."

Harry didn't respond immediately and wiped up the last of his tomato sauce with a piece of bread. "It's not like I've been ignoring them on purpose," he said, his tone a little sharper than he had intended.

Maureen looked down at her food, diverting her eyes.

"I'm sorry," he said, much softer. "I know you're not being critical."

She looked back up at him. "It's just that they miss you. You leave before they're up, and you're home after they're in bed. You're going to miss out on their whole lives."

Harry was quiet, and there was a moment of silence between them.

"I know you're right," Harry said, finally. This wasn't the first time for this conversation. "But it's a struggle when you're busy." Harry expected Maureen to continue, but she didn't. She had made her point. "Have you been instructed on the shopping?" he asked.

"Two backpacks for the girls," Maureen said. "Size, color, and styles."

"That store is just upstairs."

"And I wouldn't mind checking out the sales down at Bloomingdale's for me."

"I don't have a preference. The evening is yours."

They shopped until the stores closed and then walked down Michigan Avenue, enjoying the lights. Before leaving for home, they rode up to the observatory on the ninety-third floor of the John Hancock Center. The night was crystal clear, and the streets of Chicago extended for miles to the western horizon, marked in square grids of light. On the opposite side, Lake Michigan was dark and empty, with only the occasional flickering light of a distant ship. A few flakes of snow began to fall, disappearing below them, drifting down a hundred stories.

Watching the snow and lights and stars, Harry held Maureen from behind and felt her warmth. Maureen knew he had listened at dinner, and she wouldn't bring up the issue about the girls again—unless things didn't get better. Maureen was right, he knew that, but sometimes it just wasn't in his control. At least, that's what he told himself.

His life was good. He loved his wife and children.

He'd better make sure he found some balance.

* * *

DECEMBER 9, 11:00 P.M.
LOS ANGELES

Khalid was exhausted but relieved to finally arrive in Los Angeles, only thirty hours behind schedule. The first delay of nearly eight hours leaving Cairo caused him to miss his connection in Singapore, and then, after spending fourteen boring hours at the gate, his flight was cancelled just ten minutes before departure. He booked the next flight to Los Angeles on a different airline that left five hours later, but after pulling away from the terminal, they sat on the tarmac for another three hours while a radar unit was removed and replaced. Several irate passengers screamed and yelled at the steward-esses, but Khalid remained calm. He fully intended to avoid drawing any attention to himself, but honestly, after thirty hours, if he had been able to take a knife on board, he would have considered killing someone.

Khalid knew that Mohammed was a professional, and he had assured Khalid that every contingency was covered. Yet no one could predict airline delays, and they had become all too common. Any change of plans bothered Khalid. He would have pre-ferred to pay cash for his new ticket, but cash would have been highly unusual, especially an Arab using American currency. His credit cards were probably safe, at least he hoped so, except that he had two cards, and he hadn't been told which, if either, had been used for his original ticket. At the time Mohammed had given them to him, he hadn't consid-ered it important, but now he was worried. The card was a calculated risk.

Exiting the plane, Khalid walked briskly down the jetway and into the gate's boarding lounge, which was packed with passengers. A crowd was standing near the gate's entrance, preparing to board, and nearly every seat in the lounge was filled with travelers waiting, their carry-ons piled high around them. Proceeding past them, Khalid turned toward the concourse and followed the signs directing him to baggage claim. He stopped at a gift shop and purchased a Los Angeles Dodgers baseball cap and sweatshirt, as he had been instructed, changing into them in a nearby men's room.

Khalid bypassed the baggage claim because he had no luggage, but he noticed passengers he recognized from his flight waiting for theirs, so he was certain he was in the right location. He followed the corridor until he arrived at customs, and he took his place in one of the lines. Each line led to a booth with a uniformed official. He chose the only female, a Caucasian who was middle aged and overweight, instead of a male, though it was hard to predict if it was much of an advantage. Yet, from his experience, women were less suspicious and less paranoid, although these tendencies were not universal. Sometimes even the smallest detail mattered.

There were nearly forty people in line in front of him, and the process was slow. When it was his turn, he slid his passport onto the counter in front of the official. She wore thick glasses that magnified her eyes, but she didn't look up at him; instead she stared intently at a small computer screen in front of her. Khalid couldn't see the screen. She reached for his passport with her left hand and opened it.

"Country of origin?" she asked, glancing at the passport, still focused on the computer.

"Saudi Arabia," he answered, his voice calm. He would not smile or show any emotion.

"Is your trip to the United States for business or for pleasure?"

"Both." It was the truth as far as he was concerned.

She leafed through his passport, stopping for a few seconds at several of the pages. When she was through, she placed the passport back on the counter and pointed at his carry-on.

"No other luggage?"

"No, ma'am." The lack of luggage did seem unusual to him now, and for the first time he felt a bit awkward. "I'm expecting a brief visit."

"I see," she said, turning her eyes back to what she was reading on the screen.

Her eyes darted back and forth as she scanned the screen. Occasionally she would type on the keyboard. Khalid began to feel his heartbeat a little stronger in his chest. As he waited, he reminded himself to breath slowly. He tried to read her face, but he couldn't. She was expressionless and quite professional. He had been in similar situations several times and had never failed to pass successfully through customs. He must be patient.

The woman paused after a few minutes and picked the passport back up.

"And Saudi Arabia is also the country of your birth? Is that correct?"

"Yes, ma'am."

"Are you are traveling alone?"

"Yes, ma'am."

The woman glanced over her shoulder, and Khalid saw an armed guard make eye contact with her and move in their direction. Khalid watched as he approached. He was Caucasian as well, heavyset, thick shoulders and neck, with a holstered 9mm side arm. His badge said U.S. Customs.

Khalid's first reaction was to attack, to take advantage of surprise, and to be on the offensive. But that would ruin the plan and threaten the success of their mission. He couldn't risk that. Instead, he would maintain his composure. Answer their questions. Move to the next step.

"Sir?"

She was looking at him now, holding out his passport. Over his shoulder he saw two other guards coming up behind him.

He wished his cyanide capsule was in his hand. He wouldn't have expected to need it here.

"Sir!"

She was still holding out his passport, and he took it from her. The guard was now standing beside her.

"I need for you to accompany this officer," she said. "We need to ask you a few additional questions." The woman showed no emotion, as if she routinely directed someone to be interrogated a hundred times a day.

Khalid had instantly assessed his situation. One guard blocked his way in front, and two others were behind him. More help, as much as they could possibly need, was nearby.

"Of course," he politely answered her. He had no choice.

The guard in front turned, and Khalid followed him toward a closed, windowless, metal door. The guard quickly entered a code in a keypad on one side of the door, and an electronic lock clicked open.

Something in their mission had failed, Khalid thought. The documents. An informant. Possibly his credit card. Yet, there was still a possibility this was completely random, accidental, and he had been chosen by chance. In his heart, though, Khalid knew better.

* * *

DECEMBER 9, MIDNIGHT EST
NEW YORK CITY

It was after midnight when Vicky arrived at the apartment. The dinner with Justin had gone better than she could have hoped. She had laughed more than she had in a long time. They talked about art, music, the theater, books they had read, and all sorts of interesting topics, but the hospital or medicine didn't come up once. He was charming and his smile was contagious. She caught herself smiling just thinking about him. Against her best efforts, she had been swept off her feet, and she still hadn't decided if that was what she wanted.

She pushed the key into the lock and turned it slowly, not wanting to wake everyone up. They should all be asleep. Her next shift started at six, so she would have to leave again in five hours. She hadn't seen the kids in two days, and she felt a twinge of guilt, as if she were a bad mother who was ignoring her kids. They didn't deserve that. Life had already been tough enough on them. They should have had a normal family with two parents who loved them; a big house with a dog, a cat, and a playground nearby; dance lessons with recitals; and baseball teams with trophies. None of this was their fault. The death of their mother was a shock, and they weren't over it yet. Neither was she, she thought, as the tears welled up in her eyes. When would it get easier for all of them?

As she opened the door, she saw the light was on in the living room. Her mother was still awake. Mothers, no matter how old you were, were always mothers.

"You shouldn't have waited up, Mom."

"I didn't," she said. "I couldn't sleep, so I decided to read a little."

Vicky knew that was only partly true.

"But since I am up," her mother said, not missing a beat, "how was your dinner with your man friend?"

Tonight, as the dim light of the living room lamp softened her mother's features, her mother looked more like her sister, Kelly, than Vicky had ever noticed. Her mother had a wrinkled, round face with deep-set green eyes. Her hair, once jet black, had turned silver when Kelly died. Vicky had never thought that she looked much like her mother, yet she thought she and Kelly had always looked like twins, even though they were two years apart. That is, until Kelly had lost so much weight in her last few months. At the end, watching Kelly was like seeing herself wasting away—an image she didn't think had escaped her mother. Maybe Vicky looked more like her mother than she had realized.

"It went fine," Vicky said.

"Sit down and tell me." Her mother smoothed out a place on the couch next to her and patted it with her hand.

"Mom," Vicky protested, "I've got to get up early."

"Well, then, just the nutshell version."

Vicky shook her head and sat down. "You're too much," she said. "The truth is I had a good time."

"What does he do for a living?"

"Mom!" she said in mock disgust. "If you must know, he's been married three times and has four kids, but that's okay because he doesn't pay alimony or child support anyway. His criminal record was expunged after his probation and community service. And except for the one breakdown, his psychiatrist says he's the most stable he's been in years."

"Vicky!"

Vicky grinned. "He's an ex-navy SEAL and works as a paramedic. He's bright, fun, and dependable, but we've only been on one date, and he may never, ever call me again."

"Go to bed. You're getting grouchy."

"I wouldn't argue with that. How are the kids doing?"

"They're fine. They missed you and want you to kiss them good night."

"I will. I haven't seen them in two days."

"They'll survive. You needed the time off. I'm glad you had a good time."

"When do you get your time off?"

"I'll ask when you least expect it. Go to bed!"

Vicky peeked into John's room first. He was sound asleep and looked more precious than he probably deserved. He had a stuffed tiger under one arm and a light saber tucked under the other. She stroked his hair and gently kissed him on the cheek. Becky's room was brighter because she always slept with three night-lights. She loved flowers, and her sheets, pillowcases, and curtains were splashed with a rainbow of colors from a hundred different varieties. Becky was facing away, and Vicky leaned over her to kiss her cheek. The young girl stirred slightly, and Vicky was afraid she might have awakened her, but she was fast asleep.

Both children slept like angels, Vicky thought, so peaceful, so calm. Not a care in the world. But life wasn't always as simple as a dream.

In the bathroom, she washed off her makeup and looked at herself in the mirror. Her eyes looked tired and maybe a little sad. It was hard to hide the facts from herself.

She deserved a life like everyone else. Her medical career was fulfilling. She cherished the children. Her mother was a gift. Yet, she *was* a single young woman, and sometimes she wanted an apartment of her own, to be by herself, wrapped up in an old blanket, eating microwave popcorn for dinner, and watching an Elvis movie until the wee hours of the morning. Maybe Justin was there with her and maybe he wasn't. It was her dream, but her life wasn't simple either.

Vicky dried her face and hung her towel neatly next to the sink. After slipping on her nightgown, she flipped off the light to the bathroom and walked into the bedroom. She sat a moment on the side of the bed.

Her evening with Justin had gone great. She liked him. He seemed nearly perfect, but it was just their first date. He'd call her back or he wouldn't. Nothing she could do. She wondered why relationships had to be so complicated.

She pulled back the covers and slipped underneath. Morning and her usual routine would arrive before she knew it.

CHAPTER ELEVEN

DECEMBER 10, 7:00 A.M. CST
DAY NINE OF EXPOSURE
DEKALB, ILLINOIS

The fourth floor medical ward was being refurbished, and Harry wondered why the hospital chose the busiest time of the year to cause such a disruption. Carpet was off the floor. Painters were painting the walls. Equipment cluttered the hallways. He stepped over an open bucket of white paint and located a seat in the crowded doctors' workstation. After clicking on the computer, he brought up the record of Chester Jurney. What seemed to be a simple pneumonia on admission had taken a turn for the worse. He had now been in the hospital for five days, was on two antibiotics, breathing treatments, oxygen, and a host of other medicines, yet he was getting worse by the day. The evening before, Harry had called Dr. Naguib Abdul Haleem, an infectious disease specialist, and Dr. Haleem had seen the patient on his evening rounds. Harry noticed in the computer notes that Dr. Haleem had not changed the antibiotics, but that he had ordered some additional diagnostic tests, including a CT scan, which was done last night. The CT report showed only the pneumonia and was normal otherwise. Next, Harry pulled up Dr. Haleem's consultation note. He was reading it when he heard Haleem's voice behind him.

"Mr. Jurney has gotten sick on you."

"I was just reading your dictation. I appreciate your help."

"I think you're on the right track. You've got all the usual culprits covered. I ordered a few tests to check for some of the more uncommon possibilities."

"He didn't seem that sick when he first came in. Five days ago I thought he'd be out in a day or two. Instead, he's steadily gotten worse."

"I'm always worried when I hear that story." Haleem said. "We either have a tough bug, the wrong bug, or some complicating factor. Though the CT only shows pneumonia, it could be an obstructive process, I guess. What do you think about a bronchoscopy?"

"Wouldn't be a bad idea. Let's hope it's not cancer."

"We could set the test up for tomorrow. I can call Byrd if you want."

"That'd be great."

Harry turned off the computer screen and headed for Jurney's room, stepping around a painter or two on the way. Jurney was sitting upright in bed. He was struggling much harder for air than he had the previous day. His color was gray, and he gave several loose-sounding coughs.

"I was hoping you would feel better by now," Harry said. "I'm sorry you're not."

Jurney pointed to a basin full of mucous on his bedside table. "I'm beginning to cough up a little blood."

"I was just talking with Dr. Haleem," Harry said. "We're going to ask Dr. Byrd, he's a pulmonary specialist, to do a bronchoscopy tomorrow."

"What's that?"

"It's a scope that looks in your lungs." Harry described the test.

"Whatever you think."

"Dr. Haleem ordered a bunch of lab tests to look for rare stuff. Those won't be back for a day or two."

"He seems like a nice guy. Where's he from?"

"He's from Egypt."

"I asked him if he was one of those Muslims," Jurney said, "and he said he was. I wasn't so sure about him at first, but he seems decent enough."

"He's an excellent doctor. Very smart."

"His name's pretty tough, but I'm getting more used to these Middle Eastern names."

"I struggle a little myself."

"But if he's good enough for you, Dr. Bennett, he's good enough for me."

Harry moved to the doorway. "We'll do the bronchoscopy tomorrow. We'll call Dr. Byrd and set it up."

As Harry stepped into the hallway, he glanced at his watch. He tried not look at it in the room, but he had two more patients to see in the hospital and a drive to Sycamore before his office started.

Harry hadn't thought much about Dr. Haleem's nationality, and he hadn't ever asked if he was a Muslim. Dr. Haleem was a good infectious disease specialist. He communicated well, worked hard, and was always available.

It was odd how patients judged the doctors they saw. They often picked the best and the brightest, and saw right through the weaker ones. Harry would need Dr. Haleem's help with Mr. Jurney. Harry hoped the pneumonia was all he had.

* * *

DECEMBER 10, 9:00 A.M. EST
NEW YORK CITY

Mohammed had chosen a computer terminal that faced the back corner. He had arrived when the New York Public Library opened, and except for a couple of librarians, the place was nearly empty. The only other people there this early, it seemed, were the homeless. The library was a much more pleasant place to spend the day than the local Salvation Army facilities, and the homeless were staking out the spots where they would seek shelter from the cold weather outside. No one was near Mohammed. The homeless weren't using the computers.

The computer had access to the Internet, and Mohammed quickly typed in the address of his Internet e-mail host. The three other men were to send e-mails to Mohammed to inform him of their progress. The e-mails would appear innocent enough if intercepted but would reveal each man's status to Mohammed. Mohammed waited as the browser opened his e-mail account, and then he clicked on the first e-mail on the list.

"Saw the Capitol and the Lincoln Memorial today. Can't wait to see more. Hotel is excellent. Hope you're doing well."

Nazih Al-Sabai was in Washington, DC. Before Mohammed could click on the next e-mail, one of the street people walked behind him. Mohammed waited. The man was filthy and smelled like urine. Carrying four plastic bags filled with his worldly possessions, he shuffled behind Mohammed toward a group of chairs across the room. There he sat down and spread out his belongings all around him. The smell lingered, and Mohammed held his breath for a moment while the air cleared. He clicked on the next e-mail.

"It's snowing here in Chicago. The hotel is warm. I think I have the flu. Headaches, back pain, nausea, and some fever."

Al-Musaleh was in Chicago. Mohammed had instructed them to avoid leaving personal information unless absolutely necessary. "Muhsin must be confused about these symptoms," Mohammed thought. "Since it is probably too early for smallpox, maybe he does have the flu. Time would tell."

Los Angeles was not yet reporting. Khalid's flight was longer. Mohammed would check back later to see if there was an e-mail from Khalid. He responded to both Nazih and Muhsin, acknowledging receipt of their messages. They would now stay in their rooms until the first lesions appeared. With the men confined, there would be virtually no chance of detection. The mission was proceeding as planned.

Mohammed opened a new e-mail window and typed in the address he had memorized. His note would be copied and rerouted multiple times before it reached its final destination. He knew the recipient would be pleased.

"All but one of the Christmas presents arrived on time," he wrote. "Waiting for the last one. All is great. Regards."

The most vital part of the mission was complete. It would now be in Allah's hands.

Another e-mail was on his list, and he clicked on it. It simply had a Web site address. He closed his own Internet account, typed in the Web address on the library's browser, and watched as a Somali newspaper's site loaded. He read through the reports until he found it. The article was dated December ninth and read: "A car bomb exploded in Hargeysa, Somalia killing fifteen people at the funeral of assassinated warlord Fazul Qaarey. Killed were Qaarey's wife, six children, and eight others attending the funeral. No one has claimed responsibility for the bombing, though a rival clan is believed to be responsible."

Mohammed logged off the computer, leaned back in his chair, and smiled.

CHAPTER TWELVE

DECEMBER 11, 8:00 A.M. EST
DAY TEN OF EXPOSURE
NEW YORK CITY

Mohammed woke up with a headache. Today was the tenth day of his exposure, and this headache felt different than any he had ever had. A dull, deep painful sensation that originated from the base of his skull filled his entire head. He was queasy and also felt discomfort on both sides of his lower back. But he refused to take any medication because the symptoms meant he was infected, and he wanted to feel the full effect. He was pleased. If he had not contracted the virus from the boy, then all was wasted. In a few days, he knew, the virus would eat away at his tissues and destroy his organs, probably causing him a great deal of pain and suffering. He was ready for that. Many Muslim martyrs in history had suffered far worse fates, and they were now in paradise. Mohammed fell to the floor and faced Mecca. He prayed for courage and for strength. His jihad had begun.

After removing all his clothes, he stood naked in front of the mirror in the bathroom inspecting his body. He saw nothing. He looked inside his mouth for the first signs but found none. Though he felt that he was infected, without the rash, he was not likely contagious. He had planned a trip out into the street this morning. How great would it be if he could infect the infidels now?

He showered and dressed, and then left the Renaissance Hotel from the Seventh Street entrance. The sidewalk was packed with a constant flow of people, as was always the case in Times Square. The visitor's center was across the street, and inside he found a variety of brochures on shopping, restaurants, museums, hotels, and theaters. A sign on the wall boasted that Times Square drew thirty-seven million tourists annually. Within a few blocks were twenty-eight hotels, forty-five Broadway theaters, and five thousand businesses. He had chosen a perfect location.

The weather was crisp, cool, without wind, and not too uncomfortable. At the airport, he had purchased a New York Yankees pullover. He had actually been to a Yankees game once, but he didn't understand the rules and found it slow and boring. A street vendor near the hotel had sold him an NYFD ball cap, and he thought purchasing the hat was particularly humorous because the Americans were so proud of the firemen who were killed on 9/11. The number of their deaths was a demonstration of Islam's undeniable power. *Even more should have died.*

Mohammed walked south on Broadway to Forty-Second Street and chose a corner restaurant for breakfast. The food in America was unappetizing to him because it was too rich and heavy with animal fats and grease; although he felt a little nauseated, he needed to eat because he wasn't sure how many more days he would be able to eat. A few empty stools lined the bar, but he waited for a table and was seated near the window. He preferred not to talk to anyone, which wasn't particularly difficult in New York, especially if he was sitting alone at a table. On his previous trips, someone from the Midwest, all friendly and smiling, would occasionally try to strike up a conversation, but Mohammed would not even acknowledge the person's existence, which added to his authenticity as a native. After a few minutes, the waitress brought his order: cereal without milk, juice, and dry toast. It didn't settle particularly well.

After eating, he walked to the library on Forty-Second Street and found it was more crowded than the day before. The computer terminal he preferred was available, and he logged on. He watched his homepage load and noticed he had no e-mails. Khalid should be in Los Angeles by now, he thought, and he wouldn't have forgotten to check in. Either his flights were delayed, which was always possible, or he was detained. If any of the men were to be stopped and questioned, Khalid was the most likely. He had been involved with several operations and his background was murky. The others were essentially new recruits. But Khalid was strong, and he was a professional. Mohammed was convinced that even if the Americans used torture like they did in Cuba and Afghanistan, Khalid would not divulge any information about their mission. What concerned Mohammed the most was that if Khalid were captured and held, his smallpox would eventually become evident. Even so, it would possibly be too late, especially if the others were in place and infecting the Americans. If Khalid's circumstances had required that he take his capsule, he might even be dead.

Mohammed closed the account and logged off the computer. This would be the last time he would check e-mails. He, too, would confine himself to his room until the rash appeared and he was infectious. He left the library and stepped outside into the sunlight for the walk back to the hotel.

He hoped Khalid was not dead because if he had been captured, he would infect his captors, which would be right. In either case, he would die the death of a martyr.

* * *

DECEMBER 11, 9:00 A.M. CST
CHICAGO, ILLINOIS

Muhsin Al-Musaleh was so sick he could barely move. He had hard chills and fever, and had vomited multiple times. He felt much worse than he had expected and had a terrible, odd apprehension, almost a panic that he couldn't shake. He knew what was happening. He had smallpox. He had anticipated he would get sick, but he felt he was smothering or that his heart was failing, as if he might die at any moment.

The night before, his symptoms had been minimal, just a little nausea, back pain, and a mild, throbbing headache. He had thought he might feel better after a night's sleep, but it wasn't so.

His legs felt heavy as he swung them off the bed and pushed himself up into a sitting position. He leaned against the nightstand for support and balance; he was so weak that he was afraid he might collapse. His muscles twitched and occasionally spasmed so severely that he lost his breath. He was sweating profusely. Leaning heavily against the wall as he walked, he made his way to the bathroom, where he fell to his knees and vomited twice in the toilet. For several minutes he lay on the floor curled up in a ball, summoning the energy to try to stand again. He pushed himself away from the toilet and reached over for the sink, holding himself up with both arms. His vision was blurry, and he struggled to focus on his reflection in the mirror. He almost didn't recognize himself.

His face was ghostly pale, and his hair was soaked with perspiration that ran down his cheeks and dripped to the floor. Both of his eyes were bright red as if blood vessels had burst. He had the lesions, many of them. It was smallpox. He was infected.

Fifteen or twenty pustules were clearly evident on his face and a few more were on his arms and chest, even a couple on his abdomen. They were unmistakable, just like the pictures Mohammed had shown them. He reached up and touched one on his cheek. It was hard, firm, and slightly tender, and this particular lesion was filled with blood.

Panic welled up in his abdomen and filled his chest. The symptoms were too early. This was not what Mohammed had said would happen, but it could not be anything else but smallpox.

His watch showed nine o'clock, and the stores wouldn't open until ten. Surely he was contagious. He needed to get out among the public as soon as possible. Soon, he'd be too sick to go.

A terrible thought invaded his brain: he was dying and wouldn't have time to complete the mission. He must dress and leave, or he would fail Mohammed.

Al-Musaleh felt the contents of his stomach push up into his throat, and he vomited into the sink with such force that it sprayed on the walls and floor and splattered back up on him. The vomit was streaked with blood. The smell was awful, and he threw up again. The muscles in his legs trembled; exhausted, he collapsed, sliding down against the wall to the floor. He curled up into a fetal position. He would rest for a while. What else could he do?

Rescue me, O god of Abraham, O god of Muhammad. Rescue me from my shame.

* * *

DECEMBER 11, 11:00 A.M. CST
CHICAGO, ILLINOIS

The American Girl luncheon at the store off Michigan Avenue was every little girl's dream come true. Kathy Randall had made the reservation months earlier for her daughter, Lauren, long before Lauren's bout with chickenpox. Lauren had invited her best friend from church, Sally Miller, and the two girls had rattled on about nothing else ever since. When Lauren had broken out in the rash five days before they had planned to leave, the whole trip had been in jeopardy. But now Lauren was well, and the rash was almost completely gone; it had been just a light case of chickenpox. Their worry about missing the outing had made the event all the more special. As Kathy watched the two girls in the restaurant waiting to be served, her smile was as big as theirs.

The room was decorated in black and white with pink accents. Some chairs boasted stripes and others, polka dots. The tablecloths were solid white with lace fringe and matching napkins. Their table like most seated four people—usually two mothers and two daughters. Waitresses scurried about in charming outfits that matched the décor, serving tea biscuits, cinnamon rolls, and small cups of warm cider on monogrammed black and white china. Lauren's doll, Kirsten, and Sally's doll, Samantha, held the positions of honor at both ends of the table; the dolls sat in tiny chairs that perfectly matched the ones occupied by the dolls' owners.

"We weren't sure she could come," Kathy said, "but Dr. Bennett said it was okay."

Kathy had met Claudia Miller after the girls became friends, and the moms had become quick friends themselves. They had expected the trip would be as much fun for them as it would be for the girls.

"I'm glad she's feeling better," Claudia said. "So, she wasn't very sick?"

"The rash only lasted a couple of days," Kathy said. "Dr. Bennett said it was so light because of the vaccine. Lauren would have been crushed if she couldn't have come."

"They're having such a great time."

The two girls were chattering away, playing with their dolls, and pretending to offer them the make-believe tea in tiny doll-sized cups.

The servers brought out the main course: spinach salad, quiche, pizza, and baked chicken tenders. Drinks were pink lemonade and virgin mimosas. The girls picked at their food, too excited to eat. Dessert came last—carrot cake and pudding served in a special flowerpot.

The whole affair was a fine event and a memorable, special occasion. And for everyone, both the mothers and their daughters, it was over much too soon.

The waitress brought the girls red, miniature shopping bags imprinted with the store's insignia for their dolls, exactly matching those used for the adult patrons. The diners gathered their belongings and moved as a group toward the exit, all feeling as reluctant to leave as Lauren and her friend.

Lauren tugged on her mother's arm. "Mom," Lauren said in her soft voice, "this was perfect."

"I agree," Kathy said. "I thought it was perfect, too."

They looked around the doll store for more than an hour. The dolls were arranged in a hundred different displays, and they could have spent a fortune. Lauren and Sally repeated over and over, "I want one of those," but the mothers couldn't blame them. They wanted one of each of everything themselves. After both girls picked out a Christmas outfit for their dolls, they lined up at the registers to check out.

"If we came here often," Kathy said, "we'd be flat broke, and we haven't even started shopping for ourselves."

"Crate & Barrel is just around the corner," Claudia said. "Let's see how much damage we can do there."

"Sounds like a plan."

They stepped through the revolving door to the sidewalk outside; the two young girls walked ahead of their mothers. The girls were holding their dolls, and the mothers were carrying everything else. Their purchases completely filled two large, red sacks each.

"If we buy much more," Kathy said, "we won't have room in the car."

"We can always ship," Claudia said.

Kathy laughed. "Thank God for UPS."

* * *

The rigors woke Al-Musaleh as he jerked on the hard floor of the bathroom. He nearly panicked at the thought that he had fallen asleep, and he quickly looked at his watch. It was noon. He had been unconscious for over three hours. "What have I done?" he wondered. If he didn't leave now, he would die in this room, and he had no intention of doing that.

Al-Musaleh pushed himself up and splashed water on his face. The dry vomit in the sink almost made him retch again, but he held the contents of his stomach down. There wasn't much left. His face had more lesions now than when he had looked earlier; they seemed to be developing at a remarkably rapid rate.

After showering in cold water and changing into a fresh long-sleeved shirt and a pullover sweatshirt, he attempted to dab makeup to the spots on his face. He was sweating profusely, and though the makeup wouldn't stay on, he continued to work at it for several minutes. As bad as the lesions looked, he needed to cover them, he thought, or he couldn't go out in public.

When he had gone to bed the night before, he hadn't noticed any lesions, and now his face was covered. This was incredible.

He slid on his Chicago Bulls jacket and packed all of his belongings in his carry-on bag. After placing the Do Not Disturb placard on the door, he left the room. At the end of the hall near the elevators, he took the lid off the trashcan and stuffed the carry-on inside. He pushed the elevator button, and then he remembered something he had forgotten, the only item he needed. He retrieved the carry-on and removed the cyanide capsule, wrapped in an aspirin package. The capsule might be needed to end his life, and at this point, that possibility certainly seemed inevitable...and very soon.

* * *

Crate & Barrel, a uniquely designed, three-story Chicago landmark, was at the corner of Michigan and Erie and at the heart of the shopping district on the Magnificent Mile. The solid-glass wall that fronted the building overlooked the intersection and allowed shoppers to enjoy the view of the Christmas decorations along Michigan Avenue as they rode the store's escalators. Kathy and Claudia had started on the third floor with the furniture and home furnishings and worked their way down. On the first floor, among the seasonal china and glassware, Claudia picked out red and green Christmas plates. A long line of customers, roped off into a single file away from the crush of busy holiday customers, waited to check out. Their two daughters had become restless and were sitting on the floor at their feet, playing with their dolls. Their limited attention span would not likely hold out much longer.

"The girls are doing pretty well," Kathy said, "but they're wearing out quickly. Lauren's still not feeling all that good."

"The crowds are beginning to get to me, too," Claudia said.

"I really wanted to go to Bloomingdale's, but maybe I should wait for another time."

"I'm planning to ship these dishes so I won't have to carry them, but the car's still parked a long way from here. Should we take a cab?"

"I was thinking the same thing."

It took thirty minutes for them to reach the registers. When they finished checking out, they gathered the girls, the dolls, and the shopping bags, and stepped outside. The sidewalk was filled with a mass of people moving in both directions.

"Hang on, girls," the mothers said as they grabbed their daughters' hands tightly. The four of them squeezed into the crowd, dodging back and forth, and working their way through until they finally reached the curb.

"Take Lauren for me," Kathy said, holding out Lauren's arm. "I'll hail a cab."

Kathy stood on the curb and raised her hand. The street was full of vehicles, including dozens of cabs—all of which seemed to be occupied. She waved at each one anyway, and after several minutes, a yellow cab approached the curb and slowed to a stop. In the backseat was a single passenger. He reached over the front seat to pay the driver and then swung open the door. Kathy stepped back out of the way. The man was of Middle Eastern descent and looked to be in his twenties; he was dressed casually in jeans and a black Chicago Bulls jacket. As he passed by her, Kathy leaned into the cab, blocking a middle-aged man in a business suit who was trying to jump in front of her.

"Is this taxi available?" she asked the driver.

"It is now, lady," he replied.

Kathy signaled Claudia and the two girls, and they moved next to her. Kathy sat the red shopping bags on the seat and took Lauren's hand to help her into the car. From behind her, a man pushed her to one side and sat down on the rear seat. It was the Middle Eastern passenger who had just left. He shoved her bags out onto the curb, dumping their contents on the sidewalk.

"Excuse me!" Kathy said. "I believe we have this cab now."

"I need my taxi back," he said. "I'm too sick to get out."

"But we were—" Kathy started.

The man leaned out of the taxi and vomited on the sidewalk.

"Sorry," he said, looking up at them, wiping the vomit off his chin. "I have the flu." The man pulled the door shut, and the taxi drove away.

The vomit had splattered on the four of them and all over the sides of the shopping bags. Vomit covered their shoes and the lower portions of their legs. The two girls started crying.

"This is disgusting!" Claudia said.

Kathy instinctively wiped down the legs of the two girls and held out her hands. "I can't believe he just did that."

"That's blood," Claudia said, pointing.

"Oh, my Gosh! We need to wash this off."

"And as quickly as possible!" Claudia looked over her shoulder and motioned toward the store behind them. "We should go back to Crate & Barrel."

Kathy wiped her hands on a shopping bag, and gingerly picked up their purchases off the ground. The two mothers grabbed their daughters, pushing back through the crowd to the entrance. Inside the store, the line to the women's restroom stretched down the hall and around the corner, but when the other women in line saw them, they allowed them to move to the front of the line. Kathy washed off Lauren's feet and legs first and then her own. Claudia did the same for herself and Sally. The vomit soaked the bottom of Kathy's pants, and she attempted to wash it out with wet paper towels. The women rinsed their shoes the best they could. The smell was nauseating.

"Let's go home," Kathy said. "I can't stand this."

"I'm ready," Claudia agreed.

They went back outside and again pushed out to the curb. Kathy raised her arm and hailed a taxi. This time the first cab that stopped was unoccupied, and the four slid into the back seat.

"That's a shopping trip we won't soon forget," Claudia said.

"I'll be glad to get home and get the both of us into the shower. Maybe I should call Dr. Bennett to see what he thinks? I don't know, maybe he should check for hepatitis or HIV or something?"

"Let me know what he says. Sally and I may need to be checked, too."

"I'll call you as soon as I find out."

The smell lingered inside the enclosed vehicle. They rolled down the back windows and felt the crisp, cold winter wind, but it didn't help much. It would be a long trip home.

* * *

Al-Musaleh struggled to stay conscious.

"Take me to O'Hare Airport—long-term parking lot C." Al-Musaleh forced the words out as strong as possible, but his voice was weakening.

"You don't look so good," the driver said. "Are you sure you don't want me to take you to a hospital or a doctor?"

"No!" he said as emphatically as possible. "O'Hare Airport."

"It's your buck."

Al-Musaleh's heart was pounding, and he was sweating profusely from the fever. He was worried that his facial lesions were becoming more obvious and that this man would remember him. He pushed up the sleeve of his jacket to look at his arm. The lesions were turning a dark red and beginning to overlap each other. He could taste the blood and vomit in his mouth. He told himself that he couldn't pass out because if he did, he would be taken to a hospital where his smallpox would be diagnosed. If they did that, the whole country would be on alert, maybe even before the others became infectious. He would fail.

He must go to the airport and follow his instructions. No hospitals. No doctors. He could not pass out.

The driver left the downtown streets and pulled on to the interstate.

"Are you sure about the hospital?" the driver asked. "There is one close."

"No hospitals. I have a friend waiting. He'll take me."

"If you throw up in my backseat, I'll drop you off at the nearest curb. You understand?"

Al-Musaleh nodded

The driver was serious. The emergency room wasn't an option, but neither was losing his ride to the airport. He couldn't get sick again—that was for certain.

This was not going as planned. He shouldn't have waited so long. He might have wasted his opportunity completely, unless maybe this driver was infected or possibly the woman on the curb. Yet all this was too obvious, throwing up outside the car, too sick to stand. The woman and this driver would remember him. Who wouldn't?

The driver's voice startled Al-Musaleh awake. He must have dozed off. The driver was yelling at another taxi driver in front of him who was too slow. They were stopped in traffic and weren't moving at all. Al-Musaleh felt the panic rush up through him. He had fallen asleep and hadn't realized it. How could he be so weak and worthless? How could he die a failure and not complete his jihad?

He mustn't fall asleep again, no matter what. He must stay awake. It was imperative.

He must stay awake in order to die like a man.

CHAPTER THIRTEEN

DECEMBER 11, 11:00 A.M. PST
DAY TEN OF THE FIRST WAVE OF EXPOSURE
LOS ANGELES

Gary Roberts hated Los Angeles. He hated the traffic. He hated the smog. He hated the California lifestyle. And most of all, he hated the continuous sprawl of buildings and roads and the evidence of humanity in every direction as far as the eye could see. The whole place could drop off the edge of the United States in a giant earthquake, as far as he was concerned, and he doubted that the rest of the country would even notice or care it was gone.

Roberts's peer, the FBI special agent in charge for Los Angeles, had been waiting when he arrived LAX, and now they were on the Harbor Freeway, heading for the downtown office. FBI headquarters in Washington had called Atlanta and had insisted Roberts drop what he was doing and fly out today. He wasn't sure why. From what he had heard, the case seemed fairly routine, but they said they needed his expertise in bioterrorism. He was eager for some details.

"You don't have a name on him yet?" Roberts asked.

Two other agents sat in the back of the vehicle, but the question was for the agent in charge, and only he would answer.

"We think he's Al-Qaeda."

The agent was Dirk Swenson. The name sounded to Roberts like a Scandinavian football player turned movie star. In fact, he looked more like an accountant—a small, weasel-like man with wire-rimmed glasses and thick black hair that was slicked back. The hair was a little too long, and he was dressed much too casually, in khakis without a tie or jacket and with some sort of slip-on shoes. An agent on the East Coast or in the South wouldn't get by with his appearance for a minute, but this was California. Roberts hated California.

"What makes you think he's Al-Qaeda?" Roberts asked.

"The local CIA thought he knew him," Swenson said. "He thinks he trained with Osama in Afghanistan, but we have no direct evidence of that. We're sure the guy is dirty. Airport security thought he looked suspicious from the beginning. He came in on a flight from Singapore. He had nothing on him. The fact of the matter is he had only a carry-on with very few items; he had not checked any luggage. That seemed odd, so they detained him. It turns out his passport is fake. We arrested him and brought him to headquarters."

Swenson exited the freeway downtown and turned into an underground parking garage.

"Did the CIA want jurisdiction?"

"No. They're not interested in him until they can run him through their computers and make a definite I.D. Now that he's here, he's ours. We searched his belongings carefully, as you might imagine, and he had virtually nothing, only a change of underwear and a pair of tennis shoes. He had two credit cards, both of which were using stolen numbers, and two thousand in cash."

Roberts's interest was growing. "Sounds like he was planning a little shopping spree."

"We found several packets of aspirin, and one turned out to be a cyanide pill."

"Now, why would he need that?"

"That's why we called you. We think he's a terrorist of some sort and up to something. We wanted your help to sort it out. Besides, you speak the lingo."

They got off the elevator from the parking garage, and Roberts walked through security with Swenson, handing his weapon briefly to the agent at the metal detectors. Swenson took him down a long, narrow hallway. At the end were two examination rooms. It reminded Roberts of an old movie where the Russians, or whoever the bad guys were, tortured their victims at the end of the corridor so the screams couldn't be heard.

"So your only reason to think that this is a terrorist," Roberts said, "is the fact he had a cyanide capsule, false credit cards, a large amount of cash, and fake travel documents? We wouldn't want to jump to any conclusions if asked about this by some politician."

"For the moment anyway," Swenson said. "Maybe we should wait for the CIA documentation to come back."

"Yeah, next week."

The interrogation room was small, about fifteen feet on each side. A metal table occupied the center of the room; an Arab male sat in a chair on the opposite side of the table. The man was uncuffed. Two armed guards, both in LAPD uniforms, stood on each side behind him. Two empty metal seats were on the side of the room closest to Roberts. He and Swenson sat down. Several other agents stood behind them.

The man was dark complected and had black hair and dark eyes. He had a thin, black moustache but no beard. Roberts noted that he was sitting rigidly upright in his chair. He had an odd look—apprehensive, but not particularly scared or fearful. Roberts couldn't put his finger on it. The man stared straight ahead, looking between him and Swenson, not even glancing at either of them. Roberts noticed a thin layer of sweat covering his forehead. He leaned around the side of the table and watched the sweat drip off to form a small puddle on the floor beside him.

"Are you all right?" Roberts asked the man in Arabic.

The man did not respond.

The man was pale, and Roberts thought he looked as if he might be in pain.

"Are you sick?" Roberts asked, again in Arabic. "Do you need to see a doctor?"

The man continued to stare straight ahead, and again he did not respond.

Roberts stood and stepped toward him. He reached out and touched his cheek with the back of his hand, and quickly pulled it away.

"My God," Roberts said, "he's burning up. Did any one notice he has a fever? This man is sick."

The look on the man's face immediately frightened Roberts. His expression hardly changed, but it was his confidence. This man wasn't worried that he was sick. He knew that he was.

"Oh, my God," Roberts thought. "Maybe this was biologic. Maybe this was the case that everyone had been waiting for—and dreading."

"All of you," Roberts ordered, "out of the room! We need to isolate this man. You there," he said, pointing to one of the police officers. "You're the only one I want in here, and you watch this man like a hawk. Everyone else get out. No one comes in this room without my direct order."

Roberts led the other agents out into the hallway. He turned and looked through the one-way mirror back into the room.

"What the hell is going on here?" Swenson asked.

"Get the names of all contacts with this man—everyone. Airport security, drivers, guards, and maintenance—anyone who's been in contact."

"He came in on a flight from Singapore," Swenson said. "He was at the airport for six or eight hours."

"I don't care. Get everyone's name. Everyone on the flight— the passengers and the crew. Damn! See where the crew is now. They could be anywhere in the world. And the passengers—they're all over the U.S. by now. If this man is a biologic terrorist, and I may be jumping to conclusions here, but if he is, we could get into trouble real fast."

"Then let's get him to a doctor and find out."

"Before we move him anywhere, we need to talk to a medical expert." Roberts pointed to one of the agents. "Call the CDC in Atlanta. I want to talk to Dr. Hugh Jackson—he's the head of their bioterrorism department—and I want to talk to him now. If he's in a meeting, I don't care how important they say it is, get him out! Hell, get him off the golf course if you have to. This is an emergency!"

"So you think this is bioterrorism?" Swenson asked.

"It's a possibility. It could be anything."

"Maybe he just has the flu."

Roberts looked through the window. "Maybe...let's hope."

Roberts stared at the man. Something was wrong about this sonofabitch. He was hiding something. He didn't have a cyanide capsule because he had the flu. He looked at the man and could have sworn he saw the faintest smile.

* * *

DECEMBER 11, 1:00 P.M. CST
CHICAGO, NEAR O'HARE AIRPORT

The taxi exited off of Interstate ninety and on to the O'Hare Airport road that led to the long-term parking lots. Al-Musaleh directed the driver to parking lot C. He was fighting to stay conscious. Only a few more minutes, and he would be safely there.

The driver pushed the button at the gate and a ticket popped out as the bar rose upward.

"I told you two bucks in addition to the fare," the driver barked at Al-Musaleh. "I'll have to pay to get out, and it's cash only, buddy."

"Of course," Al-Musaleh said. He had no choice.

They turned in and headed down the first row. So many cars, Al-Musaleh thought. He had never seen so many in one place. A wave of nausea rose up in his chest again, but his stomach was empty. He had had the dry heaves on the expressway, and the driver had threatened to throw him out, but he hadn't. He needed to hold his stomach now.

Al-Musaleh debated whether or not to kill the driver. The original plan was to go to the terminal and shuttle to long-term parking. That way, no one would know where he was. But he was too weak for that. Now this foul, worthless American had seen him come here. Yet, Al-Musaleh worried that he might be too sick to kill him. He could choke him with his belt, normally a simple task, but his arms were so weak that he could barely lift them. He wanted to kill this man. This man had insulted him and threatened him. But if he couldn't complete the task, if the man was strong, or if someone saw them struggling, the authorities would come.

Better not to kill him—the driver would die soon enough if he was infected, and since he had ridden in the enclosed car with Al-Musaleh, he probably was. And if he was, he would infect other Americans before his own slow and painful death. Al-Musaleh allowed himself a smile. This driver would have hundreds of fares and maybe wouldn't remember him anyway. Al-Musaleh was sorry he wasn't strong enough to kill him. The infidel deserved it.

The driver started down the second row.

"Let me out here," Al-Musaleh said. "This is the place."

"I thought you were meeting a friend."

"This is where he will be."

Al-Musaleh paid the driver in cash, opened the door, and slid out of the vehicle. He leaned against one of the cars in the lot until the taxi was out of sight. Suddenly, a wave of nausea hit again, pushing upward into his chest, and this time he vomited several times on the ground. He had to balance himself with both hands on the car in front of him, afraid that if he fell, he could not get back up. When he had finished vomiting, he looked around. No one was nearby. Allah was protecting him.

He hoped he had the strength to find the car and to complete his final prayers.

The temperature had dropped into the twenties and the wind was blowing stiffly out of the north, but he didn't feel the cold. He looked at the thousands and thousands of vehicles stretched out in every direction. How could he find the right one? There were so many. He had the awful thought of being unable to find the car and dying on the ground; his body would be discovered by some unsuspecting traveler. If he was too weak, his only option would be to crawl under a car and hope its owner was on a very long trip.

A thick layer of snow covered most of the cars. A narrow path had been plowed on the pavement between the rows, and the pavement was dry. He stumbled along, looking for the fifteenth car in row three with the tag number he had memorized.

The pain in his back and legs caused him to groan with each step. His feet and hands had swollen to double their normal size. He coughed several times and was so short of breath that he could barely breathe. He made his way by holding on to one car and reaching out for the trunk of the next, and as he progressed across the rows, he realized he had reached the third row. He counted out the fifteenth car. The license tag matched the number he remembered. This was the car. *Praise be to Allah*.

The key should be underneath the wheel well of the right rear tire, according to Mohammed's instruction. He glanced around the lot. A few people were walking to their vehicles off in the distance, but no one was near him. There were no security cameras pointed in his direction that he could see, probably one of the reasons they had chosen this location. He shoved his hand underneath the wheel well and found the key, exactly as planned. *Thanks be to Allah*. Al-Musaleh leaned his body against the trunk, clutching the key with both hands, afraid he would drop it, and slid the key into the lock.

The key did not turn. Ice had frozen the lock.

Al-Musaleh felt a sudden panic. He had not considered the lock would be frozen. Snow was piled several inches on the top of the car, and the ice from the melted snow might not allow the trunk lid to open either. But opening the lock came first. He twisted the key hard, turning back and forth, but it would not budge. His legs began to wobble beneath him; he was so weak now that he could barely stand. He was sweating despite the cold, the sweat dripping from his forehead and freezing on the cement at his feet. Squeezing the key tightly with both hands and using his body weight as leverage, he turned it as hard as he could. He paused a moment, worrying about what would happen if the key broke. If it did, it did. He had no choice and very little time. With a loud grunt, he fell with his entire weight against the key.

A soft click indicated the trunk's release, and the lid slowly lifted a few inches. The trunk lid was not frozen. He said a brief prayer.

Al-Musaleh scanned the parking lot. He was alone. He removed the key and pushed open the trunk. After climbing inside and scanning the lot one last time, he pulled the lid closed. His jihad was complete.

CHAPTER FOURTEEN

DECEMBER 11, 2:00 P.M. EST
DAY TEN OF THE FIRST WAVE OF EXPOSURE
ATLANTA

Mike Lafitte called out three times before Jackson looked up from the laptop.

"Sorry to interrupt, Hugh, but I have a phone call I think you ought to take. Line one."

Jackson punched the button on the phone and lifted the receiver. He held a finger up. He wanted Lafitte to stay.

"This is Dr. Hugh Jackson. How can I help you?"

Jackson listened a minute or two. "My associate is in the office with me," he said. "May I put you on the speaker phone?"

Jackson pushed the speaker button and replaced the receiver. "Are you with us?"

"I can hear you," the voice said on the phone. "This is Gary Roberts, special agent in charge of the bioterrorism unit there in Atlanta. We've met, Dr. Jackson."

"I remember, Gary. We've worked on a couple of projects together, haven't we?"

"Yes, sir. I'm calling about a case here in Los Angeles, and I need your advice."

"I'm happy to help."

Roberts quickly gave the details. "And of course biologic agents, especially small-pox, have received so much media attention recently."

"So basically," Jackson said, "you have a Middle Eastern male with fever, and you have no idea where he came from."

"We now know his original flight was from Cairo to Singapore. Then he changed planes to Los Angeles. Before that we have no idea. His passport is bogus."

"Any rash?"

"I didn't see any, but he hasn't been checked that closely."

"The list of possibilities is numerous. If he originated from an Arab country or northern Africa, it could be malaria, tuberculosis, an HIV-related infection, or even a simple respiratory virus. Of course, there are many infectious agents that are not used for biologic warfare. Another good example is influenza, especially since it is December, and we're seeing thousands of cases of influenza throughout the U.S. It could be that. If it's smallpox, the rash usually first appears inside the mouth, on the face, or on the forearms, most often on the third or fourth day of a fever. And *if* it's smallpox, and he has a fever now, he would likely have been exposed seven to fourteen days ago."

"Then how should we proceed?"

"It sounds like he needs medical attention anyway. I'd recommend you put him in isolation in a negative pressure room equipped with HEPA filters at a tertiary hospital or teaching center. Let one of the local infectious disease specialists see him. We'll send a team out just in case. Of course, you need to list all his contacts."

"We're doing that," Roberts said.

"Good. The contacts should report any headaches, backaches, fever, vomiting, or blood in their stools. We'll culture up your guy and find out what he has."

"I'll get things started out here. But hurry and get here. Maybe it's just my gut talking, but something is wrong about this guy."

Jackson hung up the phone.

"Who are you sending?" Lafitte asked.

"I'm sending you."

"Me?"

"Yes, I'm sending our best. Okay, don't get a big head."

Lafitte rolled his eyes.

"This agent sounds worried and that worries me," Jackson said. "Take Jess and Cassandra. Tell them to be careful. Maybe it's nothing. Maybe it's real. The current symptoms are too minimal to be certain. And even if it's nothing, it'll be a good test of our system."

"Except," Lafitte said, "we'll catch hell for the expense."

"But if we're catching the first case of something big, not only will it be worth every penny, but we'll be damned lucky."

* * *

DECEMBER 11, 2:15 P.M. EST
NEW YORK CITY

Mohammed carefully pulled his cheek outward and inspected the lining, as he had done every hour since he had awakened. His heart was racing. He had learned the anatomy of his mouth with his regular inspections as he had never known it. The color, the shapes and contours, the consistency of the surface, the folds of tissue under his tongue, and the subtle variations of the shades of pink and flesh were all familiar to him now. His excitement grew because for the first time there was an area that was suspicious.

The spot was about the size of a pea, and it was round and gray with a distinct border. He touched it with the tip of his finger, and it felt firmer than the tissue around it.

The discovery caused him to examine his mouth and face even more closely. Just to the right of his eye, on the surface of his skin was another lesion that definitely had changed. It was also round and slightly raised, but it was red, caused by the smallest of blood vessels coursing on its surface. It hadn't been there that morning, of that he was certain.

Mohammed fell to the floor in prayer. He was contagious. The battle has started.

* * *

DECEMBER 11, 11:15 A.M. PST
LOS ANGELES

Gary Roberts hung up the phone. The two men left Swenson's office and began walking down the hallway.

"What did he say?" Swenson asked.

"We need to isolate him and transfer him to a tertiary hospital or university medical center. What are our options?"

"Probably LA County-USC or UCLA. They're both close. If he's really got anthrax or something, I want to pull the guard out of there. He's already bitching about it, and I don't blame him."

"I'm not sure that's wise. The CDC doctor said it could be a whole host of things and rattled off a long list. It may just be the flu."

The sharp crack of a gunshot pierced the hallway. Roberts and Swenson reacted instantly, running full speed as they raced down the hall. When they arrived at the examination room, they found several officers standing in front of the observation window with their guns drawn. The window's glass was shattered.

"What the hell happened?" Roberts yelled as he came up to them.

"The suspect grabbed Beeker's gun," one of the officers said, "and Hilburn shot him."

Roberts rushed into the room. The suspect lay on the floor next to the table, covered in small pieces of glass and with a gunshot wound to his chest. Blood was flowing out from under his body and already had formed a pool on the floor beside him. Officer Beeker was standing over the man with his gun aimed at his head. Roberts knelt beside the prisoner. He noticed that Swenson stayed in the hallway.

"Call an ambulance," Roberts yelled over his shoulder. "I need some help in here."

"He hadn't done nothing," Beeker muttered, "but he then went for my gun. I didn't see it coming."

The wounded man's body was shaking in small, brief spasms. His eyes were open, but his gaze was a blank stare. Roberts ripped open his shirt and exposed his bare chest. There was a hole the size of a quarter where the bullet entered to the left of his sternum. Blood, as well as bubbles of air, oozed from the wound, and Roberts heard a sucking sound. He rolled the man over. His body was limp. The exit wound was in his left lower chest wall, a couple of inches across, with ragged edges and lung tissue pushing in and out with each breath. It was also oozing blood rather profusely. Roberts pushed on both wounds, hoping to stem the loss of blood. As Roberts continued the pressure, Beeker began backing out of the room.

"Hey," Roberts said, "I need help here."

"I'm pulling my man out," Swenson said. "If he has smallpox—"

"We don't know he has anything. It could be the flu. Right now the only thing we do know is that he has a gunshot wound to his chest."

"That wouldn't have happened if you hadn't pulled the guards."

Roberts lifted his head toward Swenson, his face red. "I order you to get in here. This man is in your custody, and if he dies, there'll be hell to pay."

"The paramedics will be here in a second," Swenson said. "If you want to do mouth-to-mouth on that bastard, go ahead."

One of the agents threw in a towel, and Roberts used it to apply pressure to the chest. The man's breathing was erratic. He coughed occasionally, and when he did, blood came out of his mouth. Roberts was certain he was bleeding to death despite his efforts. He needed help, and he needed it fast.

In less than five minutes, though it seemed like thirty, two paramedics arrived and quickly went to work. Within a couple of minutes, they had taken his vital signs, attached leads for a cardiac monitor, and started two IVs for fluids. One paramedic intubated him and began ventilating him with an AMBU bag. The other inserted a chest tube. When the tube entered the chest cavity, pure red blood poured out, emptying into a container sitting on the floor.

As Roberts stood up to watch the scene, he lifted up his hands. They were completely covered in the man's blood.

"He has a sucking chest wound," a paramedic said. "I'm surprised he's not dead already."

"His pupils are fixed and dilated," the second paramedic said. "So even if he survives, he's probably brain damaged."

"I'm worried that he's infected," Roberts said. "I talked with the CDC, and he needs to be isolated."

A third paramedic arrived, pushing in the stretcher from the hallway.

"Infection is the least of his concerns," the first paramedic said.

"It's not the least of my concerns. He needs a negative pressure room and strict isolation. This could be a biological warfare agent."

"You mean like smallpox or anthrax or something?"

"We really have no idea at this time," Roberts said.

"No idea? You're just guessing?"

The second paramedic jumped in. "We always use precautions, but if we screw around too much, he'll die. You want that?"

One of the paramedics dropped the stretcher to the floor, and the other two lifted the patient in place while continuing to ventilate him using the AMBU bag. They positioned the stretcher's straps across his chest and cinched them tight.

"I don't like my prisoners dying," Roberts said, "but if he's infected, others could die, too."

"If we don't get him there immediately," the first paramedic said, "he's a dead man anyway."

"Then I'm going with you."

"I'm not sure that's—"

"I'm a federal agent," Roberts interrupted. "He's a prisoner in my custody. I think you'll regret saying no to me."

"Then stay out of the way."

The paramedics raced down the hallway and outside to a waiting ambulance. The lights were flashing, and the siren was oscillating in a high-pitched whine. After loading the patient in the back, Roberts climbed in and one of the paramedics pulled the doors shut.

The ambulance bolted out of the driveway. The first paramedic constantly ventilated the patient while the other checked his blood pressure and vitals. Both looked up at the monitor occasionally as if they expected his heart might stop.

"Pressure's sixty," the first paramedic said. "We'd better get there."

Blood was all over the front of the patient, on the stretcher, and dripping on the floor of the ambulance. It flowed freely from the chest tube. The prisoner did not appear to be conscious. Roberts thought his pale, ashen color meant he was losing a great deal of blood, and though he was not a doctor, he thought the patient looked like he was very close to death. They were losing him.

Los Angeles County Medical Center was five minutes away, and the trauma team had been activated. A crowd of nurses and doctors converged at the back of the ambulance as soon as it came to a stop. Roberts jumped out of the vehicle and held up his badge.

"This man is in federal custody. I want him in isolation, and I want a list of everyone who comes into contact with him."

The paramedics pulled the stretcher out of the ambulance, and the nurses and doctors gathered around. The paramedics gave an update on vital signs and his condition as they moved toward the ambulance entrance. No one answered Roberts.

"I am a federal officer," Roberts said loudly, "and I demand to know who is in charge here."

A tall, slender male wearing a thigh-length white coat and appearing to be in his late twenties was at the back of the group. He turned to Roberts and spoke up. "I'm the chief surgical resident. This will be my case."

"This man was infected before he was shot," Roberts said. "The Centers for Disease Control says he needs negative pressure isolation."

As the stretcher rolled into one of the emergency room's trauma rooms, fifteen staff members surrounded the patient, drawing blood, starting another IV, taking vital signs, and preparing him for surgery. The surgeon stayed just outside of the trauma room with Roberts.

"Listen," the doctor said, pointing his finger at Roberts. "We'll do the best we can when he's in intensive care, but for now he's going to surgery. We'll worry about the infection later."

"You don't understand. I'm concerned about a biologic agent."

Several staff members' heads turned toward Roberts.

"So what are you saying?" the doctor asked.

"He may just have the flu, but he could have something much more serious."

"Any particular agent you're concerned about?"

"No, that's what we need to determine."

"Dr. Ferguson," one of the nurses said, "the patient is ready and surgery has called. We can't wait."

The staff pulled the patient out of the trauma room. With a full team on both sides of the stretcher, they pushed him down the hallway, heading for the surgical suite.

The surgeon started after the staff but first turned toward Roberts. "So you're not sure of anything, right?"

"No, not positive but we need to proceed carefully as a precaution."

"Okay, we'll be cautious," the surgeon said, "but it's not going to matter if he's dead. So you'll have to excuse me, I have a surgery to go to."

"Doctor, please, ask someone to record his contacts."

"I'll do that," he said, waving his hand back at Roberts as he walked down the hall. "I'll find some nurse to do that."

Roberts wasn't convinced the doctor understood, mostly because he hadn't made himself clear. He wished he knew for sure what the suspect had, but he didn't. That didn't mean he wasn't right. He never questioned his gut, and today his gut felt certain. If this was a serious contagious biologic agent, everyone in this hospital was at risk, and that would be a disaster. The CDC wouldn't arrive from Atlanta for hours, so they wouldn't be of help for a while. The CDC would have the authority to shut down the hospital, if need be, but he had no authority whatsoever. He had hoped he could persuade these people about his concerns, but they were focused on the gunshot wound, which was an understandable but possibly tragic mistake. He might have to take matters into his own hands, at least until the CDC arrived.

It looked like he'd be watching a surgery. He hoped his stomach was up to it.

* * *

DECEMBER 11, 3:00 P.M. EST
NEW YORK CITY

The bright sunlight warmed the sidewalks of Times Square, melting the remnants of ice, creating a day of spring-like weather. The overcast skies disappeared, replaced with a crystal-clear azure blue. Mohammed breathed in deeply. He was glad to be outdoors.

It was a perfect time for him. As soon as he had seen the lesions in his mouth, he could infect others, yet the rash was minimal and unnoticeable. No one could detect his illness, but he was now highly contagious.

As always, the sidewalks were full of people, rushing off to their busy worlds, oblivious to him and the danger within him. He coughed openly. No one seemed to notice or care. Lots of other people were coughing, just as he was. The news media was full of reports on the influenza epidemic hitting the Northeast. Influenza had similar symptoms as smallpox at first: headaches, backaches, cough, and fever. He coughed again and watched others cough, too. They were infecting each other with influenza. Hopefully, he was infecting them with smallpox. With any luck, soon they would be infecting each other with the smallpox virus, too.

Mohammed looked up at the buildings. Two-story billboards with women scantily clad in lingerie sickened him, exposing only what a husband should see. The decadence of the Americans made him angry. Immorality and violence and sex were all that interested these infidels. They were a scourge on the earth.

The Forty-Second Street subway station bordered Broadway, and he followed the steps to the station deep below Times Square. After purchasing an entry card, he moved out onto the platform crowded with the waiting passengers. He mingled among them, men in business suits and in casual clothes, women in dresses and in slacks, and even a few children. He stood close and breathed, occasionally coughing, pleased to be so easily within six feet of them. A group of Hasidic Orthodox Jews, dressed in their traditional black garb, huddled near the edge of the platform, and he took great pleasure in coughing several times in their direction.

The sound of a train rumbling in the tunnel grew louder until it suddenly emerged, its brakes screeching as it slowed to a stop. The doors opened, and the crowd surged forward into the train, filling the car completely—there was standing room only. Mohammed reached up and grabbed an overhead bar. Other passengers packed in around him. Directly across the car, a middle-aged male with a bad hairpiece and a gray, pinstripe suit, typical for a lawyer or stockbroker, stood holding a newspaper in one hand and a briefcase in the other. His face was less than a foot from Mohammed's face. Mohammed coughed. "Excuse me," Mohammed said politely. The man barely looked up from the paper.

Mohammed looked to his right at an attractive woman in her twenties, blond hair and blue eyes, wearing a black leather jacket and holding the hand of a five- or six-year-old child beside her. The train rocked gently back and forth, and occasionally the rails would scrape with a shrill screech. Another train passed in the tunnel in the opposite direction, its lighted windows rushing by in a blur. The woman's face was a foot away. Mohammed coughed in her direction. She also did not notice.

Stupid Americans. They cannot stop me. They think they are safe. Their bombs and air force won't save them now.

He was traveling freely in New York City, he thought, going wherever he wanted, just as he had done before when he had ridden to the top of the World Trade Center. He had photographed every part of the buildings. There was no security. No one had stopped him then. No one stopped him now, either.

Mohammed rode the subway system for three hours, changing trains, walking through the stations, coming in contact with the wealthy, the poor, the young, and the old—even the homeless and the derelicts.

At the Times Square Station, he left the subway and walked up the stairs to the street. His back was aching, and he was growing fatigued; his illness was affecting his strength. Reaching up to his forehead, he felt the heat of his skin, and he was certain he had a fever. Occasionally, he would step into a restroom and check his face, but he still saw no obvious lesions.

After walking a few blocks along Broadway, he came to Macy's department store. A mass of white lights formed an eight-story tree on the front of the building, and bright red awnings covered each of the first floor windows. Inside, the store was jammed with shoppers. Near the front, a table was piled high with gloves and scarves in complete disarray. The value of these items alone, Mohammed thought, would provide enough money to feed a family in most Arab countries for a year. People completely encircled the table, shoving and pushing each other, and grabbing various articles. Mohammed thought he should stand in a crowded line, close to the other buyers as if waiting to pay for an item for a gift, maybe a present for a friend. This would be perfect. He reached in and picked up a wool scarf. A woman behind him elbowed her way past him as she pushed forward to the table. As he was holding the scarf, she jerked it right out of his hand.

"Pardon me," he said in perfect English.

"I had it first," she snapped.

"Madam," he said, coughing in her face as he released the scarf. "I give it to you."

She turned and walked away, acting disgusted, and he smiled. Typical, greedy infidel whore, he thought. She would pay for her rudeness to him.

The muscles in his legs felt weaker, and pains stabbed through his back in waves of spasms. His head ached. He felt dizzy and held onto the table for a moment before deciding he must leave. After making his way outside, he hailed a cab. The driver was an American.

Mohammed leaned forward. "To the Renaissance Hotel, please."

"Yes, sir."

He would rest for two or three hours, and then go back out in the evening. He only had seven or eight more days at the most.

* * *

DECEMBER 11, 12:30 P.M. PST
LOS ANGELES

By the time Roberts reached the window of the surgical suite, the procedure on his suspect had already started. The window was designed to allow a surgeon who was scrubbing in at the stainless steel sink to view the operating room. Roberts wedged himself between the edge of the sink and the wall with the window and watched. Three times a staff member told him to leave. Each time he flashed his FBI identification and refused. He wasn't going anywhere.

An older doctor, who was apparently the trauma team attending physician, joined Dr. Ferguson, the chief surgical resident whom Roberts had followed from the emergency room. They were working furiously. Four scrub nurses were assisting the doctors, and with the table blocked from view, Roberts could see little of the actual operative site. What he could see was enough. Blood was everywhere, and though Roberts had seen plenty of crime scenes, the sight of the fresh blood was making him woozy. Two large suction containers were on the floor, full of the patient's blood, and every few minutes a nurse would rush in with another couple of units to give to the patient. Roberts had counted sixteen so far. He turned away for a moment and breathed deeply.

The voices of doctors and nurses in the surgery suite could be heard through the glass. Roberts thought the tone sounded desperate.

"Suction," Ferguson said sharply, "we need more suction here. We can't see a damned thing."

"How's his pressure holding up, Dr. Harris?" the thoracic surgeon asked.

The anesthesiologist, Dr. Harris, sat in a chair at the head of the table, monitoring the patient's vital signs. "Sixty over forty, Dr. Fields," he said. "You've got to control the bleeding, or we're going to lose him."

"We know that! I need a better exposure here. Suction!" Dr. Fields held out a bloody glove. "We need suction!" One of the nurses quickly slapped the suction handle in his hand. "Dr. Harris," he said, "you just keep the blood coming."

"We're hanging it as fast as we can get it."

"The right pleural space is full of blood," Fields said. "The pericardium appears normal. He's bleeding out into the chest."

"Where's it coming from?" Ferguson asked.

"I can't tell." Fields reached down into the chest. "The wound through the upper lobe is pretty ragged, but doesn't seem to be bleeding that much. It's posterior."

"Vena cava?"

"Possibly. If I could get my finger on it." He reached in deeper. "Maybe the aorta's torn. Damn! I just can't see it."

"Pressure's forty," Harris said.

"We're losing him," Fields said.

"V-fib!" Harris shouted out. The monitor showed the typical saw-toothed pattern of ventricular fibrillation, a life-threatening, abnormal heart rhythm.

"Starting CPR," Fields said calmly. He began squeezing the heart with his hands. "Note the time and give Dr. Ferguson the paddles."

One of the nurses pushed the defibrillator unit next to the bed, and a scrub nurse handed Ferguson the paddles.

"Clear!" Ferguson said as he shocked the heart.

"Still V-fib," Harris said. "And the pressure is zero."

"Clear!" Ferguson said, and shocked the heart again.

"The chest is full of blood," Fields said. "I'm not sure that getting a rhythm will help much."

They continued CPR for several minutes and shocked the patient several times. It was futile. The wound was too destructive, and the damage too great to survive.

"That's enough," Fields said. "Let's call this thing."

"Time?" Ferguson asked.

"One-fifteen," Harris said.

Roberts pushed open the door and stepped into the operating suite, holding up his badge. "I'm Gary Roberts, FBI. I need everyone's assistance for a moment."

Fields ripped off his mask, pulled off his gown and gloves, and threw them into the corner. "Make it snappy, officer."

"I'm the special agent in charge of bioterrorism, and I need your cooperation." He pointed to a nurse. "I need your name, position with the hospital, address, phone, and social security number."

Fields stepped up to Roberts. "I don't have time for this crap. I have another surgery, if you don't mind." He started past Roberts.

Roberts stepped in front of him and held up his hand. "You go back over there. This man is a suspected terrorist, and now this is a crime scene. If you don't cooperate, Doctor, I'll be forced to arrest you. I don't think you want that."

For a moment, Roberts thought the surgeon would defy him, but he took a couple of steps backward, a sarcastic smirk remaining on his face. A nurse began writing down names.

The whole case was a complete disaster, Roberts thought. The suspect was in their custody, and now he was dead. He had committed suicide, Roberts was sure of that. The gunshot was as effective as if he had taken his cyanide capsule. Roberts remembered the smile on the suspect's face and felt a sinking feeling in the pit of his stomach. He knew he was right about the biologic agent. It was smallpox or Ebola or something... something dangerous.

"I *said* I have another surgery," Fields said angrily.

The surgeon had moved back into Roberts's face. His patience for the doctor was growing thin.

"This is complete bullshit," Fields yelled, and he pushed by Roberts for the door.

Roberts wheeled around, drawing his gun. "Freeze," he yelled, pointing his gun directly at the surgeon's head. "If you step out that door, you stupid sonofabitch, I won't just arrest your sorry ass—I'll *shoot* your sorry ass!"

* * *

DECEMBER 11, 11:00 P.M. EST
WASHINGTON, DC

Al-Sabai stood at the corner window and looked down at the intersection beneath him. Only a rare soul ventured outside at this hour, unlike during the day when the intersection was bustling with people and activity. A few flurries of snow drifted down from the darkness above him, illuminated by the bright lights of the streetlights. Across the street was the Willard Hotel, its staid architecture resembling other stately buildings and monuments that he could see up and down the street from his room. Occasionally, a convoy of black SUVs pulled along Pennsylvania Avenue at the front of the Willard, and armed guards would exit the vehicles, taking defensive positions to allow some dignitary a safe entry into the hotel. Al-Sabai wondered who the protected official was and if he might have an opportunity to infect someone important at some point…once he was infected himself.

He had spent four straight days in this room. Not only was he *not* contagious, he didn't think he was even sick. No headache. No fever. No rash. *Nothing*. He wasn't convinced he had the virus, even though he obviously had been exposed. He had been waiting patiently for symptoms, any symptoms at all, but he felt perfectly normal.

Mohammed hadn't instructed him on this possibility, and Al-Sabai wasn't sure what he was supposed to do or how long he was to wait.

The television no longer appealed to him, except for a couple of soap operas he never missed. He had stared out the window for hours each day, as he was doing now, and had learned the routine of the street below—the traffic, the vendors, the hotel service and deliveries, and even some of the people who walked the sidewalks. What appeared at first to be entirely random commotion was actually a reasonably predictable pattern, and it was his boredom that had allowed him to realize it.

The boredom was almost more than he could tolerate—the room service, the bed, the window, and the television—everything was the same. "I won't need the cyanide capsule," he thought, "because I will be bored to death."

He wanted to leave the hotel to mingle in the crowds, enjoy the fresh air, and maybe find some authentic northern African cuisine. He had endured enough.

He'd go outside in the morning…or go crazy.

* * *

DECEMBER 11, 10:30 P.M. CST
SYCAMORE, ILLINOIS

The house was dark when Harry arrived home, except for a single light in the kitchen. A note on the countertop informed him that his dinner was in the microwave. After warming it up for a couple of minutes, he ate it in almost the same amount of time. He shuffled down the hallway in the darkness, his shoulders feeling the heaviness of the day's fatigue. He had admitted two patients to the hospital after office hours, both with influenza pneumonia. The epidemic was hitting in full force, as was common this time every year. Both of these patients were elderly and extremely ill, having gone to the intensive care unit on ventilators. The winter was just starting. He was ready for spring.

As he passed by the twins' bedroom, he noticed that Amy had kicked her covers onto the floor. He picked up the floral sheets and the worn patchwork quilt lying in a heap next to the bed. Both of the girls were sleeping peacefully, surrounded by their menagerie of stuffed animals and dolls, the security blankets of a couple of twelve-year-old girls. On the walls were pictures from school and mementos from sports, plays, and recitals. Each had her shelf for her trophies and awards. He was saddened to think that he had missed too many of the events represented by their collection. Harry spread the sheets and quilt back over Amy and gently tucked her in. He squeezed the quilt in his hand and felt the texture. His grandmother had made it when he was twelve—the same age Amy was now. Every evening for the week he had stayed with his grandmother one summer, he had watched her tacking the quilt on a wooden rack while the TV blared in the background. Lifting the old quilt to his face, he drew in a breath. It still smelled the same. He missed her.

Harry tenderly stroked Amy's blond hair for several minutes and listened to her quiet breathing. He leaned forward and lightly kissed her forehead. He did the same for Audrey. They were asleep now and had been asleep when he had left for work in the morning. He had kissed them both then, too, but now felt the guilt of not talking to them once today, not being home when they were home, not eating dinner as a family. Too many days repeated the same story.

Harry walked down to the end of the hallway to the master bedroom. The pale light of the moon through the south windows outlined his wife sleeping in their bed. He crossed to the bathroom and changed clothes in the adjacent closet. After preparing for bed, he stood next to her a few minutes, listening to her breathing and watching her chest and shoulders rise with each breath. She was beautiful when she was sleeping. He bent over and softly kissed her cheek. As Harry slipped beneath the covers, his wife stirred. He reached over and touched her shoulder, and she slid next to him.

"Long day?" she asked.

"Sorry to wake you."

"I wasn't sleeping. I was waiting for you to come home."

Harry smiled. "You were waiting very quietly."

"Did you get your patients taken care of?"

"Yes, both with the flu. Both sick. I'm not sure either one is going to make it."

"I'm sorry to hear that."

"They may be calling me back in."

She slid against him and pulled him close to her. She pressed her lips against his. "I need to feel you," she said. "I missed you."

Harry slipped off his shorts and helped her to lift her nightgown over her head. Their lovemaking was slow and gentle. He felt a deep passion for her, and when they made love, he felt again the softness of her lips, the fullness of her breasts, and her warmth as he entered her, always as if for the first time. They gave of each other, slowly building until reaching together, and making their closeness complete. He held her against him, staying inside her until she fell asleep. He gently touched her cheek with his lips, kissing her good night.

Harry lay still beside her in the darkness, his workday removed from his thoughts, feeling her chest rise and fall, hearing her breathing soft and gentle, a peace coming over him and filling him with contentment. His mind drifted to the night prayers he had so often repeated with his daughters down on his knees beside their beds, a familiar prayer for protection against the unknowns of life, the fears and dangers seemingly so far from him at this moment.

Now I lay me down to sleep.

I pray the Lord my soul to keep.

And if I die before I wake,

I pray the Lord my soul to take.

Harry held Maureen tightly and kissed her gently. He quietly rolled over on his back and stared at the ceiling. "Don't take either of us now," Harry prayed, "for the sake of our children and for the sake of the two of us." As a physician, Harry knew better than anyone the uncertainty of health, the fragility of life, and the guarantee of death. And he felt unprepared, just as his two patients who were dying in the hospital and their families were probably feeling now. Despite what he had said many, many times in the childhood prayer, he simply wasn't ready.

Harry prayed again for protection, for the desired but elusive security in troubled times, for life's unknown future, and to be placed in hands greater than his own.

And if I die before I wake…

CHAPTER FIFTEEN

Mohammed watched outside his hotel window as the ticker tape of lights swept past on the building across the street, displaying the day's stock market prices. Each of the three massive signs was a story tall and a block long, and they were suspended eight or ten stories above the ground. Mohammed was intrigued with the stream of lights, yet this was simply another crass display of American wealth. New York was the pinnacle of American financial power. The towering buildings, the mass of people and cars, and the extremes of materialism in the advertisements and stores—all these trappings of the American way of life would come crashing down as millions died of the disease he carried. New York City was a world apart from the desolate desert of Somalia, where the young child had lain in agony. The very same fate awaited these people, caused by the same hands that choked the life from the boy. But their pain would not be relieved. They would die slowly, with great suffering, and with little benefit from all the modern medicine their Americans doctors had to offer. There was no cure for smallpox, and there was no treatment. There was only deformity, pain, or death.

The lights on the building would flash the names of the dead as fast as they now were displaying the prices of stocks. *Praise be to Allah*.

Mohammed showered and dressed. A few more of the spots, now small, red, and slightly raised on his skin, were showing on his arms and face, and he noticed two or three on his chest. The medical term was papules. In a couple of days, they would change to blisters called vesicles, and then a couple of days later they would fill with hard, firm pus. By then, the pustules could not be hidden, and it would be time for him to leave for the airport. But for now he would use his time wisely and spend full days among the shoppers and the crowds on the streets and in the subways.

His symptoms were worse, but two ibuprofen had helped. He was nauseated and had eaten little. His muscles ached, especially his back, and he felt an increasing fever. Despite the symptoms, he was ready, and he left the hotel for the day.

Along the streets of Broadway and Seventh Avenue, the crowds were continuous, as they had been every day. The wind whipped along the sidewalks, and as a result, it was much cooler than it had been previously. With his fever, Mohammed's Yankees pullover was warm enough. The chill in the air was comfortable.

He would pace himself today, and he would expose many, many Americans.

* * *

"A million stores in the Bronx," Vicky said to her mother, "and we have to go downtown to shop."

"It's a tradition," her mother said. "I've been a New Yorker all my life, and I've never missed Christmas shopping on Fifth Avenue. Besides, the kids love the toy stores, and if you're good, maybe I'll buy you something at Tiffany's."

"Mom, I can't afford to check my coat at Tiffany's."

Her mother gave her a quick smile. "Let's go, kids," she hollered out. "Time to leave."

John and Becky chattered with excitement while Vicky and her mother bundled them up. They walked the few blocks to the Morris Park Station to take the five train to Manhattan. The morning was brisk. The forecast was for sunshine and light winds, and half the city would likely be out shopping.

As the train rumbled along the elevated tracks through the South Bronx, there were plenty of abandoned brick warehouses and tenements, with their windows bricked shut and graffiti defacing the walls, and vacant lots strewn with trash and weeds—a sight Vicky saw daily yet barely noticed. At the Third Avenue Station, the subway plunged into the tunnel that carried them beneath the Harlem River and into Manhattan. When they first boarded the subway car, it was relatively empty. But by the time they were close to their destination, their car was full of determined, serious shoppers jammed in elbow to elbow. Vicky set her young nephew on her lap and pulled her niece in close to her side. The car was much too crowded for her liking.

"We should do our Christmas shopping in October," Vicky said, "when everyone else is thinking Halloween."

"We're here for the decorations," her mother said.

"And Santa Claus, Aunt Vicky," Becky added.

"I can't wait," Vicky said, wrinkling her nose.

"Vicky, you sound like Scrooge," her mother said. "Get into the Christmas spirit."

"Bah, humbug," Vicky said.

The train pulled into the Lexington Avenue Station, and they were jostled out of the car by the mass of humanity exiting onto the platform. They followed the crowd up the stairs and into the sunlight. A short walk away was FAO Schwarz, their first stop; it was unmistakable with its giant bear and rocking horse at the entrance. It seemed every school-aged child in the five boroughs was there. Employees were scurrying about, replacing the toys knocked over or tossed on the floor; their efforts to restore some order in the midst of chaos nearly futile as the ravaging hoard of children disrupted all in their path like an F-5 tornado. Vicky and her mother allowed the kids to run free, but they followed close behind, fearing they would lose sight of them. John and Becky picked out a couple of toys and added a hundred or so to their Christmas wish lists.

After Vicky and her mother waited interminably in line to pay for their purchases, they were rewarded with a return to the mob of bodies outside on the sidewalk.

"Where to next?" Vicky asked her mother.

"I definitely want to see the ice skaters and the Christmas tree at Rockefeller Center."

They crossed over in front of the Plaza Hotel and walked up Fifth Avenue to Rockefeller Center. Despite her humbuggery, Vicky had to admit that the eighty-foot Norway spruce, blanketed in thousands of multicolored lights, was magnificent and the skaters floating on the ice of the rink were lovely. The two children hung on every view with the excitement of Christmas in New York.

They purchased chestnuts and a soda at the corner, and sat down on the edge of a brick wall for a few minutes to map out their strategy. Their feet were already tired, and the kids were beginning to lag. Vicky and her mother decided they would skip the most expensive stores and work their way to Macy's. The kids would only last so long, and after all the shopping, they would have to make the trip back home, with the kids no doubt cranky and exhausted. Vicky could hardly wait.

* * *

Mohammed walked around Times Square several times, entering the stores and shops, mingling with customers, coughing frequently. How could he not infect hundreds, even thousands? This was much too easy.

When he had grown tired of walking, he entered the subway at Times Square Station and caught the first car that arrived. On the subway, the masses of people came to him as he sat resting. Thousands and thousands crammed on, and then as quickly got off. Mohammed rode back and forth the full length of Manhattan for several hours and, as he expected, went unnoticed. He was completely ignored. No one spoke to him. No one even looked at him. They were minding their own business like good New Yorkers and oblivious to his presence. He was quietly infecting many of them, and they would soon be victims of the war they had declined to notice—the war against the people of the Islamic Nation. They had chosen to ignore the crimes of America, just as they were ignoring him. Now Mohammed had brought the battle to them.

Mohammed had decided not to take the trains that traveled off of Manhattan. If he went to Flatbush Avenue or the South Bronx or Coney Island or Jamaica in Queens, he might find his nationality would attract attention. He could hide amidst Manhattan's cultural diversity. He was ordinary, common, and invisible there.

After spending the morning below ground, he left the subway at Penn Station and walked along Thirty-Fourth Street to the east. He thought he was hungry and stood in a packed line at a fast food restaurant selling processed beef in stale buns and fried potatoes dripping with oil. But by the time he reached the counter to order, the smell was so nauseating that he nearly vomited on the floor. He pushed his way outside into the cool, fresh air, and the nausea eventually passed. Any meals he ate now would be light grains and water.

His symptoms were causing him to feel worse, his stamina was declining. His last stop would be Macy's, and then he'd take a taxi back to the hotel.

* * *

The shoppers at Macy's were slightly more controlled than the crowds on the streets. Of course, Becky and John insisted on going straight to the Ben & Jerry's, and Vicky and her mother agreed. The two adults would sit and take a rest while the kids ate ice cream—John chocolate and Becky chocolate chip. Vicky thought her mother would be exhausted by now, but she seemed to be holding up better than she was, even with the long walk. Vicky slipped off her tennis shoes and rubbed her feet. She was used to standing at the emergency room for ten, twelve, and even twenty-four hours, but after only a few hours of shopping, her energy was gone.

Lugging shopping bags was her least favorite task, and carrying them on the train home was going to be a challenge. Why was it that children's toys were always so big and bulky? She and her mom already had three or four sacks each, and they weren't finished yet.

By mid-afternoon and after three hours in Macy's, all four of them were dead tired and ready to go home. Vicky and her mother rounded up the two kids, along with the boxes and bags, and found the elevator. Vicky pressed the down button, and only a second or two passed before the chime rang and the doors opened. The elevator was full, but a couple of mothers with strollers exited, and Vicky and her family crowded in. Vicky was glad their shopping adventure was nearly over. The subway station was close, and they'd soon be on their way home.

As the doors closed in front of her, Vicky heard a person coughing in the back of the elevator. He coughed two more times; it was a dry cough like she had heard a hundred times a day in the emergency room during the past two weeks. Today was her only day off this week, and her next shift started in the morning. She hoped to go home and watch TV, and maybe take a long bath. She hadn't thought of work all day.

The man coughed again, and she glanced back over her shoulder. She hoped he was covering his mouth because that was how germs were spread. Both her mother and she had their flu shots, but the children hadn't, and the flu shot wouldn't help any of them if the man coughing had one of the hundreds of cold viruses. She instinctively held her breath as she sometimes did in tight quarters when someone coughed, an old habit she had begun in medical school when she had sat through hours of lectures on the horrible variety of viruses and bacteria that inflicted mankind. The elevator was approaching the first floor where they would exit. She wouldn't have to hold her breath long.

She also noticed the smell. It was sickly sweet, foul, and distinctly odd—almost putrid. In the emergency room, she frequently smelled the body odor of patients up close, unavoidable in her occupation. But this smell was different. Someone in the elevator, possibly the man who was coughing, had an abscessed tooth or a lung abscess or maybe a colostomy bag or something.

The doors opened on the first floor, and Vicky stepped out. She extended her arm to hold the door for her mother and the two children, and they followed her out. She was glad to be in the fresh air and on their way home.

Next year they'd stick to the Bronx. She smiled at that thought. Her mother would never agree to it.

* * *

DECEMBER 12, 3:00 P.M. PST
LOS ANGELES

The morgue at the Los Angeles County Hospital was in the basement, as morgues should be. The tables, cabinets, basins, and equipment gleamed of stainless steel, resembling the surgery suite, but the morgue smelled of formaldehyde, disinfectant, and old blood. And the pace was slower than surgery—much, much slower.

Jackson and Lafitte had arrived from Atlanta an hour earlier and were whisked to the hospital by Roberts. The other two men in the room were Dr. Stephen Vincent, the pathologist who would perform the autopsy, and his assistant, Chad Ferraro. All five were in complete isolation gear brought by Lafitte from Atlanta. Jackson had urged the highest precaution level, and every effort would be made to follow the protocol in the morgue. After the fiasco in surgery, Jackson would take no chances with further contamination. If this man were infected, they would have a gigantic mess to clean up.

"I hope we're not wasting your time," Roberts said.

"From what I see here," Jackson said, "you had every reason to be concerned."

Each of the men wore a full body suit with its own air supply, a hood with a clear plastic shield, boots, and puncture-resistant gloves. The pathologist would perform the actual autopsy, but for now he stood back and allowed Jackson to inspect the body.

Jackson had insisted on coming. He had seen more contagious diseases in his lifetime than the entire hospital staff combined.

"The patient, identity unknown," Jackson said, recording his examination into a microphone inside the suit, "is of Middle Eastern descent. His origin is unknown, but based on his body size and complexion I would guess Arabian Peninsula—Saudi, Kuwaiti, or possibly Yemeni. He is about forty or forty-five years old, one hundred seventy centimeters in height, and seventy-five kilograms in weight." Jackson described his facial features, hair, and complexion. "He has a gunshot wound to the chest and a midline surgical incision of the chest, and these will be described further by the pathologist, Dr. Vincent, in the autopsy report." Jackson leaned over and began inspecting Khalid's face. "He has a fine petechial rash consistent with his resuscitation. Multiple small, superficial lacerations on his face, neck, and forearms from flying glass, by history. I see no lesions of the conjunctiva, nares, or ears." He opened Khalid's mouth and looked inside, pushing the tongue to each side and pointing a light toward both cheeks. "Nor in the oral cavity." Next, Jackson examined the entire skin surface, including between the fingers and toes. "I see no vesicles, rash, pustules, ulcerations, or suspicious lesions."

With the help of the pathology assistant, Khalid was turned over, and Jackson inspected the neck, shoulders, and back and spread the buttocks to inspect the anal region. Jackson dictated his findings as he went. He completed his examination and Lafitte stepped forward, obtaining specimens from various body fluids and orifices.

"We'll check him for everything," Jackson said. "Ebola, smallpox, tuberculosis, and fungal infections, as well as HIV and hepatitis."

"Maybe I was overreacting," Roberts said.

"No," Jackson said, "I think you were wise to be cautious."

"He probably just had the flu."

"Maybe. But even if everything is negative, this is good practice for us. This is exactly what it will look like when a bioterror event does happen."

Roberts remained quiet a moment at that remark.

"You've listed all the contacts?" Jackson asked.

"No, actually we missed some. Maybe quite a few."

"Don't be discouraged. That happens a lot. In this case, most of the contacts will be law enforcement or health care personnel, and they should be pretty easy to track down. The ones at the airport will be tougher, especially any contacts in the terminal.

When they are in police custody like he was at the end, the tracking will be relatively easier."

Dr. Vincent began the autopsy. Ferraro started with a midline incision through Khalid's chest and abdomen. Dr. Vincent probed the two cavities with his hands, then stepped aside as Ferraro began the systematic process of removing the individual organs. As each body part was handed to Dr. Vincent, he examined and weighed it, occasionally slicing an organ open with a scalpel. He recorded everything.

"I think he committed suicide," Roberts said to Jackson as the pathologist continued. "He knew exactly what he was doing. I would have preferred to have interviewed him, but I'm not certain I would have gained much. I'd give my left nut to know what he was up to."

"If these specimens don't give us a clue," Jackson said, "we'll never know, will we?"

"No," Roberts said. "If you don't find an answer here, we won't know about this one. But sooner or later we'll have the very situation we all fear, and I'm afraid we may well be powerless to stop it."

No one in the room said a word. The possibility was too dreadful to consider.

CHAPTER SIXTEEN

DECEMBER 19 (SEVEN DAYS LATER), 10:00 A.M. CST
DAY NINE OF THE SECOND WAVE OF EXPOSURE
SYCAMORE, ILLINOIS

Lauren Randall was sitting in her mother's lap when Harry entered the exam room. He knew at first glance that she was ill. Nothing specific, but even when she had been in the office earlier with chickenpox, she wasn't too sick to jump up and give him a hug. Today she sat in her mother's lap, cuddled quietly against her mother's shoulder, tightly clutching her doll.

Harry sat on his rolling stool and slid up close to her. He touched her forehead lightly. "I'm sorry you're not feeling well, Lauren," he said. Her skin was warm and dry, he noted, but she didn't have a fever. "Tell me, Kathy, what's going on with Lauren?"

"Lauren's really been acting odd the last twenty-four hours. She's complaining of a headache but nothing else. She wants me to hold her constantly, yet it's almost as if she hurts when I touch her. Her appetite is off, and she vomited once last night. She ate a little bit this morning, so maybe her appetite's better. You know she had chickenpox recently. Could it be that?"

"I don't think so. It would be unusual for her to have such a mild case and develop problems this late."

"A bunch of the kids at the school are out with the flu."

"We're certainly seeing flu in the office, too."

Harry lifted Lauren up gently and laid her on the exam table. He examined her carefully, looking in her eyes, nose, and throat, listening to her heart and lungs, feeling her lymph glands and abdomen. "Nothing looks particularly out of the norm." The chickenpox rash he had seen earlier was entirely gone, and she had no new rashes.

"I could have it, too," Kathy said. "I'm just a little achy today and have a mild headache."

"I want to order a few tests, checking for influenza, strep throat, and white blood cell counts. It'll take thirty minutes to do all these, and I'll be back when they're done."

"Thanks, Dr. Bennett."

Harry went into the hallway and gave his nurse the orders on Lauren. He'd likely see a number of similar cases today. "Who's next, Jill?" he asked.

"I squeezed in Lydia Atwood. She's sick, too, and you're already twenty minutes behind."

"Thanks a lot."

"I had to stick her somewhere."

"Oh, that's fine. Now's as good a time as any."

"I swabbed her nose for influenza, so at least that's pending and should speed things up."

Harry entered the room. Lydia Atwood was a twenty-five-year-old petite blond who worked as a teller in the local bank. He had delivered her in the first year or two of his practice and had watched her grow up in Sycamore. She was curled up on the exam table, bundled in a couple of blankets, chilling.

"Good morning, Lydia."

"Good morning, Dr. Bennett."

"You're looking pretty puny this morning."

"I'm feeling terrible."

Harry stood next to the bed and touched her forearm. "When did this start?"

"Yesterday. All of a sudden I started coughing. I was sick to my stomach and threw up a couple of times. High fever. Headache. Every muscle in my body aches."

"Chest pain?"

"Maybe a little."

"How high was the fever?"

"I didn't have a thermometer, but it was pretty high, and I'm having some chills. I can't keep warm."

Harry opened the chart. "The nurse took your temperature here, and it's a hundred and three. That's pretty high. Has anybody you've been around had similar symptoms?"

"No, Dr. Bennett. Not a soul, but I'm in contact with a lot of customers at the bank."

Harry asked Jill to step in, and Harry examined Lydia. Except for the fever, the exam was otherwise negative. Just as he finished, the lab technician knocked on the door and stuck her head in the room.

"Influenza A positive," she said.

"Good job, guys," Harry said.

"Does that mean I have the flu?"

"Yep, and since we're catching it early, I can give you some medicine that will help." Harry turned to Jill. "Let's start her on oseltamivir seventy-five milligrams twice daily. If we have some samples, let's give her one right now and call in a prescription for five days."

"Thank you, Dr. Bennett."

"You're welcome, Lydia. I hope this helps."

Harry stepped into the hallway, and the lab technician handed him Lauren's lab slip. He spent a few seconds reviewing the results before going back into Lauren's room. Lauren was on her mother's lap, sleeping.

"The strep screen is negative," Harry said, "and so is the flu test. Her white blood cell count, which is an indication of infection, is only four thousand, but there are two band cells. That's a little worrisome. The band cells generally indicate a more serious infection. She probably has a virus of some sort with the total count being so low. Usually with bacteria it will be elevated."

"Are you going to give her an antibiotic?"

"Not at this point. I think this is a virus. Antibiotics don't help viruses." Harry stood and washed his hands at the sink. "I want to get a blood culture, which unfortunately means we have to stick her again. When you get home, I want you to give her plenty of fluids and acetaminophen for fever or her headache." He turned to Kathy as he dried his hands. "Call me back if she's worse. She certainly doesn't look like she feels good, so watch her closely."

"Okay, I'll give you a call."

"I'm on my pager all night."

Harry walked to the lunchroom and poured himself another cup of coffee. The five calls after midnight were taking their toll. The schedule was packed, and he was already forty minutes behind. He suspected it would only get worse.

Lauren didn't have the flu, but whatever she had was probably contagious, and he didn't want it. Yet he was the most susceptible when he was tired from the lack of sleep. Even with the flu shot he had received in November, he had no real protection against the variety of viruses and bacteria he typically treated in the office.

The last thing Harry needed right now was to get sick.

* * *

DECEMBER 19, 11:00 A.M. EST
WASHINGTON, DC

Gary Roberts's flight from Atlanta to Washington, DC, was an hour late, which was not at all unusual, but fortunately the trip from the Reagan National Airport to the FBI headquarters on Pennsylvania Avenue only took twenty minutes. Roberts would have time to catch a quick cup of coffee before his meeting with Edward Mold, the deputy assistant director of the FBI's Counterterrorism Division, and Roberts's immediate supervisor. Mold was in charge of the four FBI operational sections on terrorism, and he had responsibility for all international and domestic terrorism investigations, including those involving weapons of mass destruction. He was a hard-nosed agent and smart, and Roberts was hoping to convince him to allow some manpower to investigate the Los Angeles suspect, even though Roberts himself wasn't completely sure if there was anything to investigate. Yet he had that recurring feeling in his gut that the suspect, a prisoner in his custody, was the real thing. Roberts trusted his instincts, and his instincts were shouting at him, but he had come up with nothing so far. The preliminary lab was negative. The man's credit cards were false accounts, his passport was fraudulent, and his background was untraceable. "It's all *too* professional," Roberts thought. The man had traveled alone, originating in Cairo, Roberts had discovered, but calls to the stewardesses on each of his flights had yielded nothing. Not one had remembered him. He was an invisible man without a past.

Roberts didn't have much to go on, and he was going nowhere fast with what he had. He was convinced that the man who died in Los Angeles, whose last breath he watched, had the perfect bioterrorist profile, if Roberts had ever seen one. Now if he could only prove it.

And another odd thing that bothered him: the CIA was of no help. On the way from LAX he was told that the CIA had initially thought that the man in custody was Al-Qaeda, but later the CIA told him they had no information on his suspect. Al-Qaeda and then nothing? It didn't make sense, and when spook central denied everything, his gut yelled all the more.

He hoped Edward Mold would help, but even if he didn't, Roberts wouldn't let this go—help or no help.

The taxi dropped Roberts off on Pennsylvania Avenue in front of the J. Edgar Hoover Building, an ugly cement structure he thought looked like a parking garage with windows, and he walked a short distance along Tenth Street under the row of American flags mounted on the building until he came to the west entrance. Roberts wore a dark suit and tie but no overcoat, and it was a bit cool, the forecast calling for a few flurries and temperatures much colder than those in Atlanta. The wind whipped up a stiff breeze down the street, blowing right through him, and the sun was hidden behind dreary clouds. It was a good day for a meeting and almost nothing else.

After passing through security, Roberts took the elevator to the administrative level. He located a coffee pot, poured himself a cup, and found an empty chair near Mold's office. Before he could enjoy even half of it, Mold was ready to see him.

Mold was in his mid-fifties, balding, with a slight build, and wearing thin-framed glasses. He motioned for Roberts to take a seat as he shut the office door. The office was plain like most FBI executives' offices and held a boxy, wooden desk in the center, a brown leather chair for Mold, two wooden chairs for visitors, and several bookshelves full of law books. The wall behind Mold had two rows of black-framed certificates surrounding a large copy of the FBI seal.

Roberts waited for Mold to move around the desk and sit down before he took his seat.

"I got your packet," Mold said, tapping on a manila folder on his desk. He was all business.

"What did you think?" Roberts asked.

"You're worried about the suspect you had in LA that was shot and killed?"

"Yes," Roberts replied, "very much." Roberts noticed that Mold didn't exactly answer his question.

POX

Mold slid the papers out of the folder and began reading intently, making no comment as he looked at the pages, flipping each one over as he finished it. Roberts waited patiently. He was certain Mold knew the contents of his packet well.

"How would you proceed?" Mold asked as he continued to thumb through the packet without looking up.

Roberts had considered this possible question carefully. "He was working alone, and that would be unusual for a terrorist. I'd check similar patterns—single Middle Eastern males traveling alone on that same date. Start with the major airports and check for passengers without luggage—maybe all originating from Cairo. I'd check for Middle Eastern males going to emergency rooms with illnesses, at least in large cities. And I'd check all documents from that region used on that date for validity. Other than that, I'm not sure."

Mold glanced up at Roberts over his glasses. "You said he was alone. So maybe he's not a terrorist."

"Maybe," Roberts said. Roberts was trying to read Mold, but his face was blank and uncommitted. Roberts waited.

Mold slipped the papers back into the folder and pushed the packet toward Roberts. "Sounds like you're asking for some resources?"

"Yes," Roberts said. "I know I've got something here. I haven't proven it yet, but I just know."

"On your hunch?"

"Yes, sir. On my hunch."

Mold paused a moment. "Okay," he said, "but a preliminary investigation. Finances are limited. Unless, of course, you find something."

"Yes, sir."

"Make out a budget, and I'll review it. Be reasonable, okay?"

"Yes, sir," Roberts said. "Thank you, sir."

Roberts stood and held out his hand, and Mold shook it.

"Don't find anything terrible, okay?" Mold said.

"I hope not, sir," Roberts said, "but you never know."

Mold nodded his head slightly as Roberts spoke.

No one ever knows for sure, Roberts thought, but terrible things were exactly what he'd be looking for.

136

Roberts left Mold's office, took an elevator to the street level, and hailed a cab to the airport.

The meeting went well, and he was pleased. The taxi driver was talking about the weather, but Roberts wasn't listening. His thoughts were preoccupied with the details.

He had some terrorists to catch. He hoped he wasn't too late.

* * *

DECEMBER 19, 11:30 A.M. EST
DAY EIGHTEEN OF THE FIRST WAVE OF EXPOSURE
WASHINGTON, DC

Nazih Al-Sabai wasn't even sick, and for the last seven days he hadn't stayed in his room. He occasionally wondered what Mohammed would say, but he really didn't care. He would have gone crazy in his tiny room. A person could only look out a window so long.

If he left his room, how would that jeopardize their mission? He only looked like a tourist. No one would know or likely care.

The location of his hotel on Pennsylvania Avenue was ideal for sightseeing. He had visited the Smithsonian museums and was most fascinated with the Natural History Museum, especially the dinosaurs and the minerals. He spent hours studying the precious gems, including the Hope Diamond, and he was amazed at the moon rocks. He wandered aimlessly through the art galleries, mostly looking at the American women who were there; many were very beautiful, and all were unveiled, with tight clothing that accentuated the features of their bodies. Many of the paintings and sculptures had nude women. He had heard about the degraded American morals but was surprised to see such examples in their governmental museums.

Late one evening, Al-Sabai had gone to a bar in Georgetown and drank a beer—his first taste of alcohol. A woman there approached him, but he refused to talk to her, and she eventually gave up. The encounter unnerved him, and he left soon after to return to the hotel.

He was uncomfortable out at night anyway. Mohammed had warned him about the crime in Washington, and he had seen many examples of it on TV. After that night he resolved to only venture out in the daylight.

Each day he walked at least five miles. Today he had left the Marriott, walked down Fourteenth Street past the Washington Monument, and circled around the Tidal Basin. He crossed back across the Mall at Seventeenth Street and walked to the White House, spending several minutes looking at the south lawn through the fence. It was a popular tourist spot and many took pictures. He decided to walk down Pennsylvania Avenue toward the Capitol, bypassing his hotel, until he found a place to eat lunch. He was hungry. At some point he had expected he would lose his appetite, but it hadn't happened so far.

Pennsylvania Avenue was wide and busy, and lined with governmental buildings. He stopped at a small, uncrowded café near the Internal Revenue Service building, across from the FBI headquarters. The wind was brisk, and he felt a chill run through his body and thought it odd. Earlier that morning, he had inspected himself carefully in the mirror, as he always did, but today he saw a small, red spot on his cheek that he had not previously noticed. It could be smallpox, he thought, but he wasn't sure. If it was, he was already contagious. But how could that be if he didn't feel at all sick?

It had been seventeen days since he had breathed near the mouth of the poor, sick child. Al-Sabai had expected much more by now.

The restaurant's choices were mostly sandwiches, and Al-Sabai ordered off the menu. The waitress was young, blond, and pretty. She leaned close to his face and was friendly.

Was he infecting her while she was helping him? Would he kill her with the smallpox virus? Was this woman an infidel whore? Or was she innocent like his own mother and sister were innocent?

He would finish eating and return to his room. He was tired, and he would rest.

He would pray and think, and then decide what he would do.

CHAPTER SEVENTEEN

DECEMBER 19, NOON EST
DAY EIGHTEEN OF THE FIRST WAVE OF EXPOSURE
NEW YORK CITY

Mohammed's lesions had spread. They were now on his forehead, cheeks, chin, and neck, and inside his mouth. He also had some lesions on his chest, arms, and abdomen, and a few on his legs. They were hard, firm, and painful pustules, and soon there would be many more. He carefully covered each one on his face with makeup, but the makeup wouldn't work much longer. Soon the spots would be too noticeable to hide—maybe even today. This would be his last trip out.

The smallpox virus was destroying his body. He was wracked with pain, especially in his back and neck, and his fever was very high. The nausea was constant, and he had vomited twice. He hadn't had anything to eat or drink in thirty-six hours. His legs were weak, and he felt woozy. He worried that he might not be strong enough to go back out, but he had no choice.

The end was close. He would go out on the street, but this time he would leave and go directly to the airport, and he would not return.

Mohammed rolled out his rug and faced Mecca. As he pressed his forehead to the rug, he felt the tenderness of the pustules and the aching in his neck. He prayed earnestly, asking for the strength to finish, to complete his mission against the infidels, and for his rightful place in paradise, where he would taste the sweet, clear water and rich, abundant fruit. For his family, he asked for nothing, for they would never know his fate and would not grieve for him if they knew.

When he had finished, he packed his clothes and personal items in his carry-on bag and left the room for the last time. Near the lobby, he entered an elegant men's room. He removed the cash and the cyanide capsule from the carry-on and then stuffed the bag in a trashcan.

Every muscle in Mohammed's body hurt. His head throbbed, and his vision was blurry. For the first few days, acetaminophen and ibuprofen had helped, but he had been unable to take anything for the past forty-eight hours. His weakness worried him, and he thought about a cab, but he wanted to walk. He would expose more people if he walked.

He passed numerous pedestrians on the sidewalk. Some glanced his way, so he knew he must look different. Near Forty-Second Street and Sixth Avenue, he felt exhausted and decided to stop at Bryant Park; he chose a bench beneath an old syca-more that had a three-foot-thick trunk and white bark that was gnarled and peeling off in pieces as big as his hand. He sat alone for nearly an hour. As he looked around, he realized that most of those sitting on the benches near him were homeless and had probably spent the entire day camped out there. The weather was unseasonably warm, apparently causing the shelters to empty. Hardly anyone had come close to him, and no one was within six feet, so there was only the slightest chance for infection. He was wasting his time, except that he needed to gather his strength. If he didn't get much stronger, he'd need to leave.

"The homeless would be ideal vectors," he thought. "Perfect for smallpox." He was surprised he hadn't considered it earlier. In this country the rich and middle class rushed to the doctor with every sniffle, but the poor seldom sought medical treatment, especially the homeless. When they did, they delayed until they were deathly ill and then waited for hours in a jammed emergency room rather than sit in the quiet solitude of a private physician's office. These were the people he should infect.

Mohammed thought about the cash he was carrying. He still had the lion's share left in his wallet in crisp American hundred-dollar bills. He only needed enough for a taxi to the airport. Mohammed reached into his wallet, took out the bills, and slid them into his pocket. He stood and moved close to the man nearest him. The man was a Caucasian with a full, ragged beard and was covered with several layers of dirty, worn coats. He had pulled a blanket over his head, and he was surrounded by plastic bags stuffed full of his possessions. He was alert and awake but was staring blankly forward, talking to himself. Mohammed held out a hundred-dollar bill, and the man took it.

Mohammed leaned into his face. "Merry Christmas," he said politely, and then he coughed.

Mohammed moved to the next bench where an African American man who looked and was dressed remarkably similar to the first man was curled up on his side, covered with a blanket. He, too, had all his possessions in plastic bags within his reach. Mohammed leaned over and touched his shoulder, but the man didn't move, though Mohammed could see his chest rise and fall with every breath. He slipped money in the man's coat pocket, and coughed close to his face several times. The man still didn't move.

As Mohammed reached the third bench, he became aware that the first man was standing behind him. The man's hands were cupped together and extended, as if he expected an offering. While he wasn't uttering a word, his lips were moving, and he still seemed to be conversing with himself. The man who was on the third bench stood up and approached them. He also was holding out his hands. Mohammed could see other homeless men looking his way. These were the most disgusting of the Americans. They were vile and smelled of the filth in which they lived; they were probably drug addicts, alcoholics, or mentally ill. Several of the men farther away were now moving in his direction. "Handing out money to the homeless," he thought, "is like feeding pigeons." A flock of these men were ambling his way, chirping and flapping their wings like stupid, inconsequential birds. They encircled him, preparing to ask for a handout, a tidbit, a treat, and then fly off to wait for the next opportunity.

He passed out the money and coughed in each of their faces as he wished them a joyous holiday; he hoped that in two weeks their lives would be consumed by disease and pain.

From across the park he saw a police officer on foot who seemed attracted to the commotion. Benevolence in a New York City park was an infrequent event, he guessed. The police would find it unusual and come to investigate.

Mohammed ducked down, passed through the crowd of the homeless men, and walked toward the street in the opposite direction from the officer as quickly as he could. He hailed a taxi and slid into the passenger seat. His next and final stop would be John F. Kennedy Airport.

* * *

The ride to the airport took an hour. Mohammed's dilemma was where exactly to go. He looked grotesque. He had many pustules now, and their number was increasing at a rapid rate. The ones on his face were more and more noticeable, and the makeup wasn't helping because the sweat was washing it off. He was worried that someone would notice him and recognize the illness. He didn't speak to the taxi driver and pretended to be sleeping so the driver wouldn't pay much attention to him. Though he was only a few feet away, the driver spent most of the trip on his cell phone, ignoring Mohammed. Just as well. At the airport, however, the level of security would be much higher. He had originally intended to be dropped off at the terminal and take the shuttle to long-term parking. The advantage would be that the taxi driver would not know where he went, and he could get lost in the airport crowds. But the disadvantage was that he could be discovered by the security officials and held for questioning. That, of course, would be unacceptable.

As they reached the airport drive, Mohammed needed to make a decision. The large green signs over the highway announced the various exits and that the terminal was just ahead. They were fast approaching the parking exit.

"Here," he said, "turn here."

The driver turned into long-term parking and let him out at the shuttle stop. After Mohammed paid the fare, the taxi left. Mohammed surveyed the sea of cars that extended for nearly a mile in all directions. He had memorized where the car was located, and although he was extremely weak, he had enough strength to reach the vehicle. He looked up at the tall light poles; each pole had a sign identifying that section of the lot. Several times before, he had parked here to familiarize himself with this part of the plan. The other men he had traveled with would be doing as he was doing now. Had they all already died? He had not seen any mention of smallpox in the news media. The first cases had not been identified, yet he was confident this was not because they had failed, but because they had succeeded. The massive wave of the second generation of smallpox would overwhelm the Americans. He had come in contact with many Americans, and he hoped they had all become infected. The infection could spread worldwide, but the Americans would be devastated, and the Islamic nation would rise from the ashes, according to Allah's will.

Mohammed found the car in the designated spot. The key was beneath the wheel well as planned. He looked around and saw no one. After opening the trunk, he crawled inside and pulled the lid closed.

Inside, he found the plastic bag and the rope he would use to tie it off. He took the cyanide capsule out of its wrapper and held it in his hand. His thoughts went to his family, but he had no regrets. His father was misguided and weak. His brothers were without courage or honor. He would not see them in paradise.

The men and women he would see were those who had been martyred for the faith. He was responsible for some of their deaths—like the shopkeeper in Djibouti and the mother and child in Somalia. He saw their faces in his mind. He recalled a young woman, a poor Palestinian living in the squalor of a refugee camp, to whose body he had helped tape explosives before she sacrificed herself for her faith. He would never forget her face as she thanked him, sincere and smiling for her opportunity. He remembered the martyrs in Afghanistan and the exploding American bombs—the deafening roar, the choking dust, the destruction, the debris, and the bodies. He would join them all in paradise.

He slid inside the plastic bag then tied it closed with the rope. The cyanide capsule would kill him long before he would suffocate. He knelt in the trunk as best he could and said his final prayers. He was not afraid for he had served Allah well.

The cyanide capsule felt smooth as he rolled it between his fingers and placed it on his tongue. His mouth was dry from the lack of fluids, but he managed to swallow it. Within a few short seconds, he experienced a bitter taste and a slight warmth over his entire body. It would be over soon.

The pain in his body eased as the numbness rushed over him. He heard a soft roar in his ears. He smelled an unpleasant odor— a very odd scent that was both sickening and faintly sweet.

It was the smell of death; Mohammed had smelled it once before.

CHAPTER EIGHTEEN

DECEMBER 21, 3:00 A.M. CST
DAY ELEVEN OF THE SECOND WAVE OF EXPOSURE
SYCAMORE, ILLINOIS

The sharp, piercing sound of the pager awoke Harry with a start. In the darkness, he reached to the floor, groping around until he found the pager, and turned it off. Maureen groaned softly; the noise or his jerking had awakened her, but he knew she would quickly fall back asleep. He, on the other hand, always stayed awake. Though some doctors had to be paged twice to be certain they would answer, he never did. It was a trait that was invaluable for his decision making but disruptive to his sleep cycle. The pattern hadn't changed in his twenty-five years of practice.

He lifted up the pager and read the number. It was the DeKalb emergency room. After dialing the number, he rested his head back on his pillow. Within the first ring or two, the nurse answered. Dr. Solomon was calling, and she went to fetch him.

"Dr. Bennett?"

"Yes."

"This is Solomon in the ER. I have two of your patients here, a mother and daughter, Kathy and Lauren Randall. You saw the daughter in your office two days ago."

"Yes, I know them."

"The daughter's worse—fever of one hundred and three, backaches, headaches, myalgias, and nausea. The mother is also sick. She's had the same symptoms but not quite as bad. Chest X-ray and lab on both of them are negative. I checked a strep screen, influenza A/B, and complete blood count. All normal except for a few band cells on Lauren."

"How many?"

"Six."

"She only had two in the office."

"I'm not sure what that means."

"So what are you thinking?"

"We're seeing a lot of cases of influenza down here and these look similar. I told them it was probably a virus and recommended fluids and acetaminophen, but the mother is rather insistent that you come in and see them. She says something is really wrong, and she's worried. Seems rather excessive. Neither looks *that* sick."

"What time is it?"

"Three in the morning."

"She's not one of those moms who usually panics. I guess I can come in to see them."

"I don't think she'll leave until you do."

"Okay, thanks. I'll be there in twenty or thirty minutes."

Maureen rolled over at the sound of him hanging up the phone. "Do you have to go in?"

"It's Kathy and Lauren Randall. They have some sort of infection, and she's asking me to see her."

"It can't wait until you're in the office?"

"They went to DeKalb, and she wants me to see them, so I guess I'll go in."

Harry wandered into the bathroom and threw on some clothes. The trip to DeKalb was ten or fifteen minutes, and he had driven it many times at this hour. As he left his house in Sycamore, the streets were clear. No one was awake except him. When he turned onto the highway, he picked up speed. He could go as fast as he wanted. The local cops would never stop him, and they were the only ones on this stretch of highway. He treated most of the local guys and their families, and they would always assume he had an emergency at this hour. They would be right.

When he arrived, the emergency room was basically empty. Only a couple of cars were in the parking lot, and no one was in the waiting room. Dr. Solomon updated him on the condition of his two patients. Solomon was a moonlighting resident who worked nights for extra income and was a regular at the DeKalb ER. The nurses handed Harry the two charts, and he found their exam room.

Lauren was sitting on the bed. Her father, Frank, was sitting on one side of the bed, and Kathy was sitting on the other. Lauren smiled briefly when Harry walked in, but the smile was short-lived and seemed forced. He could tell she didn't feel well.

"Lauren got worse this evening," Kathy said. "We tried to put her down, but she wouldn't go to sleep. She threw up a couple of times before we came, but she seems to be holding down liquids now. I think I have the same thing. My head is throbbing, and my muscles are aching. I'm sick at my stomach, but I haven't thrown up."

"Dr. Solomon repeated all the tests I did in the office and they're negative again, except for the band cells I told you about. The blood culture wasn't growing anything as of yesterday afternoon. Jill should have called you."

"Yes, she said it was okay."

Harry examined Lauren. Her throat was slightly red, but her eyes and ears looked normal. He listened to her lungs, and they were clear. Her heart had a regular rhythm and no murmur. She seemed to have some mild tenderness in her abdomen, but it wasn't localized, as one might suspect with appendicitis. He felt no lymph nodes and saw no rash. Her neck was soft, which was not consistent with meningitis.

After examining Lauren, he asked her dad to hold her and requested that Kathy climb up on the bed. He examined her carefully and found nothing of particular concern.

Both Lauren and Kathy appeared quite restless and anxious throughout the visit. It was odd. He hadn't seen either of them act quite like this before. Lauren would cry easily and was very nervous. Maybe it was the emergency room or being in the hospital again.

Harry asked about their possible exposures. A number of students were sick at school, and several neighbors were ill. It was that time of year. He asked about food and travel, but they hadn't done anything unusual.

"I'm not certain what you have," Harry said. "I still think it is some sort of virus. Dr. Solomon thought so, too, and he wrote out prescriptions already for oseltamivir, which is for the flu, and azithromycin, which is an antibiotic. It would seem reasonable to start those. I want to draw a set of blood cultures on both of you. Frank, do you think you can take them home?"

"I can try."

"I want to see you both back in the office tomorrow."

"I'll call and make the appointment," Kathy said.

Harry nodded at her. "You be sure to call me if anything changes."

"Don't worry, Dr. Bennett," she said. "You'll be the first to know."

Harry stepped out of the room and began writing his progress note. Solomon walked up to him.

"What do you think?" Solomon said. "Do you think she's a squirrel?"

"No, not usually. I think they have something. Maybe it's a virus. I bet they'll be over it within the week."

"Yeah," Solomon said, "like fifty percent of the stuff we see here."

Solomon talked to Harry about a couple of other cases he had seen that night, mostly, it seemed, because he was eager to have an interaction with another doctor who happened to be awake during his night shift. After a few minutes of listening and yawning, Harry gathered up his hat, gloves, and coat, and headed for the doctors' lounge. It was four o'clock and too late to go home. He'd grab a quick nap and make early rounds, and then stop by the house for breakfast, a shower, and a change of clothes before going to the office.

These middle-of-the-night emergency room visits were harder on him as he grew older. It wasn't just the lack of sleep. It was the disruption of his schedule. The older he got, the less he could tolerate messing with his daily routine.

The two sleep rooms for physicians were adjacent to the doctors' lounge. At this time of the night, he had the place to himself. He stripped to his underwear and slipped into the bed. The small room was plain with just the bed, a bedside table, a phone, and a lamp. No decorations. Over the years he had spent a fair number of nights in this room, especially years ago when the staff physicians covered the emergency room every night. Though he was usually comfortable enough to sleep easily here, this morning his mind refused to drift off. The look on Lauren's face worried him. He saw something in her eyes that bothered him. They usually sparkled and were bright, and even when she had been so deathly ill after the near drowning, the spark had still been there. He wasn't so sure he had seen it today.

He wondered if he should have done more. Should he have admitted her to the hospital? Or started an IV antibiotic? Solomon was probably right, though. It was likely a virus, and she'd be better in a couple of days.

He lay awake and stared at the ceiling. It was her eyes that worried him.

* * *

DECEMBER 21, 10:00 A.M. EST
ATLANTA

Jackson gazed out the window over suburban Atlanta at the dusting of snow covering the trees, fields, and buildings. A rare inch of snow caused panic on the streets in Atlanta, but in Boston a flurry this light wouldn't have been noticed. Nonetheless, it reminded him of the winters in Boston, and he missed the cold weather he remembered during his years at Harvard. But more than that, he missed the walks in the snow-covered parks and the skating in the crisp evening air linked arm in arm with his wife. His world was lonely without her.

Lafitte was sitting in the chair across from his desk, rattling off the usual mundane reports. Lafitte hadn't bothered to move Jackson's pile of mail, which had a perpetual presence on the chair. Jackson was half listening. He was waiting for the report on the Los Angeles case. It had continued to weigh heavily on his mind.

Ten days had passed since the man had died. The early specimens were all negative: gram stains, histology, blood smears, and urinalysis. The white blood cell count from the lab drawn in the emergency room was normal at 8,000, which wasn't very helpful. The drug screen was negative. Initial bacterial cultures, both aerobic and anerobic, were no growth on a variety of culture media. Toxicology; virology; and the fungal, mycobacteria, and atypical cultures were still pending.

"Mike," Jackson said finally, "I'm sorry to interrupt. Can you give me an update on the LA case?"

"There's not much to say, really. Everything's negative so far after ten days. The toxicology came back this morning, and it was negative. We're still processing the viral cultures, but they would have likely grown something by now."

"Most likely."

"I suppose it could be tuberculosis. The initial acid-fast smears were negative, but sometimes the TB cultures will grow despite that. The fungal cultures are the last."

"Clinically, it didn't look like a fungus. We're going to come up empty handed, aren't we?"

"It looks that way," Lafitte said. "So what do you think? You've seen everything there is to see. You lived in the part of the world this guy came from. Was this biological or was he just sick?"

Jackson moved from the window and sat down in his chair. "I wish I knew."

Lafitte rattled off the rest of the report, and when he finished, he left. Jackson hadn't listened to a word. He leaned back into the soft leather and sighed. "It's tough to diagnose a dead man," he thought. They'd have to be very lucky. He wished he'd seen this man alive. If he had seen him alive, he could have looked in his eyes. The eyes said everything. No one could hide their disease from him. He had seen far too much.

His thoughts drifted to the eyes of the smallpox victims in Africa. They were staring at him—infants, children, mothers, fathers, grandparents, and the elderly—all wanting help and all wanting a cure. Of course, he and the others had done much good. The ring vaccination finally eradicated the disease. They prevented death for many who were doomed to die. Some of them had already been exposed to the disease but lived. Millions of lives were saved, yet those eyes still haunted him…every single day…and every single night.

* * *

DECEMBER 21, 2:00 P.M. EST
WASHINGTON, DC

Roberts had arranged for the meeting before the assistant deputy director had actually approved his budget, and the calls went out moments after the confirmation fax arrived. Roberts had permission to include the three operational sections of the Counterterrorism Division—International Terrorism, Domestic Terrorism, and Terrorism Financing—as well as several of the terrorism task forces. The agents all knew each other, and they knew Roberts. He thought they would trust that he'd have a good reason for his suspicions, but convincing them to use their time and manpower was a challenge.

Ten people were at the meeting. Roberts had flown in from Atlanta earlier that morning. The meeting was held in the administrative conference room on the third floor of the Hoover building. The room was plain, with white walls and no windows, and the only decoration was the FBI seal hanging near the head of the table. Roberts started by explaining in detail the situation he had encountered in Los Angeles. He showed photographs of the body of the suspect, but no one recognized him. Roberts updated them on the leads he had so far, or actually on the lack of them, and outlined his plan for the investigation. All in all, they didn't seem too convinced but agreed to contribute the necessary resources.

He didn't blame them. The premise was weak. Yet the truth of the matter was that results didn't usually come from some foreign agency or a walk-in informant, but rather from agents in the field making their contacts and doing their homework, and mobilizing them for his investigation was the key.

After the meeting, Roberts had scheduled a few minutes with Edward Mold. He was certain the assistant deputy director would also want an update. Mold shut the office door before he sat down behind his desk.

"I've been thinking," Mold said, "about your man in Los Angeles and those patterns you were talking about."

Roberts listened. He was impressed that Mold had considered his investigation and thought about it at all.

"We've been most worried," Mold continued, "about two major types of bioterrorism: a release of a biologic agent such as anthrax spores in a population and a contamination such as water or food supply. Correct?"

Roberts nodded.

"And you're suggesting a third. You were saying your man was already sick, and so he may have been on a suicide mission, like a suicide bomber in a sense, walking among crowds. Is that what you're thinking?"

"Exactly."

"I thought to myself: how would *I* do that if I were him? Where would *I* go? The whole notion is pretty scary, really." Mold stopped a moment then pointed to Roberts. "Where would you go?"

"I'd go to where the population is. Maximum effect."

"Me, too."

"We know Los Angeles," Roberts said, "but if it were me, I'd definitely go to New York or Chicago."

"Or maybe Philadelphia or Houston or possibly here in DC. You should consider these places first."

"Right. Makes the most sense."

"What agencies will you notify?"

"Interpol, British MI-6, and the French Sûretté."

"The CIA?"

"That's where I need some help," Roberts said. "It's bothered me that the LA suspect got caught in the first place. How do you explain that? At the time, I was told it was his passport but later—nothing. Why was he picked out? What tipped them off?"

"And who else has come into the country with documents that meet similar criteria."

"Exactly."

"I'll see what I can do. Maybe we'll get some help from the CIA, maybe Immigration, maybe Customs, but don't hold your breath."

Mold was right, Roberts thought. He wouldn't be holding his breath. The investigation would be easier if he had a suspect, a photograph, put out an APB, and checked cellular conversations. If he only knew for whom he was looking. If he had the biologic agent—an anthrax spore, a vial of smallpox, or anything at all. If he even knew for sure that a crime was being committed!

"One last thing," Mold said.

"Yes, sir?"

"Be culturally sensitive," Mold said. "This isn't a witch hunt."

Culturally sensitive? Yeah, right, Roberts thought. Ignore that his man was an Arab? Is that what he wants? Disregard the facts?

"We have many allies in the Middle East," Mold added. "Not everyone is a bad guy."

"Okay, boss," Roberts said. "I get it." But I don't like it, he wanted to say, but he kept the thought to himself.

That *was* the problem, though, wasn't it: picking out the bad guys? "The terrorists knew how to look and act like normal Americans," Roberts thought, "and they took full advantage of it. Hiding as regular people, disguised by our diversity." Diversity was one of America's strengths but also one of its weaknesses. Roberts's job was tougher because of it, but that wasn't anything new. He was certain terrorists were out there, and they were most likely from the Middle East—that was just a fact. He'd be culturally sensitive because that was his job, but if the bastards were really out there, he'd find them. That was his job, too.

CHAPTER NINETEEN

DECEMBER 21, 5:00 P.M. CST
DAY ELEVEN OF THE SECOND WAVE OF EXPOSURE
SYCAMORE, ILLINOIS

The last patient of the day was an easy appointment, and Harry thought he'd be home in time for supper for the first time in a month. Emma Lou Greer had been a patient for twenty years, and she was one of his favorites. She was approaching a hundred years old and had been treated for stable hypertension and mild congestive heart failure as long as either one of them could remember—maybe even before they invented medication, Harry had joked. I'm as old as the hills, she'd say at every visit. You're not that old, Harry would protest each time. You said *that* when I was eighty, she'd reply, and I were old then, and I'm old now. She lived alone. Her mind was sharp as a tack. And though thin and sinewy, she was still strong. Harry truly believed she could take him down in an arm wrestle. Easily.

"I ain't going to live forever, Dr. Bennett," she said. "Since I'm going to be a hundred soon, I've been thinking about having one of them living wills."

"Not a bad idea, Emma Lou."

"Wouldn't want you to shock me with one of them gadgets. It'd be a waste of electricity. Besides, I'm so ornery, I'd probably break it."

"We can get you the forms."

"She should have signed one ten years ago," her niece said. Her niece had brought her to the office and was sitting in the chair next to Emma Lou. "But you know women. She didn't want to admit to her age."

Harry laughed. "That's true at any age."

A rap on the door interrupted their conversation, and Jill stuck in her head.

"I have an emergency, Dr. Bennett," she said. "Lauren Randall's having a convulsion. Frank's on his cell phone."

Harry looked at Emma Lou. "I'll be right back."

"Sure, Dr. Bennett, you go take care of that."

Harry quickly left the room. Jill was holding out the phone at the nurse's desk.

"Frank, what's going on?"

"Lauren just had some sort of seizure." His voice sounded frantic. "She was shaking and convulsing. It only lasted a minute. We're in the car now on our way to DeKalb. Kathy's so sick I had to help her to the car. I'm taking them both to the hospital."

"That's exactly what you should do."

"Will you meet us there?"

"I'm on my way, but I'll also call and have the ER doctor see you the minute you arrive."

"Something is really wrong."

"Frank, you drive carefully. The last thing we need is all of you in a car wreck."

"Okay, Dr. Bennett. I'll be careful."

Harry hung up the phone and turned to Jill. "Call the emergency room. Have the ER doctor see them on arrival. Tell them I'm finishing up with my last patient, and I'll be there within thirty minutes."

* * *

When Harry arrived in the emergency room, the place was busy. The waiting room was full, which was a bit unusual at six in the evening. People were coughing and hacking, and everyone there looked sick. As he approached the nurses' station, the unit secretary saw him coming and pointed him to the Randalls' room. Lauren was lying on the bed. She was breathing normally and was alert but certainly appeared much sicker than when he had seen her previously. Frank was standing next to Lauren, holding her hand. Kathy was at the head of the bed, sponging Lauren's forehead with a washcloth. Kathy didn't look much better than Lauren.

"Kathy," Harry said, "you're going to fall down. We need to get you into a bed."

"I'm staying right here," she said firmly.

"It's not going to help if you collapse on the floor."

"The nurses tried to get her to leave," Frank said, "but she wouldn't budge."

Harry stepped into the hallway and arranged for a second gurney to be brought in alongside Lauren's. It would be a tight fit, but at least she would be in a bed. When Harry returned to the exam room, he asked for an update.

"She was on the couch watching TV," Frank said, "and suddenly began convulsing. Her eyes rolled back up into her head and her arms and legs were shaking. It scared me to death. She was turning blue, and I thought I'd have to give mouth-to-mouth, but then she quit the convulsions. It was maybe a minute. It seemed like thirty."

"She's never had a seizure before, right?"

"No, never. The nurse said her fever was a hundred and four, but it wasn't very high this afternoon at home. She was having some chills, and she also started having diarrhea. We were going to call you, but we have an appointment in the morning."

Harry began examining Lauren while Frank was talking. Her eyes were clear but dull. Her throat was still slightly red. Her ears were normal. When he moved her neck, it wasn't stiff, and he didn't feel any swollen lymph nodes. When he listened to her heart and lungs, her lungs were clear, and the heart sounds were normal. Her abdomen was soft and had some mild diffuse tenderness. On her upper thighs he thought she might have a very fine, faint redness, but he wasn't sure if it was significant.

"She says her headaches are terrible," Frank said, "and her back seems to be worse. We gave her acetaminophen."

"You did fine. This could be a febrile seizure," Harry said. "Sometimes children will have a seizure when their body temperature spikes upward. We'll watch her very carefully. I might need to do a lumbar puncture to draw some fluid off from around her spinal cord. We may need to do a CT scan. For now, we're going to repeat all her blood work and start an IV to give her some fluids. She looks a little dry, and I want to give her some IV antibiotics."

Harry moved next to Kathy and began examining her. She told Harry her symptoms, and they were nearly identical to Lauren's, except she didn't have the diarrhea and her fever wasn't as high. Her exam was about the same as Lauren's with mild dehydration and some abdominal tenderness. Neither had a definite rash. In fact, neither had any physical findings that Harry was particularly worried about, except for the fact they both looked so sick. That was enough for him to be concerned.

"Do you think it's the chickenpox again," Kathy asked. "You know Lauren had her shot, but I've not had the shot, and I don't think I've ever had chickenpox."

The thought had crossed Harry's mind. "It's a consideration," he said.

Kathy had the same restlessness that he had noted before in Lauren. Now Lauren was lethargic enough that she didn't appear to be as anxious. This had to be some sort of virus, he thought, but he was becoming more and more worried because he was so unsure as to the cause of their illness.

"I did notice this," Kathy said. She reached over her bed rail and lifted the hair up on Lauren forehead. "She has these places."

Harry slipped in next to Lauren's bed and examined the area of Kathy's concern. Just below the hairline was a series of blisters. He hadn't lifted her bangs before, so he had missed them. He leaned over to take a close look and adjusted the light so that he could see. There were eight or ten along the hairline. They were definitely blisters, but these were deep-seated, and all of them were in the same stage of development, unlike chickenpox. In chickenpox, the rash was in crops, some red bumps, some blisters, and some pustules all mixed in the same area. This didn't look like chickenpox. The situation was beginning to scare him. There had been a two-day prodromal of mild symptoms; followed by the onset of fever, chills, backache, and headache; and then convulsions. And now, deep-seated vesicles that were all the same stage along the forehead. Yet it was hard to diagnose anything with only eight lesions. Was it a virus? Was it an allergy? His mind began racing as he considered the different causes, and he kept coming back to the same conclusion: this *had* to be chickenpox. What else could it be? Lauren had experienced a typical light case recently. The mother might never have been exposed before.

Harry stepped back from the table, and they must have seen the concern on his face.

"What do you think, Dr. Bennett?" Frank said. "Is this serious?"

"I'm not...I'm not certain," Harry said. "I want all of you to stay in this room. Please don't leave. I'm calling Dr. Naguib Abdul Haleem. He's an infectious disease specialist."

"What do you think it is?" Kathy said.

"I'm just not sure. I need to run some tests."

Harry stepped into the hallway and signaled the nurse over. "I want them all together in isolation," he told her. "Don't let anyone else take care of them. No other personnel to come in. No equipment. It's important that they're in total isolation for now."

"Yes, Doctor. What are you thinking?"

"I don't know yet, but it could be highly contagious. I'm calling Dr. Haleem. Please do exactly as I ask."

Harry walked to the nurses' station to page Dr. Haleem. It wasn't chickenpox, he thought. That just didn't fit. But what he *was* thinking worried him, and his gut was telling him that his concern was legitimate. His heart began pounding as he thought about it more. If he were right—and surely he wasn't—but if he were, this was a terrible situation. He had to be correct about this. He'd ask for help to confirm what he feared was happening, but he knew in his heart of hearts that he was right. Yet she had vesicles and not macules, the red bumps that often occurred first. The vision of Jackson's slides flashed in his mind: the rash, the patients, the children's eyes. This could be smallpox.

Damn it to hell! This could be smallpox!

* * *

Harry poured two cups of coffee and handed one to Haleem. The staff's break area in the emergency room was convenient— better yet, it was empty. It consisted of little more than a large closet with a small, round table, four plastic chairs, and a wall of narrow cabinets with a coffeemaker and compact refrigerator. The walls were still yellow from the years of cigarette smoke before smoking was banned inside the hospital. The room was an afterthought and not part of the original floor plan, but it was necessary since ER personnel seldom had time to walk to the cafeteria on the opposite side of the hospital for meals.

Haleem had interviewed and examined the Randalls, and Harry thought the break room was a good place for a private conversation about Haleem's findings.

Within the hour that Haleem had driven from home, Lauren had developed new vesicles on her face and upper arms. Haleem had also noticed several on the insides of her cheeks. Nothing else had changed, and she had not had any further seizures. Lauren's white blood cell count that Solomon had ordered was 3,500, which was slightly lower than normal and consistent with a virus but not especially helpful. She now had fifteen band cells.

"What do you think?" Harry asked, sitting down at the table.

"It's confusing," Haleem said, sitting next to Harry. He paused a moment as he took a sip of coffee. "She had the chickenpox earlier. The rash is breaking out in phase, not crops, so it's probably not chickenpox."

"What else could it be? Early disseminated herpes?"

"Both patients at the same time? That would be unusual. And neither is immuno-compromised, right?"

"No, they've both been in good health. I told you about Lauren's near drowning four years ago, but she's fully recovered from that. It's not likely measles. She's been immunized."

"Right. You can see vesicles from a drug eruption but not usually with these associ-ated symptoms."

"Monkey pox?" Harry offered.

"I think they're too sick for that. Meningococcemia is a possibility, I guess, but I'd expect hemorrhagic lesions."

"Yet, if we're even considering a bacteria that could cause meningitis, especially with the seizure, should we do a spinal tap?"

"No, not clinically yet. I agree with you, it's probably a febrile seizure. This really is a puzzling case. If we had forty-eight hours to watch the rash, it'd be easier."

"We don't have forty-eight hours," Harry said. "I kind of feel like the medical student who reads the textbooks and can't make a reasonable diagnosis because he's considering all the wildest possibilities. Common things are common."

Haleem did not reply, and they were both quiet for a few seconds.

"What we have," Harry said, "is a patient with three days of a febrile illness with the fever greater than one hundred and one degrees *and* headache, back pain, chills, vomiting, and a convulsion. She has deep-seated, well-circumscribed vesicles, and the lesions so far are in the same stage of development. And her mother is sick with simi-lar symptoms. Maybe I'm just biased by the lecture I had three weeks ago, but I think Lauren meets the major criteria for smallpox."

"This is unbelievable," Haleem said. "We're here in DeKalb, Illinois. Where would this come from? No other cases have been reported."

"We would have heard about any if there were."

"You did the right thing by isolating them. We need to be sure. As soon as we initiate the smallpox contingency plan, all hell will break loose."

"It's a clinical diagnosis at this point. How sure are we?"

"What else could it be? It meets the major criteria. I think we have to call it."

"This is bad, really bad," Harry said, standing. "We should inform the administrator and chief of staff."

"I agree."

"I'll give Powell and Lucas a call."

"I have a buddy," Haleem said, "a fraternity brother over at Chicago University. They have an electron microscope, so at least we may be able to tell if it's an orthopoxvirus. I can swab one of the lesions and take it there myself."

"You'll have to be sure the technician gets vaccinated."

"Of course. If we confirm this, we'll need to move the Randalls to the intensive care unit. We only have one negative pressure room equipped with HEPA filters."

"We can put them both in the same room, but the ICU staff won't be comfortable with a pediatric case."

"Then we should isolate an area on peds for Lauren and use the ICU for Mrs. Randall. That ICU room is occupied with a patient on a ventilator, so it may take a while to move him."

"I'll take care of things on this end," Harry said. "You call your buddy in Chicago."

Haleem stood to leave. Harry tossed the cups away.

"I do have a connection, sort of, at the CDC," Harry said as they moved toward the door. "I met Hugh Jackson at a conference recently."

"I've heard of him."

"I'll give him a call. They're supposed to have a rapid response team, but I think that takes twelve to twenty-four hours. Once we start this, it's going to snowball."

"The possibility of smallpox scares the hell out of me, but I don't see we have a choice. This case meets the criteria."

"Then we should act on it," Harry said.

"I agree."

"If we're wrong, we'll look stupid, but what the hell—I've done that before."

"Me, too."

Harry swung open the door and held it open for Haleem. "Drive carefully," he said, "and call me as soon as you get the results."

"Don't worry. I'll let you know."

* * *

Harry stood outside the curtain of the Randalls' exam room, waiting to go in, collecting his thoughts. He had already called the president of the medical staff, Dr. Duncan Lucas, a surgeon he had known for twenty years; the hospital administrator, Stanley Powell, who had been head of the hospital the entire time Harry had practiced at DeKalb; and the director of nursing, Carolyn Perkins, a crusty nurse who had worked at DeKalb since her graduation from nursing school thirty years earlier. Harry had insisted they come in from home because of an emergency, without telling them any specifics, and they had agreed. After all his years on staff, they trusted Harry and knew he was serious. They'd be at the hospital within thirty minutes. He also had called the ICU to clear the room upstairs. They were reluctant at first, but he demanded it, though he didn't actually have any administrative authority. He could be intimidating when it was necessary.

The first thing Harry did once he was back out in the emergency room was to confirm whether the staff had followed his instructions on the Randalls' strict isolation. They had, and signs to that effect were posted next to the room. Of course, the ER staff was smart and beginning to formulate their own diagnoses. Harry would need to include the staff at his next meeting or rumors of everything under the sun would be racing like wildfire throughout the hospital before he could stop them.

Harry slipped on gloves, a mask, and a gown. He slid open the curtain a bit and stepped into the Randalls' room.

Lauren's rash had worsened at a remarkable rate. Since he had first seen her, the vesicles had spread over her entire face. Her general condition had not changed and neither had Kathy's. Lauren had not had any more seizures.

Frank looked up at Harry as he entered. "Have you found out anything, Dr. Bennett?"

"Not yet, but we hope to have some answers shortly."

"What are you thinking this is?"

"We're not sure. We'll be running some tests. To be honest, we think it could be something really rare and quite contagious."

Frank and Kathy listened intently as Harry spoke.

"We must isolate both you and Lauren," Harry continued, looking at Kathy. "No visitors. And Frank, you need to stay in here, too. Just a precaution. You've been exposed to whatever they have."

"I know. The staff wouldn't let me go to the bathroom. They made me use a urinal."

"I'm sorry about that. We'll be moving all of you to a room out on the floor in a little while. You'll be more comfortable there."

"I'm not complaining," Frank said. "I'm just worried."

"I know. I am, too."

"Everyone's wearing the gowns and gloves," Frank said. "It's pretty scary."

"It's standard procedure, at least until we find out more."

"Let hope it's just the flu," Kathy said, "or something you can treat."

"That'd be good," Harry said.

Harry stepped out and placed his gown, gloves, and mask in a receptacle marked biohazard outside the door. The ER staff were already preparing for something serious, which was appropriate.

As Harry thought about the conversation he had just had with the Randalls, recalling all they had been through already, he felt a heaviness in his heart. As soon as he knew what this was, they would be the very next to know. He owed them that much.

* * *

When Harry opened the door, the entire emergency room staff was crammed into the small break room. Powell, the administrator, and Lucas, the president of the medical staff, were seated, but most of the ER crew was standing. Solomon, the physician on duty, Perkins, the director of nursing, three ER nurses, the lab tech, the X-ray tech, and two of the receptionists were present. Harry knew most of them, had worked with them for years, and was the personal physician of several of them and their families. He had decided to be brief—they couldn't ignore the patients very long at all—and be directly to the point. Harry remained standing. All eyes were on him.

"Dr. Haleem and I believe we have two cases of smallpox in the emergency room."

Harry waited a moment for their response, but only the administrator and president of the medical staff gasped. It was as if the ER staff already knew.

"Dr. Haleem is at the University of Chicago as we speak. We hope to have a report within an hour."

For the benefit of those who just arrived, Harry gave a summary of the Randalls' illness, and how he and Dr. Haleem felt their case met the major criteria for smallpox. Although some of the staff may have suspected it, no one spoke or asked questions. Harry understood. The possibility was stunning, dreadful, and terrible to consider; it took a moment for all of them to comprehend and sort out their emotions, including Harry.

"Dr. Haleem is taking a specimen to Chicago to be examined by an electron microscope. We hope to determine whether or not it is an orthopoxvirus, which is the family of viruses that includes smallpox. I've already put in a call to the CDC, and I'm expecting a call back shortly. I'm certain they'll send a response team up here, and the actual confirmation will be done at the CDC laboratory in Atlanta. Our job now is to treat this as a probable case of smallpox and limit its spread."

Harry wasn't sure what he had expected from this group—panic, fear, or disbelief? But they took the news well and appeared professional and determined. Maybe the gravity of the situation hadn't sunk in.

Harry continued. "Our isolation has to be perfectly strict. We'll have to use the emergency personal protective equipment."

"I'll make sure those are available," Perkins said. "I'll also make sure everyone has a copy of the emergency smallpox response plan."

"Why don't you and I review that," Lucas said, "before we start leaving copies lying around—at least until we confirm this."

"Dr. Bennett," Powell said, "I think it's important that we don't tell anyone until we are absolutely sure this is smallpox. We shouldn't tell other staff in the hospital, not any of the patients, and especially no one on the outside. We need some time to be prepared. Dr. Lucas, let's you and me set up a situation room in the hospital boardroom, and as soon as we get this microscopic confirmation, we can call an emergency meeting. I need your help to create the list."

"Sure, Stanley," Lucas said. "Good idea."

"Is anyone here vaccinated?" Harry asked.

No one raised their hands.

"That's what I was afraid of. We'll be asking for volunteers to take care of the Randalls."

A nurse from the ER spoke up. "That shouldn't be a problem, Dr. Bennett."

"Why don't we just transfer them," another nurse asked, "like to a university hospital or someplace?"

"That's a good question," Lucas said. "But a transfer is a logistical nightmare, especially if we don't know what the disease is yet. And who would accept them at this point? I think that'd be the Commissioner of Health's call."

"So do we lock the place down?" Solomon asked.

Harry looked over at the president of the staff. "It's not my call," Harry said, "but I would think we should delay everyone's discharge until we find out. Then we could make that decision. If it's confirmed, we'll probably have to hold everyone here until they are vaccinated."

"I'd have to agree," Lucas said.

"What we must do right now," Harry said, "is create a list of all the Randalls' contacts—anyone who's had face-to-face contact within six feet. I mean *anyone*, including nurses, lab, X-ray, receptionists, security, even housekeeping—no exceptions. We'll vaccinate every one of those people, I assure you, and all of you."

"Absolutely," Lucas agreed.

"The CDC should be calling soon," Harry said, "I'm definitely planning to address the process of vaccinations."

"Fortunately, they came in by ambulance," Solomon said, "so it's not as worrisome for the patients in the waiting room tonight. But the Randalls were here early this morning on my last shift."

"That's right," Harry said, "so we need a list of everyone who was seen last night and all the staff on duty then, as well as those on duty tonight. Also, we need the EMS that brought them in tonight."

"I'll take responsibility for that," Perkins said.

"Good," Harry said. "Dr. Haleem and I decided that the best thing to do is use the negative pressure room up in the ICU for the mother and clear an area on peds for Lauren. It'll take a while to get that done. In the meantime, both patients will stay down here."

No one offered any comments.

"Okay, what have we forgotten?" Harry asked.

There were no questions. The staff was ready.

"Then back to work," Powell said. "We have patients out there who need you. And remember, absolutely no one can know about this until we have a confirmation. Understood?"

* * *

In all his life, Harry would never have expected to receive a phone call like the one from Haleem, and his heart sank at the words.

"It's orthopoxvirus," Haleem said. "It's definite. It's smallpox until proven otherwise."

"I'll take care of things here. We'll initiate the emergency smallpox response plan and call the Health Department."

"Good idea. I'll be back in an hour."

Harry glanced at his watch. "I'll call the meeting for ten o'clock."

Harry hung up the phone and walked to the Randalls' exam room. All the staff stopped working as he walked by, trying to read his face. They probably knew the answer, but he had promised the Randalls they would be the first to know, and he would keep his promise.

Perkins had placed the personal protective equipment outside the room as she promised. He donned the disposable long-sleeved gown and latex gloves, and then slipped on the respirator mask and eyewear with side shields. Kathy and Frank would know immediately when they saw the equipment that it was serious, but his words would still be devastating to them. He had learned over the years to quickly get to the point and allow people to react. When they had steadied from the blow, then they would ask questions.

Harry pulled the curtain aside and stepped through. Frank was sitting next to Kathy, pressing a wet compress on her forehead. Kathy had several lesions on her face. She hadn't had any when he was in the room earlier. Lauren looked worse. Now the vesicles were on her arms and neck. Neither Frank nor Kathy said a word when Harry entered, but both looked up at him expectantly.

"I'm sorry to tell you this," Harry said, "but we think you have smallpox."

"Smallpox?" Kathy said. "How can that be?"

Frank stood. "I've heard of smallpox, but wasn't it…like…eliminated years ago?"

"We thought so."

"I'm having trouble understanding this," Kathy said.

"I know," Harry said. "It's hard to comprehend, but the test we did is highly suspicious."

"But if it's been eliminated…?" Kathy said, pausing a moment. "Are you saying we have smallpox?"

"Yes," Harry said. "That's what we think."

"But isn't that impossible?" Frank said. "It would have to be from a terrorist or something, right?"

"We're not sure about where it came from, but the symptoms and signs meet the criteria for smallpox. So this *must* be our tentative diagnosis until we do the tests that confirm it."

"When will that be?" Kathy asked.

"I'm sorry, but I just don't know. I've put a call in for the CDC, the Centers for Disease Control. They do the tests."

"I'm not believing this," Frank said.

Kathy's eyes filled with tears. "Dr. Bennett," she said, "please tell us there's a mistake."

"I wish I could."

"What is smallpox?" Lauren had spoken with her soft, sweet voice.

Harry's attention turned to Lauren. She was looking back and forth at her parents. He felt a stab in the pit of his stomach.

"Lauren," he said softly, "it's an infection."

"Okay," she replied.

It was a simple statement of trust. She was trusting in her doctor while not understanding the problem at all; Harry didn't completely understand the situation yet, and none of them could predict the consequences of such a diagnosis. Harry could barely imagine the possibilities—the medical treatments, the isolation, the crush of the media, the political implications, the criminal investigations, and the disfigurement, even death, of the patients—but he wasn't sure the Randalls could understand it. Not yet. This was not an ordinary diagnosis, and the whole scene was almost surreal.

"How can this be possible?" Frank asked. "How could they have gotten this?"

"I can't answer those questions. Like I said, we can't even confirm it for certain until the CDC comes and obtains some specimens and runs some tests in Atlanta. In the meantime we have to isolate you. Frank, we have to quarantine you, too. We can give you the vaccine as soon as it's available."

"I'm *not* leaving my family," Frank said.

"I'm not going to ask you to do that right now, but when the Health Department gets here, I'm sure that question will have to be answered."

"I don't give a damn what they say. I'm *not* leaving my daughter and my wife."

"I know, Frank. I don't blame you. I may be criticized for telling you it's smallpox before it's confirmed, but I thought you deserved to know. But you have to promise me—and this is *very* important—not to tell anyone. You can't call anyone and talk about this. No family, friends, or neighbors. It is absolutely essential that we know what we are dealing with before it becomes public."

"We understand," Frank said.

"I also promise you that I'll let you know the results the moment they are confirmed. I won't leave you in the dark on this."

"We appreciate that," Frank said.

"The other thing I'm asking of you, and this is also very important, is that I want you to make a list of all the people you've had contact with the last seventy-two hours. Everyone— friends, neighbors, and family. I need to know all the places where you went shopping or went to eat. This is very important because we need a list of everyone who may have been exposed."

"We haven't been many places," Kathy said, "because Lauren's been too sick, but we've had some friends over."

"Please be as complete as possible. It's very important."

"This *can't* be smallpox," Kathy insisted. "You must be wrong. This is all a big mistake. Check your tests again. It's some sort of flu. How could we have smallpox? It doesn't exist. You have to be wrong!"

Harry felt her pain and worry, and he couldn't blame her for her disbelief. He could barely believe it himself.

"I hope you're right," Harry said, his voice soft with emotion. "I hope you're right with my whole heart."

A nurse called Harry's name from the outside of the curtain, and he peeked out.

"A Dr. Hugh Jackson is calling for you from Atlanta. He says he's returning your call."

"Tell him I'll be right there."

Harry removed the protective equipment outside the room. He washed his hands at the sink and crossed the hallway to the phone.

"Hugh," Harry said, "this is Harry Bennett.

"Hi, Harry. I got a message that you had called."

"Thanks for calling back." Harry briefly explained the situation. "We just found out fifteen minutes ago that it is an orthopoxvirus."

"Harry, this is very important. You have to assume this is smallpox until we can confirm it here. Notify your State Health Department immediately now that you have a tentative diagnosis."

"I definitely will."

"You should start any smallpox response plan that you have in the hospital."

"That's underway."

"I'll send up an Epidemic Intelligence Service Team and get them there as soon as we can. I'll also send Gary Roberts. He's the FBI agent in charge of bioterrorism here in Atlanta. We just had a case in Los Angeles ten days ago that we were both concerned about. We didn't confirm a causative agent, but now I'm worried, and there definitely could be a connection."

"We look forward to any help you can send us."

"Any idea where they may have had contact?"

"No, not at all."

"I don't mean to worry you, but you must be prepared for additional cases."

"I've already thought of that."

"Once this is confirmed, we will rapidly vaccinate everyone in contact. I think we can guarantee a rapid deployment. I'll fax or e-mail the entire CDC protocol to you."

"I appreciate your help."

"The team should be there in a few hours. I'll get it started the second I'm off the phone."

Harry gave him the fax number and said good-bye. He started to hang up the phone but heard Jackson speaking.

"Oh, by the way, Harry," Jackson said.

"Yes, Hugh?"

"Good job, Doctor!"

CHAPTER TWENTY

DECEMBER 21, 10:00 P.M. EST
DAY ELEVEN OF THE SECOND WAVE OF EXPOSURE
ATLANTA

The bowl of microwave popcorn in Roberts's lap was his second. The first bowl at eight o'clock was dinner and this one was dessert. He had tuned in to ESPN SportsCenter hoping to find out more about the rumored off-season, two-pitcher trade to the Atlanta Braves, but they had said nothing, and Roberts would have to wait for the morning paper to check on any more late-breaking news. Roberts had to admit he was a Braves fanatic. As far as he was concerned, the first and foremost reason anyone would ever live in Atlanta was Atlanta Braves baseball.

Ready to go to bed, Roberts flipped off the television. His suitcase was packed and sitting by the front door, still warm from his trip home from Washington, DC. He had wasted no time setting up his first meetings and had scheduled an early flight for New York City in the morning. The New York regional office probably had more experience on terrorism than anyone, and their agents had some of the best contacts. He would brief them, pick their brains, and hope to send them out as converts to his theory. They'd know the rocks to look under, he thought, and were up to the task. Since 9/11, the daily fear of another terrorist attack was not a hypothetical exercise for law enforcement in New York City, but a constant, pervasive reality.

As Roberts turned off the lamp in the living room, the telephone rang, and he flipped the light back on.

"Hello," he said, answering.

"Gary Roberts?"

"Yes?" The voice on the phone sounded familiar.

"This is Hugh Jackson...from the CDC."

"Hi, Dr. Jackson. How are you?"

"Fine, thanks. We have a situation, and I need your help."

"What is it?"

"We have a report of two possible cases of smallpox at a hospital in DeKalb, Illinois."

Jackson paused. He was waiting, knowing Roberts needed a moment to grasp what he had just said.

"Are you sure?"

"Not yet. They haven't been confirmed, but they meet the major criteria."

"Source?"

"None, but it's early. It would seem that Los Angeles is a connection."

Roberts had thought of that instantly.

Jackson continued, "We're sending the team in immediately. I think you should go."

"Absolutely!"

"But since it's not confirmed yet," Jackson said, "you should divulge this information on a need-to-know basis."

Roberts understood. "I do have a question," he said.

"What is it?"

"Where the hell is DeKalb, Illinois?"

"I'm not sure. Not too far from Chicago is what I was told. We'll get that information to you."

"What a coincidence," Roberts said. "The CDC is in DeKalb County here in Atlanta."

"That is odd."

Jackson and Roberts finished their conversation, and Roberts hung up the phone. He'd go to bed, not that he'd sleep, and leave early in the morning—not for New York City as he had planned, but unexpectedly for Chicago and DeKalb, wherever that was.

Roberts thought about the suspect in Los Angeles, the sweat dripping off the man's face on to the floor and the look in his eyes. Now this!

Dammit! I hate being right!

* * *

DECEMBER 21, 10:00 P.M. CST
DEKALB, ILLINOIS

Harry had sat in the boardroom of DeKalb County Hospital and had seen a number of contentious issues over the years—a move to unionize the nurses, a state senator who threatened to close the hospital after his mother fell out of her bed, a male nurse accused of raping a patient, a doctor operating stone drunk—but none of these issues compared to the topic they were preparing to discuss tonight. After tonight, the hospital, his life, and the lives of these people sitting around the table would never be the same. Harry watched as they waited for the meeting to start. Only a few in attendance were talking. Most were sitting quietly, keeping to themselves. It was the proverbial calm before the storm.

The boardroom was stylishly decorated with dark paneled walls on three sides and a wall of glass on the fourth that overlooked the college and downtown DeKalb. A large oval table of pecan occupied the center of the room and was surrounded by twenty chairs, about half of which were filled. One wall at the far end was covered with portraits of former administrators and the presidents of the medical staff. Harry's portrait, as staff president, would most likely hang there in a couple of years.

Everyone who was called was present without knowing the reason for the meeting, but Harry wasn't naive enough to think the rumor mill wasn't already churning. Around the table sat Powell, Dr. Lucas, Perkins, and Dr. Haleem, who had rushed back from Chicago. They had been joined by Virginia Gentry, the hospital epidemiologist, Keith Steidley, the vice president for public relations, Martin Phillips, the hospital's general counsel, Todd Owens, the hospital engineer, and Dr. Gregory Ingram, the chief pathologist. The board of the hospital was represented by Eric Ness, who served as chairman of the board of trustees and who owned Ness Electrical Supply, one of the largest employers in the county. Ness was efficient as board chairman but wasn't particularly liked by the physicians at the hospital because they thought him to be prohospital at the expense of the physicians. Ness sat at the head of the table.

Lucas walked to the lectern and asked for everyone's attention. "I thank you all for coming on such short notice," he said. "We have a grave crisis in our hospital. Two of Dr. Harry Bennett's patients are in the emergency room, and they meet the major criteria for smallpox."

Just as Harry had paused when he made the announcement, Lucas did as well.

"We are initiating the emergency smallpox response plan and closing the hospital. We are considering this a disaster of the highest level. In a few minutes, the commissioner of the State Health Department, the state epidemiologist, and the chief of staff of the governor's office will be joining us by conference call. I'll wait for Dr. Bennett to discuss the details of the case when they are on the phone, but for now I believe we have several issues related to the care of these two patients.

"We have already begun making a list of contacts, both from their admission today and also from their ER visit last night. I made several phone calls regarding the possibility of transfer and, for the time being, that option seems to be unavailable. It is recommended that patients with smallpox be placed in what are called negative-pressure rooms that pull the air out of the room and filter it. Ideally, we would place the mother in the negative pressure room in the ICU and the daughter in a negative pressure room in pediatrics, but we are not equipped for that. I've asked Todd Owens to discuss our options."

"The only solution we have at this time," Owens said, speaking from his seat at the table, "is to put one of them in the negative pressure room in the ICU and the other in an adjacent room. We'll have to close down that area of the ICU and block the inflow and outflow heating ducts of the entire area, but it can be done. It would be difficult to safely do this in both the ICU and Peds. If necessary, we can heat the rooms with space heaters. I think this will be a good temporary option."

"Are you suggesting we close an entire area of the ICU?" Ness asked.

"Yes," Lucas said. "It seems best since we must not allow the virus into the ventilation system."

"What happens to the patients already in the ICU?" Ness asked.

"We'll transfer them to the floors," Lucas said.

"We'll have to bring pediatric staff to this area," Perkins said. "The adult-care nurses won't be comfortable treating the girl."

"We anticipate some anxiety from the nurses and other staff," Lucas said, "which is expected, so we plan to be absolutely clear that working in these areas is voluntary. No one will be forced. And we will assure them that they will receive the first vaccine that arrives." Lucas turned to Keith Steidley. "Keith, I'm sure we will need a press release sometime in the next few hours. Would you work on the wording and show it to Mr. Powell and me?"

Steidley nodded.

The participants from the conference call came on the line and were introduced to the group. Dr. Kenneth Illig, the commissioner of the State Health Department, spoke first. Next was Victor Cox, the state epidemiologist, and last was David Choate, the chief of staff of the governor's office.

Harry provided a summary of his patients' symptoms and signs. He emphasized the electron microscope findings of an orthopoxvirus and his conversation with Jackson.

"I hate to throw an egg on this deal," Ness said, "but I think they shouldn't even be here. We should send them to Cook County or University Hospital in Chicago right now. That way we don't have to worry about ventilation in the room or nurse exposure or all that other stuff. We're not a tertiary hospital. We're a community hospital, and a damn good one, but this deal is way over our heads. These people need specialists and experts we don't have—no offense to our doctors. Surely there's someplace that has treated a few cases of smallpox or even specializes in it and knows what to do. Smallpox here will shut down this hospital. You think anyone will bring their family members here? I wouldn't, and I'm the chairman of the board. I think we should move them and do it pronto, *before* we confirm it's smallpox. Then it looks better."

"We can't do that," Lucas said. "I made those phone calls already."

"So what?" Ness said. "Do it anyway."

"We can't," Harry responded, "for three important reasons. First of all, no doctor has treated a case of smallpox in this country in over fifty years. Second, we'd have a considerable legal liability to put a receiving hospital at such a substantial risk, especially the risk to their staff and other patients. Lastly, this is a national disaster, and until we know the extent of this from a national view, we should wait for the CDC's input on this."

"I couldn't articulate it better myself," Dr. Illig said over the phone. "The State Health Department will investigate all those options."

"I don't care what you say," Ness said. "Then tell them it's smallpox. A tertiary hospital can't refuse a transfer. It should be the decision of the board of this hospital, and I can have the board together within the hour to decide. This will destroy the hospital financially. What would our community do then?"

Illig spoke again, now with a degree of irritation in his voice. "Mr. Ness, I think you should carefully weigh that decision before you make it."

"It's out of the question anyway," Harry said.

"Why is that?" Ness said sharply.

"Because Kathy and Lauren Randall are too unstable to transfer."

"What the hell has that got to do with it? We send people out of here all the time in worse condition."

"That's my opinion as attending physician."

Ness stood and pointed at Harry. "What are you trying to pull?"

"Mr. Phillips," Lucas said, "you're our legal counsel. What are the legal ramifications here?"

"This whole case is a legal nightmare," Phillips said. "It's making my head spin. There's no precedent for any of this. There's no precedent for closing the hospital. There's no precedent for holding people here against their will. Mr. Ness may be right that a tertiary hospital can't refuse a transfer, but Dr. Bennett is correct in that the patients have to be stable for transfer, and that's his call as attending physician. The law is clear on that point. We have all sorts of issues regarding informed consent. Who needs to be vaccinated? Who's responsible for the side effects of the vaccination? From my understanding there are some very serious side effects, sometimes even death. We have employee safety issues, OSHA, and workers' comp. The quarantine laws in this country are antiquated and fuzzy—maybe even unenforceable. When the story hits the news, we'll have more media in our parking lot than patients, and I anticipate media challenges regarding the right to have access to information or maybe even access to our facility. It would help if the governor would declare a state of emergency. Most courts would allow the governor to have broad powers in circumstances such as this—powers that we as a hospital won't have."

"So what's the rationale for closing the hospital," Ness persisted, "especially if there are legal issues?"

"I'll answer that," Lucas said. "This is a serious situation, and we don't have a handle on it yet. People coming and going, trying to run an emergency room, attempting to control access to the hospital, particularly if word should get out—these are big problems."

"And what will you tell the visitors?" Ness said.

"That we have an infectious disease emergency, which is true, and they have to spend the night. All of us should plan to do so as well."

A voice broke in on the speaker phone. "This is David Choate, the governor's office chief of staff. As soon as this meeting is over, I'll be contacting the governor, and though I can't promise a state of emergency, I'm certain he'll be involved. On behalf of the governor's office, I want to commend you for your efforts, and I think the governor would be pleased with your concerns about the people of the State of Illinois as well as the welfare of your patients. If there is nothing further that you need from the governor's office, I'm will disconnect at this time and immediately call the governor."

"Thank you, Mr. Choate," Lucas said. "We appreciate your being a part of this conference."

"Victor Cox and I are hanging up, too," Illig said. "We all have a lot of work to do. The Health Department will take full responsibility for administration of the vaccines, and according to our legal interpretation, the hospital will have no liability for the side effects of the vaccines. We'll be sending our people to your hospital within a few hours. I think we should conduct another conference sometime tomorrow morning. If you would, call my office about eight o'clock to set it up."

"We'll be happy to do so," Lucas said.

The conference phone clicked, and the line went dead.

"I think we have a lot of work to do ourselves," Lucas said. "The decisions are to keep the patients here and move them to the ICU, start the smallpox protocol, close the hospital, and vaccinate everyone indicated when the CDC arrives. We can't let anyone into the hospital without special permission, and we can't let anyone leave. I think we can anticipate that a lot of the decisions will be taken out of our hands once the Health Department and the CDC arrive. Any questions?"

"So you're sure," Ness said, "that you want to close the hospital?"

"I think it's the best decision," Lucas said.

Ness stood and pounded his fist on the table. "I go on record right now against closing the hospital. These two patients should be transferred to Chicago." He pointed his finger at Lucas and Powell. "When the hospital is bankrupt, and you're scrambling for your jobs, I'll remind you of this."

"Mr. Ness," Powell said, "this is out of our hands."

"We'll just see about that," Ness said as he gathered up his coat and gloves. Just before reaching the door, he turned back to face them. "This conversation and this issue are *not* over!" he said. "That I promise!" The door slammed behind him as he left.

They all remained silent for several seconds, mostly in disbelief.

"He should tell us what he *really* thinks," Lucas said finally.

For a moment there was some nervous laughter.

Lucas looked around the room. "Any more questions?" he asked.

"Just have one," Perkins said.

"What's that?"

"Where are all these people going to sleep?"

"A good task for the director of nursing."

"Oh, thanks," she said. "Finding a place for all of them means I won't get much sleep."

Lucas gave her a quick salute. "Your dedication is appreciated in advance. Just don't use *my* room in the doctors' lounge, okay?" Lucas looked around the table. "If there's no further business...the meeting is adjourned."

Harry walked out into the hallway with Haleem. Many of the others stayed to talk, but Harry had talked enough.

"I'll bet things are going to get worse," Haleem said.

"I bet you're right," Harry said. "Probably worse than we can even imagine."

CHAPTER TWENTY ONE

DECEMBER 21, 11:30 P.M. CST
DAY ELEVEN OF THE SECOND WAVE OF EXPOSURE
DEKALB, ILLINOIS

The intensive care unit was ready for the Randalls. They would place Lauren in the negative pressure room since she was the sickest, and Kathy would be moved into the adjacent room. Engineering had sealed all the ducts in Kathy's room with plastic to prevent circulation of contaminated air. Harry and Haleem were personally overseeing the transfer. They decided to install an orthopedic frame over each of the beds and completely encase the beds with a plastic covering. After securing an elevator, they emptied the corridor in the ER and all the hallways between the second floor exit and the ICU. Everyone involved in the transfer wore the personal protection equipment, including Harry and Haleem.

Harry helped push Lauren's bed, and Haleem helped with Kathy's. Outside the elevator they stopped. Only one bed would fit in the elevator at a time. Lauren's bed went in first, and Harry rode up to the second floor with her. After exiting the elevator, they waited for Haleem and Kathy's bed. Once both patients reached the second floor, they were ready to push the beds to the ICU.

Harry walked down this second-floor hallway every day. Yet tonight, the hallway was completely different. All the doors were closed and sealed with tape. The nurses' station on this floor, normally abuzz with nurses and staff, was totally empty. They didn't see a soul. And except for the bed wheels squeaking and their footsteps echoing on the tile floor, there was no sound. Harry knew that the patients and nurses were there but separated from them by the walls and metal doors, protected from the deadly virus that was traveling down the hallway.

In a way, the trip was history in the making.

When they arrived in the unit, a full complement of adult and pediatric nurses and support staff were in the ICU, to Harry's pleasant surprise. Dressed in protective equipment, they took control of the beds and maneuvered them into the two rooms.

The head nurse, Janet Hernandez, greeted Harry. He had known her for ten years. She was fortyish, slender, with striking red hair. She was 100 percent Irish, she would say, notwithstanding her husband's Hispanic surname. Her husband was a good golfer, a two handicapper, and Harry had played with him numerous times.

"We'll get them in the rooms," she said, "unwrap these Christmas presents you brought us, and check their vital signs."

"I'm glad that you and your staff are taking this on," Harry said. "Everyone in here right now should be commended. I know all of you are a little uncertain and scared, but you're doing the right thing."

Janet shrugged her shoulders. "We'll see how these expensive masks work."

"I'll make sure that anyone who hasn't had a vaccine gets one as soon as the CDC arrives."

She nodded as she went into Lauren's room.

Haleem and Harry sat at the nurses' desk and watched as they prepared the patients, completing their nursing assessments and determining their current needs.

"They look worse, don't they?" Harry said. "Both of them."

"It's amazing how fast the rash is spreading," Haleem said. "What is worrying me is that I noticed one of Lauren's lesions had some blood in it."

"You think this is hemorrhagic smallpox?"

"Like I've ever seen a case. It could account for why this is progressing so rapidly. I gave them both the first dose of their antibiotic down in the emergency room. The big question now is do we start cidofovir?"

"What is that? I've never heard of it."

"I researched online and copied some information." Haleem handed Harry some papers. "It's an antiviral used for HIV, but it hasn't been used in smallpox, of course. Two problems: it may not help once their viral load is this high, and the second is that it is nephrotoxic."

"I think some kidney damage may be worth the risk right now."

"I would agree. We don't routinely stock it in the pharmacy here, so we'll have to order it in. I'm not even sure how fast we can get it."

"We're breaking new ground," Harry said. "No one has treated smallpox in half a century."

"In the morning I'm going to make some phone calls. We're going to need some help."

Harry glanced around to check that none of the staff was nearby. "I'm worried about the exposure to the employees," he said. "The Randalls' blood went to the lab without any special precautions."

"Smallpox isn't supposed to be passed in the blood. It's the surface of the transport tubes that I worry about. We'll need to double bag all of them. I'll call the lab and make sure they're absolutely prepared for additional specimens before we draw any more blood."

"We're really flying by the seat of our pants, aren't we?"

Janet stuck her head out of Lauren's room. "Lauren is looking sicker," she said. "I think one of you needs to come in and check her."

"Sure," Harry said, glancing at Haleem. "Be right there." He moved toward the doorway.

Janet stepped out and began removing her protective equipment. "They need several things," she said. "Both of them are vomiting, so we should give them something for that. We'll need an order for a pain med, too. What they gave them in the ER is wearing off. And they could use a sedative. They're going to wear out quickly."

"If you'll write those orders," Harry said, "I'll sign them in a second."

Janet nodded and stepped aside as Harry slipped on his protective equipment. He entered Lauren's room first. She was more lethargic but recognized Harry through the mask and smiled. Harry spoke in a soft, gentle voice while he examined her again. The rash was worse on her legs, but only a few vesicles were on her abdomen. He had read about the extreme cases where the pox lesions were extensive, including the mouth, the ear canals, the cornea, sometimes even the bronchial tubes, the esophagus, and the rectum. He thought about this being the fate of his two patients. Inflammation could occur in almost any of the body's organs—the brain, liver, or pancreas. And the list of complications was long: meningitis, pneumonia, encephalitis—all caused by the virus.

Harry lightly touched Lauren's face, and she closed her eyes. She must be exhausted, he thought.

The blood in one of the lesions on Lauren's face worried him the most. If she had hemorrhagic smallpox, she would probably die, despite all they did, despite the best of modern medicine. They would be helpless to stop the inevitable.

Harry listened to her heart and lungs; he gently pushed on her abdomen and found nothing different.

Kathy was next. After changing to a new set of protective gear, he went into her room.

"How's Lauren?" she asked.

"Seems to be settling in. She's sleeping right now."

"Good. She's so tired."

"Both of you need to get some sleep."

"Dr. Bennett, this is really very scary. Is everything going to be all right?"

Harry didn't want her to feel hopeless, but he also wanted to be honest. His philosophy in twenty-five years of family medicine was that truth dispensed with compassion was always the best approach.

"To be honest, Kathy, this is a very dangerous infection, and we'll do everything we can to help you and Lauren."

"I know you will, Dr. Bennett. Thank you."

Kathy's examination was unchanged. Her condition was more stable than Lauren's. Harry was much more worried about Lauren, not only because it could be hemorrhagic, but also because smallpox was tougher on kids.

He stepped back out into the hallway and placed his protective equipment in a special receptacle. Their smallpox plan had a process for disposal of the trash, the linens, the body fluids, and the wastes. If they missed one thing that spread the disease, a disaster would result. They had to think of everything.

Janet was at the desk charting on her nurse's progress notes when he sat down.

"Your staff is the best," Harry said.

She shrugged again. "It's what we do," she said. "We have serious infections up here all the time. What's the difference?"

She was a professional, and so was Harry, and he knew it had not seriously entered her mind to decline treating these patients. But this *was* different. This was smallpox, and she and Harry both knew that this day would change their lives forever.

* * *

Lucas posted a sign on both the inside and outside of the main entrance to the hospital and locked the door, the last of all the entrances to be secured. The hospital was closed. Powell had arranged for additional security guards and had positioned one at each door. They had not as yet encountered any resistance.

"That went well," Lucas said.

"Better than I expected," Powell said.

The security guard pointed to the sign. "Do you want me to have them read that or just tell them what's on it?"

"Either way," Powell said.

The guard read the sign slowly. "By orders of the Illinois State Health Department. An infectious disease emergency."

"Right," Lucas said.

"What is that, Doc?"

"We're worried about an infection in the hospital, so we're closing it."

"Oh," the guard said, still a puzzled look on his face. "Then, is it dangerous?"

"We hope not," Lucas said. "Just a precaution."

"So don't let anybody in or out, okay?" Powell said.

"Okay," the guard said, "that's what I'll do."

An elderly couple was sitting across the lobby. While the three of them were talking, the couple made their way toward them. The old man looked like he was eighty. He was using a cane and walked with a decided limp, as if his hip was completely deteriorated. The woman was every bit as old, and she wore dark, wraparound glasses. She clung to the old man's arm. It was hard to tell whether he was her guide or she was his balance.

The couple walked past them, and the old man pushed on the door, attempting to open it. When it wouldn't budge, he began rattling the door back and forth.

"Excuse me. Excuse me," the guard said several times until the rattling stopped. "The hospital is closed."

The old man held his hand up to his ear. "What?" he said loudly.

The guard cupped his hands around the man's ear. "The hospital is closed!" he yelled.

"What?" the old man said. "I can't hear you."

"We need to go home," the woman said, "and the door seems to be broken. I'm late for my insulin."

Lucas and Powell looked at each other.

"Let them out," Powell said to the guard.

"I thought we were closed," the guard said.

"We are," Powell responded, "but go ahead and let them out."

"Whatever you say," the guard said. "You're confusing me."

"But no more exceptions," Lucas said.

The guard shook his head, and let them out. Lucas and Powell watched a few seconds as the old couple walked away down the sidewalk.

"This may not be as easy as we think," Lucas said.

Powell shrugged his shoulders. "The tough stuff never is."

* * *

Harry slid out of his clothes and slipped into bed in a sleeping room next to the doctors' lounge. He hadn't prepared to spend the night again at the hospital, and he had brought nothing with him—no toothbrush, toiletries, or fresh clothes. Fortunately, the hospital had some personal items, but he would have to wear the same wrinkled clothes in the morning. On the way to the hospital he had called Maureen on his cell, but he hadn't talked to her since. She would probably be in bed by now but would worry if he didn't call. He propped himself up on pillows and dialed the phone. After a couple of rings, Maureen picked up. Her voice was sleepy. He had awakened her.

"I'm sorry to call so late," he said softly.

"Are you still at the hospital?"

"Yes. Lauren and Kathy Randall are really sick, and we have a serious emergency here. I'm going to have to spend the night in the call room."

"You sound worried. Is everything all right?"

"I'm fine. Just some very sick patients. I'll call you in the morning."

"That'd be good."

"Sorry to wake you."

"You didn't. I was awake."

He knew better. She was being sweet.

"I love you, Harry."

"Love you, too, Maureen."

Harry hung up the phone and switched off the lamp. The room was dark, but the light from the lounge slipped under the doorway, reflecting on the shiny tile floor. Usually, he was the only one in the call rooms, except maybe for an obstetrician or another family doctor. Tonight, he heard soft voices in the lounge outside. Perkins would probably utilize any empty bed anywhere in the hospital, which was fine with him. Lucas was in the room next door, and Harry could hear him snoring through the wall. He hoped the snoring wouldn't keep him awake. He needed some sleep tonight.

It had been an incredible day. He could not have dreamed up a worse scenario. Precious little Lauren Randall diagnosed with smallpox and growing worse every hour. Her mother was ill as well. Yet with all the advances of modern medicine, there was absolutely nothing he could do that would cure either of them. This helpless feeling was what the doctors and healers had felt for centuries: standing by with ineffectual remedies as their patients were ravished by smallpox; watching powerless while the victims died in front of them; witnessing a family's devastation; and burying those they knew, young and old, healthy and infirm, who didn't deserve such an awful destiny.

He stared at the ceiling and felt the tears well up in his eyes. The nightmare that everyone had been dreading was happening. And he was in the middle of it.

When the announcement was made tomorrow, the panic would begin, and it would all be worse.

* * *

The phone rang at two A.M. and startled Harry awake.

"Dr. Bennett?"

Janet was calling from the ICU. He could hear the stress in her voice.

"Yes," he said as he switched on the light.

"You need to come up here right now."

"Are the Randalls okay?"

"It's not about their medical condition. That hasn't changed. There are some army people demanding to see them. I refused to let them in. They've got guns. Now they're demanding to speak to you."

"Call security. I'll be right there."

Harry hung up the phone, quickly dressed, and hurried to the second-floor ICU. As he rounded the corner and entered the unit, Harry saw the nurses standing in front of the Randalls' rooms in a line of defiance, their arms folded across their chests. Across from the nurses, closest to him, stood four men in military uniforms. Each of the men carried a holstered Beretta 9mm pistol, and one was holding an M-16 rifle.

"I'm Dr. Bennett, the attending physician," Harry said as he approached. "Can I help you?"

The four men turned around. Three of the men were white males wearing uniforms that denoted their status as officers. The soldier with the M-16 was an intimidating African American male and looked like a TV commercial for the U.S. Army. He moved behind the officers and stood at the ready. The officer in the middle stepped forward toward Harry. He extended his hand, and at first Harry thought he was offering to shake hands, but instead he was holding out an envelope. Harry let him hold it in the air without taking it.

"How can I help you gentlemen?"

"I'm Colonel Fredrickson. I am a physician with the U.S. Army Medical Corps, Fort Detrick, Maryland, and I have been authorized to obtain specimens from two of your patients, Lauren Randall and Kathy Randall." He never dropped his arm. "These are our orders."

The two officers on each side of Fredrickson were captains, and they didn't speak. They wore camouflage battle dress uniforms with the Army's Medical Corps insignias on the collars. The soldier behind them was a staff sergeant, and he hardly blinked. His M-16 spoke to the seriousness of their request.

Harry took the envelope and opened it. Inside was a one-page letter addressed to him personally and signed by General Andrew Wykoff, whose name meant nothing to Harry. The letter looked official—it was on U.S. Army letterhead and signed by a general. But Harry thought it odd that there was no address or location identified. The request was written in polite and formal language and to the point, asking permission, not demanding. A request, Harry thought. That was the reason they sent four armed men to deliver it.

"I guess I'm just confused," Harry said. "Where are you sending these specimens?"

"I'm not at liberty to say, sir."

"And you'll send us the results when the tests are completed?"

"Your results will come through the CDC."

"So *we* won't know the results?"

"Like I said, your results will come through the CDC."

The military had likely been alerted, Harry thought, as soon as the CDC or a state health department was notified of smallpox. He just hadn't anticipated the arrival of the military, and especially so quickly.

"We're happy to help in any way we can, Colonel," Harry said.

"Dr. Thomason," the colonel said, nodding to the captain on his left, "will obtain the specimens. Would it be possible to use your protective equipment?"

"Nurse Hernandez, would you please provide the doctor with those items? I'll be going in with him."

"If you must, Doctor," the colonel said.

Harry heard a little annoyance in his voice.

"I insist," Harry said.

Both men slipped on gowns, gloves, and masks. Harry led him into Kathy Randall's room first. She was awake, lying on her back with a white sheet covering her from the neck down, her arms out of the bedding. The rash now covered her face and upper arms with blisters. She was very anxious and fidgeted constantly in bed; the sedatives were only helping slightly.

"Kathy," Harry said, "this man needs a specimen. He's going to remove some fluid from one of your lesions, if that's okay."

She nodded.

Thomason laid a plastic container about the size of a large book on the table next to the bed and folded it open. It was labeled Biohazardous Materials. He removed three microscopic slides and three clear plastic tubes and laid them out side by side on the table. The kit also contained a syringe for blood and a tourniquet, a scalpel, and some material for dressings.

"This shouldn't hurt at all," Thomason said.

The officer held the scalpel in his right hand and moved it close to her face. She watched him closely as the scalpel approached. Skillfully and gently he unroofed one of the blisters on her face and expressed the fluid on one of the slides. After allowing it to air dry for a couple of minutes, he placed it in a clear plastic sleeve and slid it into the container. He repeated the procedure two more times, opening a different vesicle each time. Next he opened a package of cotton-tipped swabs, unroofed another lesion, and rubbed one of the swabs along the surface, soaking up the fluid. He stuffed the swab into one of the tubes, snapped off the swab's plastic shaft, then screwed on the lid. He repeated this procedure twice more. Finally, he drew blood into three vials. He gathered up the vials and all of his supplies and placed them in the container.

"Thank you, Mrs. Randall," Thomason said. "We appreciate your assistance."

Thomason checked to see if all the specimens were marked, and then he closed the container. He opened the door to the exam room and held the container out. The second captain was holding open a larger bag, and Thomason dropped it in. The second officer closed his bag and then dropped it into a silver metal case. He closed and locked the case. Thomason removed his protective equipment and then replaced it with new equipment before moving to Lauren's room. Harry did the same.

Lauren was more lethargic than she had been earlier. Harry hoped it was a reaction to the sedative and not the illness. He explained to Lauren what they were planning. Thomason repeated the entire process with a new container. He obtained the fluid for the three slides and for the three tubes. After placing the tourniquet around Lauren's upper right arm, he picked up the blood vial and held it in his right hand.

"Okay, Lauren," he said softly. "I'm going to draw some blood now."

Lauren's eyes opened widely and she began screaming. "No, no, no," she yelled. "Please, no blood, please, please, *please...*" Lauren jerked her arm away, out of the grasp of Thomason and began thrashing around in the bed.

Her reaction caught both of them off guard.

"Lauren," Harry said, attempting to reassure her, "we need to draw some blood."

"No, no, *noooooo...*"

Now her voice pitched up an octave and she began jerking back and forth. Thomason caught her arm and pushed it down on the bed, positioning the needle above the vein he intended to pierce. Lauren's eyes were wild with fright, and she began pulling her arm away. Thomason held tight and made a quick stab. He missed the vein, and she screamed again.

"We should wait," Harry said. "You're hurting her."

Thomason was preparing another attempt. Lauren was thrashing wildly in the bed, but Thomason would not relinquish his grip. Harry heard Kathy next door, and the nurses outside the room, asking them what was wrong.

Harry moved next to Thomason. "Please stop," Harry said firmly. "That's enough!"

"I'll be done in a second," he said, not looking up. Thomason started to push the needle into her arm again.

With a quick, sudden blow, Harry rammed him with his arm, knocking him backward away from Lauren. Thomason took a step back, lost his balance, and fell to the floor. He jumped up instantly and grabbed Harry by his chest.

"You bastard!" he yelled in Harry's face.

Thomason had both of his hands on Harry's gown, pushing him backward. Harry felt his feet sliding out from under him.

"Captain!" Colonel Fredrickson was in the doorway, holding open the door. He was not wearing a gown or mask. "Stand down, Thomason."

"He was interfering—"

"I said stand down! And that's an order!"

Thomason released Harry but gave him a quick shove when he did so. Harry almost punched him.

"This is ridiculous!" Harry said as he moved toward Fredrickson, pointing his finger at his face. "I refuse to allow any more specimens. I don't care how many generals order it."

By now the nurses were in the doorway. If there was going to be a fight, Harry wouldn't be alone.

"I think, Dr. Bennett," Fredrickson said, "that we have all the specimens we need. Captain, bring the container here. You'll not be drawing any blood."

"Yes, sir," Thomason said. He wasn't happy.

"Don't you touch my baby."

The voice came from behind them. Outside in the hallway, Kathy Randall was standing by herself, wearing only a hospital gown, her IV pulled out, a thin stream of blood trickling down her arm. She was as pale as a ghost.

"You leave my baby alone!" she said. "You leave her alone!"

The nurses turned to help her, but before they could, her eyes rolled upward in her head, and she collapsed on the floor.

* * *

"Frank?" Harry knocked softly on the door. "Frank, it's Dr. Bennett." The nurses had found Frank an empty room a few doors down the hallway. They had insisted he try to sleep. Technically, Frank was in isolation, though he didn't have a rash or fever. Harry thought it best, considering his certain exposure.

Harry realized Frank may have heard the commotion in Lauren's room, and even if he hadn't, Frank deserved an explanation. Harry knocked again but didn't hear a response, so he cracked open the door.

"Frank, it's Dr. Bennett. I need to talk to you."

Frank was sitting in a chair. He was bent over with his hands covering his face. The room was dark, except for the soft light from a table lamp next to the bed.

"Sorry to disturb you, Frank."

Frank looked up at Harry. "That's all right," he said as he sat up. His eyes were red. "How are they?"

Harry pulled up a chair next to him. "I wanted to talk to you about Lauren."

Frank slid to the edge of his seat. "What's going on?"

"She's having some problems," Harry said, "and I wanted to update you."

Frank sighed in relief. Harry realized Frank was expecting worse news. Harry felt a jab in his stomach. Unfortunately, that could come later.

"We had to sedate her heavily," Harry said gently. "She was becoming delirious. She seems to be more comfortable now, though she cries out occasionally in pain. I've ordered the nurses to treat her whenever she seems to be uncomfortable."

"Thank you, Dr. Bennett."

Frank was looking down at the floor. Harry could see the tears welling up in his eyes.

"I'm worried that she may be developing pneumonia," Harry said. "Her respirations have increased, and her breathing seems more shallow. I've ordered a chest X-ray and some more blood work. I'll have Dr. Byrd, he's a lung specialist, here in the morning."

"Will he see her?"

"What do you mean?"

"You know, with the smallpox."

"Of course he will!"

"I wasn't sure."

"I don't think that will be a problem with any of the doctors I ask to help. I also wanted to tell you, Frank, that the military was here a few minutes ago and took some specimens."

"They did?"

"I was with your wife and that went smoothly, but when they tried to draw Lauren's blood, she became very upset, and I had them stop. But your wife heard her and came out of her room. She was so weak she passed out on the floor. She's okay."

Frank's expression did not change. Harry was wondering if he was listening or was in his own world, thinking of his wife and daughter, and possibly of their future. For several minutes, Frank did not speak. Harry did not rush him.

"Don't let anybody," he said finally, "hurt my family."

Frank's tears began to flow freely. He covered his face with his hands, leaned forward, and sobbed. Harry reached out and gently touched his shoulder.

"That's a promise, Frank," Harry said. "That's a promise."

It was several minutes before Frank was ready to ask a few questions, and Harry answered all of them. Frank understood how serious the situation was.

When Harry stepped back out into the hallway, Janet was walking toward him.

"Dr. Lucas needs you in the emergency room," she said. "He asked me to come get you."

"Did he say what it was about?"

"No, just that it was urgent."

"Okay, I'm on my pager. Call me if you need anything at all."

"You know I will."

Harry left the intensive care unit for the emergency room and was about halfway there when he caught up with Lucas walking down the hallway. Lucas was moving fast and looked upset.

"Solomon called me," Lucas said, somewhat out of breath, "and said there is some ruckus going on, and he needs our help."

"You can't handle it yourself?" Harry asked as he came abreast of him. "You're really slipping."

"I was thinking about slipping," Lucas said, "right out to my cabin at the lake."

"You won't be the only one when the word gets out. It's going to be pretty crazy around here."

"I heard you assaulted an Army officer."

"He ticked me off."

"The nurses think you're a hero."

"I don't know what the heck I was doing. The man was armed."

"They told me they came in a convoy of Humvees and pulled into the circle drive."

"So much for being subtle."

Rounding the corner to the emergency room, they saw a group of about thirty people massed just inside the entrance to the hospital. Powell, the administrator, stood precariously between the crowd and freedom, attempting to block their exit. He had his arms forward, pleading with them. The security guard stood next to Powell, his right hand resting lightly on his gun.

"Please be patient," Powell said. "We need for everyone to step away from the door and go back to bed. We have an emergency situation, and we will provide more information in the morning."

A young man with a scraggly beard, wearing a gray sweatshirt and a ball cap turned backward, stood closest to Powell. "I'm supposed to be on the job in an hour," he said. "If I don't leave now, I'm going to lose my job."

"We'll notify your employer."

"That won't do one damned bit of good," he responded sharply. "They'll just fire me."

A middle-aged woman moved in front of Powell. "I have two teenagers at home by themselves," she said. "You don't understand."

A big, burly male in the back yelled out, "We want to know *right now* what's going on. We don't want to wait until morning."

A chorus of agreement rose up. The crowd surged forward.

"Wait a minute. Wait a minute," Lucas yelled, holding his arms up in the air. "Please listen to me."

The crowd turned to face him.

"We have an emergency here," Lucas said. "*No one* can leave."

Lucas's statement caused an angry reaction, and the crowd began pushing back toward the exit.

"People, people," Harry heard himself say. "I am Dr. Harry Bennett. I am a family medicine doctor here. We *do* have an infectious disease emergency. Please, everyone, listen."

The crowd stopped and turned toward Harry.

"We're not sure what we have yet," he said, "but we really need to keep everyone here until we find out if, and I said *if*, there is any danger at all."

"We have homes to go to," a man yelled.

"I have family at home," Harry said, "and I'm staying here. So are the other doctors and administrators. The patients who are sick are my patients. You may have been exposed, and you may need medication or a vaccine." Harry pointed to the woman who spoke. "Would you want to take this home to your children?" He pointed to the man who needed to be at work. "Would you want to make your coworkers ill? The State Health Department is coming in a few hours. We'll find out as quickly as we can what we need to do. It's not just for *your* benefit but for the benefit of your families and our community that we are doing this."

"First thing in the morning?" the woman with the teenagers asked. "You promise?"

"First thing in the morning." Harry spoke with confidence. He hoped it was true.

The crowd slowly began to disperse. When they were gone, Powell crossed over to Harry and Lucas.

"Good job, Harry," Powell said.

Lucas patted Harry on the back. "You're a politician!"

"Let's not get tacky," Harry said.

"I'm calling the police department," Powell said. "Should have done it earlier. We need the police at each of our entrances."

"Look out there," the security guard said, motioning to them as he stood by the entrance.

The three of them stepped to the doorway and looked outside. In the circular drive in front of the building a CNN news truck had just pulled up, and the bright lights of a camera illuminated the front of the hospital. A story was breaking, and the media vultures were beginning to circle.

CHAPTER TWENTY TWO

DECEMBER 22, 7:00 a.m. EST
DAY TWENTY-ONE OF THE FIRST WAVE OF EXPOSURE
WASHINGTON, DC

The morning sunlight cracked through the window, creating a soft glow in Al-Sabai's hotel room, but he didn't move. He had slept fitfully and had hoped the curtains would shut out the light, but they hadn't, and he was awake again, just minutes after dozing off. During the night, any movement of his body caused excruciating pain, interrupting his chance to sleep. His muscles and joints ached terribly. He had vomited twice. The smallpox lesions on his face and arms were slowly accumulating, changing from the red spots to blisters as he had expected. He still only had a few, but he knew there would be more.

Mohammed's instructions were for him to leave the room and infect the Americans, but he wasn't so sure he could. And maybe he didn't want to.

He felt sick...finally. It had taken much longer than he had expected. Mohammed had said about two weeks, but for him it had been nearly three. Now was the time he needed to be walking around, riding the subway, and mingling with the crowds.

Al-Sabai had prayed to Allah five times a day, praying for strength and for wisdom, praying to do Allah's will. This morning, he had decided he would pray from his bed. He was too weak to get up, may Allah forgive him.

He had been among the Americans, those who resisted Allah and his messenger, as he had always been taught. At the beginning in Cairo, Mohammed said that it was the defeatists and hypocrites who waivered from the divine orders. The messenger's principles were not open to negotiation or compromise. To fail was disgrace.

Yet the clerics taught that Islam is a peaceful faith. Isn't Islam for all nations?

What must he do? Should he leave or should he stay?

Yes, the Americans resist Allah. Now, do I?

Al-Sabai pulled the pillow over his head to shut out the light. If he could fall asleep again, he'd feel better.

Maybe in a dream Allah's will would become clearer. He prayed it would.

* * *

DECEMBER 22, 6:00 A.M. CST
DAY TWELVE OF THE SECOND WAVE OF EXPOSURE
DEKALB, ILLINOIS

Harry was up and had showered before the alarm on his watch went off at six. He had slept relatively well, not much different than most call nights. After receiving a couple of calls on the Randalls, he was awakened by a nurse who had a cancer patient die on the floor. Since the hospital was closed and the patient's personal physician couldn't come into the hospital, Harry was called in to pronounce the patient dead. The family was upset that the body couldn't be removed to the funeral home and that they couldn't leave. It was one of the many dilemmas the hospital administration would be facing.

He called Maureen and talked with his two daughters. They were preparing for school. His daughters missed him, they said, but he was sure he missed them more. Maureen was in a good mood. He'd better be alone in that call room, Maureen joked with him. She was the prettiest nurse in the hospital, he joked back. He wondered how many days his only contact with his family would be by phone.

His schedule at the office was full. He called Jill O'Dell at home and had her cancel the patients or shift them to his partners. After only a couple of weeks back from vacation, he was dumping the load on them again. It couldn't be helped.

When Harry arrived at the intensive care unit, he found a table with a security guard at the entrance. The guard knew Harry and waved him through. Limiting access to this area was important, and Harry was glad Powell had thought of this, especially with a news media truck parked outside. Four nurses were standing at the nurses' station, and he suspected that none of them had slept at all. Eventually, the staff rotation for the care of these patients would be an issue. The nurses reported that Kathy was worse, but that Lauren was holding her own. Lauren's fever had dropped, and she was feeling somewhat better. After gowning and gloving, he slipped on the mask and went into Lauren's room first. A large number of new blisters covered her face. He noticed quickly that her arms and legs were also much worse, with a lesser number on her abdomen and back. This was a common distribution for smallpox. She had lesions in her ear canals and nostrils and inside her mouth.

"Hi, Dr. Bennett." Her voice was hoarse, so she likely had lesions on her vocal cords.

"Good morning, Lauren. How are you feeling?"

"Not so good."

"We're giving you some medicine that we hope will help."

"The nurses are nice, but I'm ready to go home."

Her voice was sweetness, the voice of a precious, innocent six-year-old. Harry felt a deep sadness. "We're all hoping that will be soon."

What worried Harry the most was how dense the lesions were on her face. Several appeared to be coalescing, and he counted three blisters that were filled with blood. The changes were consistent with hemorrhagic smallpox, and though, of course, he had never seen a case, he knew it was invariably fatal.

As he left Lauren's room, he removed his protective equipment, washed his hands, and regowned and gloved, hoping to avoid any cross-contamination between mother and daughter, though they likely had the same illness. Kathy was much worse than when he had seen her last. Her face was covered with vesicles, and she also had more on her arms and legs. She was sitting in bed, leaning forward, breathing rapidly, and almost panting as if desperate for her next breath. She appeared panicked, her eyes wide and darting back and forth. Harry didn't like that look.

"How is…Lauren?" she asked between gasps.

He wasn't surprised that her first concern was her daughter, even as sick as she was.

"I think she's a little better today. Her fever is down. How are you feeling?"

"I'm not feeling so good."

He listened as she relayed her symptoms.

"Do you think this is smallpox, Dr. Bennett?"

"We expect the CDC here any minute. They'll be the ones who help us confirm this."

"I'm sorry about this morning."

"What's that?"

"You know, with the military man and Lauren."

"No, that's my fault. I should have had the nurses draw her blood."

"I think I contaminated everyone," she said.

Harry reached out his gloved hand and touched her arm. "Kathy," he said gently, making contact with her eyes, "I would have done exactly the same thing."

When Harry left Kathy's room, Haleem was at the nurses' station.

"You don't look like you got much sleep," Harry said as he sat down next to him.

"I didn't. I spent most of the night on the Internet. There's basically no information in the last thirty years on the treatment of smallpox, which of course is understandable because everyone thought the disease was eradicated from the face of the earth. We have no idea which antivirals, if any, are helpful. We have no experience treating the complications with modern antibiotics, which of course didn't exist back then. I'm not sure our safety precautions have been adequately tested for a respiratory-based virus as vicious as this one is. The universal precautions we use are mostly directed at blood-borne infections. This is respiratory, and it looks like it can spread through the ventilation system. When they had the last cases in Africa, they didn't have central forced heat and air like we do. The virus can live on bedding, towels, and clothes for weeks. I was reading about cases of smallpox that weren't diagnosed by doctors who saw smallpox frequently. I saw where patients had been sent to smallpox hospitals but were found to have measles. Then they contracted smallpox in the hospital and died. All this seemed theoretical until now. I can think of a hundred problems with our smallpox protocol that I hadn't given one second of thought about before."

"I think Lauren's is hemorrhagic," Harry said. "She has more bloody lesions."

"That's bad. You know the prognosis."

"Yes, and I think it's likely Kathy has the same strain."

"It wouldn't surprise me. I expect the CDC to be here shortly. I hope we benefit from their assistance, but to be honest, they may not know much more than we do."

"Any help will be appreciated."

"Dr. Bennett," Janet said, "Mr. Randall is in his room, waiting for you."

Harry's heart was heavy as he walked the hallway to Frank's room. At some point he would need to prepare Frank but at the same time not destroy his hope. He could lose his wife and daughter, and soon. Harry would have to choose his words carefully.

Frank was sitting in a chair in the corner of his room. Normally, friends, cow-orkers, and/or church members would surround the families of ICU patients, but Frank was alone. With the hospital closed and no visitors, the social isolation for him approached cruelty. Frank looked up expectantly as Harry entered.

"Lauren seems to be holding her own," Harry said. He sat on the bed next to Frank. "Her fever is down, and she is more alert and less anxious. Kathy's rash is worse, though, and I'm worried about her breathing. She seems to be struggling a little more."

He appeared to take the news well and asked a few questions.

"They haven't let me in to see them. I feel stuck here in this room."

"The nurses are so busy with them now. I'm sure you can visit in a little while."

"I shouldn't be contagious until I break out in a rash, isn't that right?"

"That's correct."

"And I've been exposed already, right? So if I get into the gown, gloves, and mask and I can't expose anyone else, what harm would it do? I should be in there with my family. What good is it that I wait?"

He had a point, Harry thought.

Harry nodded his head. "I'll see what I can do. How are you feeling?"

"My back's a little sore, but that could be this bed. No other symptoms...yet."

It was the *yet* that worried Harry, too. "I hope that's all it is," Harry said. "Let me know if you begin to feel worse."

Harry stood to leave.

"Dr. Bennett," Frank said, "assuming it's smallpox, what's the prognosis?"

Harry's mind flashed back to the slides at the conference, the terrible scars on the faces of the survivors, the picture of the beautiful young girl blinded, and the eyes of the children dying. "It's hard to answer," Harry said gently. "But even before our antivirals, strong antibiotics, and improved technology, the majority of smallpox victims survived." Harry could see his relief. "But Frank, let me tell you something. If it is smallpox, this is a serious illness, and you must be prepared for the worst."

Frank looked down and a tear flowed down his cheek.

"If this is smallpox," Harry continued, "the situation at the hospital will be confusing and complicated, but I promise you my top priority will be the medical care of your family." Harry's voice dropped softly. "I have a wife and two twelve-year-old daughters."

Frank looked up at him. "Yes, I know. My wife told me. Thank you, Dr. Bennett."

"You're welcome." Harry felt like crying, too.

* * *

The meeting in the boardroom started at eight, and Harry saw that all the same players were there: Powell, Lucas, Perkins, Steidley, public relations, Phillips, legal counsel, and Owens, the hospital engineer. Everyone was supposed to have spent the night at the hospital, and from each person's crumpled clothes and disheveled appearance, everyone must have. As Harry entered, Lucas was talking to a man he didn't recognize at the head of the table. He wore a black business suit, sharply pressed, with a red tie, dressed like a banker or a lawyer.

"As you are aware," Lucas began, "the hospital is secured. Police are guarding all entrances and exits. We did have one arrest. A young man who was insisting he would lose his job if he didn't leave tried to push his way out, even after we offered to call his employer. He was arrested, but he is in a lockup here in the hospital. We have talked with the CDC this morning. They are on the ground in Chicago and are being transported here as we speak; we anticipate their arrival in a few minutes. It may not have been necessary to lock down the hospital, but we'll get to that in a moment. The rumors are rampant. Two major news agencies arrived early this morning and demanded entry for interviews. We refused. However, a report is already out that we closed the hospital because of smallpox and that it is spreading rapidly throughout the hospital and killing everyone. After the CDC arrives, we'll hopefully issue a press release." He nodded at Steidley. "Keith is working on it now."

Lucas motioned to the man in the business suit. He stood and approached the lectern.

"I want to introduce Gary Roberts," Lucas said. "He's with the FBI's division on bioterrorism and arrived this morning from Atlanta. Good morning, Agent Roberts, and welcome."

"Thank you," Roberts said. He waited for a moment as Lucas took his seat. "Dr. Lucas and Mr. Powell were kind enough to update me on the situation here. Though it is yet to be confirmed, we are going to assume this is smallpox. The FBI considers smallpox to be an agent of terrorism until proven otherwise, and the FBI assumes jurisdiction for domestic terrorism. Thus, I am beginning a criminal investigation. Of course, no one at the hospital is a suspect, but I do ask for everyone's cooperation. I understand the two victims' attending physician, Dr. Bennett, is here." Roberts looked around the room. Harry raised his hand. "Good. Dr. Bennett, I'll be interviewing the victims after this meeting."

"Mr. Roberts," Harry spoke up, "with all due respect, one of the *patients* is a six-year-old girl and the other is really too sick to be interviewed."

"I understand, Doctor, but this *is* a matter of national security. Surely, a few minutes."

Of course Harry realized it was important, but he couldn't see how Lauren could be helpful. Kathy was probably too sedated and if her condition deteriorated much more, might soon be on a ventilator and unable to talk at all. "It'll have to be brief," Harry said.

"That's fine."

Harry had the sense it didn't matter what he thought. Roberts would do as he pleased.

"Once the CDC is here," Roberts continued, "I think we can begin to allow the visitors and nonessential staff to leave. We have a window of four days from the time of exposure to vaccinate, and I would imagine the CDC will bring plenty of vaccine with them. We should be able to list the names and numbers of the contacts, vaccinate them, and let them leave. Those who refuse or who are unable to be vaccinated for some reason pose a different problem. We may need to quarantine them somewhere. I doubt you want to house and feed all those people."

"We've probably violated all sorts of civil rights," Phillips, the legal counsel, said. "Any advice?"

"I'm not the person to ask," Roberts said.

"I called the governor's office early this morning," Powell said, "hoping they could declare a state of emergency or something, but they're reluctant until the 'situation is clarified.' In the meantime, we're left hanging. Of course, the hospital is relying on our medical staff to guide us."

Harry wasn't sure what Powell meant, but the tone seemed to implicate Haleem and him. If it wasn't smallpox and the hospital violated someone's rights, could it be his fault for misguiding them? Is that what he was saying? Harry didn't like the sound of that. If it *was* smallpox, though, the issue would be irrelevant.

"I put in a call to the Illinois attorney general's office for some guidance," Phillips said. "Surely, we'd have some latitude."

"If this *is* smallpox," Roberts said, "you've acted promptly, and I can't believe it would be a problem."

But then again, Harry thought, what if it wasn't smallpox?

"The chairman of the hospital board," Lucas said, "was insisting we move the two patients to a Chicago Hospital."

Harry noticed for the first time that Eric Ness wasn't in the meeting. He had probably slept in his own bed.

"That would have been a bad idea," Roberts said. "I would think isolation even in less-than-ideal circumstances is better than the chance of exposures during transportation. I'll be updating the FBI director in Washington in a few minutes. In regards to your closing the hospital, I'll have him call the U.S. attorney general."

Phillips piped up. "I'm not sure that there is any federal jurisdiction on that particular issue. This is probably a state matter."

"Domestic terrorism," Roberts said, "is federal, so this is a federal case nonetheless, and I'm extending that jurisdiction to all related matters." He looked up at Harry. "I'm ready to interview your patients now."

Lucas wrapped up the meeting, and before they adjourned, all agreed to meet daily. As they broke up, Roberts approached Harry.

"I know you're reluctant," Roberts said, "and I'll be brief and respect your concerns, but it is critical that I gather as much information from them as possible. It could save a lot of lives. And it sounds like, if they're getting worse, that we may not have much time."

Harry escorted Roberts to the intensive care unit. Roberts wanted to see Kathy first. Before Harry could assist him with putting on the personal protective equipment, Roberts was nearly ready. At least, Harry thought, he appeared to have some experience in isolation techniques.

Roberts turned to him. "I'm going in alone. This is a criminal investigation."

"I don't care," Harry said. "I'm going in with you."

"No, it's not allowed. You know, national security."

"These are my patients, and I am responsible for them. I'm sure you understand."

"Dr. Bennett, with all due respect—"

"I let the army in. I won't do it again."

"I'm not drawing blood."

How would Roberts know about that? "No, you won't," Harry snapped. "And you won't be going in without me either."

Roberts remained firm. "I'll get a court order if I need to."

"Then get one. How long will that take?"

"Okay, Doctor," he said sharply, pointing his finger at Harry. "You can come in, but I don't want to hear a peep out of you."

Harry glanced at Roberts's sidearm, and he knew he was pushing. It was the second time Harry had challenged an armed man in the last few hours. "I don't want to make the FBI mad at me, but if *my patients* wear out or become too weak, I *will* peep and the interview *will* be over."

Roberts rolled his eyes. "Okay, Dr. Bennett, come on in. You're more than welcome. I won't draw blood, and I won't cause a problem. Satisfied?"

Harry heard clapping behind him. The nurses were applauding. He shrugged his shoulders and put on his protective equipment.

As they entered the room, Roberts coughed and instinctively covered his mouth, though it was already covered with his mask. The smell was peculiar, Harry thought. Roberts probably had never smelled or seen anything like this. But then again, neither had he.

Kathy Randall looked terrible. Her breathing was rapid and shallow. The rash was dramatically worse, now covering nearly every square inch of her face. She was very restless, unable to lie still, but she also appeared sedated and mentally confused. She didn't seem to grasp who Roberts was when he introduced himself, or what he was doing there. Initially her answers were garbled, but as Roberts continued, she seemed to clear a bit. Still, she didn't seem to remember many details.

"Any exposure to vapors or powders?"

No, she couldn't remember.

"Any odd tastes, smell, or odors?"

No, none that she could recall.

"Travel outside the country?"

No, never.

Roberts paused a moment. "Have you noticed any strangers get especially close to you," he asked, "uncomfortably close, especially anyone of Middle Eastern descent?"

At first she didn't answer.

"Anyone? Anywhere?" Roberts repeated.

"Dr. Haleem." Her voice was soft, weak.

Roberts looked up at Harry.

"He's our infectious disease specialist here," Harry said.

Roberts turned back to Kathy. "Did you see Dr. Haleem before coming to the hospital?"

"No."

"Any others?"

She thought a moment. "In Chicago."

Roberts perked up. "Chicago? Tell me about Chicago."

Kathy related the story about their shopping trip, her speech broken into phrases by her labored breathing. She told them about the man who stepped out of the taxi and vomited on the sidewalk right in front of them, about the blood, and how they went back into the Crate & Barrel to wash off their shoes. As she continued, she grew weaker, her strength fading.

"What did this man look like?"

"I don't know," she said. "I only saw him...for a second."

"Any body features you remember?"

"No."

"Did he say anything?"

"Something like 'excuse me' is all...then he threw up...and pushed his way back into the taxi."

"Do you remember the taxi company?"

"I don't know."

"Mr. Roberts," Harry said. "She's getting tired."

"Just a couple more. This is important. Try to remember the taxi company."

"I don't know."

"What color was it?"

Kathy closed her eyes and didn't answer.

"Mr. Roberts," Harry said again. "I'm not sure she can continue. You need to finish."

"Sorry, Doctor, just another one or two, then I'm done. Please, Mrs. Randall, anything you can remember. Anything at all. It's very important."

"I think it was yellow," she said, not opening her eyes. "Yes, it was yellow."

Even Roberts could see she was exhausted. "Thank you, Mrs. Randall," he said. "You've been very helpful."

After they left Kathy's room, Roberts decided not to interview Lauren. She was sound asleep, and Roberts was doubtful she could add anything of value. Instead, he left the unit to interview Frank Randall and make a phone call. Harry sat at the desk to complete a progress note in both charts. To put into writing a description of the seriousness of their situation was discouraging. Harry wished it weren't so.

"Dr. Bennett, I presume."

A tall, slender male stood across the counter from him. He was holding out his hand.

"I'm Mike Lafitte from the CDC," he said as they shook hands. "Dr. Jackson sends his regards."

Lafitte introduced his team of six, and they spent the next hour examining the patients, collecting samples, and taking digital photographs. After a brief meeting with his cohorts, Lafitte called together Harry, Haleem, and Lucas. They met in an empty room not far from the ICU.

"The first samples are on their way to Atlanta," Lafitte said, "and we've e-mailed the pictures to Dr. Jackson. The samples at USAMRIID confirm it's an orthopox, but your tests already showed that."

"USAMRIID?" Harry asked.

"U.S. Army Medical Research Institute of Infectious Disease. That's a mouthful. It's at Fort Detrick, Maryland. From our exam and the initial tests, we're calling this *highly suspicious* for smallpox and initiating a full response. I'll be calling Dr. Jackson in a couple of minutes. We want to begin vaccinating everyone in the hospital ASAP. We have adequate vaccine for that with us. Then we'll decide who's next—certainly this entire county and maybe the entire Chicago metropolitan area. The State Health Department will help coordinate the vaccinations. We'll have to educate the public about the vaccine's side effects. The vaccine immune globulin, which we'll need to treat any serious reactions, is still in very short supply. But, even without adequate VIG, it is *crucial* to begin immediately. We'll keep all of you informed."

And with that statement, the meeting was over. Lafitte stepped out of the room and started down the hallway.

"Thank you very much," Lucas said.

Lafitte stopped and turned back. "Oh," he said, "Dr. Bennett and Dr. Haleem." He took a few steps toward them. "You did an incredible job. Very good work, gentlemen."

Lafitte shook both of their hands. Harry felt relieved at Lafitte's comment. Up to that point, he hadn't been sure he'd done anything at all right, or for that matter, that they really even had the correct diagnosis. Part of it was, though, that the diagnosis was still very difficult for him to believe.

CHAPTER TWENTY THREE

DECEMBER 22, 4:00 P.M. EST
DAY TWELVE OF THE SECOND WAVE OF EXPOSURE
ATLANTA

Jackson stared blankly out the window as the rain spilled from the gray sky. The clouds were crying, as his wife would say, and today they had good reason. The lab had confirmed smallpox. Lafitte had called him from DeKalb, Illinois, a small town he had never heard of, but in a few hours, he and everyone else in the country would know and never forget DeKalb. Twenty days ago he had shared lunch in the sunshine of a magnificent Colorado sky with Harry Bennett, who had joyously introduced his family and shown hospitality to a stranger; now Harry was crossing his path again. This time for disease, for suffering, and for a tragedy as only Jackson had seen. A single circumstance in a single city was not the ending, but rather the beginning. The infliction of many, maybe a multitude, had begun. His life's work would be a waste—his effort defeated by an act of terror. It was not only a callous act but also stupid—possibly unleashing a fury on mankind not seen in a half-dozen centuries. He slammed his hand against the thick pane of glass and felt it vibrate against his palm. The cruelty of man knew no bounds.

Containment was crucial. The loss of life in the U.S. would be devastating, but the infection would likely expand worldwide. He could see it now. The number of deaths around the world would be catastrophic.

"Dr. Jackson?"

The voice of his secretary brought Jackson back to reality. "Yes, Nellie?" he said, turning to the doorway.

"Your driver is here for your flight to Washington."

"Thank you. I'll be along in a minute."

He turned back to the rain. He would go to Chicago where he could help, but first he must go to Washington to inform and advise the president. It was imperative that the president make the announcement promptly. All the emergency rooms in the country must be notified immediately. They must all go on alert, along with the family physicians, the internists, and the pediatricians. Every state must begin its plan for the inevitable vaccinations. A rapid response was essential.

After advising the president, he would set up a phone conference on the president's authority of the most powerful of the most powerful government in the world: the FBI director, the White House chief of staff, leaders of Congress, the national security advisor, all the cabinet members, the joint chiefs of staff, the U.S. attorney general, and the director of the CIA.

Next, a conference by phone with the governor of Illinois, the mayor of Chicago, the Illinois congressional delegation, the Illinois state health commissioner, and all the others who needed to know.

Last, a blast fax from the CDC to all fifty states and the territories, to Customs, Immigration, police departments, VA hospitals, medical and nursing professional organizations, and military hospitals.

He had spent four years thinking of little else, hoping to never use the plans he had created, hoping to retire and die thinking maybe he should have chosen to be productive, to be useful, to accomplish something, anything, rather than waste his time on a contingency that never would and, more importantly, never should occur. Who would be so crazy as to unleash smallpox on mankind? What kind of evil was this?

"Dr. Jackson," his secretary said, standing in the doorway, "I'm sorry to bother you, but you'll miss your flight."

"That's fine, Nellie. I'm ready."

He picked up his case with his laptop and a small overnight bag. He looked around his office at the stacks of clutter, the piles of knowledge unread, and the letters unanswered.

"I could have done more," he thought. "There's so much to do, but I could have done more."

His efforts were coming to a test, a trial by fire, but rather than feel even the smallest bit of satisfaction, he felt only the greatest of sadness.

Containment was key. The preparation was over. The battle had begun.

* * *

DECEMBER 22, 5:00 P.M. EST
NEW YORK CITY

Vicky opened the cardboard box of Chinese takeout and dumped a portion of cashew chicken on a paper plate.

"How'd you know this was my favorite?" she asked Justin.

"Lucky guess," he said. "And I figured that since you're working a double shift *again*, anything's better than hospital food."

"You figured right."

She and Justin were fast becoming the hot item in the emergency room. Since he had asked her out to dinner two weeks earlier, she had shared more meals with him than she had with her mother or the kids. She hadn't planned it that way, but her schedule was unbelievably busy, and Justin had made an effort to bring in food while she was working. If she had to be at the hospital, at least she was enjoying mealtime.

She missed Becky and John more than they seemed to miss her, but like all children, they seldom verbalized their emotional needs. Her job was interfering with the relationship she wanted with them, and if they didn't build trust and friendship now, the tough teenage years when kids often pushed away would be a problem.

To complicate matters, she was falling for Justin, and the whole idea of that scared her. Besides enjoying his company and his conversation, she felt comfortable in his arms. He was on her mind constantly, and when she thought of him, she smiled. She noticed she was smiling a lot lately, especially when he showed up unexpectedly with six cartons of Chinese food, egg rolls, and a few fortune cookies.

"How much time do you have?" he asked.

"About the same as usual."

The ER never stopped. There were always people waiting to be seen. In the past, she had simply skipped most of her meals, occasionally grabbing a sandwich when there was a lull. For the past month the ER had been insane, and there was never even a moment's lull, but with Justin, she would just stop and take a few minutes regardless. But she always felt guilty about the time.

She smiled at him. "Thank you for dinner, Justin. I'll enjoy every minute of it."

"You're welcome. I don't know how you keep up this pace. It would kill me."

"You're working your fair share of doubles."

"But I don't have any one else to take care of...yet."

"You're embarrassing me."

"Doing my best."

Vicky's pager beeped as she took a bite of an egg roll. "A few quiet minutes for dinner," she thought, "was too good to be true." She glanced at the pager and noticed the number was outside the hospital.

"Excuse me a second," she said as she moved to the phone. The name on the pager was Dr. Greg Winner, a former classmate in her emergency medicine residency. He now worked in downtown Chicago. As she dialed, she wondered why he was calling. She hadn't talked to him in three or four years.

"Greg?" she said when he answered.

"Vicky," he said. "Good to hear your voice."

He exchanged small talk for a couple of minutes and asked about her sister. He hadn't heard. She glanced over at Justin and shrugged her shoulders.

"I got a call a few minutes ago," Winner said, coming to point of his call. "A friend of mine is moonlighting at one of the community hospitals not far from here. He was in the ER when a woman and her daughter came in with a rash. They think it may be smallpox. The hospital is closed, and everyone is quarantined. He said the place is going crazy. He called out and was surprised the phone system wasn't shut down."

"Smallpox? Is he sure?"

"He said they're ninety-eight percent certain. Confirmation is pending."

Vicky looked up at Justin, and their eyes met. "Do they know the source? Bioterrorism?"

"No one knows. I called all of our classmates I could think of. This is the real thing."

"Why hasn't it been in the media?"

"My friend said it will be very soon."

Vicky thanked Winner for calling. She stepped back to the table and sank into her seat. She knew Greg Winner well enough to know that he was reliable, but his source was a friend of his she didn't know. Smallpox in some small town? That seemed unlikely. "Did you hear that?" she asked Justin.

"Couldn't help it, really. What do you make of it?"

"I don't know. If it's confirmed as smallpox, I'm sure we'll hear about it soon enough."

"This is a big deal. If it's smallpox, it's bioterrorism. That's for sure. There would be no other source. You know I was active duty—Gulf War and the Middle East—and we trained for bioterror contingencies. It's scary stuff."

"Were you vaccinated?"

"That was before it was really available. Have you been?"

"No. They don't consider our hospital a first responder."

The door to the break room opened, and Newton walked in.

"It's stacking up out there," Newton said. "Is your lunch about over?" Newton looked directly at Vicky, ignoring Justin as if he didn't exist.

Justin stood. "I need to get back myself." He leaned over and gave Vicky a kiss on the cheek before excusing himself.

Vicky didn't like the intrusion or Newton's attitude, but he was right about the patients. "I just had the weirdest phone call," she said.

Newton sat at the table and held up a carton of chow mein. "Are you going to eat all this?" he asked as he began spooning some vegetables onto a plate.

She ignored his question but briefly related the conversation with Winner. After she finished, he pondered her story for a moment.

"Smallpox? Seems rather preposterous."

"He's reliable—that's what worries me. Maybe we should initiate our plan."

Newton laughed. "Our plan? We don't have a plan. In fact, our committee is full of idiots! We've been working on a smallpox response plan for twelve months, and it's still not finalized. Isn't that ridiculous? Everyone's too busy, and I can't get anyone to agree on anything." He shoveled noodles into his mouth as he spoke.

She had heard that Newton had never called a meeting.

"I guess we'd better finish it," he said as he stood. "I need to make a few calls to light some fires under the butts of a few people in this hospital, and I probably should call the directors of all the city's ERs. Wouldn't be a bad idea."

Newton grabbed a fortune cookie off the table, opened the plastic wrapper, and cracked the cookie open. "A gentle touch moves the heart more than the hardest push," he read aloud, holding the paper insert. He looked up at Vicky. "I'm trusting you on this one," he said as he stuffed the cookie in his mouth. "I hope you haven't screwed up."

Vicky watched him leave and shook her head. A new work environment with less stress, more time for family and newfound friends, and *less* time with Newton wouldn't be such a bad idea.

* * *

DECEMBER 22, 6:00 P.M. CST
DEKALB, ILLINOIS

Harry leaned forward on the couch in the doctors' lounge as the president of the United States came on the TV. Lucas, Haleem, and several other doctors were seated on the couch or had pulled up chairs. Harry had been talking with Maureen on the phone when the president's coverage had broken in on the regular programming, and she remained on the phone with him. It was not a press conference. The president was addressing the nation from the Oval Office. He sat at his desk, grim faced and serious with his hands folded in front of him.

"Good evening, my fellow Americans," he said. "I am addressing you tonight on the gravest of circumstances, a serious crisis for our nation. Today, two American citizens in a town outside Chicago have been confirmed to have smallpox. No other cases have been reported, and we believe this could be an isolated event. The two people, a mother and her daughter, are at the DeKalb County Hospital and are receiving the best of care from the brave doctors, nurses, and staff there. I've authorized the release of the smallpox vaccine to the Illinois State Health Department to be available to the Chicago metropolitan area immediately. We must presume that the source of the infection is a terrorist attack, and I have every confidence that the source will be found. This new terrorist attack on our freedom will test our resolve and our strength, but we are a strong nation. We will prevail. It is essential that we are prepared. We must be alert, and we cannot panic. We have the greatest scientific minds and the best doctors in the world, and we will conquer this challenge. Each of us must do our part, and I will be asking you to be brave, to be calm, and for some of you, to serve your country, our great nation."

The camera zoomed out, showing Dr. Jackson sitting in a chair next to the president.

"Good gracious," Maureen said over the phone.

"I have asked Dr. Hugh Jackson," the president continued, "the head of bioterrorism at the Centers for Disease Control and Prevention in Atlanta, to address you tonight. He is the foremost expert on smallpox in the United States." The president leaned forward and looking intently into the camera, said, "My fellow Americans, we must join together and fight the evil nations in the world who are terrorizing those of us who love peace, democracy, and freedom. Good night and God bless."

The camera moved to Jackson. Harry noticed that he was wearing the same crumpled suit he had worn in Vail. His hair was in disarray, and he looked like an absent-minded professor. He wore no makeup, unlike the president, and he appeared nervous, which Harry thought was reasonable because a billion people were watching.

"That's the man we met in Vail," Maureen said. "And the president of the United States is talking about *your* patients, honey."

"I know. It hardly seems real."

"Are you in danger?"

"I'm fine. I got the vaccine this afternoon."

Jackson started by detailing the symptoms of smallpox and recommending that those with symptoms should report to their local health department, to their local doctor, or, if they had no other option, to a hospital emergency room.

"This will be a mess," Harry said. "Everyone will think they have smallpox."

Jackson outlined the CDC response. No other cases had been identified, he said, but he suggested that everyone should be on the highest alert. When Jackson concluded, the networks immediately switched to their talking-head "experts," who seemed to Harry to have been rapidly assembled to fill time. He wondered how they always seemed to know what the president was going to announce.

"Maureen, I've got to go back to the ICU. It will be chaos."

"I've never worried about you being in danger, Harry, but I'm worried now. Be careful and come home safely to me."

"I'm not nearly as brave as the president makes me out to be. I'll be careful. It's my nature."

"I love you."

Harry heard her kiss the phone. He kissed back.

"I love you, too."

* * *

DECEMBER 22, 7:00 P.M. EST
NEW YORK CITY

For the first time in recent memory, the ER of Saint Joseph Hospital had stopped. Everyone—nurses, techs, EMS, and doctors, including Vicky—were glued to the TV. Other than the president's voice, there was complete silence. Despite the advance warning Winner had given her, Vicky could not believe it: the first cases of smallpox, a disease eradicated from the face of the earth, in the United States in more than fifty years.

Vicky observed those around her. Their reaction was relatively minimal, yet these medical people understood the importance of the announcement. If the number of cases was high, their facility and staff would quickly become overwhelmed, but the exact effect would be difficult to judge in advance. Even if no additional cases of smallpox were reported, their situation in the ER wouldn't be much better if the country panicked, and hundreds of people flocked in complaining of all sorts of symptoms. Who would blame them? How would they know? Vicky expected an interesting few days ahead of her.

The president finished and Jackson began. When Jackson finished, Newton flipped off the TV and addressed the staff.

"I would like to meet with the supervisors and staff physicians within the hour. This is why I've been insisting we complete our response plans. I heard a rumor about the Chicago hospital, and I reacted swiftly to be prepared. I know we are swamped, but each of us needs to learn to recognize this disease. Maybe it's isolated in Chicago, but we must always be ready here in New York City. Now everyone, get back to work."

The staff dispersed, leaving Newton and Vicky alone.

"I guess my tip was correct after all," Vicky said. "I'm glad you've been working so diligently on this."

"I'm not sure what you're referring to," Newton said sharply. "I've been hearing rumors for a couple of days now. You're not the only one who has friends around the country." He pointed to the stack of charts on the workstation. "Don't you think you should be clearing out some of these patients before the onslaught of *smallpox* comes in?"

Newton turned and walked away.

That's exactly what she would do. While Newton went back to his office to work on "the plan," she would see the patients and prepare the staff for the inevitable hordes of concerned and worried New Yorkers, the hundreds who would be descending on them because they thought they were infected with smallpox. And from among them, like a needle in the proverbial haystack, she must be prepared to find a case of smallpox, an unimaginable possibility—not because Newton wanted them to, but because it was absolutely critical to do so.

* * *

DECEMBER 22, 7:00 P.M. EST
WASHINGTON, D.C.

Al-Sabai turned off the television after the president's smallpox announcement and rested his head back on his pillow. Two cases of smallpox near Chicago—it must be Muhsin Al-Musaleh who had infected these people. The epidemic had started.

"Al-Musaleh has been the faithful one," Al-Sabai thought. He had carried out his mission, his jihad—*their* jihad. He wondered if Muhsin was now dead? Had his death been terrible? Had he swallowed his cyanide capsule in the trunk of a car as they had been instructed? Surely Mohammed had followed the instructions. Al-Sabai was certain that Mohammed would.

Al-Sabai took the cyanide capsule from the aspirin package and held it in the palm of his hand. He rolled it between his fingers, feeling its smooth texture. It was smaller than he had expected. It must be a powerful poison. At least he hoped it was. Should he take it now? Would that end it all and make it easier?

Smallpox vesicles covered his face, arms, and trunk, and they had begun spreading much more quickly during the last twenty-four hours. His fever had been high, and he had sweated profusely, soaking the bed; the pain had been nearly unbearable. This afternoon he thought he might be better. He drank some water, and it had stayed down. He hadn't vomited since midnight, and the fever seemed lower. Even the pain was better. He wondered if it was too late for him to leave his room. The lesions were noticeable and would probably be easily recognized by anyone who had seen the news reports.

Only a third of people with smallpox would die, Mohammed had told them. Would he die or would he survive?

He slid the capsule back into its envelope and hid it beneath the Gideon Bible in the drawer of the bedside table.

Maybe he would save the capsule…for later. For now, his fate was in the hands of Allah, as it had always been. *Allah is the great one. Praise be to Allah.*

Al-Sabai covered his face with his hands and sobbed. He had failed Allah. He had failed and would be punished.

CHAPTER TWENTY FOUR

DECEMBER 23, 8:00 A.M. CST
DAY THIRTEEN OF THE SECOND WAVE OF EXPOSURE
DEKALB, ILLINOIS

Harry woke up again in the doctors' lounge, but for a moment he was disoriented and forgot where he was. It only took a second to remember, and the reality of the reason he was in the hospital weighed heavily on his heart. Before he called Maureen and the girls, as he had done every morning, he slid out of bed and knelt on the floor to pray. He prayed for Kathy and Lauren and any others who might become infected. He prayed for the doctors, nurses, and other caregivers, and he asked for wisdom, guidance, and strength. He prayed for the nation and for peace in the world. And last, he prayed for himself because he felt completely unprepared to be in the midst of an international crisis. He would need all the help he could get. Today, the result of malice and hatred was hitting close to home. He hoped God would hear and intervene because man was doing a terrible job.

Harry showered, shaved, and changed into the fresh clothes that Maureen had dropped off at the hospital. It was a sweet gesture. She didn't call or tell him that she was coming. She told him later that he would have insisted on seeing her and kissing her and holding her, and that wouldn't be a good example for the others. And she was right on all counts.

After eating a couple of bagels and drinking a glass of milk in the cafeteria, Harry walked down to the ICU. Haleem was already there. Harry sat beside him at the nurses' desk.

"Guess it's official now," Haleem said.

"We're in the news," Harry said. "Not that it's such a good thing."

To Harry, the ICU didn't seemed to have changed much in the last few hours since the announcement by the president, but it truly had. Everything had changed, and the whole world would now be watching every single detail of what they did and what happened here.

"Kathy's getting worse," Haleem said, "and quickly. She's bleeding from just about everywhere—her nose, gums, and from her bowels. She's had four transfusions and ten units of platelets. Her urine's bloody, too."

"If her kidney function declines much more, we'll need to consider dialysis."

"I'm worried it could be the cidofovir," Haleem said. "Renal failure is a known side effect."

"Should I call nephrology?"

"Wouldn't hurt."

"Her breathing is better," Harry said. "I'm glad we didn't need the ventilator."

"So far. She's on antivirals, antibiotics, and sedation, and I just started dopamine to maintain her blood pressure. I don't know what else to do. She can't talk—probably because of the lesions in her throat—but she is alert. She must be miserable."

"The lesions are coalescing and filling with blood. Is this a case of hemorrhagic smallpox?"

"It looks like one, but how would I know for sure?"

"Lauren's lesions are changing to pustules," Harry said, "but she doesn't look as bad as Kathy. Maybe her condition is peaking."

"I hope so."

"Dr. Bennett," a nurse said, "you have a phone call."

"Who is it?"

"A Dr. Hugh Jackson. He's calling from Washington, DC. He told the operator it was urgent *and* private."

"Sure," Harry said. He walked down the hall to an empty room and waited a moment as they switched the call to him. Within a couple of seconds, the phone rang.

"Harry, how are you doing?"

"Fine, Hugh, doing as well as can be expected. Hey, you looked good on TV last night."

"Thanks. Piece of cake. I'm calling because the president wants a press conference at the hospital within six hours. The media is aggressive and will make up stories if they have to. He wants the attending physician and the CDC head of bioterrorism together."

"The attending?"

"That's you and me, Harry. You'll be a celebrity. The president says it will have a calming effect. You know—educating the public and all. It will be limited to medical issues, and the press will be forewarned. It's too early to speculate about the terrorists, and that kind of information will come from one of the agencies here in Washington. I'll be leaving in twenty minutes by military jet. At the conference, the president wants some other doctors and nurses behind us. You've seen the drill before."

"How about our chief of staff and the infectious disease specialist on the case?"

"Your choice. The White House will notify the media, the hospital, and everyone else to set it all up. All you do is show up."

"That sounds simple enough."

"Of course, since all of you are considered contacts, we will have to separate you from the press."

Harry hadn't considered that. "Are you sure it's wise to bring the press into the hospital?"

"It's what the president wants. You and I understand the dangers of smallpox, but the public will take that and multiply it many, many times to an unreasonable level. And the press doesn't help. It's less scary if they see you and hear you."

"I'm saying something?"

"It'll be simple. We'll script it for you." Jackson paused a moment. "How are the patients doing?"

"The mother is much worse and going downhill quickly. She may be septic and in early renal failure. Her lesions are coalescing, and she's bleeding from multiple sites. Looks like your slides of hemorrhagic smallpox."

"You think it's hemorrhagic?"

"I've never seen a case of smallpox. I think so, but I'm not sure."

"If it is, the prognosis is terrible."

"I know."

"Everyone in your hospital should be receiving vaccinations by about now. Did you get yours?"

"Yes, yesterday afternoon. Mike Lafitte gave it to me personally. He said it was a direct order from you."

"Good man. Your community will have the vaccine in a couple of hours."

"I'll let the Health Department know that. They'll be the ones administering it, right?"

"I'm sure they already know. We were considering vaccinating all of Chicago, but I hate to until we know the full extent of the outbreak. We're certainly vaccinating all of the hospital staff, the EMS, all visitors to that floor, and all patients and visitors to the ER both times the Randalls were there. We hope to finish by today. After that we'll vaccinate the whole county, and I suspect it'll take four or five days, depending on the manpower available. If we vaccinate Chicago, it'll be another ten to fourteen days at best. That will be a massive undertaking. We figure it'll take 5,000 personnel for every million people to vaccinate in seven days."

Harry thought he heard Jackson sigh.

"Too bad you're stuck in the hospital," Jackson said. "You won't have time to get a haircut before you go on TV. I didn't."

"And to be honest, Hugh, it looked like you needed one."

Jackson laughed. "That's what they all said, including the president. See you in a few hours, Harry."

"See you, Hugh."

Harry hung up the phone and leaned back in the chair. He felt a brief spasm in the muscles in his back. For the last couple of hours his back had been aching. Maybe it was the bed in the doctors' lounge or possibly the vaccine he received yesterday or the tension and stress. He hoped it was nothing.

* * *

The hospital cafeteria was completely empty except for Harry, Haleem, and Lucas at one table and a couple of nurses at another. The three doctors chose a corner table that overlooked the front of the hospital. The midday sun bathed them in bright sunlight, and it almost felt warm. It was as close as they would get, Harry thought, to outdoors for a while.

"The hospital is a ghost town," Lucas said. "Not once in my twenty-five years of practice have we had anything close to this."

"And look out there," Haleem said, pointing out the window. "There're more people on the grounds outside than here in the hospital."

Harry had never seen so many media in one place. "I'd guess forty vehicles and three hundred reporters."

"At least," Haleem said.

"It's been quite a job to keep them out," Lucas said. "Last night, security caught two reporters trying to sneak in some windows on the first floor."

"Hernandez confiscated a camera from one of the X-ray techs," Harry said. "He was fired, of course. How much is a picture of Kathy or Lauren Randall worth?"

"Everything about this is a tragedy," Haleem said.

They sat in silence for a full minute, lost in their own thoughts.

"I hate to admit this, but maybe Eric Ness was right," Lucas said, "about the effect of panic on the hospital."

The public was avoiding DeKalb County Hospital, as Lucas would say, "like the plague." The hospital had reopened after the CDC arrived, but it had not had a single admission nor had the ER had a single visit.

"I saw Ness being interviewed on CNN," Haleem said.

"I know," Lucas said. "I was embarrassed for him. They're really scraping the barrel."

They all laughed.

"There's been nothing but smallpox on the news since the president spoke," Harry said. "They're running out of people to interview."

"The constant coverage is scaring the staff," Lucas said. "After receiving their vaccines this morning, five employees walked off the job."

"Actually," Harry said, "I'm surprised by the number who've stayed, especially after the two ER nurses."

Harry was worried about them. Two of the nurses had started having backaches and fever. They had been admitted to the hospital and placed in strict isolation. One had been in the ER both nights the Randalls were seen, but the other wasn't and that was causing more concern. Lafitte was investigating. Harry had also been worried about his office staff. He had spoken to Lafitte, and Lafitte had personally taken the vaccine to his office and had administered it to Harry's employees himself.

"The bent of the news coverage," Lucas said, "has been particularly negative on Middle Easterners. They're acting like it's a forgone conclusion that a country in the Middle East is behind this."

Harry remembered Roberts's questions to Kathy about the man in the taxi. "Does all that bother you, Naguib?" Harry asked.

"I've gotten used to it," Haleem said.

"You mean since September eleventh?" Lucas asked.

"It's been worse since then, but it's always been bad. I remind myself that I chose small-town America, but maybe it's no better anyplace else. I said it's a free country, and it didn't really matter what other people thought. But it *does* matter when my wife has been personally threatened. And we don't let our children out of our sight."

The men fell silent.

"I'm sorry," Harry said. "I didn't realize."

"No apology, Harry. My colleagues don't treat me as a suspect. I am very satisfied. It's just out there." Haleem pointed out the window. "For the most part."

Harry felt sad for him and his family. Hatred, unfortunately, wasn't isolated to only one part of the world. If the smallpox was the result of an attack by terrorists from the Middle East, a wave of resentment would likely touch Haleem and his family.

The three looked toward the doorway as Powell entered the cafeteria. He waved at them and approached.

"I just received a call from the state police," he said without sitting. "Dr. Hugh Jackson from the CDC will be arriving in three minutes, and I thought you might want to be there."

The four men rode the elevator to the first floor and followed the hallway to the hospital lobby. The lobby was empty except for the two police officers guarding the front doors. Outside, the media must have gotten word because they were massing around the circle drive like a pack of hyenas waiting for their prey. Sirens wailed softly in the distance, growing louder as the convoy approached. Three black Humvees surrounded by a dozen police cars pulled into the circular drive and stopped. Ten or twelve men dressed in military uniforms and carrying M-16s piled out of the Humvees and set up a defensive perimeter. The passenger door opened and Jackson stepped out. The mass of reporters immediately converged on Jackson, stuffing microphones in his face and yelling out questions. The soldiers quickly created a corridor, and Jackson, without issuing any comments to the press, walked through it and into the building.

Once inside the lobby, Jackson recognized Harry and walked straight up to him.

"Good to see you, Harry."

"Welcome to DeKalb, Illinois," Harry said. "Looks like you brought some protection."

"It's not for me. We are a military power and this is a war. The president wanted it to look like a war."

Harry introduced Jackson to all those around him: Lucas, Haleem, Powell, Perkins, and the others present. Jackson shook hands and said a few words to each person. He was personable and friendly, more like a politician than a doctor. After the introductions, the group moved to the boardroom, now referred to as the situation room. Lafitte greeted Jackson, and Jackson spoke a minute to each of the CDC staff. When he had greeted each one personally, he sat down at the head of the table. Harry chose a seat nearby.

"Let me tell you how the press conference will go," Jackson announced and then waited for the room to settle down. His manner commanded everyone's attention.

"The White House wants the press conference at four Central Standard Time, which is five Eastern Standard Time, and it will last about forty minutes. That gives the networks twenty minutes of expert commentary and advertising before the early evening national news. It will provide prime-time coverage, and the eyes of the entire nation will be watching. I will speak for twelve minutes. Dr. Kenneth Illig, the commissioner of the Illinois State Health Department, will speak for five minutes. Dr. Bennett will speak for three. Dr. Lucas, would you be willing to give a sixty-second description of the hospital and the staff here?"

Lucas nodded.

"Good. I'll give you some pointers." Jackson looked around the room until he found Haleem. "I think just a couple of words from you, Dr. Haleem, would be good. Would you be willing to do that?"

Haleem also nodded.

Jackson continued. "That will leave about twenty minutes for questions. Dr. Illig and I will answer those. I'm sure you are aware of the seriousness of the situation. Our attitude should reflect that, especially those standing in the background. If any of you have been watching the media coverage, you've noticed a lot of discussion about this being the act of Middle Eastern terrorists. Off the record, there is evidence that this may in fact be true. I am pleased that Dr. Haleem is willing to stand up with us. I believe the diversity he brings will be beneficial to the country. So does the president. Thank you all for your help." Jackson stood. "I'm hoping now, Dr. Bennett, with your permission, to examine the patients."

"Certainly, Dr. Jackson, and any suggestions you may have would be welcomed."

"Then let's go," Jackson said.

Jackson led an entourage from the situation room to the ICU. Harry and Lucas walked beside him, the others behind. Jackson kept up a friendly conversation, asking about the hospital, its staff, and the community. Harry appreciated Jackson's demeanor. He was relaxed, confident, and interested, and he was calming to everyone around him.

In the unit, Jackson introduced himself to each of the nurses and other staff, shaking their hands and thanking them.

"Have you had your vaccinations?" he asked as they gathered around him.

They answered in the affirmative.

"The president of the United States gave me a message to deliver to those of you who are caring for the Randalls—you who are on the front lines, who have not left your posts, and are willing to place these patients and our country above your own personal considerations. The president wants me to thank you for your dedication, your professionalism, and your bravery. Because of people like you, our country is great. It is why our nation is so strong. The president is proud of you." Jackson nodded at Harry and Haleem. "Would you doctors please join me as I examine the patients?"

"Dr. Jackson?" Janet said.

"Yes, Ms. Hernandez?"

"Mr. Randall wanted you to know he would step out while you were here. He's been here constantly. But he asked if he could speak with you and Dr. Bennett after you're finished."

"Yes, of course. I'd be happy to."

The three doctors dressed in protective equipment outside of Kathy's room.

"Notice the odor?" Jackson asked them before stepping in.

"Yes," Harry said, "we had noticed."

"It's unique. I could many times diagnose smallpox by this smell. It's not well understood." He placed his hand on the door but did not open it. "How is Mrs. Randall doing?"

"Very poorly," Harry said in a low voice. He detailed her condition: dopamine drip, dialysis, two antivirals, three antibiotics, and multiple transfusions. She was bleeding everywhere, even under her skin. Oddly, though, she was still alert.

They entered Kathy's room. She lay motionless on the bed. The white sheets covering her were soaked in blood, though Harry was certain the nurses had changed the bedding just before they had arrived. Her face was now one continuous, draining, pustular scab, swollen and unrecognizable. The whites of her eyes were black. Her breathing was shallow and rapid. Jackson introduced himself to her; he looked into her eyes, spoke in a soft, kind voice, and treated her with respect and dignity. Harry was impressed.

After examining Kathy, Jackson stepped back out into the hallway. He removed his gown and gloves, and waited for Harry and Haleem to do the same. He leaned forward and talked to them softly so only they could hear.

"It is hemorrhagic," Jackson said. "Her prognosis is very poor. She's unlikely to make it much longer. You need to prepare her husband. She doesn't need to be transported to another facility. She's much too sick, and it would be too risky. You're doing a fine job. There is nothing else to offer her."

Jackson waited for them to respond or ask questions, but both knew that what he was saying was true.

The three redressed in protective equipment to see Lauren next. Since the morning, her condition had dramatically worsened.

"It looks like hemorrhagic as well," Harry said. "She's now bleeding from multiple sites and requiring transfusions, too. Her breathing is okay, but her kidneys are failing. She's on the same medications as her mother—basically everything Dr. Haleem and I thought might help. Honestly, we don't know what else to do."

Jackson went into the room to examine Lauren. Harry had rounded on Lauren at least three times a day, and each time she was worse. The skin on her face was nearly as bad as her mother's, and Harry could barely look at her. He felt his eyes fill up with tears. He turned away a moment to compose himself and took a slow, deep breath. He remembered her sweet, beautiful face; her soft, innocent voice; her laugh and smile; and her hugs. His sadness for her was almost overwhelming, yet he also felt terrible outrage. Who could do such a thing to a precious child? This wasn't some accident or some rare infection she had acquired someplace. This was an intentional, murderous, evil act. He was angry with those responsible and also angry because of his helplessness.

Harry turned back to watch Jackson. He was touching Lauren's face and gently stroking her hair, talking softly, and encouraging her. Jackson finished his exam, and he gathered the two of them in the corner of the room.

"Before we leave, I want to tell you something important." Jackson's voice was very low, nearly inaudible. "This is a difficult situation even for experienced doctors and nurses. It is easy to feel despondent, to be overwhelmed, and even to get angry."

Harry felt Jackson was reading his mind.

"I felt the same in Africa," Jackson said. "Smallpox is a terrible disease. If we have many cases, it will be easy to become callous or withdrawn. I want both of you to remember how you are feeling right now. Don't let the anger or hurt control you, but rather let the caring and sensitivity come out." Jackson reached out and touched both of their shoulders. "Think about the patients, your job, and your duty to them and their families. Think about your own families and your community. Retain your humanity in all of this. It is what you are. Remember—doctors don't just cure the sick. They help the dying, too."

Neither Harry nor Haleem spoke. Harry knew that Jackson was preparing them for the inevitable. Jackson's experiences in Africa, though years ago, had prepared him and had etched an everlasting impression on him. Harry remembered the sadness in Jackson's eyes when they had first met in Vail. Now he understood why.

A hard rap on the door broke the silence.

"Dr. Bennett!" Janet said, opening the door. "Mrs. Randall is coding!"

Harry and Haleem rushed into Kathy's room. A nurse pulled in the crash cart behind them. One of the nurses was leaning over Kathy, pushing sharply down with her outstretched arms, compressing the chest in short bursts. Another nurse was squeezing an AMBU bag tightly fitted on Kathy's mouth and nose, pushing the soft sides in and out, breathing for her.

"What happened?" Harry asked.

"It was a respiratory arrest," Janet said, and then she turned and pointed to the monitor, "but as you can see, she went into V-fib."

Harry moved to the head of the bed, and Haleem stood along the side. Jackson stayed closer to the door and watched. Harry glanced up at the monitor and noticed the typical pattern of ventricular fibrillation.

"Hand me the paddles," he said.

"The defibrillator is charging," Janet said.

She handed Harry the paddles. The steady whine of the device increased in pitch and intensity. Janet lifted Kathy's gown and placed two pads on her chest. The whining sound stopped, signifying the defibrillator was fully charged.

"It's ready," Janet said.

"Clear!" Harry yelled.

The nurses stopped the CPR, and the staff backed away from the bed. Harry positioned the paddles, one on each side on her chest, and simultaneously pushed the buttons. Kathy's back arched suddenly as the current surged through her.

All eyes turned to the monitor. No change.

"Three sixty," Harry said calmly.

Janet increased the voltage and the defibrillator's whining resumed. In a very few seconds the whining sound stopped.

"Clear!" Harry yelled, and then he released the charge.

Again, Kathy's back spasmed upward and dropped back to the bed.

"Still V-fib," Janet said.

"Continue CPR," Harry said. "Let's give her epinephrine one milligram and try again." He pointed to the crash cart. "Hand me the laryngoscope. I'm going to intubate her."

Harry noticed the nurses had brought in the ventilator, anticipating such a possibility.

The nurse held out the laryngoscope and an endotracheal tube. As they briefly stopped CPR, Harry slid the blade into Kathy's mouth and lifted her jaw forward. Pox lesions covered her trachea. Further down, the vocal cords, two narrow bands of grayish material, were covered with pustules as well. If he missed, the pustules would bleed, and he might not have a second chance. With his right hand, Harry slid the endotracheal tube in place.

"She's intubated," Harry said. "Restart chest compressions."

"Good work," Jackson said.

After the nurse connected the endotracheal tube to the flexible tubing of the ventilator, Harry adjusted the settings, and the ventilator began its steady clunking, pushing air into Kathy's lungs.

Harry allowed the epinephrine to circulate a few minutes while the nurses continued chest compressions. He knew a code blue on this young woman ravished by hemorrhagic smallpox was unlikely to be successful and at best might only delay the inevitable outcome. But what else could they do? Harry observed the grim faces of the nursing staff and Haleem, and thought his own must look the same. The loss of this one patient would be tough enough. While he hoped there would be no more, he knew there would be.

They worked furiously on her. Her abnormal heart rhythm was shocked ten times but to no avail. They tried multiple medications, but none helped. She was septic and in shock. All they were doing was useless. After forty-five minutes, Harry called the code, and they stopped.

Kathy Randall was dead.

"Time?" asked Janet, her voice choked with emotion.

"One-fifty P.M.," Harry said. He reached over and turned off the ventilator.

The room was silent. The nurses began the process of cleaning up, picking up syringes, removing the defibrillator pads, and disconnecting the ventilator. Harry removed the endotracheal tube from Kathy's throat and the IV from her arm. They were all slow and deliberate in their actions. There was no hurry now. As the nurses worked to make the body as presentable as possible, Harry heard their quiet sobs through their masks. The doctors removed their protective equipment and stepped into the hallway. Haleem crossed to the desk without saying a word and began charting a progress note on what had just happened.

"I'll go talk with the husband," Harry said to no one in particular.

"I'm sorry," Jackson said.

"Me, too," Harry replied.

"I need to call the president," Jackson said. "He'll want to know about this. When you're finished, please tell Mr. Randall that I'd like to meet with him. Afterward, you and I will need to talk about the press conference."

The press conference was the furthest thought from Harry's mind. He walked slowly down the hallway toward Frank's room. He had done this enough times over the years to know there was no easy way. It was best to be direct, yet over and over his mind thought through the words he would say. Even with the preparation, it didn't get any easier.

Harry knocked softly on Frank's door and opened it a crack. Frank was on the bed and sat up when Harry entered. His eyes looked up at Harry with a knowing expression, a fear of what Harry might say.

"It's about Kathy," Harry said gently. "I'm sorry. We lost her. She's gone."

For a brief moment, Frank's disbelief froze him, but then he cried out in agony, "No, no, no, it can't be." He covered his face with his arms and slumped forward. "It can't be true," he said. "It can't be true." His chest heaved as he began sobbing, his body rocking back and forth.

Harry sat down next to him on the bed and lightly touched his shoulder. Harry's heart was aching, but he could only imagine the depth of pain Frank was feeling. He had no family with him here. No friends. He would grieve alone, except for Harry. Harry was in no hurry to leave.

Frank raised his eyes toward Harry. "I was hoping she'd pull through," Frank said through the tears, "but I knew it was bad."

"We did everything we could."

"I know you did. Thank you for that."

"I'm so very sorry."

"Me, too." He sighed. "Me, too." Frank wiped his eyes. "When can I see her?"

"Whenever you're ready."

"You know I was in there a few minutes ago."

"Yes, the nurses told me."

"After I see Kathy, I'm going to see Lauren."

"I'm sure that's okay."

"And I'm staying...no matter what."

Harry didn't blame him. If it were his daughter, he would do the same.

"Give the nurses a few minutes, then you can come down. I'll have them put a comfortable chair in Lauren's room."

"Thank you, Dr. Bennett."

"You're welcome."

Jackson's words about helping the dying and their families echoed in Harry's mind. He felt privileged to be present during such an intimate and personal moment, to be trusted to share the private tragedy and the pain. It was the hardest part of being a doctor.

* * *

The press conference was held in the hospital's education auditorium and started at exactly four o'clock. Those from inside the hospital stayed on the stage, while the press sat in the rows of seats normally reserved during medical programs for doctors and nurses. The reporters, occupying nearly every seat, were separated from the stage by a temporary barrier of folding chairs more than fifteen feet from the front. The chairs would not be seen on the broadcast. The cameras and microphones from every major network had been hastily set up during the previous two or three hours, connected by heavy cables to the satellite trucks outside. Bright, portable floodlights illuminated the entire auditorium.

Jackson would be the first to speak. He stood at a lectern in the center of the platform. Harry, Lucas, Haleem, Illig, Lafitte, Roberts, Janet Hernandez, and two other ICU nurses were in a line behind him. A network staffer silently counted the final seconds to go live.

"Good afternoon," Jackson began. "I am Dr. Hugh Jackson, and I represent the Centers for Disease Control and Prevention. We are in DeKalb, Illinois, at the DeKalb County Hospital where two days ago a mother and her six-year-old daughter came into the emergency room and were subsequently diagnosed with smallpox which, I might add, was done in a remarkably rapid and proficient manner. The diagnosis was confirmed at the CDC. In the meantime, the two patients were appropriately placed in strict isolation and treated. However, it is with the greatest sadness that I must now report to you that the mother, Kathy Randall, has died of smallpox. This occurred about two hours ago."

A murmur of voices rippled through the room. Jackson waited for them to quiet down.

"Kathy Randall lived in Sycamore, Illinois, and was a mother, a wife, and a second-grade school teacher, and, in my opinion, a hero. She will be missed by her friends, her family, and all who knew her. Her daughter, Lauren, is now fighting for her life. We are hopeful for Lauren's recovery, but her condition is critical."

Jackson gave a brief, pertinent summary of smallpox, including the course of infection, its transmission, the vaccine, and the treatment. After about ten minutes, he turned the podium over to Illig, who described the State Health Department's involvement and response. Roberts gave a brief discussion of the FBI's criminal investigation but stated he would not at this time provide any specific details. Next, Lucas described the hospital and its staff, and Haleem read a brief statement about smallpox provided by Jackson. After Haleem, Harry approached the lectern. Jackson had given him an outline for his remarks, summarizing the diagnosis of the Randalls. Harry slid the paper out of his pocket and placed it on the lectern. He paused for a brief moment, and then crumpled the paper in his hand.

"I am Dr. Harry Bennett," he said, looking out at the reporters, "the family physician for the Randall family. I have known Kathy and Frank Randall for about seven years. I cared for Kathy when she was pregnant with Lauren, and I delivered Lauren and held her in my arms when she was a tiny baby. She was one of the prettiest babies I have ever delivered. I watched her grow as an infant and a toddler. Four years ago Lauren nearly drowned, and by God's miraculous healing, she made a full recovery. Today I watched her mother die from a disease that we thought was long ago erased from existence. Now Lauren's condition is critical, and we as her physicians and nurses are helpless against this terrible disease. I ask now for your prayers for Lauren and for her father, who is grieving the loss of his wife. I ask you to pray for a miracle because a miracle from God is all that will save her now."

Harry stepped away from the microphones and stood quietly for a moment. Jackson allowed a few seconds, and then he approached Harry.

"Thank you," he whispered to Harry.

As Jackson returned to the lectern, Harry took his place.

"Now we have time for a few questions," Jackson said. "Who will be first?"

The reporters' arms shot up. Jackson pointed to a reporter in the front row.

"I'm Lisa Kravitz, *New York Times*. Dr. Jackson, are there any other cases now in the U.S. that are being investigated for smallpox?"

"No," Jackson said, "not at this time." He pointed to another reporter.

"Thank you, Dr. Jackson. Charles Mueller, CNN. What are the specific plans to prevent the spread of smallpox here in this hospital and elsewhere?"

"We have had a response plan developed for some time now. In fact, parts of it are similar to the plan used successfully to eradicate smallpox thirty years ago. We will initiate specific public health actions that will utilize local and state health departments."

"What specific actions?" Mueller asked.

"The plan utilizes contact tracing—that is, identifying the people who were in contact with the smallpox patient—and ring vaccination, which is a strategy to vaccinate those identified in outward rings of contacts. We will provide a copy of the plan to you." Jackson pointed to another reporter.

"Ralph Hembree, ABC News. Who are you planning to vaccinate—the population of DeKalb? Chicago?"

"We have already vaccinated all those in contact with the two patients here at the hospital. We made the decision to vaccinate the population of DeKalb but not Chicago."

Hembree raised his hand. "A follow-up?"

Jackson nodded.

"Why not Chicago? Surely people here in DeKalb have been to Chicago in the last few days."

"The implementation of control measures for smallpox is very much dependent on the number of cases and location. Let me say that even though our society is mobile, I think there is a misunderstanding about how widely the virus could be spread. If someone becomes infected, he will have an incubation period of ten to twelve days, during which he feels normal and is not contagious. Then he becomes very ill. After several days of what is typically a serious illness, a rash develops. It is only when the rash begins that he is contagious. Most people become quite ill and, just as in the case of the Randalls, they don't travel but stay home or seek medical care. Vaccinating Chicago would be a massive undertaking, and with only two cases here, it isn't warranted." Jackson selected another reporter.

"Ray Seidel, MSNBC. Dr. Jackson, how close a contact? Is it passed through blood products? Sheets? Towels? Clothing?"

"It is airborne and is passed by a contact within six feet. No, it can not be passed through blood. Yes, it can be obtained through bedding and clothing, so special precautions must be taken." He pointed at another raised hand.

"June Elsberry, *Wall Street Journal*. Thank you, Dr. Jackson. My question is, if someone has been directly exposed to smallpox and needs the vaccine, but he has undergone chemotherapy or is infected with HIV, would he be forced to receive the vaccine? What will be done in that situation?"

"I'm not sure we can force anyone, but the issue is different with a direct exposure than with routine vaccinations. The risk of smallpox to a person who has been directly exposed is much greater than the risk of the vaccine. In addition, if that person were to develop smallpox, his underlying illness would increase his chances of a worse case of smallpox. Therefore, those people in the situation you describe should be vaccinated. Last question." He pointed to another reporter.

"Thank you, Dr. Jackson. Aaron Sterling, CBS News. Are plans in place for quarantining the population, and if so, under what legal authority are they based?"

Jackson paused at this question. "Your question is a good one, and I'm not sure I'm the one to answer it. We're hoping the public understands the very serious nature of this disease and would voluntarily isolate themselves when requested by a health official. Without the public's cooperation, control measures may well be in jeopardy. Since the first cases of smallpox have now occurred, I wouldn't be surprised if additional legal clarification was not forthcoming. Ladies and gentlemen, this concludes the press conference. Thank you for your attention."

Most of the reporters left to record their stories. A few remained, hoping Jackson would answer more questions, but he quickly left the stage and walked through a doorway to the hospital. The doctors and nurses followed him.

"Thank you for your help," Jackson said to them as they gathered around him. "No more press conferences, I promise you. I think all of you have much more important things to do now."

Harry left the group as most of them either headed for the ICU or the situation room. He decided to go back to the doctors' lounge where he had some acetaminophen in his bag. His back was aching worse, and now he also felt some nausea. Still, it could be the vaccine.

"Dr. Bennett?" Roberts approached Harry. "Can I walk with you?"

"Sure. What's up?"

"I wanted to tell you how sorry I am about Kathy Randall. It's such a shame."

"I appreciate that."

"And thanks for allowing me the few minutes with her."

"You're welcome. Was it helpful?"

"We have so little."

"I know, you can't say anything."

Roberts stopped and faced Harry. "Actually, Doctor, I believe your patient gave us a lead. We were able to track down the taxi, but the driver's out with the flu. However, the records show the fare was dropped off at O'Hare."

"He went to the airport? It would seem unlikely he was well enough to travel."

"How so?"

"You saw Kathy Randall. I doubt he would have looked much different. He must have been pretty sick."

"I hadn't thought of that. If he didn't fly out, and we're checking the flights, why would he go to the airport?"

"I don't know. You have to remember, though, that if this was a terrorist, he wouldn't want to be diagnosed with smallpox. If he was, we'd know he was here, and we'd track down the contacts and vaccinate them. I think he only wanted us to find the people he infected. We call them the second wave, like Lauren and Kathy Randall. So maybe this man was going someplace to die."

"At the airport," Roberts said. "Maybe a hotel? A trash dumpster? Or a parked car?"

"From Kathy's description, he probably had just a few hours, if that."

Roberts started down the hall. "Thanks, Dr. Bennett. You've been very helpful."

An image of Kathy's body arching as he pushed the buttons on the paddles flashed through his mind. "You're welcome, Mr. Roberts. Anytime. Oh, and Mr. Roberts?"

Roberts was already several feet away but stopped and turned. "Yes, Dr. Bennett?"

"You really should find that taxi driver," Harry said, "and be sure it *is* just the flu."

Roberts's face showed that he understood Harry's concern.

"That's right," Roberts said, nodding. "I'll do that. Thanks."

Harry walked alone to the doctors' lounge. He needed the acetaminophen. If it didn't help, he thought, he probably should mention his symptoms to Jackson. But the last thing he needed right now was to be quarantined.

CHAPTER TWENTY FIVE

The line of people outside the Saint Joseph emergency room stretched for three city blocks, and Vicky heard it was the same at every ER in the United States. The news media blitz was constant—every minute on every station. No new cases had been reported so far, but the authorities were expecting many, many more. At least that was what the media was reporting.

The ER was mostly taking names. The CDC had recommended that every patient with a fever of greater than one hundred and one be isolated at home, if feasible, and monitored. Vicky had decided to run influenza tests on all the patients with fever, and quite a few had been positive. So far in her ten-hour shift, she had seen a hundred and twenty patients who thought they had smallpox. Several had rashes, including one with poison ivy and two with eczema. Many were simply frightened, and some were just plain hysterical. One patient pointed out a tiny bump he had found, and she had to use a magnifying glass to find it. Some only had a few muscle aches, and a number had no symptoms at all. All wanted to be checked. And all wanted the smallpox vaccine. Several demanded it and made threats. One patient even brought his personal lawyer. There were so many worried about smallpox that the staff couldn't even see the really sick patients.

Vicky stopped at the workstation and tossed five charts down on the counter. At least most of these visits were quick—the fewer the symptoms, the shorter the visit. Yet she was certain that every doctor in America was worried just as she was that the next simple, straightforward patient or the one with a slight, minor rash was actually the next case of smallpox—easy to overlook but serious consequences to miss.

As she grabbed five new charts, she looked up to see Justin's face grinning at her.

"Life is wonderful," he said.

"Even in this mess?"

"Because of this mess. We'll never have to worry about unemployment, right?"

"That's the least of our worries."

"Can I bring you some lunch?"

"Food? What's that?"

"You have to eat."

Vicky looked around at the hoards of people and at the furor and turmoil of the emergency room.

"Call me later," she said. "I don't know."

He kissed her lightly on the cheek. "I will. I'm in and out. Call me if you need anything."

Vicky reached out and held his sleeve. "Justin, what did you find out about your vaccine?"

He smiled. She knew the smile was for her benefit.

"We're high on the list," he said. "That's all they'll say, being new on the job and all."

"I'm worried. You should already have had one."

"I'll get in line when they're available."

"Justin, please be careful. This is serious."

He continued to smile, but she could tell he was concerned. He didn't want to worry her. It wasn't working.

"You be careful, too," he said.

He pulled her close and kissed her. She was in the middle of a packed emergency room and probably everyone was watching, but she didn't care. His kiss felt soft and sweet, and was simply wonderful. His arms were strong, and she felt safe. After the kiss, he stepped back and smiled again.

"Okay, Justin, bring me some lunch."

"You got it, babe."

She watched him go. She wished she had a normal life. She hadn't been home since the president's announcement, but neither had nearly every doctor and nurse on staff, and there was no end in sight. She was glad she had spent some time with Justin before all this. He had met her mother and the kids, coming to their home, Justin enjoying her mother's home-cooked meal. Her mother had liked him. So had Becky and John. And he had been great with the kids. She worried, especially if more smallpox were found, that it would be a long time before she'd see a normal life again.

"Dr. Anderson?" The unit clerk was holding up the phone. "It's for you."

Vicky answered the phone. It was her mother.

"Vicky, how are you?"

"Fine, Mom. Anything wrong?" Vicky heard concern in her mother's voice.

"Nothing serious."

"The kids okay?"

"Yes, yes, they're fine."

"Mom, I'm busy. It's packed here. What is it?"

"I'm not feeling so good. My back's been aching since yesterday, and this morning I started running a fever."

"How much?"

"A little over a hundred. Is that anything to worry about?"

Vicky certainly hoped not. "Why don't you come in and let us check you out. We'll run an influenza test. Make sure everything's okay."

Vicky hung up the phone. Her first thought was that her mother's symptoms were perfectly consistent with smallpox, but so were the symptoms of most of the patients she had been seeing in the ER. Every person in America with a backache or a headache or a little temperature was worried. Where would her mother get exposed? It would seem unlikely. Yet, when it was someone close, she thought, it was easy to worry. Her mother would feel better after Vicky had examined her, and so would Vicky, and that was the same reason all these patients were in the emergency room. She hoped the only thing her mother needed was a little reassurance.

* * *

DECEMBER 24, 9:00 A.M. CST
DEKALB, ILLINOIS

Harry woke up, checked on Lauren, and then returned to the doctors' lounge for a few minutes of privacy and his morning call to Maureen. Lauren's condition was deteriorating, and he could barely enter the room because she looked so terrible. He spent fifteen minutes with Frank outside the room. Frank was holding up pretty well, considering the circumstances.

Harry missed Maureen and wanted to go home, but his symptoms were worse. His back ached more, and he was nauseated. He had decided to isolate himself in his room as much as feasible, and he watched carefully for any lesions. He had his vaccine, so it was probably a simple virus.

He hadn't told Maureen.

He dialed the number. The phone rang twice before Maureen answered.

He was glad to hear her voice. "Hi, darling," he said. "You sound out of breath."

"I just walked in the door," she said. "I went to the grocery store, and it was wild—nearly a riot. The shelves are empty. Everyone was shoving and shouting."

"Because of the smallpox?"

"It's unbelievable. People are frantic. Some are leaving for the country. Half of our neighbors are packing up."

Harry wasn't surprised. If more cases were discovered, the *real* panic would begin.

"How's Lauren doing?" Maureen asked.

"She's worse."

Maureen was quiet a moment. "I'm sorry, honey. Are you okay?"

"It's getting tough. I need to come home. I need to see you and the girls."

"We miss you, too. You could leave for a little while. You could rush back for an emergency."

"I think I'd better stay."

With Lauren so critical, he wouldn't leave until she was better, or until he knew for sure she wouldn't ever be.

And he couldn't go home until he was certain his symptoms weren't caused by smallpox or until his family was vaccinated. Even then, no one was certain if the vaccine was completely protective, especially with this strain. And if his symptoms were smallpox, he didn't want to think about what that would mean.

"Then I'm coming to see you," Maureen said.

"I don't know. I'm not sure you should go out."

"Is the hospital closed?"

"No, not actually."

"Then it's settled."

It was hard to say no to Maureen. He felt sick and was sure his fever was increasing, but he shouldn't be contagious until he had a rash.

"Please, don't bring the girls. I want to see them so badly, but I'm not sure it's safe. Please."

"Okay, if that's what you want, but they'll be upset."

"I know, but it's for the best."

"I'll bring you supper. It *is* Christmas Eve."

"Thank you. That would be nice."

After Maureen hung up, Harry fell back on the bed. He hoped he wouldn't risk Maureen's health by seeing her. He couldn't live with himself if he infected her with smallpox.

He prayed to God that he only had the flu.

* * *

DECEMBER 24, 10:00 A.M. EST
ATLANTA

Jackson had three hundred e-mails on his computer, and the clutter in his office had doubled since he had left. He had six important phone conferences scheduled before five o'clock, including one with the president.

The president was considering a mass vaccination for the entire country, but Jackson was advising against it. It might be politically correct, but he argued that it wasn't particularly good health care policy. Though the number of vaccinations in DeKalb for only two cases of smallpox was relatively small, Lafitte had already notified Jackson of several reactions. One was serious enough to require VIG, which was the only known treatment. Reactions were expected, and most would be mild, yet the media maximized the dangers of the vaccine and the critical shortage of VIG. Several of the people who were thought to be smallpox contacts in DeKalb had refused to be vaccinated, and the law was unclear about the consequences. Jackson had hoped the educational materials would be encouraging, but with all the legal requirements, the side effects of the vaccine sounded worse than the disease itself. If multiple cases of smallpox occurred, the fear of the vaccine would be a problem.

"Dr. Jackson?" His secretary was calling on his speakerphone.

"Yes, Nellie."

"It's the president. Line two."

Jackson picked up the phone.

"Yes, Mr. President."

"Jackson, any more cases?"

"No, sir. If we learn of any, we'll notify you immediately."

"I think we should make plans to vaccinate the entire country, just in case."

"Mr. President, those plans are in place and can be instituted at any time you deem appropriate."

"Good. I need you in Washington tonight. I'm calling an emergency meeting. I know it's Christmas Eve."

"That's not a problem."

"My staff will make arrangements."

"Thank you, Mr. President."

Christmas Eve really wasn't an issue. He wasn't in the mood to celebrate anyway.

* * *

DECEMBER 24, 11:00 A.M. EST
NEW YORK CITY

Vicky's next patient was another person with fever, chills, and backaches. Of course, as with every single patient she had seen, she considered smallpox a possibility. The worry about smallpox was beginning to interfere with her judgment. Not all of these people could have smallpox, could they?

Vicky's mother had come to the emergency room earlier with the same symptoms as everyone else. Vicky had checked for influenza, and the test was negative. As with many of the patients, her mother's symptoms were consistent with smallpox, but her exam was normal, and Vicky had sent her home. She wished she could have vaccinated her mother, but there was no vaccine available. No new cases of smallpox had been reported anywhere, so Vicky reassured herself that her mother would be fine. She hoped she was right.

Vicky stepped into the exam room. The patient was a Pakistani and spoke no English. He looked ill. She checked him very carefully, examining his ears, nose, and throat; his heart and lungs; and his abdomen. She especially checked for even the slightest rash. He was sick enough to order a variety of tests, and his influenza A was positive. He had the flu and went home with a prescription for an antiviral.

The next patient was a thirty-year-old white male, a well-dressed, affluent lawyer. He complained of two days of fever, vomiting, and backaches, and he was absolutely positive that he had smallpox.

"Have you been around anyone with the flu?" she asked.

"Yeah, about ten thousand people on the subways, on the sidewalks, and in the streets. I live in New York."

Vicky ignored the sarcasm. She started at the top of his head, and then examined his ears, nose, and throat. Next she listened to his heart and lungs, and examined his abdomen. As she had done on every patient, she looked closely at his skin for a rash.

She almost missed them. Behind his left ear were two vesicular lesions, small blisters—definitely suspicious. With the two cases in Chicago, his symptoms, and these vesicles, this was smallpox until proven otherwise. She had most likely found the next case of smallpox!

"Have you ever had chickenpox?" she asked, attempting to sound calm.

"I think so...when I was a kid. Why?"

"You have two lesions behind your ear that I'm a little worried about."

"What is it?"

"I'm not sure. I want one of our other doctors to look at it."

"You think it's bad? Is it smallpox?"

"Listen, I'll be right back. Please be patient. Okay?"

Vicky stepped out into the hallway. "Where's Newton?" she asked one of the nurses at the desk.

"He's in his office," she answered. "Where else?"

The office door was closed. Vicky knocked and cracked it open.

"Come in," Newton said.

"Jack, you need to come see this. I think it's smallpox."

"Really?"

"Thirty-year-old white male with fever, backache, and vomiting. He has two vesicular lesions behind his ear."

"None in his mouth? No other locations?"

"No, just the two."

"Okay, let's go take a look."

Newton followed her into the exam room, and she introduced him to the patient. The lawyer was anxious, she noticed, and with good reason.

Both she and Newton examined the lesions. Now there were three, a change in only ten minutes, and they were all in the same phase. Vicky and Newton looked at each other. Vesicular lesions. Same phase of development. It was smallpox!

"I'll call infectious disease," Vicky said. "We'll admit him to the ICU negative pressure room with HEPA filters."

"I'll call the CDC," Newton said. "We'll need confirmation."

Vicky thought that it was most certainly smallpox, and if it was, all hell would break loose. Two sites confirmed a terrorist attack.

Her heart sank. Her mother had the exact same symptoms.

CHAPTER TWENTY SIX

DECEMBER 24, 6:00 P.M. CST
DAY FOURTEEN OF THE SECOND WAVE OF EXPOSURE
DEKALB, ILLINOIS

Harry checked his temperature. It was one hundred point five. He was nauseated and had vomited once, and his back was hurting much worse. He had carefully inspected himself for a rash in the doctors' lounge and saw absolutely nothing. He wasn't contagious until the rash broke out, and he couldn't confirm his diagnosis until that time either. Maybe it was just the flu. He hoped so.

He left the hospital by the door to the doctors' parking lot at the rear of the building. Only one guard was on duty, and he was there to keep people, especially reporters, out. The guard greeted Harry by name and wished him a good evening. Harry informed him he'd be coming back inside in a few minutes.

The sky was pink and blue along the western horizon. The air was cool and crisp but refreshing. For twelve years on this evening, he had left work early to celebrate Christmas Eve with his wife and daughters. They'd have a candlelight dinner prepared by Maureen's expert hands, take a drive to view the lights, and then snuggle together in front of the fire until the girls, and usually Maureen, fell asleep. Santa came in the morning at their house, and they enjoyed a private family time. Christmas was their special holiday.

Not this year.

Harry scanned the parking lot for Maureen. She was standing next to their car, and she was alone. As he had wished, the girls did not come, yet he so desperately wanted to see them. Harry embraced her and held her tight. He hadn't held her in what seemed forever.

"I brought you some food from home," she said. "I didn't want you to miss our traditional dinner."

"Thanks. I do appreciate it."

She held out a paper sack full of containers. "I thought you might be tired of hospital food."

Harry took the sack. He didn't have much of an appetite. "This is really sweet, but I'd much rather be at home."

She touched his forehead. "You're warm. Do you have a fever?"

"I think so."

"Is it smallpox?"

"Probably not. I had the vaccine. Maybe it's the flu."

"I knew something was wrong. Can you be tested?"

"Not yet, but I'm not contagious."

"That doesn't matter to me. You think it matters to Frank?"

"No," Harry thought, "it didn't. Of course, it wouldn't matter to her either."

"Is there someone there you can see?" she asked.

"Probably Naguib Haleem."

"Promise me you'll talk to him."

There was no sense arguing with Maureen. She was a bulldog when she made up her mind.

"If I break out in a rash, then it's definite. I'll be hospitalized in isolation and treated."

Her silence meant she knew how serious that would be.

"I'll see to it," he said, "that you and the girls get the vaccine. You'll be okay then. Mike Lafitte is here, and he'll do that for me."

Maureen reached out and held him tight. She kissed him, unafraid. He felt the warmth of her lips and the passion of her kiss.

"I might not see you for awhile," he said.

"I don't want to hear that. I'll be praying for a miracle."

She opened the car door and then kissed him again. She slid into the front seat, and he gently shut the door and watched her drive away. He wanted more than anything to get in the car with her and go home to spend Christmas Eve with his family. He wanted to sleep in his own bed and make love with his wife.

Harry turned back to face the bright lights of the hospital complex etched against the black sky. As he approached the door to the hospital, a man was leaning against the brick wall of the building, smoking a cigarette.

"Where are you going to work when this is over, Dr. Bennett?"

"Pardon me?" Harry said. The voice sounded familiar, but Harry didn't recognize the man in the darkness until he was closer. It was Eric Ness.

"Of course, because of you," Ness said, "our hospital won't survive, just like I predicted."

"Don't you think that's a bit premature, Mr. Ness?"

Ness dropped the cigarette onto the sidewalk and rubbed it out with his foot. "You don't have a clue as to what it takes to run a hospital, do you?" Ness took a couple of steps out into the light toward Harry. "We have only one patient now. No one else will come here. Will that pay our bills? I don't think so."

"It was the right thing to do."

"For whom? Have you asked your colleagues? They're traveling thirty miles to other hospitals to admit their patients. Our community will likely lose its medical facility. In fact, even the Randalls would have been better off. In Chicago, they would have the *appropriate* specialists on the case."

"You're an ass!"

Ness laughed. "I've been called worse. If we do survive, Dr. Bennett, you can kiss *your* career here good-bye." He pointed his finger at Harry. "Try and get privileges at this hospital to do anything. It won't happen."

Harry shook his head. "You'll have to excuse me," he said. "I have more important things to do than talk to you."

Harry turned his back on Ness, passed the security guard, and entered the hospital. He walked to his room by the doctors' lounge and opened the paper sack of containers with Maureen's Christmas Eve meal. It smelled good, but his nausea lessened his appetite. He would eat it anyway because Maureen's hands had made it.

Harry took his first bite. Ness didn't intimidate him, he thought. Lauren needed care, and she might as well be here. No doctors anywhere had any better treatment than they did. That was the shame of it.

Maureen had prepared glazed ham, broccoli and cheese casserole, green beans, and a garden salad with homemade Italian dressing. The meal was much better than any hospital food he had ever tasted, and Maureen's efforts made him yearn for his home and family.

Regardless of what Ness believed or what his colleagues thought, if indeed what Ness said about them was true, Lauren should be here and so should he.

He took another couple of bites but then stopped. The nausea was worse. His head was beginning to throb more, and the muscles in his back and limbs ached. He closed the containers for later and stretched out on the bed to rest.

He should be here, of that Harry was certain, but if he had smallpox, he knew in his heart that he might never leave.

* * *

DECEMBER 24, 7:00 P.M. EST
NEW YORK CITY

The Saint Joseph emergency room was in pandemonium. Six cases of fever and vesicular rash were seen in the ER and admitted to the hospital. All were extremely ill. The local news media reported that all the other ERs in New York City were seeing cases of smallpox—unconfirmed, of course. So far, thirty-four. Three were also reported in New Jersey, and one in Connecticut. Thirty-eight total.

Vicky was in an examination room with a young woman whose vesicular rash had developed on her face and neck in the past six hours. She saw her exact rash on a TV picture and rushed to the ER, only to wait six hours in line to be seen.

"Is it smallpox?" she asked Vicky, her voice shaking with fear.

"We can't be sure until we do some tests to confirm it, but we do need to keep you in the hospital."

The woman didn't move for a couple of seconds then suddenly threw herself backward and howled a blood-curdling scream. "Noooooo!" she yelled. Her arms began flailing and flapping.

"Nurse!" Vicky shouted. "I need sedation in here. Now!"

Three nurses and two orderlies rushed in, and it required all five to hold her down while the sedative took effect. She was case number thirty-nine. Vicky was told eight similar cases were in the waiting room. Many more like this one, Vicky thought, and she'd be exhausted.

In the hallway, five nurses took Vicky aside. They were upset.

"We've seen six cases of smallpox in this ER," one of the nurses said, "and none of us has yet to be vaccinated. Newton said we would get it today."

"You should have four days," Vicky said. "I'm sure it'll arrive."

"Four days," the nurse said, "that's assuming we haven't had any cases in here that we missed, and how can you be so sure it'll be here? This could mean our lives."

Another nurse pointed her finger at Vicky. "We've heard the shipment was diverted."

"I can't believe—"

"The mafia," she interrupted, "or the black market."

Vicky thought it wasn't out of the realm of possibility. She needed hers, and Justin needed his, too.

"You tell Newton," the first nurse said sharply, "two hours or we're walking, and we mean it!"

"Please, don't do that. We need your help. I'll talk to Dr. Newton."

"We mean it, Dr. Anderson," the second nurse said a little softer. "We have families."

"I know. I'll talk to him. I promise."

* * *

DECEMBER 24, 9:00 P.M. EST
WASHINGTON, DC

The emergency meeting called by the president of the United States was held in the cabinet room in the Executive Office Building adjacent to the White House. Thirty people were in the room with the president—the cabinet members, military, congressional leaders, the vice president, director of the FBI, and Jackson. Jackson had attended numerous meetings at the White House and at Congress but never one this intense.

The president had asked Jackson to give an update. Jackson was standing next to the president, who was seated at the head of the table.

"Do we know how many cases?" the president asked.

"Yes, sir. We have, of course, the first two cases in Chicago from three days ago. The first case in New York City was diagnosed at eleven A.M. this morning. Now we have sixty cases in New York, New Jersey, and Connecticut, ten more in Chicago, five here in Washington, one in Miami, three in Boston, and two in Wyoming. Eighty-three total. There will be more."

Everyone in the room stayed silent.

"No pattern yet," Jackson continued. "We're vigorously collecting epidemiologic information."

One of the generals spoke up. "We need to do more than collect data!" he said.

"Who has done this?" the president asked.

The director of the FBI answered. "We don't know, Mr. President. We think it is unlikely a single release. It's more consistent with multiple individuals who made multiple contacts. The victim in Chicago stated that she remembered contact with a man of Middle Eastern descent who was very ill. We are investigating this."

"Is that all we have?" the president said sharply. "That's it?"

"The virus is likely the same," Jackson said, "since the infections have all occurred at the same time. All the specimens were sent to Atlanta for confirmation. We'll know the strain tomorrow or the next day. Both the CDC and USAMRIDD are working around the clock. If it is a bioengineered strain, one where the virus has been altered to make it more virulent, it may be even more dangerous. The first cases in Chicago were very, very aggressive."

"How many more cases are we going to have?" the president asked.

"Unknown. We're probably seeing the second wave."

"What's that?"

"The first wave was the original cases—the terrorists, we presume. The second wave is those who were infected by the first wave. The second wave is the cases currently being reported, and this hasn't peaked yet. Before the third wave we'll have a lull, then about two weeks later an explosion of cases."

"Of course, this is serious," the president said, "but we don't want to panic either."

"Mr. President, I'm not. We now have nearly one hundred second-wave cases in multiple sites, and we expect more. Our models show that with a thousand initial cases, each infecting three other people, and assuming no interventions, we will have 7,000 infected in thirty days and 450,000 in ninety days. Of course, we will intervene as best we can. We must remember, however, that the number of people susceptible to small-pox is now very large, so the transmission rates for this epidemic could be much greater than the rates in the past. Also, large-scale interventions are an enormous undertaking. In 1947, in an outbreak of eight cases in New York City, it took over a week to vaccinate six million people. If the disease spread is very rapid, it may outpace our ability to vac-cinate the population, even with a mass vaccination program. This is a possibility we must be aware of, Mr. President. I don't think we are panicking."

There was a complete silence in the room.

"Dr. Jackson," the president said finally, "what should we do?"

Jackson hadn't slept a wink in two days, but he was remarkably alert. He was not fatigued. His thinking was crystal clear. "Mr. President," Jackson said, "it is my opinion that it is time to vaccinate everyone in the nation. It's our only chance."

"Voluntary?"

"Not my decision," Jackson said. "In addition, we should quarantine New York City and Chicago, which have reported cases, and maybe Washington, DC."

"Impossible!" one of the cabinet members said loudly. "You're suggesting we shut down travel in and out of New York? In and out of Washington? That's impossible. We might as well destroy our entire economy."

"Mr. President," Jackson said calmly, "at least until everyone in those cities is vac-cinated."

"How long will that take?" the president asked.

"Two weeks would be an optimistic estimate."

"That would require the National Guard to cordon off those cities," the president said. "We'll have to declare martial law." The president directly faced Jackson. "Now is the time? Are you sure?"

"Yes, sir. A hundred Spaniards conquered twenty million Aztecs, and our popula-tion has the same poor immunity to smallpox as the Aztecs did."

"How many will die from the vaccine?"

"One to two per million vaccinated. Also, we are about out of VIG, which is what we use to treat a serious reaction to the vaccine. We have only enough VIG in the U.S. to treat two or three thousand serious reactions. Then we'll be out."

The president was quiet. No one spoke or shuffled papers or made any noise at all.

"Jackson," the president said.

"Yes, Mr. President."

"Begin the vaccinations. I want a legal opinion and an opportunity to talk to the mayors of those cites and their governors before we close them." The president stood and everyone in the room stood with him. "God help us all," he said.

The meeting was over.

* * *

DECEMBER 24, 10:00 P.M. CST
CHICAGO O'HARE AIRPORT

The howling Chicago wind blowing off Lake Michigan was miserably cold, and after twelve long, continuous hours outside, Roberts was exhausted. The temperature had been above freezing most of the day and much of the ice and snow was melting; it was the wind chill that made him so uncomfortable. Roberts stamped his feet and covered his face with his glove, hoping to warm himself up until they were finished. This was the last of the long-term airport parking lots they would search. So far, their efforts had been wasted. The chances of finding the body were poor—not knowing if it was here at O'Hare or if a body even existed at all.

A gust of wind forced Roberts backward, almost knocking him off his feet. *Damn Chicago and its windy city!* This weather was why he preferred Atlanta.

In his entire career at the FBI, he had not organized such a large group and certainly never as quickly as this one had been pulled together. Nearly two hundred law enforcement officers had been searching since ten o'clock that morning. Roberts had simply made three or four phone calls, and all of the people he had called had agreed to help. In turn, each of them had enlisted other volunteers, and within two hours they had assembled more than they could use—FBI, Chicago PD, DEA agents, U.S. Marshall Service, and a variety of others. Even more amazing, they all came on Christmas Eve. In addition, a dozen search dogs were offered, which Roberts thought were a whole lot more important than the men. They were looking for a dead terrorist who had crawled into a hole to die. The hole could be anywhere and was likely well hidden. The dogs were essential. The sooner they found the body, the better. If they could confirm that the smallpox cases were caused by a terrorist attack, especially finding clues as to the network involved, it would be invaluable.

Roberts divided the volunteers into ten teams. They searched parking lots, sewer and drainage pipes, storage sheds, and trash dumpsters. The parking lots around O'Hare were huge, and they had required the most time and manpower. If this last lot, parking lot C, was unsuccessful, Roberts wasn't sure where to look next.

"Bitchin' cold, hey boss?" said the man standing next to Roberts.

Blake Walker was a burly Chicago PD sergeant who was one of the first to volunteer and was the dog handler for Jazz, a black Labrador retriever. Roberts had always thought black Labs were pretty stupid, but this one clearly wasn't. He sniffed out and investigated his assignments with a boundless energy, never resting, checking every nook and cranny. Jazz worked hard, as his handler said, like a dog. Roberts was impressed. If the terrorist's body were here, this dog would find it.

"Too cold for me," Roberts said to the officer. "The wind is blowing right through me."

"You become acclimated after a few years."

"I'll pass."

"You southern boys are wimps."

"Sensitive is what they tell me," Roberts said. "And the southern girls love it."

"No accounting for taste," Walker said.

Roberts smiled. He pointed down a row. "Take Jazz down there," he said. "Then we'll come back up that one, and we'll be done."

The second team was directed by one of the agents from the Chicago FBI office. They were gathered on the opposite side of the lot and would work to the middle toward Roberts's group.

"You'd think Jazz would be freezing," Roberts said to Walker, "but he doesn't seem to mind."

"Tolerates it better than we do," Walker said. "If he didn't, I wouldn't have him out here."

Roberts didn't doubt it. He probably treated the dog better than he did his own kids. "Shouldn't be much longer, then we'll all go indoors."

The plan was simple. They'd identify a suspicious vehicle, don the bioprotective suits, and pry open the trunk. Roberts's biggest fear was the possibility that the terrorist had rigged the trunk with explosives before he died. It didn't seem likely—would a man dying of smallpox have that capability? Yet anything was possible. Roberts would check, but if the trunk was wired, it would probably be on the inside and undetectable. The unknown was the part of the job he hated.

Walker directed Jazz toward each vehicle, and the dog would circle it casually, acting almost disinterested. Occasionally, Jazz would stop and examine more closely, but no car had yet caused Jazz much concern.

Roberts noticed about halfway down the row that the lighting seemed less bright. Security cameras faced several directions but were too far away to provide good coverage of this area. If he were to choose a spot, this one seemed among the best. Roberts tried to think through the process from the view of the criminal. What type of car would he use? New? Old? Would it be a rental? Stolen? Many criminals were predictable and logical. Some were not—either too clever or too stupid to follow a pattern. This criminal, Roberts thought, would not be stupid.

As he thought about it, the cyanide capsule they found in California now made more sense. He remembered the odd smile on the face of the man in custody. Though Roberts had suspected it at the time, it was clear to him now that the man was a terrorist. The man had been prepared to die by poison, but they had accommodated him with a gunshot wound. Here in Chicago another man who was likely a terrorist, probably an accomplice of the one who died in California, had slipped through. This sonofabitch had successfully infected the mother and child, and then crawled into a hiding place, maybe the trunk of one of these cars, and taken the pill. The poison, as far as Roberts was concerned, was too easy.

Jazz stopped and began pawing at the rear tire of a late-model white sedan. He was on to something. The team moved closer and watched. After circling the car twice, Jazz came to the rear and faced the car, stretching down to the pavement on his front paws. He held that position and began barking loudly.

This was the one.

Walker moved the dog away. His job was done. Now the men would take over.

Roberts pulled his radio off his belt. "Randy," he said into the microphone, "bring the van over." He gave the driver their position. "Okay," he told the team, "set up a perimeter around this car." He pointed to one of the officers. "Run that vehicle's tags."

The van turned into the lot and stopped about a hundred yards away from the target. The driver swung open the back doors and the team carried out the blast shield, just in case of explosives. Roberts changed into the bioprotective gear. The men grew serious, and no one said much—no chatter, small talk, or laughter—only a few brief exchanges. This was strictly business.

Roberts pulled the hood over his head. The plastic facemask allowed a clear vision. A microphone and radio were attached to the inside of the hood, enabling communication with the team. He slipped on the gloves and locked them into place. The suit wasn't insulated, yet as his adrenaline began to flow, he didn't feel nearly as cold.

Several tools were set out on the ground if he needed them. He lifted a thick, black pry bar over his shoulder. Roberts was ready. He gave a thumbs up and moved into position. About three feet from the car, he stopped and inspected the underside with a small, round mirror attached to the end of a ten-foot length of rod, specifically looking for a battery, plastic explosives, or any unusual wiring. He saw none. He approached the rear of the car and slid his hand along the bottom of trunk lid, gently feeling for any loose objects, wires, or anything out of the ordinary. He peered through the crack, but it was tight, and he could not see inside. Standing back for a moment, he breathed in deeply and released it slowly. His pulse rate was up, and he felt the thump of his heart in his chest. Relax, he told himself. Keep breathing. Roberts glanced behind him at his team. "It's a go," he said. It was time.

The trunk lid popped open easily with the pry bar. Inside was a black garbage bag extending the length of the trunk. As soon as Roberts saw it, he knew it was the body. It was lying crossways and the top was tied from the inside. Glancing quickly around the interior of the trunk, he saw nothing suspicious for explosives. He reached out and lightly touched the bag with his finger, feeling the softness of flesh through the thin plastic, confirming what he expected. The body was slightly warm, and it felt bloated and squishy, like rotten fruit, and he thought he felt the tissue sliding off the bone as he gently pushed. The sensation made him queasy.

From a pocket on his suit, he took a pair of scissors and held them near the top of the bag. Sitting a hundred yards away and directly behind him, Jazz began crying in a high-pitched whine.

"Can you smell that?" one of the officers asked through his headphones. "We can smell it from here."

Roberts couldn't smell anything but his own body odor in the suit. "No, I don't," he said.

"Man, that smells terrible."

Roberts reached out and held up a section of the black bag. He took the scissors and cut a small slice across the top then turned the scissors perpendicular and slit the plastic lengthwise. As soon as he did, a putrid material oozed outward, a mass of foul, decomposing flesh, formless and liquefied, as black as death. At the sight, Roberts's stomach swelled upward into his chest and he vomited into his mask. He stumbled backward a few steps and ripped off the hood, coughing out the material from his throat. In all his years he had seen nothing like it. Turning away, he bent over and vomited several more times, emptying his stomach on the ground. The smell from the vehicle behind him was disgusting, and he felt even more nauseated. He stood and walked several yards toward the van, attempting to catch his breath. The nausea had caught him off guard. The image of what he saw in the trunk continued to flash in his vision.

Roberts sat on the ground. The others kept their distance, which was probably wise. He might have contaminated himself by pulling off the hood, but he couldn't help it. It was a stupid thing to do, he told himself. He hoped he wouldn't regret it.

"Gary?" It was Walker's voice behind him, several feet away. "Are you okay?"

Roberts turned to Walker. "I'm fine. I don't know what I was expecting, but it wasn't that."

"What's over there?"

Roberts slowly shook his head. "The very gates of hell itself," he said, as he looked back over at the car. "May God help us all!"

Roberts stood and removed the equipment, and then wiped his face. They had found the man they were seeking, or what was left of him. The answers they needed were in the trunk, and, despite the mess, they had the means to discover the truth. It was only a matter of time.

* * *

DECEMBER 24, 11:00 P.M. CST
DEKALB, ILLINOIS

Lauren looked worse when Harry made rounds just before bedtime. Haleem had already been there and had gone to bed. Her breathing was shallow, and her rash had become a solid sheet of pustules on her face. The nurses had dressed the weeping wounds, and she was wrapped up in white gauze like a mummy. Harry ordered more sedation. She wouldn't suffer.

Frank was at the bedside, and he barely spoke. He was on a death watch.

"Call me if you need me," Harry said to Janet. "I'll be in the doctors' lounge."

She nodded but didn't speak. The nurses were despondent, too.

The walk to the doctors' lounge was quiet. The hallway was deserted. Most of the units were completely closed, and the staff had been sent home. He undressed and washed his face. His back ached worse and his fever was higher. Harry carefully examined his face and mouth but saw nothing.

Lucas was snoring next door. He had stayed in the hospital even though he wasn't treating anyone, feeling a responsibility. Haleem did, too. Lafitte said they could go home since they were immunized, but Harry certainly didn't want to. The others were staying for their own reasons.

Harry's symptoms were becoming harder to ignore. He took two acetaminophen and slipped under the covers, finally drifting off, thinking of Lauren and his own daughters. He dreamed of sunshine and skiing and his girls laughing and playing on the beach. He was holding Maureen in their bed and kissing her deep and long, making love in the darkness of their bedroom.

The loudspeaker startled Harry awake. "Code Blue ICU. Code Blue ICU." Immediately his pager began beeping as well.

It was Lauren.

Harry rushed out of bed and down the hallway. As he reached the unit, Frank was outside the room, slumped on the floor, his face covered in his hands. Harry quickly gowned and went into the room. One nurse was compressing Lauren's chest, and one was using the AMBU bag to deliver oxygen. Janet was pushing a medication from a syringe into Lauren's IV line.

"She had a respiratory arrest first," Janet said, "but then her monitor went flatline. We started CPR, and I gave her one dose of epinephrine. We're not getting a good seal on the AMBU."

Harry noticed the rubber edge did not fit tightly around her mouth because of the dressings.

"We need to intubate her," Harry said.

Janet handed Harry the laryngoscope and a small, pediatric endotrachael tube. The nurses were prepared for the possibility. Harry took the equipment from Janet, but then he dropped his arms to his sides. He wasn't sure he wanted to do this. It wouldn't change her condition. It wouldn't help anything—only prolong the inevitable. If the epinephrine didn't restart her heart rhythm, intubating her wouldn't really matter.

"Dr. Bennett?" Janet said. She was waiting.

Harry looked at Lauren. She was covered in gauze, dying of a fatal disease, a precious child victimized by a horrible fate. Was it right to do this?

"Dr. Bennett!" Janet said. "We're not making a good seal."

"We can't quit," he thought. "She deserves every chance."

Harry lifted her jaw and positioned the laryngoscope. The nurse stopped compressions. Smallpox lesions covered her mouth and were oozing. Blood pooled near her vocal cords, obscuring his view.

"Suction!" He held out his right hand.

Janet slapped the suction tip into his palm, and he cleared the area of blood. For a brief time, the vocal cords were visible, and he pushed the endotracheal tube forward, slipping it into place.

"Restart the compressions," Harry said, "and connect the ventilator."

The nurses scurried to complete his orders. The monitor showed continuing asystole—a flatline, no electrical activity.

"Give a second dose of epinephrine," he ordered.

Janet did as Harry asked. They both watched the monitor. No change.

Haleem arrived. Harry updated him on Lauren's condition.

"Any other thoughts?" Harry asked. "Should we shock her?"

"Don't think so," Haleem said, "but we might as well repeat the epinephrine. We have nothing to lose."

Janet gave another dose. Each nurse took turns at the chest compressions while Harry and Haleem observed the monitor. Hardly a word was spoken. The nurses, as regular caregivers in the intensive care unit, had participated in far more codes than Harry or Haleem, but they remained silent. There was nothing left to do. Both doctors ordered several more doses of medications, but it was futile. Nothing worked. She was not responding. They were losing her.

"Time since arrest?" Haleem asked.

"Thirty-five minutes," Janet said.

Harry saw the monitor was still flatline. "Should we continue?" he asked.

"No." Frank was standing in the doorway. "It's time to stop." He was out of his gown and mask. His eyes were pleading. "No more. She's gone, Dr. Bennett, she's gone."

Harry slowly nodded his head. Frank was right. It was time to stop.

Harry faced Frank. A tear fell from Harry's eye and he was not ashamed. "I'm sorry, Frank," Harry said.

"It's not your fault, Dr. Bennett, or yours, Dr. Haleem."

Frank walked up to the bedside.

"Mr. Randall," Janet said softly, "you should have your gown on."

He ignored her and began gently stroking Lauren's hair. "I don't give a damn about that," he said, without harshness or anger.

"It's okay," Harry said. "Frank, take your time."

The nurses, Haleem, and Harry left him alone and closed the door. Harry removed his equipment, placed it in a biohazard container, and wrote a final note in the chart. The nurses were sad, crying softly, and Harry thanked them for their help. After talking briefly with Dr. Haleem and thanking him, too, Harry left the ICU, walked down the hallway, and went into the nearest men's room. It was empty. Harry opened the stall and sat on the toilet. He covered his face and sobbed deep and hard, as if he might never stop.

CHAPTER TWENTY SEVEN

DECEMBER 25, CHRISTMAS DAY, 9:00 A.M. EST
DAY FIFTEEN OF THE SECOND WAVE OF EXPOSURE
NEW YORK CITY

The solid line of humanity waiting to be seen outside Saint Joseph Hospital stretched two miles. Vicky looked out the window on the eighth floor to see. She couldn't believe it. The line was four or five people wide and followed the sidewalk straight up the street uninterrupted, blocking the intersections. No one was willing to leave a space and lose their place. It was an amazing sight.

The media had reported the Randall girl's death. One patient in New York City had died but not in Vicky's hospital. One other death, in Chicago, was now reported to be the taxi driver who took a terrorist to O'Hare Airport. The media was reporting that the terrorist's body had been found at the airport in a car trunk. Though the details were pending, the reporters speculated at length, even to the point, Vicky thought, of making up what they couldn't confirm.

Rumors were rampant. Thousands were leaving the city. The interstates and bridges were totally blocked. Airline tickets were selling for five thousand dollars each. The mayor of New York had announced the entire city would be vaccinated, and a mass of people were camping out at the health department, anticipating the start.

In the past two hours, Vicky had diagnosed eight new cases. Saint Joseph had already isolated an entire floor for smallpox, and the administrators were talking about turning the hospital into a smallpox facility. Newton had come through, and the entire ER staff had been vaccinated. A few hours later, one nurse started having nausea, back pain, and fever, so she was isolated as a potential early case. That sent a panic through the staff, and the other nurses were threatening to walk off the job. Vicky couldn't blame them. She was scared, too.

When Vicky returned to the ER, she saw Justin pushing a stretcher into a room. He saw Vicky and smiled, but it was a weak smile, and that worried her.

"How are you feeling?" she asked.

"A little fluish. I got my vaccine—finally. Hope it's the flu."

"But you got your flu shot?"

"Doesn't matter," he said. "Can't stop. No one to replace me. How's your mother?"

"She's not feeling very good. Now her fever is one hundred and two. No rash yet, but I'm pretty worried."

"All you can do is wait. Did she get a vaccine?"

"It's not available yet."

"That's not right. What are they waiting for? It's crazy out there. The streets are jammed, and it's hard to get the ambulance anywhere. Have you been watching the TV?"

"Bits and pieces."

"Did you see the pictures of the looting in the South Bronx? One of the grocery stores on Westchester has been ransacked and is on fire."

"That's getting pretty close to home."

"They were reporting the entire water supply was contaminated. Now they're saying it's okay. I'm drinking bottled water anyway."

"They stationed a couple of National Guardsmen in the ER here about an hour ago. Now that's scary!" She reached out and touched his arm and leaned toward him. "Justin," she said softly, "I'm not sure what's going to happen. Mom's sick, and I'm stuck here. I'm thinking about leaving."

"I don't blame you. If you need me to take you anywhere, let me know."

"Thanks, Justin."

He walked away, and she stood alone. She needed a few minutes of privacy with him, a moment to touch him, to kiss him. But that wouldn't likely happen. She couldn't stop her work for her personal needs. Yet she was torn about going home. A number of the employees in the emergency room and other places in the hospital had already left. For now, she had a job to do, and no one else could do it for her.

Her next patient was a middle-aged male. He had fever, backache, and obvious pox lesions on his cheeks. Case number nine in two hours. The very first case was the toughest to diagnose. After that, it was think smallpox first, and then consider other possibilities.

"I'm sorry, sir," she told him. "It looks like smallpox. We'll need to keep you in the hospital."

He seemed to take the news better than the others. Maybe it was becoming more expected and not such a great surprise.

She wrote out a quick note and some orders, and placed the chart in front of the unit secretary.

"Another admission to the smallpox wing," Vicky said.

A loud crack came from the room she had left. Vicky rushed in. The man she had just seen was slumped over in the bed. He had a gun barrel in his mouth, and his blood and brains were scattered on the wall behind him. She moved to his side and checked his vital signs. He was dead.

Several of the nurses came into the room to help. Vicky shook her head. There was nothing for them to do.

"We could have helped you," Vicky said aloud to him, though she wasn't sure in her heart it was true. As she looked at the man's face, the tears gently rolled down her cheeks. "You could have at least let us try."

Vicky lifted the sheet and covered his head. The tragedies were only beginning.

* * *

DECEMBER 25, 10:00 A.M. EST
WASHINGTON, DC

Roberts's temporary office at FBI HQ, actually more a converted closet that Edward Mold had found for him, overlooked the corner of Tenth and E Streets toward the Ford's Theatre and the house where Abraham Lincoln died. That event, occurring years ago only a few hundred feet from where Roberts sat, began a national mourning unlike any known in the history of the United States. Now this event, an epidemic of smallpox, could potentially cause the largest loss of life ever seen in modern times. Both were deliberate and premeditated. The nameless terrorist Roberts had found in Chicago was a murderous, ideological madman, not unlike a John Wilkes Booth, a Hitler or a Stalin, a Timothy McVeigh, or an Osama bin Laden. Roberts was too late in Chicago, basically got lucky in Los Angeles, and had likely missed one in New York. How many others were out there?

The body from Chicago had so far provided few clues. Crime scene analysts had lifted two fingerprints from the trunk lid, but they had matched no known database. Though the body was badly decomposed, forensics hoped the DNA would yield results. The suspect's clothing was being thoroughly analyzed, and Roberts expected some helpful information about things like fibers, particles, and pollen. Eventually, they might know where he traveled and, if fortunate, where he originated.

Agents had spent hours reviewing surveillance tapes from the O'Hare Airport and from cameras around Michigan Avenue where the terrorist's taxi ride began. Unfortunately, and probably not by coincidence, the video of the airport parking lot where the car was parked was of little value. The taxi was seen arriving and leaving, but the suspect was not observed entering the trunk. The taxi company and the driver were clearly identified, but too late to help the poor driver who was already dead by the time the tapes were reviewed. Roberts had interviewed the driver at Dr. Bennett's suggestion, but he was already extremely ill, alone in a tiny apartment, covered with pox lesions, twice sent home from the emergency room with antibiotics. He was too sick to be helpful and had died a few hours later. Roberts had viewed the parking lot tapes himself, but the disfigured face of the man at the apartment looked nothing like the images on the video.

Roberts and every FBI agent in America were working today, Christmas Day, and would be working 24/7 for weeks to come. The budget was no longer an issue.

The phone on Roberts's desk rang. The caller, Lance O'Neal, identified himself as a local field agent in Washington, DC. He said his supervising agent thought his information might be important to Roberts.

"What have you got for me," Roberts said.

"I'm at the Marriot at Fourteenth and Pennsylvania. I've interviewed one of the maids here who told her supervisor about a guest who's been here for three weeks. He's a Middle Eastern male. She thought his activities seemed suspicious after seeing the smallpox reports. Her boss called our local office, and I came down to talk to her. I think we have a possible terrorist here."

"I'm three blocks away. Don't let her leave. I'll be there in five minutes."

Roberts exited the Hoover building into the December chill. The snow was falling lightly, melting on the warmer pavement of the sidewalks and streets, but starting to form a thin layer on the parked cars and benches. Since it was a holiday, barely a car passed him on Pennsylvania Avenue, and only a couple of pedestrians had ventured out. Roberts clutched his blue blazer, thinking it would have been adequate for a three-block walk, but he had forgotten he was in Washington, DC, and not the warmer climate of Atlanta. By the time he reached the Marriott, his fingers were going numb.

The revolving doors were off Fourteenth Street. He was greeted by the bellman as he entered the lobby. The registration desk, empty of guests, was to his right. A grand staircase reached downward to a lower level in elegant style straight ahead of him. He saw O'Neal at the bottom of the stairs, and though they had never met, he instantly knew O'Neal was FBI.

Roberts walked down the staircase and shook hands with O'Neal. The lower level held the administrative offices, and O'Neal led him into a small room off a narrow corridor. Inside the room, sitting behind a metal table, was a petite, Filipino woman, probably in her fifties, dressed in a gray maid's uniform, with a white collar. She was nervous to the point of visibly shaking. Roberts extended his hand, smiled, and introduced himself. He sat across the table from her. O'Neal remained standing. Roberts attempted to appear relaxed, paused frequently, and deliberately spoke slowing and softly, hoping his witness would relax because she would remember more if she did.

"The whole country is worried about an outbreak of smallpox," Roberts began. "Your willingness to tell us what you've seen is greatly appreciated by the FBI. We never know if what you've noticed will be helpful or not, but it's very important for us to investigate each and every lead."

The maid nodded and briefly smiled at his comment. "Thank you, officer," she said.

"You're welcome," Roberts said. "Now, please, tell us what you've seen."

"Okay. I called about the man who checked in three weeks ago to room six-oh-seven. He hasn't had his room cleaned once. For the first five days he never left, but then he went outside every day and was gone most of the day. I don't think he ever had a visitor. He orders room service often but doesn't allow delivery in the room, and he puts the tray in the hallway when no one is around. After ten days, I told the supervisor about it and we went into the room while he was gone. The room was messed up. He was sleeping on a bare mattress. The bathroom was dirty and trash was everywhere. I wanted to clean it up, but my supervisor said no. He said he hadn't harmed the hotel property, and he had his rights."

"Did you ever see him?" Roberts asked.

"Yes, a couple of times as he was leaving."

"What did he look like?"

"Young—in his twenties. He looked like an Arab, but he wore American clothes."

Roberts asked several questions about his description—his height, his weight, his facial features, and his hair. She answered quickly. She had been observant.

"He was out all the time before, but he hasn't left the room once in the last three days. Seems odd."

"Are you sure he's still in there?"

"Of course. The reason I called now is because I thought he might be sick."

"How's that?"

"The last time I saw him he looked bad. I don't know—pale, sickly…something. He just didn't look right."

"Did he have a rash?"

"I don't think so, but I only saw his face. The other thing I noticed was that he quit eating. When I picked up his trays, the food had barely been touched, and he hasn't ordered room service at all in twenty-four hours. I saw the reports of smallpox on TV, and that's when I called."

"We're very glad you did."

Roberts thanked her and ushered her out of the room. O'Neal shut the door and sat in the chair across from Roberts.

"I would consider this highly suspicious," Roberts said. "Check with hotel registration. We might get lucky if they have his passport."

O'Neal nodded.

"I'll call the director," Roberts continued. "I think we should go in with a SWAT team. We don't want this one to get away."

"Probable cause?"

"I don't think we'll have any trouble getting a court order. It's a clear case of national security."

O'Neal nodded in agreement. "I'll check the documents."

"I'll call the director," Roberts said. "Let's meet back here in half an hour."

* * *

DECEMBER 25, 10:00 A.M. CST
DEKALB, ILLINOIS

The light of Harry's flashlight hovered over a small vesicle on the inside of his cheek. There was no doubt. It was smallpox.

Despite a careful exam of the rest of his mouth and skin, he saw no other lesions. He was sicker, had vomited twice, and was chilling from the fever. He'd page Haleem and tell him, but he must tell Maureen first.

His home phone rang a couple of times before Maureen answered it. He asked about her and the girls. They were fine.

"Oh, Harry," she said, "it's really getting scary. I stocked up on groceries and supplies. The stores are empty. There's a black market for food, and gas is twenty dollars a gallon. I finally turned off the TV. Looting, cars on fire—it was too much to watch. I've been playing card games with the girls."

"I need to tell you something, Maureen." Harry wasn't sure he could tell her.

"What is it?"

"I'm sorry, sweetheart," he said, "I'm infected."

"Oh, my God, Harry," she said. "Are you sure?"

"Sure as I can be."

"I can't believe it. If you have smallpox, what does that mean?"

Harry wanted to assure her that he was fine, but he wasn't convinced himself. "It's too early to know," he said.

"I'm so very sorry. Are you all right?"

"I'll need to stay here."

"Then I'll come down there."

He could tell she was fighting back the tears. She didn't want him to hear her cry.

"No," he said gently. "It's too risky. I want you to stay home. I wish you would stay inside until Lafitte gives you your vaccine. He said he would be there today."

"I'll do whatever you want. I just feel so helpless."

"Me, too. I just wanted you to know." Harry's voice trailed off. He could hardly go on. "You must be prepared for the worse," he said. "This strain has been tough."

There was silence. She understood what he was saying.

"Harry," she said, "I'm worried sick."

"I think it will be a light case. I had the vaccine, so I'm expecting a lighter case."

Maureen was holding the phone away, but he could hear her softly sobbing.

"I'll be isolated," he said, "but I'll try to call. I miss you so much."

"I miss you, too," she said. "I love you. You have to get better."

"I will. I promise you."

"Don't give up on us."

"I won't." His voice became raspy. He was barely able to speak. "I have too much to live for."

She was crying. "And don't you forget it."

He smiled. "I love you."

"I love you, too."

He replaced the receiver and then lay back in the bed. He was infected with small-pox! At that moment, he felt more scared than he ever had in his life.

* * *

DECEMBER 25, 5:00 P.M. EST
WASHINGTON, DC

Roberts had made the arrangements for the raid on room 607 within two hours after talking to the maid, and three hours later, everyone was in place. Nobody felt like celebrating Christmas this year anyway, and with fear and smallpox spreading rapidly across the country, this was the only concrete lead anyone had.

Roberts had immediately called the FBI director from the Marriott and within a few minutes the Crisis Management Team was selected. Roberts was assigned as the on-site commander, special agent in charge (SAC), though he was from outside the local division. As the commander SAC, he was responsible for the overall assault as well as for any loss of life, if that was at all possible. Roberts reported his plans to Edward Mold, and Mold reported to the FBI director. The FBI director, Roberts had been told, had personally called the president and the U.S. attorney general. The White House wanted to be informed of every detail, no matter how small. Of course, the director had agreed.

No one knew what to expect, and Roberts had prepared for many contingencies. The team would be ready for a biologic agent, particularly smallpox, and that had been practiced multiple times in training, though none of the agents had made an actual assault in full biologic protective gear in a real situation. The harder part, and certainly unknown, was the possibility of armed violence. Did the suspect have a firearm? Had he utilized a tripwire to trigger explosives? Could he even have a radioactive dirty bomb? Anything was possible.

Instead of the Washington district SWAT team, the director wanted to deploy the FBI's Hostage Rescue Team (HRT), a counterterrorist unit with responsibility for high-threat tactical missions. When Roberts called, the HRT was on a biologic training exercise at Quantico. They told Roberts they'd be ready and at the hotel in two hours.

The HRT's education at Quantico would quickly be tested.

Despite the urgency, Roberts felt his preparations were as thorough as possible. They needed a fast response. He couldn't overthink this...or second-guess his decisions. Every minute delayed was wasted.

"Roberts, what do you think we'll find?"

The question was asked by SAC Rick Shelby of the FBI Washington Metropolitan Field Office, commander of the HRT. Shelby's voice was soft and low. He and Roberts were crouched in the hallway, around the corner fifty feet from the suspect's room; they were dressed in full biologic protective equipment, as well as flack jackets and body armor. They communicated by radios inside their headgear but still talked softly to avoid being heard down the hallway. Eight other agents, all heavily armed and most with automatic assault weapons, were either crouched down or standing behind them. Next to Roberts stood a muscular, six-foot-three agent, a former college weightlifter, holding a battering ram. A second team of agents was positioned behind the door to the stairwell at the opposite end of the hallway, prepared to begin the raid on Roberts's command.

Typically, the on-site commander did not participate directly in the raid, but Roberts would have none of that.

"I don't know," Roberts answered Shelby. "Maybe we'll find a sleeping tourist or a man sick in bed with smallpox. I hope we don't find a bomb."

"Me, either."

"Maybe he hasn't come out of his room because…well…maybe he's dead."

"I hope he'd not dead," Shelby said. "I want the sonofabitch alive."

"So do I," Roberts said. "I hope we keep *everyone* alive."

"Roger that."

Before the HRT arrived, the hotel was evacuated. Roberts encountered several logistical problems. If the suspect had smallpox, the guests and employees must be presumed to be exposed, possibly by the spread of the virus throughout the hotel through the ventilation system. The FBI transferred the guests to a nearby hotel and requested that they to remain quarantined until their risk was determined. It was particularly challenging to remove guests from the sixth floor and the rooms adjacent to the suspect, without alerting him to their activities. A skeleton crew of employees volunteered to stay on duty, but FBI agents manned the phones in case the suspect called the front desk or room service.

Outside, out of the view of room 607, Roberts had the streets cordoned off. In case the suspect was monitoring the streets and sidewalks, undercover agents and unmarked vehicles were used to mimic the patterns of traffic within his view. At the Willard Hotel across the street, guests whose windows faced Fourteenth Street were moved to other rooms in the hotel. HRT snipers were placed strategically in the Willard's rooms and on its roof.

Overall, the preparations went smoothly, and the guests and employees were surprisingly cooperative.

Roberts had tried to think of everything, and the input of others had been helpful. HRT and SWAT raids weren't too infrequent, and Roberts had planned several in the past, but never did one have such significance.

"I think we're ready," he told Shelby.

Shelby went through a radio check position by position, and each agent signaled back that he was good to go.

Roberts felt the tension in the hallway. Each agent knew the danger. They were ready. Whoever or whatever was in there, they'd know in a few seconds.

"On my count," Roberts said, holding up his hand. "One…two…three."

Both teams of agents left their positions and moved without a sound toward Room 607, one coming from around the corner and the other from out of the stairwell. The agent holding the battering ram stood in front of the doorway, waiting for the other agents to move into place. Roberts would lead and Shelby would follow directly behind him. Eight total agents would move rapidly into the room, and the rest would remain as backup in the hallway.

The agent with the battering ram glanced over at Roberts, awaiting his signal.

Roberts stood to one side and knocked on the door. "Housekeeping," he said. He knocked again a little firmer. "It's housekeeping." Roberts gestured to go.

The agent swung the battering ram back and forth a couple of times, and then with a powerful release slammed it into the door. The door ripped off its hinges and flew a few feet inside the room. Roberts tossed in the flash bomb and turned away.

Crack! A brilliant white light instantly burst from the room, filling the hallway. Immediately, Roberts and the agents rushed in.

In the center of the room was the suspect on the bed, an Arab male, completely naked, his entire body covered with smallpox pustules. He was holding his arms over his face, a reaction to the light. The room was in total disarray with trash and bedding flung everywhere. It smelled terrible. The curtains were closed, but the lights were on. The agents surrounded the subject with their weapons pointed at his head. He weakly dropped his arms and looked around at the agents.

"Don't shoot me," he said, raising his hands upward.

Roberts saw that he had no weapons or detonators. He was terribly sick, much too ill to resist. His smallpox lesions were textbook, impossible to confuse. This was their terrorist.

"Please don't kill me," he said, his voice weak, but his English perfect.

His mouth was parched. His lips were cracked and bleeding. The suspect was looking from agent to agent, pleading for his life.

"I won't hurt you," he said, "I promise. Please, I don't want to die."

Roberts watched him beg, wondering how many people he had infected. He wondered how many would die because of this terrorist's actions. The man looked pitiful, naked, helpless, weak, but the disease was dangerous, as powerful as any other weapon he could have used.

No, Roberts thought, this man would not be killed. He would be held and inter-rogated. He would go to the most modern of hospitals and receive the best medical care in the world.

He would not be killed, Roberts knew, but this man, the most despicable human he had ever seen, certainly deserved to die.

CHAPTER TWENTY EIGHT

DECEMBER 28, 9:00 A.M. EST
DAY EIGHTEEN OF THE SECOND WAVE OF EXPOSURE
WASHINGTON, DC

The President of the United States appeared grim faced and determined as he sat at the head of the table. He had called the meeting of the Joint Chiefs of Staff, the director of the CIA, the national security advisor, and the secretary of defense, and they were meeting in a secure area deep beneath the White House. This was not a meeting for a political solution but to define a strategy for retaliation. The casualties of this war would not go unanswered.

"The evidence points to an Islamic extremist group," the director of the CIA said. "We were holding a suspect in Los Angeles, but he was killed in an altercation. We've identified him and linked him to terrorist activities in the Middle East and Europe. He probably has Al-Qaeda connections. An FBI agent in Chicago started checking parking lots at O'Hare Airport and found a dead terrorist with smallpox in a plastic bag in the trunk of a car. We're now checking Kennedy, La Guardia, Dulles, Baltimore, Reagan, Boston Logan, and several other airports. Three days ago on Christmas, the FBI apprehended a terrorist at the Marriott on Pennsylvania Avenue covered with smallpox lesions."

"My God," the president said, "that's three blocks away."

"Yes, Mr. President," the director said. "The suspect is being held in strict isolation. It's been difficult to interrogate him because he's so sick, but the doctors think he might survive. A full investigation is underway."

"Who's behind this?" the president asked. "That's what I want to know."

"We do, too, Mr. President," the director said. "We hope to have the answer soon."

"I want to protect our food and water supplies, as well as our transportation and power."

"We're on full alert," the chairman of the Joint Chiefs of Staff said.

The president nodded. "I saw that the National Guard has been activated in Chicago, Washington, and New York. We may need armed convoys of food and supplies to those cities. I plan to stay here in Washington. It will look better."

"Yes, sir," the chairman said.

"I don't think we need to wait until we find all the dead bodies in the trunks of cars to begin our plans for a response. It's a short list of organizations and nations who are capable. Let's begin our preparation."

The men in the room nodded in agreement.

"This is an attack on America," the president said, "and we will not rest until we prevail."

The president stood, and the men stood with him.

"God help us all," the president said. "God help us all."

* * *

DECEMBER 28, 10:00 A.M. CST
DEKALB, ILLINOIS

Haleem was standing at the nurses' station when Jackson came into the unit.

"Good to see you, Dr. Haleem," Jackson said.

Haleem stood. "Thank you. It's nice of you to come see Harry."

"How's he doing?"

"He doesn't look so good. He's on antibiotics and antivirals."

"He had a vaccine as a child?"

"When he was ten. And he had the vaccine your team gave him six days ago."

"The vaccines should help."

"Maybe. I hope so. That's really the only chance he has. We're almost out of medications and won't get any additional supplies. I'll be lucky if I can give him a couple more doses. We have three ER nurses and one ICU nurse with smallpox. The hospital staff is panicked. I know all four personally. It's tough. In fact, you met the ICU nurse, Janet Hernandez."

"I remember her. I'm sorry."

"We have another mother and daughter. They are friends of the Randalls and had gone to Chicago with them."

"How about Mr. Randall?"

"He's devastated, of course, but he's not showing any signs of smallpox—although it's still too early to be certain."

"We needed to react more quickly, but I'm not sure how we could have."

"How many cases nationally?"

"Nearly three hundred, and we're expecting more."

"I'm sure other hospitals have it as bad as we do."

"The plans are underway for the president's mass vaccination program. It'll take three or four weeks. As I'm sure you've heard, he's closed New York City, Chicago, and Washington. We're vaccinating them first."

"Incredible times."

"You look exhausted," Jackson said.

"I've been going nonstop."

"Thanks for taking care of Harry."

"You're welcome."

"Take care of yourself, too."

Haleem nodded.

Jackson slipped on the personal protective equipment before entering the ICU exam room. Harry was in a hospital bed with two IVs, a heart monitor, and oxygen attached. His eyes were closed, and his breathing was rapid. His face, neck, and arms were covered with discrete pustular lesions, none hemorrhagic. Maureen was sitting in a chair opposite the doorway. She started to stand, but Jackson motioned for her to remain seated.

Harry's eyes remained closed. Maureen told Jackson that he had been asleep for several hours.

"Thanks for coming," Maureen said. "It means a lot."

Jackson moved to the side of the bed. "How is he doing?" he asked softly.

"They have him heavily sedated. Dr. Haleem says he's doing everything he can."

Jackson turned away from the bed and sat down on the chair beside Maureen. "Dr. Haleem is doing a fine job. I'm sorry to see Harry so ill. I feel like we should have gotten the vaccine here faster."

"You did your best. We had the first cases. Dr. Haleem said Harry was likely infected before we knew the diagnosis was even possible."

"I'm still sorry, and I'm sorry about your nurses, too."

"Did we have a chance to stop it here, anyway? It was already spreading."

"You're right. Probably not."

Maureen reached out and gently touched Jackson's arm. "I wanted to thank you for the vaccine for me and the girls, and for Jill, Harry's nurse. The vaccine is getting scarce."

"You're welcome. I was worried all along that the demand would outpace the supplies, and it surely might. Fortunately, I have connections."

"Harry appreciated it, too."

"You know, your husband is remarkable. He was the first doctor to see smallpox in thirty years, and he immediately diagnosed it."

"He went to an excellent lecture on the topic."

"And he was listening!"

"When we first met, I told you that I hoped your plans would be a complete waste of time. Remember?"

"Yes, I do. We were on the top of a mountain in Colorado with your family. It seems like forever ago."

"I'm sorry your plans weren't a complete waste of time."

"Me, too."

"Smallpox is a terrible disease. It should be destroyed, and this time forever."

"It'll be my mission, I promise."

The two of them sat in silence, watching Harry as he slept, his body struggling with an illness that was consuming him, fighting against an enemy inside that was set to destroy him. Harry was at war with the virus, not some unknown terrorist, and the heart and tenacity of the fragile battlefield of Harry's body would determine the victor.

All any of them could do now was wait.

* * *

DECEMBER 28, 11:00 P.M. EST
NEW YORK CITY

Vicky was exhausted, both physically and mentally. The emergency room was packed. She had not been home in three days. She had eaten little and had hardly slept. The noise in the hallway was at its usual feverish pitch, but it was relatively quiet in the break room.

Becky and John were sitting at a small table in the center of the room, both in their pajamas, eating from a bowl of popcorn Vicky had fixed. Vicky wasn't at all hungry. The two children were talking softly in their sweet voices, unconcerned, unknowing, and innocent. Vicky was sitting on a couch, her face on her hands, her heart heavy with worry, her next task the most difficult of any in her life.

The door opened and she looked up. The kids smiled and shouted out Justin's name as he entered the room. She stood, and by the look on his face she knew he saw her concern.

"Thanks for coming, Justin," she said. "I appreciate it."

"How is she doing?" he asked.

Vicky glanced at the children. "We're running tests now. I'm glad you could be with Becky and John for a few minutes while I admit my mom to the hospital. I didn't know who else to call."

He nodded his head. "I'm glad you called me."

He went to her and held her. She felt his strength. She would need more.

Justin pulled up a chair and sat between the kids. "Hey, guys," he said, "you going to hog all this popcorn?" He grabbed a handful and stuffed it in his mouth. "Or do I have to steal some."

Vicky watched a moment as the two children laughed with Justin. It was good that he was here, that he had come when she needed him. She would need him now more than ever.

Outside in the hallway, Vicky stepped into the rush of the commotion of the emergency room, but she didn't really notice. She walked down the hall and into the first exam room. Her mother was resting with her eyes closed, but she opened them when Vicky entered.

Her mother looked very ill. She had several red papules on her face. She was feverish, her hair soaked with perspiration, and she appeared pale. The fever had started three days earlier, but without the rash it was hard to know. Vicky had hoped it was just the flu.

A few days earlier, Vicky had obtained three doses of the smallpox vaccine and given it to her mother and the children, but apparently it was too late for her mother, probably given too long after her exposure, whenever that was. They did not have a clue who had transmitted the virus to her. Vicky had also hoped that her mother's childhood vaccination would have helped. She had received a vaccine when she was five, nearly sixty years earlier. Though everyone was expecting that the childhood vaccines would provide some protection, it was becoming evident that only about half were helped.

Vicky hadn't told her mother yet, but her mother knew. It was obvious. The television had shown hundreds of pictures. Vicky herself had seen dozens of cases, several an hour now, and she was certain she would see more.

Her mother was smart enough to know not only the diagnosis, but the prognosis as well.

"Is Justin with the children?" her mother asked.

"Yes, he's in the break room fighting over popcorn with them already."

"I like that boy."

"Me, too, Mom."

"He will be good to you."

"Yes, Mom, I think so, too."

Her mother paused a moment as she raised herself up to a sitting position. "So, does my doctor," she said, "have some bad news for her patient?"

Vicky thought about her mother's symptoms. She had broken out with red papules earlier that morning after three days of backaches, headaches, and fever. She had a few lesions on her face and some on her arms. In the midst of an epidemic, confirmation was not required. The problem now was that so many patients with smallpox had been admitted to the hospital that they were completely out of supplies—no antivirals, no antibiotics, and the IV fluids were running low. An entire wing of the hospital was devoted to smallpox, yet most of what could be done was only supportive care. Some of the nurses had left, but many had stayed. How her mother would fare was truly unknown.

The words lay heavy on Vicky's heart as she spoke them. "You have smallpox, Mother."

"I know, Vicky. Thank you for telling me. I'm sorry."

"Me, too, Mom."

"What happens next?"

"We admit you to the hospital. Hopefully we can find some medications and treat this."

"I know you'll do your best."

Vicky reached over the bed and hugged her mother. Now Vicky's tears came. Her mother held her a long time. After a while, Vicky stood and wiped her eyes.

"Don't let the children see me when I look bad."

"Okay, I won't."

"You keep working. I'll be fine."

"I don't know, Mom."

"Who else is there? They need you more than I do."

Vicky knew she was probably right, yet her heart wasn't in it.

"Promise me?" her mother said.

"Okay, I promise."

"No, really. I want you to really promise me."

Vicky sighed. "Okay, Mom, I will."

"Good," she said softly. "That is very good."

Vicky expected the next few days or weeks would be a struggle for her mother and for all the dozens of smallpox patients in her care. It would likely be worse than she could imagine. In those difficult days ahead, it was the promise she made to her mother that would keep Vicky going.

CHAPTER TWENTY NINE

JANUARY 4 (ONE WEEK LATER), 10:00 A.M. EST
ATLANTA

Two governors had already called Jackson and threatened his job; he was quickly growing tired of the phone conversation he was having with governor number three. He knew that these discussions were essential, but they were also a complete waste of his time. He had much more important business on which to focus.

Jackson leaned his elbows on his desk. He was feeling the fatigue of the past week.

"Yes, Governor. I'm very aware of the number of cases being reported in your state," Jackson said. He paused for the governor's response. "Yes, sir. I *do* know how fast it's spreading." Another pause. "I assure you we're doing the best...Yes, sir. I have been in contact with the president."

Jackson glanced up. Mike Lafitte was standing in the doorway. Jackson waved him in.

"It's a matter of...Yes, sir...I understand."

Lafitte sat on the stack of mail in Jackson's chair, the pile several inches higher than usual. Jackson looked up at him and rolled his eyes.

"Of course not, Governor...Yes, I'll keep you informed...Thank you, sir...You, too, sir."

Jackson hung up. He was getting too old for this. In Africa, he had worked nearly twenty-four hours a day, in stretches that sometimes lasted months. But he had been forty years younger back then. Now, the pace was killing him. Everyone was working hard without a break, bringing cots up to the office to sleep, and never leaving. It was a sign of the increasing sense of urgency, as the epidemic quickly grew out of control. Yet, he was certain that the worse was yet to come. There was too much to do, everything was vital, and everyone was hoping the effort was not too late.

Jackson shook his head at Lafitte. "They think we'll waste our vaccine where it's not needed." Jackson pointed to the phone. "I'm not cut out for the diplomatic thing."

Lafitte smiled. "I'm glad it's your butt and not mine."

"Thanks. What've you got for me?"

"Have you noticed that things aren't going as planned?"

"I was trying to ignore that fact," Jackson said, "but a half-dozen politicians have called to remind me."

"You want the good news first?"

"I was hoping there was some."

"A little," Lafitte said. "Jacobs and her group have nearly completed the DNA sequencing on the smallpox isolate. In addition, all the samples have shown to be identical."

"So the virus is from one source."

"That's right, and it appears the isolate is very similar to Somalia seventy-seven."

"Really? That's the strain I saw in Eastern Africa in the nineteen seventies. In fact, my presentation on smallpox has pictures of cases of Somalia seventy-seven."

"They think it's probably a wild *Variola*, *not* a laboratory release, and fortunately, *not* a genetically engineered variant."

"Thank goodness for that."

"We should have confirmation within a few days."

"If it's a virus from the wild," Jackson said, "it has survived forty years. Amazing."

"How could it do that?" Lafitte asked.

"We've always known the scabs were durable. Maybe someone dug up some dead bodies—a mass grave of smallpox victims, perhaps. Then they became infected. Somalia is in a terrible situation right now. If it were going to happen somewhere, Somalia would make sense."

"Smallpox virus hiding forty years without detection? That's frightening."

"So what's the bad news?"

"To be honest, there's a lot. First of all, we had to abandon the twelve-hour push packages."

"Then how can we set up the vaccine clinics?"

"We are able to fly in the fifty tons of supplies by wide-body cargo jets. That's not the problem. We don't have the eight tractor-trailers on the ground to move the supplies to the vaccine clinic sites. We're looking into railway access."

"I'm not sure that would work, unless we set up the clinics right next to the tracks. Are there any other alternatives?"

"I'll check. In addition, in the plan the vaccine kits were to be shipped separately, but that's been a big problem. Transportation is so bad that many times the kits aren't arriving within the seventy-two hour window. Those kits can't be used. Of course, they shouldn't be frozen, but one large shipment was left out overnight—guarded, mind you—and was totally wasted. And the plan called for local acquisition of certain supplies like gloves, tape, gauze, and bandages, but they've been impossible to obtain. We didn't anticipate that."

"Those are all logistical problems," Jackson said, "and should be solvable."

"I would hope so," Lafitte said. "Another problem is determining how much vaccine is needed. It was supposed to be a state public health responsibility. We're finding their estimates totally unreliable. Sometimes falsified reports. There's even been instances of fraud."

"Do you have a solution?"

"No, not yet, but we're working on an action plan."

"So, how many vaccine clinics are up and running?"

"Actually, none."

"Not any?"

"I mentioned the distribution issues. Coordinating the clinics themselves has proven to be a challenge. Each site requires twenty to thirty personnel—clinical managers, schedulers, medical screeners, data entry, security, etc. A number of these positions are volunteers. It's been more complex than we anticipated. And yet, even worse than that, some of the vaccine and supplies have been intentionally diverted."

"I expected that might happen. I've already spoken to the president about using the military for distribution. There'll be pros and cons about it in the media."

"Speaking of the media. Communications have been difficult. Our Internet site is up and down. Our phone system is completely jammed. We've had near constant requests from the media for all sorts of information such as the number of cases of smallpox, of people vaccinated, and of those who have suffered reactions. Just fielding the questions is a full-time job. All in all, though, the media has been more helpful than I expected."

"The truth of this situation is sensational enough, newsworthy even, for the media."

Lafitte paused a moment. Jackson could read his reluctance to continue.

"What is it?" Jackson asked.

"You want the really bad news?"

"It gets worse?"

"Much worse." Lafitte reached down and picked up a manila folder he had put in the chair beside him. He handed it to Jackson. "These are the latest computer models."

Jackson nodded as he took them. He noticed the confidential stickers that sealed the folder.

"The previous computer models that we had done in the planning stages," Lafitte said, "were based on an initial release at one location. These reflect a more widespread release."

Jackson held on to the folder, preferring to allow Lafitte to explain rather than to open it.

"The latest models," Lafitte continued, "show that the new case rate will definitely outpace our vaccine rates for some time. It's not the amount of vaccine we have available—that should be adequate. It's the ability to give it effectively."

"How many deaths?"

"I've asked them to recheck the numbers."

"They *did* recheck them, didn't they?"

Lafitte nodded.

"How many?"

"In the U.S., two hundred and forty thousand. Eleven million worldwide. Eradication—fifteen years. Of course, these are only estimates."

Jackson sighed. "We have a lot of work to do, don't we?"

Jackson handed the folder back to Lafitte. He didn't need to read it. He had expected as much.

"It'll be easy to get discouraged," Jackson said softly, "but the task is not impossible."

"It'll be hard to convince some people of that," Lafitte said.

It was true. Jackson had seen it when they had eradicated smallpox before—the first time. "Yes, I know," he said. "Not everyone will believe it."

"The devastation and chaos," Jackson thought, "had only just begun. It was imperative that they remember that *every* life counted and *every* vaccine given was disease prevented. It was the attention to those details that would make the difference."

"For you and me, my friend," Jackson said, "what matters most now is that *we* believe it."

Lafitte nodded his agreement.

"Without that belief," Jackson thought, "we'll never get through this."

* * *

JANUARY 10 (SIX DAYS LATER), 2:00 A.M. EST
NEW YORK CITY

Vicky had been sitting at her mother's bedside for twenty-four hours straight, since the moment her mother had slipped into a coma. Her pulse was thready. Her breathing was shallow and erratic, and every time there was a pause, Vicky feared it would be her last breath. For the past ten days, her mother had cried out in continuous pain. It had been a living hell. But thank God, she seemed comfortable now. The morphine had helped, and Vicky was grateful for it.

Even after two weeks of her mother's illness, Vicky could not accept that she was going to die. Just days ago, her mother had been so vibrant, so alive. How could this be? How could she be in this bed, sick as she was, looking like this—smallpox pustules covering her beautiful face, her neck, her arms? How could someone do this?

Vicky had seen a lot of death in the last two weeks. New York had nearly 25,000 cases of smallpox and over 5,000 deaths; Vicky had seen hundreds of people with small-pox in the emergency room. By the fifth day of the epidemic, it became obvious that the hospitals would soon be completely full of patients with the virus. Saint Joseph Hospital was converted to a smallpox hospital two days later, and the emergency room was closed. Vicky's duties were shifted to the wards. When the beds were completely full, the hospital brought in cots. When the cots were full, they brought in pallets for the floor. Saint Joseph was housing nearly three thousand people in a facility originally designed for eight hundred beds.

Most of the doctors and nurses had stayed to help, many working continuously, including Vicky, never leaving the hospital. The doctors had little to offer. The care of the patients was almost entirely supportive, providing comfort measures mainly, with only time deciding who would live and who would die of the disease. Most of their medications, bandages, and disposables had run out days earlier. Vicky felt very fortunate to have some morphine for her mother. Though the epidemic was primarily concentrated in New York, isolated cases occurring around the country caused hospitals everywhere to horde their supplies, and virtually nothing was being shared.

Vicky had checked on her mother frequently. The nurses had taken special care to watch her, doing what they could to help her, and Vicky was so very grateful.

The city of New York, hit the worst by the epidemic, was closed. The trains weren't running. Boats didn't dock. The airlines cancelled all flights. Truckers, even those who the government had vaccinated, refused to drive anywhere near the city. Food was becoming scarce. Medical supplies were nonexistent. The government promised that the trains would bring in food any day now. Vicky knew all the medicines in the world wouldn't help her mother, anyway.

New Yorkers who could leave had left. Those who stayed remained indoors. When Vicky looked out the window or took a quick walk around the block, she saw no one except the soldiers. New York was a ghost town.

The National Guard, Vicky thought, was truly a godsend. On the fifth day of the epidemic, the riots began and lasted three days and nights. The fires threatened the entire city, and rumors circulated that people with smallpox were being specifically targeted to "burn them out" and free the city of the disease. The reports created tremendous panic. Everyone believed Saint Joseph could be next and Vicky thought about taking her mother home, but the National Guard took defensive positions around the hospital late that evening. Everyone, including Vicky, was greatly relieved.

Vicky's mother took a breath and then paused. Vicky held her own breath. When her mother began breathing a few seconds later, so did Vicky.

Justin had simply been wonderful. He had visited every day. The ambulances continued to deliver patients to the hospital, replacing those who died, and when Justin came he would spend as much time as he could with her, always asking about her mother's condition. She appreciated his genuine concern.

Vicky longed for the day when she and Justin would have normal lives again, spending time together, having dinner, sharing a sunset, holding each other close. It wouldn't happen for a while.

Becky and John were staying with a trusted neighbor. Vicky called them six times a day. Their lives had been disrupted by the epidemic, as had those of many families. Every day in New York, mothers or fathers were lost. Children were orphaned. Friends or neighbors or people from church or work were stepping up to help. Vicky couldn't leave the hospital. There was no one to replace her. As much as she missed the children, she wouldn't see them, and they wouldn't leave their neighbor's home until it was over.

Today on the phone, Becky asked to talk to her grandmother, but Vicky said she couldn't come to the phone. Becky began to cry and said that she and John missed their grandmother so much.

Vicky wasn't sure how she would tell them—first their mother and now their grandmother. It would be hard.

Two orderlies in the hallway carried a body away in a black, plastic bag. Vicky had seen it a hundred times, and as she held her mother's hand, she knew in her heart it would soon be her mother's turn.

Vicky looked sadly at her mother's face. She would choose to remember her without the scars and without the disease; she would always see her with her eyes bright, smiling and laughing in a better time.

Her sister, Kelly, and her mother would soon be together. No pain for either of them.

Her mother took in a breath and let it out with a soft, hissing sound. Vicky waited. After a few seconds of silence, Vicky knew it was over.

She was gone.

Vicky leaned over her mother and quietly sobbed, holding on to her one last time. She didn't know how to let her go.

Vicky had seen death many times, but that didn't make any of this any easier.

CHAPTER THIRTY

JANUARY 13 (THREE DAYS LATER), 7:00 A.M. EST
NEAR FREDERICK, MARYLAND

Roberts watched the wiper blades slap the ice off the Hummer's windshield and was glad he wasn't driving. The sleet, falling faster than when they had left Washington, DC, had formed a solid sheet of ice on the interstate, and had tripled the time of their trip to Fort Detrick. The driver, a staff sergeant who had come to fetch him, seemed experienced, and Roberts felt as safe as possible considering the circumstances, but the constant slide of the vehicle on the road was still a bit unnerving.

When they had called him and woke him up at three A.M., they told him that the suspect had asked for him personally. He wasn't sure why. He had only seen him for the short time at the Marriott before he was whisked away to some unknown location. Roberts had wondered how the suspect had fared; the man had appeared so ill at the Marriott, but Roberts knew he would not ask and would only be told if he needed to know. It appeared he needed to know.

When Roberts heard that the destination was Fort Detrick, he was surprised. He would have expected Bethesda or one of the other military medical centers. Fort Detrick wasn't a hospital. It was known for medical research, home to USAMRIID, the U.S. Army Medical Research Institute of Infectious Disease, and housed the nation's experts in biological warfare. Why was the suspect at Fort Detrick? He would find out soon enough.

The driver hadn't said two words, which suited Roberts. He didn't much like small talk, and he couldn't imagine there was anything he particularly wanted to know about the sergeant. Roberts suspected the feeling was likely mutual. Besides, the last thing he wanted was a distracted driver in this weather.

The sun had cracked above the horizon a few minutes earlier, coloring the dark sky with a bit of light gray as the sun penetrated the dense clouds. As the Hummer's headlights cut into the darkness, Roberts noticed an odd illusion. The sleet appeared to be falling only in their path, the blackness outside the light of their headlamps hiding the rest from view, as if nature had chosen only them for its wrath. They were the target of an icy attack.

No one else was foolish enough to be on the roads.

Fort Detrick, located near Frederick, Maryland, was about forty miles from the center of Washington. Through the years Roberts had made the short trip several times to attend a conference or a strategic planning session. The place had always given him the creeps. There were too many dangerous bugs in the hands of a military that knew how to use them. Maybe it was the perfect place for a smallpox terrorist.

The driver slowed as they pulled up to the front gate and stopped. A sentry came up beside the driver's side window and stood in the sleet, carefully examining both sets of their credentials with a flashlight. The sentry, dressed in a hooded camouflage uniform with heavy gloves, with an M-16 slung over his shoulder, appeared to be unfazed by the weather. As he held open the documents, little pellets of sleet bounced off the sheets and scattered in all directions. Two other soldiers watched from behind the glass partition of the guardhouse, both also heavily armed. The sentry asked the driver several questions about their destination and the purpose of their trip. Both were classified, the driver said. The interchange between the two was polite but curt. The sentry handed the driver back both their papers and stepped away, waving them through.

The road into the base was heavily sanded and Roberts felt better. They passed by a series of buildings including a modern two-story structure that served as administrative headquarters. The USAMRIID sign was prominently displayed on this building. Turning into a parking lot, they followed it around to the back until they reached a much smaller, windowless building of brown brick sitting by itself, completely surrounded by a twelve-foot fence topped with razor wire. A single streetlamp illuminated the sidewalk leading to the only gate. A sign on the fence named the structure Building 377. The driver rolled the Hummer to a stop and flipped off the ignition.

"They're waiting for you inside, sir," the driver said.

"Thanks for the ride."

The driver gave a quick nod. Roberts guessed that was all he deserved as a civilian.

As Roberts slid out of the front seat of the car, he saw a man in a military uniform exit the building. As Roberts approached, the man unlocked the gate and swung it open.

"Welcome to Fort Detrick," he said.

"Thanks," Roberts said.

The man extended his hand. "I'm Captain Thomason. I'm a physician with the U.S. Army Medical Corps."

"I'm Gary Roberts, special agent, FBI."

"Yes, I know."

Roberts followed Thomason into the building. Just inside was a tiny waiting room with two or three chairs, and a metal door in the center of the wall facing them. Thomason glanced up at a camera that Roberts hadn't seen, and he paused briefly, waiting for the buzz of the lock's release.

In the light, Roberts could see Thomason's rank of captain on his uniform and the insignias of the Army's Medical Corps on his collar. Roberts followed him through the door into a larger room. Along one wall were two desks, several bookshelves, and a wide, metal cabinet. A young man dressed in white, an attendant or nurse, was sitting at one of the desks, typing on a computer keyboard. On the opposite wall was a large window with a view into an area that looked like a typical hospital room, and Roberts could see the suspect inside lying on a bed, covered to the chest with white sheets.

"It's a one-way mirror," Thomason said, watching Roberts as he looked through the window, "and he can't see us from his side. His name is Nazih Al-Sabai. He grew up in Libya. That's about all he's told us. We think he knows English, but he has only spoken in Arabic. He hasn't said much."

"He used English when we arrested him."

"I heard that." Thomason pointed to the four cameras mounted in the corners of the ceiling. "Everything's recorded," he said. "It's sent off somewhere and instantly translated and broadcast back to us on our computer monitors."

"What's his medical condition?"

"Young, healthy, except for the smallpox—*Variola major*, but a relatively light case. No complications so far. Our facility appears simple, but we basically have unlimited capability here."

Roberts didn't doubt it.

Thomason nodded at the attendant who stood and opened the cabinet. "You'll need personal protective equipment. His lesions have pretty much crusted over, but we're playing it safe."

"Of course," Roberts said.

The attendant handed Roberts the equipment.

"You're free to ask anything," Thomason said.

Roberts thanked him. But he didn't need the doctor's permission, and he'd ask whatever he wanted.

Roberts dressed and stepped through the door into a small negative pressure chamber. He waited a moment, watching a red light on the wall turn to green as he heard a rush of air. When he entered, Al-Sabai looked up, smiling. His reaction was friendlier than Roberts would have expected.

"Thank you for coming," Al-Sabai said in Arabic.

He spoke with an accent unfamiliar to Roberts. Thomason had said he was from Libya. Roberts noticed a chair along the wall and pulled it up next to the bed.

"My name is Gary Roberts," he said as he sat. "I'm an agent with the Federal Bureau of Investigation."

"I know the FBI," Al-Sabai said. "I walked by your headquarters on Pennsylvania Avenue every day."

The suspect had a number of smallpox lesions on his face and arms, all with a crust as Thomason had pointed out. Al-Sabai was at the end of his illness. He had survived.

Roberts wondered why he had asked for him. He had only seen him a few minutes at the Marriott. After the arrest, Roberts read him his rights in English and then again in Arabic, just to be safe. From Roberts's point of view, this was simply an investigation, actually an interrogation, and with the suspect's Miranda rights already read, Roberts could afford a few minutes to be friendly.

"Are they treating you well?" Roberts asked.

Al-Sabai smiled. "Like a king. First class." He paused and the smile faded. "For as long as I'm sick."

He was probably right, Roberts thought. A lengthy stay in a federal prison was likely in his future.

"You could have killed me," Al-Sabai said, "but you didn't."

Here was the bond, Roberts thought. "It would have served no purpose," Roberts said.

"Maybe I'd be better off if you had," Al-Sabai said. He pointed to the mirror. "Now *they* have me."

It was a choice Al-Sabai had made. "Only God knows the way of a man," Roberts said. "We are all in darkness."

Al-Sabai nodded. "You're with the FBI," he said, "and you're hoping I'll tell you something I wouldn't tell them, aren't you?"

"I won't lie to you," Roberts said. "Anything you want to talk about, I would appreciate."

Al-Sabai didn't respond immediately. Roberts wondered if Al-Sabai was thinking there was a price they'd be willing to pay for information. If so, Roberts knew he was wrong—at least from the view of the FBI—but who knew about the politicians, the CIA, or the military.

"It seemed simple at first, Al-Sabai said, "but I didn't realize what we were doing."

His comment caught Roberts a bit off guard. "What do you mean?" he asked.

Al-Sabai turned to Roberts. "I wasn't thinking we'd be killing people—just infecting them. You may not believe that. In Somalia, it seemed like two different things." He looked away.

Roberts stayed quiet and let him talk. Somalia?

"How many have died?" he asked, looking back at Roberts. "Can you tell me?"

Roberts didn't think it was classified, and to him it seemed that Al-Sabai was feeling remorse. Maybe he was simply planning to gloat about the number of Americans he had killed, but Roberts doubted it. He thought that maybe Al-Sabai should know.

"As of yesterday," Roberts said, "more than six thousand people have died."

Al-Sabai slowly shook his head. Roberts saw the sadness.

"I'm sorry," he said. He closed his eyes and said nothing. After several minutes, Roberts wondered if he had fallen asleep, but then Al-Sabai opened his eyes again and began speaking.

"Our journey began when we found the sick child and his mother in the desert of Somalia on the second day of December. I have never seen anyone so ill as that young boy. He was pitiful. What I remember the most was the terrible smell. I had never smelled anything like it. It made me sick, and I retched several times outside the hut until my stomach was empty. I wish now that I had never stepped one foot inside that place…"

* * *

Eight hours had passed before Roberts left the building. The sleet had stopped. The clouds had thinned to a mist of gray, and the sun had warmed the air to allow a decent day. The ice was melting. The drive home would be much easier.

The details of the suspect's story were completely filling Roberts's head; it was frightening in its simplicity. He would sleep little tonight and would have a full report on Edward Mold's desk by morning.

Roberts had been right about the suspect killed in Los Angeles. His name was Abdul Bin Khalid, at least that was the name he used. The body at O'Hare was Muhsin Al-Musaleh, an Egyptian. The terrorist they had missed in New York City was the leader, Ahmed Musa Mohammed. Al-Sabai claimed he knew nothing of the details of any network, and Roberts wasn't certain whether or not to believe him, but it was obvious to Roberts that the attack was coordination, well planned, and professional.

Four terrorists were sent to America and had caused one of the most terrible epidemics in human history, simply by walking around in the crowds, themselves infected with smallpox, the virus raining death on humanity, falling like the sleet in the headlights, killing thousands, maybe millions by the time it was over—if it would ever be over again.

Four men had done this—*four*!

My God, he thought, what if there had been more!

* * *

JANUARY 27 (TWO WEEKS LATER), 10:00 A.M. CST
DEKALB, ILLINOIS

Harry pushed up on to the arms of the walker but was too weak, and he fell back into his chair.

"You're going to have to do better than that," Maureen said, "if you're ever going to leave the hospital."

"And if you don't try," Haleem said, laughing, "Maureen's going to pester you until you do."

Harry grinned, nodding. "I know," he said. "I survive smallpox, and then my wife harasses me during recovery!"

Haleem and Maureen both smiled at Harry. At least he had improved enough to have some sense of humor.

"I called the Hillside Rehabilitation Center," Haleem said. "You know they refused to take smallpox patients at first, but now they will."

"I don't see how they could legally refuse," Maureen said.

"I'm hoping," Haleem said, "that you will be ready in a week or two."

Harry knew that the last four weeks, since the epidemic began, had been difficult for Haleem. DeKalb County Hospital had twenty patients with smallpox, which didn't seem like many, but almost all of them were nurses, doctors, or paramedics. Janet Hernandez was one of them, very ill in the ICU. In a small hospital, staff couldn't be replaced. Dr. Haleem was the personal physician of all the smallpox patients, but often he was so worn and ragged that he could barely stand. The load of the epidemic at DeKalb had rested entirely on his shoulders.

Everyone had hoped that the contacts of the Randalls had been vaccinated quickly enough but apparently that was not the case. The CDC was investigating intensely. Harry had been told that most of the nearly one thousand cases in Chicago were traced to the Holiday Inn where the terrorist had stayed. Even guests several floors away from the terrorist's room were infected. The ease of transmission of smallpox was unlike any illness Harry had ever seen.

Harry watched Maureen's smile, and he was glad she was there. Once Mike Lafitte had vaccinated her, Maureen had remained by his side and only rarely left the hospital to attend to the girls. Harry had worried that the vaccine wasn't a 100 percent effective, and that despite receiving it, Maureen could still contract smallpox. Several stories were reported in the press where that seemed to be the case. Maureen had refused to leave, as stubborn as always, so Harry prayed the vaccine would work.

With Maureen's not-so-gentle urging, Harry felt he was finally making some progress in his recovery, but it was distressingly slow. The first two weeks of his illness had been the worst. His memory of those days was a hazy cloud because of the medication and the disease. The past two weeks had been better, but the pain continued, not just the pain from the lesions and scars on his skin, but in every joint and in every muscle of his body. The virus was especially damaging to the nerves, and Harry thought it must be similar to the shingles pain that he had seen some of his patients suffer.

Haleem sat down, and Harry saw his shoulders slump. He was exhausted. Harry knew that after the media had reported on the Middle Eastern terrorist in Washington, DC, Haleem had suffered from the anti-Muslim backlash—his car tires were slashed, a brick was thrown through a window in his home, and he'd received threatening phone calls—but Haleem hadn't left. He had stayed at the hospital. If only they knew how many patients Haleem had helped, would they still throw their rocks?

"How are you holding up, Naguib?" Harry asked.

"I'm making it. I could use some help, but I don't expect any. If I could work a few hours less each day, I'd have a first-year intern's schedule again."

Harry knew Haleem was only partly joking. "Who'd thought it'd be this hard in private practice, right?"

"Okay, Harry," Maureen said. "Enough of your stalling. You need to get to work."

"Let's stand him up," Haleem said. "He won't get stronger sitting there."

Haleem positioned himself next to Harry's chair. Maureen moved to the opposite side to help. With some effort, they lifted Harry up to his walker.

"You're walking to the bathroom door," Haleem said. "The nurses are tired of bringing you a bedpan."

"I don't blame them one bit."

Harry took a step forward and a hard, sharp pain shot through his leg. He grimaced, paused a brief moment, and then took a second step. Haleem held one arm, and Maureen held the other. The road to recovery would be long and difficult, but Harry would do his best. That was about all he could do.

EPILOGUE

APRIL 5 (TEN WEEKS LATER), 7:00 P.M. CST
SOMEWHERE IN RURAL WISCONSIN

Harry cherished the solitude of his parents' log cabin more than he would have ever expected, and though it had been nearly ten years since his last visit, the view out to the lake from the wraparound porch was just as he remembered it—pristine, unspoiled, and absolutely perfect. A century-old forest of maple, pine, and spruce framed both sides of the property as a thick mass of woodlands running down to the rocky shore. The lake's flat surface shined like a mirror, reflecting the evening sun as it dropped from the edge of a low mountain along the horizon and slowly skinny-dipped into the water and out of sight. The sky was a deep blue, streaked with the colors of the sunset.

The grand view of nature he was witnessing was a world away, it seemed, from the sterile hospital room where he had been bedridden for so many weeks and where, he was convinced at the time, he would die.

Out on the lake an occasional fish jumped high into the air before flopping sideways on to the water, creating a series of concentric wrinkles on the smooth surface. At the base of a nearby pine, an energetic squirrel foraged noisily for a buried nut, unfazed by Harry's presence or the rhythmic creaking of his wooden rocker on the porch's oak slats. A bright red cardinal flitted back and forth on the bare branches of a maple; Harry thought it was most likely guarding a nest nearby.

The winter was over, and life had begun awakening; the spring faithfully and steadily unfolding as he watched, miles from DeKalb and Sycamore, miles from the confines of the hospital, and miles from the ravages of the disease and death of the smallpox epidemic.

Maureen was curled up on a small wicker love seat a few feet away, quietly reading a book to him. The soft light from the table lamp bathed her body, gently outlining her

293

beauty, and he was glad she was close by, near enough for him to touch her if he felt the need. She glanced up at him, sensing that he was looking at her, and she smiled before returning to the story.

Down the hill, the two girls were scampering along the shore, throwing sticks into the water. Harry had shown his daughters how to skip stones on the lake's surface—how to pick out a perfectly flat, smooth specimen and use a flipping motion to catch the water low and level, creating a short succession of skips until the stone was grabbed by the lake, tumbling down to the bottom. Though he showed them over and over the secrets of the skill he had learned through the years, the girls for some reason preferred to throw sticks.

When he had first arrived a month earlier, after six weeks in the DeKalb County Hospital and three weeks in the Hillside Rehabilitation Center, he was too weak to walk from the porch to the water's edge. Despite his lengthy convalescence, he continued to have multiple symptoms, and the return of his strength was far from complete. His progress was slow, but he *was* improving. The wounds were healing, but the scars would remain. He was lucky. Many had died.

"Can I get you something?" Maureen said. She had stopped reading and was looking up at him.

"No, honey. I'm fine."

She smiled again and returned to the book. He caught the brief look of worry on her face, as if she knew his thoughts. She probably had sufficient reason for concern. Since they had arrived, he had been preoccupied with his illness, thinking of almost nothing else, and only in the last week or so had he allowed himself the possibility that he might ever recover. He had even considered for the first time that he might at some point go back to work.

The particular strain of the virus at DeKalb was virulent and deadly, but Harry thought he had survived probably because his childhood vaccine had provided him with some degree of immunity. Yet the effects of the disease would be evident all his life. Every square inch of his body contained at least one pox scar—his arms, his legs, his abdomen, his back, and especially his face. He didn't consider himself vain, but the scars so changed his features that he struggled to look at himself in the mirror. It helped that those he loved the most, Maureen and the girls, had adjusted to his appearance. Maureen said they were the marks of a hero. Though as his wife she might be expected to say something like that, he appreciated her words of encouragement more than she would ever know.

Harry heard the sound of gravel rattling on the driveway out in the front yard, signaling an approaching car. He glanced at Maureen, and she shrugged. They had not had a visitor since they had arrived. Grabbing his cane, he used it to stand, pausing a few seconds to balance. Maureen tucked his arm under hers, and they maneuvered carefully down the wooden steps to the back lawn. The girls heard the noise, too, and joined them as they rounded the corner of the cabin. The lights of a vehicle, a black Mercedes, illuminated the driveway as it rolled to a stop behind their minivan. Harry waited. The lights flipped off, the driver's door opened, and after a moment, Hugh Jackson stepped out. With a big smile on his face, he held out his arms and gave Maureen and the girls each a hug. He turned to Harry and did the same.

Harry thought Jackson's embrace felt almost odd. Since his illness had begun, few people other than his family had touched him—even those he had known personally at the hospital. Most had avoided any close contact, fearing the consequences, even weeks after he was no longer contagious.

"What brings you to these parts, Hugh?" Harry asked.

"Came to see how my sick friend is doing," Jackson said. "So, may I ask, how *are* you doing, Harry?"

"I'm getting there. Slower than I'd like."

Jackson reached his arms around Harry and Maureen and walked with them to the back of the cabin. After a brief conversation with Jackson, Maureen disappeared inside and returned with two lemonades. She asked the girls to join her indoors, leaving the men on the porch.

For several minutes Jackson and Harry sat in silence, looking out into the last glimmer of the pink and purple sunset. The air was clear and crisp. A frog's harsh croaking came from somewhere near the lake's shore. Lightning bugs hovered above the lawn and flashed in brief bursts in a random chorus of pulsating lights. A soft breeze whistled quietly through the pines, a distinct soothing sound, and a distant owl called out a lonely cry into the darkening night.

"This is a lovely place," Jackson said.

"I feel fortunate to be here."

Jackson didn't immediately respond, and Harry realized his words had two meanings.

"You could have phoned to see how I was doing," Harry said after a bit. "It's a long trip out here."

"Yes, I could have," Jackson said, leaning back in the love seat. "But I'm here to extend to you an invitation, and I wanted to do that in person."

"Invitation?"

"It's a good thing. You're invited to a dinner at the White House—at the request of the president of the United States."

"That's certainly not what I expected you to say."

"Actually, more than that," Jackson said. "The dinner's in your honor."

"You're kidding, right?"

"No," Jackson said, "not in the least."

"I'm not sure I understand. Why me?"

"Because, my friend, you're a hero."

"Nonsense!"

"No, it's true. The whole country watched the press conference at DeKalb. They know about your illness, and they want to know you're okay. You're like a nine/eleven fireman going back into the towers, risking his life to do his job."

"I shouldn't be compared to the nine/eleven firemen. I'm not a hero like they were. I didn't do anything special. Any doctor would have done the same. In fact, doctors, nurses, and other caregivers are out there right now. And some of them have died—Nurse Hernandez for one—that's a far greater sacrifice than mine."

Jackson paused a moment. "You're right," he said softly. "And even more will probably die, despite our vaccines. Those people *are* the front lines, and they're scared to death. Your story gives them hope...and courage."

Harry stayed silent for several minutes. Jackson respected the silence and said nothing, waiting for Harry's response.

"I was just unlucky," Harry said. "I was at the wrong place at the wrong time, and then the training took over."

"We both know it wasn't that simple. You battled the disbelief of others. You refused to ignore what seemed impossible. Your efforts were remarkable, and the president wants to recognize that. So what do you say?"

Harry turned to Jackson and shrugged. "If that's what the president of the United States wants, who am I to argue?"

"Good," Jackson said, nodding. "I'm glad you've agreed. The president will be pleased. Your family, of course, is invited."

"They'll enjoy that. The White House? Are you kidding? They'll think that's very cool." Harry rocked back into his chair. "Hugh, there is something I need to ask you..."

"Yes, Harry?"

"The smallpox epidemic," Harry said, "it's bad now, isn't it? Maureen and I decided some time ago to stop listening to the news."

"It's worse than we could have ever expected. In the U.S. alone, we've had a hundred and twenty-seven thousand cases of smallpox reported, and the mortality rate is nearly fifty percent—not the twenty to thirty percent we had anticipated. Our vaccination program may be finally turning the tide, but it's been incredibly slow to do so. One thing we did right was our plan to send vaccine and supplies into the cities by trains, though even that was done too slowly. The roadways at first were inaccessible. Amazingly, even now some people are refusing the vaccine, fearing its side effects. I can't understand that in the face of an epidemic."

"And outside the U.S.?"

Jackson sighed heavily, and his face showed the weight of his concern. "Spreading rapidly," he said. "Most countries in Europe, South America, and Africa are reporting cases. With the first cases in the U.S., Japan and China immediately closed their borders, but smallpox is there, too. It will be truly catastrophic—a global disaster—and without the natural immunity we had in the past. I never saw anything like this in Africa. It's almost as if we did a disservice by eradicating the disease."

"No, it was the right thing to do. Who could have foreseen a terrorist act like this?"

"Unfortunately, this is what I always dreaded. It came true despite our best plans."

"It was unthinkable."

"You would have hoped so." Jackson stood and leaned his back against the porch's railing, facing Harry. "There is another reason I came to see you."

"And what would that be?"

"Are you ready to get back to work?"

"I don't know," Harry said. "I've thought about it a little, but I can't even walk around the block yet."

"I expect you will be able to soon enough, and if I know you, you can't sit on your butt around here all day. Of course, I'm sure you'd be welcomed back to your old practice in Sycamore, but I have something more important in mind."

"Oh, yeah? More than a family physician helping people in rural Illinois?"

"On a larger scale then—affecting millions of lives."

"You want me to write a book about my story?"

"No…well, maybe yes, that too." Jackson saw Harry smiling and he laughed. "Hey, I'm offering you a job."

"I kind of figured that."

"I want you to come work for the CDC. We're being asked to integrate the nation's efforts—vaccine programs, prevention, research on treatment, and public education. Thousands of people like yourself have had the disease and will likely need treatment for various complications—vision loss, nerve injuries, plastic and reconstructive surgery, and psychological and social support. Coordinating all of this will be a massive undertaking."

"Sounds like it."

"Best of all," Jackson said with a smile, "your office would be down the hall from mine. We'd be working closely together, though my focus will be international. You could begin when you're medically ready but the sooner the better."

"I'd have to ask Maureen."

"I would expect so. We need your help, Harry. This nightmare isn't close to being over. In many ways we're just getting started."

"Yes, I know."

"So?"

"Give me a few days. I'm not saying no."

"That was the best I could hope for." Jackson leaned out over the railing. He took in a few deep breaths before turning back to Harry. "It is truly beautiful here," he said, "and I can see why you'd want to stay forever. The sky is clear, and the air is clean. Who could blame you?" Jackson gently pointed at Harry. "But you're different, my friend. You have a calling."

"I'm not so sure about that. My life is what's here now." He swept his arm back toward the cabin. "It seems more precious after what I've been through."

"I know we're asking a lot. The country is in a crisis and the American people need you."

"My patriotic duty?"

"Yes, your patriotic duty and your professional duty—all of that. I won't belittle it. We're at war. Not just with the terrorists who did this, but also with this virus."

"Biologic warfare…aimed at the defenseless."

"Exactly," Jackson said. "Some of us just can't sit back and let them win."

Harry reached for his cane and stood, taking a moment to steady himself. "Let's go inside, Hugh," he said. "I'm getting chilled. This time of year the temperature drops pretty quickly after the sun goes down."

Jackson held out his arm for Harry. "Fine with me," Jackson said. "This old goat doesn't tolerate the cold either."

Harry grabbed his arm, and they walked together toward the door.

"Besides," Jackson said, "I hope that's the smell of homemade chocolate chip cookies coming from your kitchen!"

Harry smiled. "Knowing my wonderful Maureen," he said, "I wouldn't be a bit surprised."

The End

ACKNOWLEDGMENTS

So many people helped and encouraged me as I wrote this novel, and I will be forever grateful. They include Kathy Pile, for her early read and excellent advice; Brig. General Ed Wheeler, USA, ret., for thoughts on Somalia and the Middle East; Dr. Stan Schwartz, for encouragement and thoughts on infectious disease; Dr. Scott Sexter, family doctor, partner, and friend; Dr. Ed Hirsch, family doctor, for inspiring me; Lucas Ortiz, for trying your best; and the many, many family, friends, and patients, including Bob and Joyce Reinking, Linda Reinking, Donna Williams, Paula Alfred, Eugene Scott, Claudia and Wayne Woody, Vicky Bridges, Katie Banas, Herman and Lee Meyer, Pierre and Sharon Smith, Harrison and Terry Townes, Donna McCandless, Randy Bissey, Bob Tumilty, Mike Iverson, Bill Allen, Isla and John Joyce, Janis David, and Gene and Shirley Bedingfield. If I didn't name someone, it wasn't because I am unappreciative, but rather because the process was too long and my memory too short.

Most importantly, for all the love showered on me even when I was spending my time hidden away in my study pecking away on a computer keyboard, I am deeply blessed and thankful for my wonderful family, Amy, Rachael, and Daniel, and my amazing wife, Karen. I love you all.

ABOUT THE AUTHOR

Dr. Reinking received his doctor of medicine degree from the University of Oklahoma and is a Fellow of the American Academy of Family Physicians. He is currently practicing medicine in Tulsa, Oklahoma, as a member of the Warren Clinic, a two-hundred-fifty physician medical group, and at Saint Francis Hospital, where he serves as a medical director. Among his many honors and privileges, Dr. Reinking has served as president of the Oklahoma Academy of Family Physicians, taught medical students and residents, given lectures on a variety of clinical and medical administrative topics at local, state, and national forums, and has been a contributing author for several national publications of the American Academy of Family Physicians. Dr. Reinking was named the 2011 Oklahoma Family Physician of the Year.

In the community, Dr. Reinking has provided medical care at free clinics in the Tulsa area; coached his son's baseball teams; presented tobacco-free programs for elementary students; mentored youth on mission trips to assist the poor of rural Kentucky, innercity Houston, and Reynosa, Mexico; and traveled to Africa on multiple occasions to provide medical care in rural Tanzania. He is currently serving on the boards of two charitable organizations: the Executive Committee of Montereau, a not-for-profit senior living facility, and as chairman of the board of Literacy & Evangelism International, with the mission of improving literacy among the world's poorest nonreaders, particularly in Africa and Asia.

Dr. Reinking and his wife, Karen, have three children—Amy, Rachael, and Daniel—and live in Tulsa, Oklahoma. When not writing, Dr. Reinking spends his free time reading, and enjoying golf, landscaping, and local youth sports.

Made in the USA
Lexington, KY
16 July 2013